Please return this item to any Poole library
by the due date.
Renew on (01202) 265200 or at
www.boroughofpoole.com/libraries

boroughofpoole.com

By the same author:

The Madam

The
ALIBI

JAIME RAVEN

avon

AVON

A division of HarperCollins*Publishers*
1 London Bridge Street,
London SE1 9GF

www.harpercollins.co.uk

A Paperback Original 2016
1

Copyright © Jaime Raven 2016

Jaime Raven asserts the moral right to
be identified as the author of this work

A catalogue record for this book is
available from the British Library

ISBN 978-0-00-817149-0

Set in Minion by Palimpsest Book Production Limited, Falkirk, Stirlingshire
Printed and bound in Great Britain by Clays Ltd, St Ives plc

To Lyanne, Ellie and Jodie – my three wonderful daughters.

PROLOGUE

'Don't look at me like that, you pathetic bitch. You brought this on yourself.'

The words fell out of his mouth on the back of a ragged breath.

Through the tears that blurred her vision, Megan Fuller watched him straighten up and step away from her. She wanted to plead for her life, to beg for forgiveness, but she couldn't speak because her mouth was filled with blood and fragments of broken teeth.

She had never known pain like it, and it pulsed along every nerve in her body. From the demented look in his eyes she could tell that he had completely lost it. The red mist had consumed him. He was in the grip of a dark rage, and not for the first time. She'd seen it happen before and had likened it then to someone being possessed by the devil.

He gave her a look of sneering contempt as he stared down at her, his face tense, jaw locked, blue veins standing out on his neck.

'I warned you,' he yelled. 'It didn't have to be like this.'

Every molecule in her body was screaming, and hot tears spilled from her eyes.

She should never have let him in. It had been the mother of all mistakes. He was fired up before stepping over the threshold, intent on making her regret what she had threatened to do to him.

After slamming the front door behind him, he had launched into a furious rant, accusing her of being a money-grabbing whore. She had tried to calm him down by offering to make him a cup of tea.

But it wasn't tea he was after. He wanted her to tell him that she was backing down and that he didn't have to worry. But her refusal to do so had wound him up to the point where he'd snapped.

He'd smashed his fist into her face. Not once but twice. The first blow struck her mouth and stopped her from screaming. The second blow broke her nose and sent her sprawling backwards onto the kitchen floor.

Now she was at his mercy, unable to cry out as she watched him reach towards the knife block on the worktop. He withdrew the one she used for cutting vegetables. The sight of it paralysed her with fear.

'You were a fool to think I'd let you get away with it, Megan. The others might cave in, but I fucking won't.'

His voice was high-pitched and filled with menace, and his chest expanded alarmingly with every breath.

Panic seized her, and she tried to push herself up, but he responded by stamping on her right arm.

There was no stopping him now, she realised. Even if she could talk he was too far gone to listen to reason.

'You've always been a frigging liberty taker,' he fumed. 'But now you've overstepped the mark big time.'

The knife was above her now, and as he squeezed the steel handle the blood retreated from his knuckles.

She tried again to scream but it snagged in her throat and suddenly she couldn't even draw breath.

At the same time he lowered himself until his knee was pressed into her chest and his weight was threatening to crush her breastbone.

Face clenched with murderous fury, he moved his hand so that the tip of the knife was pressed against her windpipe. She could actually feel the adrenalin fizzing through her veins like a bolt of electricity.

A voice in her head was pleading with a God she had never believed in.

Please don't let him do it.

Please make him see sense.

She managed to swallow back the blood in her mouth and let out a strangled sob. But that was about all she could do.

'I can't let you live, Megan,' he said, and the harsh odour of his breath caused her nostrils to flare. 'I realise that now. If I do I know you'll make it your business to destroy me.'

She arched her body, desperate to throw him off, but he was too heavy and too determined.

Suddenly all hope took flight and she felt herself go limp.

Then she closed her eyes because she couldn't bear to look at his face as he plunged the knife into her throat.

1

Beth Chambers

I jolted awake to the sound of my mother's voice and the earthy aroma of instant coffee.

'You need to get up,' she said. 'The paper phoned and they want you to call them back straight away.'

I forced my eyes open and felt a throbbing pain at the base of my skull, made worse by the harsh sunlight streaming in through a gap in the curtains.

'Oh, Jesus,' I groaned.

'Let me guess,' my mother said, placing a mug on the bedside table. 'You've got a hangover.'

I rolled on my side, squinted at the flickering numbers on the digital clock.

'Bloody hell, Mum. It's only half eight.'

'That's right,' she said, her tone disapproving. 'It's also Saturday – one of only two days in the week when Bethany Chambers gets to spend quality time with her daughter.'

'I hadn't forgotten,' I said. 'Is she still in bed?'

'You must be joking. She's been up for an hour. I've washed

5

and dressed her and she's having breakfast. She thinks you're taking her to the park.'

I felt the inevitable wave of guilt wash over me. It had been a mistake to drink so much last night. But then how else would I have got through what had been such a tiresome ordeal?

'How bad is it?' my mother asked.

I closed my eyes, held my breath, tried to assess the level of discomfort.

'On a scale of one to ten I'd say it's an eleven,' I said.

My mother exhaled a long breath. 'Then sit up and drink some coffee. It'll make you feel better.'

I hauled myself up and placed my back against the headboard. I had to close my eyes again to stop the room from spinning. When I opened them my mother was still standing there looking down at me. Her arms were folded across her ample chest and she was shaking her head.

I sipped at the coffee. It was strong and sweet and I felt it burn a track down the back of my throat.

'When did the office call?' I said.

'A few minutes ago,' my mother said. 'I answered your phone because you left it in your bag – which you left on the floor in the hallway, along with your coat and shoes.'

I couldn't resist a smile. It was like going back to when I was a wayward teenager. Most weekends I'd roll in plastered, barely remembering what I'd been up to. My poor mum had put up with a lot in those days and even now, aged 29 and with a kid of my own, I was still a bit of a handful. Still cursed with a reckless streak.

'So how did it go?' she said. 'Was this one Mr Right?'

I shook my head. 'I should be so lucky. Suffice to say I won't be seeing him again.'

She gave a snort of derision. 'I told you, didn't I? The only blokes you'll meet on those internet dating sites are losers and cheats. It's a waste of time and money.'

And with that she turned and stepped back out of the room.

'Can you get my phone for me?' I called after her.

'No, I can't,' came the reply. 'If you want it you'll have to get up.'

I took a deep breath and let it out in a long, tuneful sigh. It was becoming increasingly difficult not to accept that she was probably right about the dating thing. Last night had been awful. Another date, another disaster. The guy's name was Trevor and in the flesh he looked nothing like his profile picture. Most of his hair had vanished since it was taken and he'd also grown a second chin. He said he was an IT consultant, and I believed him because he spent the whole time talking about what he did with computers.

It became obvious early on why he was still single at the age of 35. And if it hadn't been for the fact that he'd gone to the trouble of travelling all the way across London to meet me I would have left sooner than I did. But that would have been impolite, perhaps even a little cruel. So I'd stuck it out while knocking back the Pinot in an effort to numb my senses.

Over the last five months I'd dated seven men through online dating sites and Trevor was the dullest. He'd been even less entertaining than Kevin the chiropodist who had offered on our first date to examine my feet. When I wouldn't let him he went into a sulk and accused me of being a snob.

No way was I a snob. When it came to men I'd always been happy to cast a wide net. I'd never discriminate against race, colour, or class, and I accepted that most guys around my age had baggage from a previous relationship. I just wanted someone who was honest, open, reasonably intelligent and with a sense of humour. It would help, of course, if there was also an instant physical attraction. But so far those I'd met online had lacked most or all of those qualities.

'I suppose it's time I called it a day,' I said aloud to myself, knowing I didn't really mean it.

The trouble was I missed being in a relationship. The divorce was two years ago and I hadn't slept with anyone since. It wasn't just the sex though. I missed being part of a couple. I missed the companionship, the intimacy, the stream of pleasant surprises that were part and parcel of a burgeoning relationship.

Of course being a single mum with a full-time job kept me busy. In fact I had hardly any time to myself. And that was essentially the problem. I wanted more fun and a touch of romance in my life. I wanted to fall in love again and maybe have another child. I wanted a home of my own and to share it with someone who'd get to know me as well as I knew myself.

My mother didn't really understand me, or so she said. She reckoned I was being selfish, that I should forget about men and focus on bringing up Rosie.

'You already work far too many hours,' she told me when I first joined the dating scene. 'You haven't got time for a boyfriend or a husband.'

Then again she had her own reason for wanting things to stay as they were. As long as I remained unattached she got to have us living with her. Not that I'd ever complain. If it wasn't for my mother I'd probably find it impossible to look after a 3-year-old *and* continue to work as a journalist.

Thanks to her I didn't have to pay for childminders or meet the high cost of living in London. While married my husband and I had shared the exorbitant rent on a property in Dulwich.

But Mum owned outright this three-bed terraced house in Peckham, and my contribution to the outgoings was relatively small.

She was also on hand to take care of Rosie. That was important, given the fact that my job entailed horrendously unsocial hours.

Take this morning, for example. I had a horrible feeling that the newsdesk wanted me in on my day off. Why else would the office call me at this hour on a Saturday morning? Had something happened? Was there a breaking news story they wanted me to get across?

There was only one way to find out, of course, and that was to get up and phone them back. But it was the last thing I wanted to do. My head was hurting and I felt more than a little nauseous. Plus I didn't want to have to tell my daughter that I might not be taking her to the park after all.

As if on cue the bedroom door was flung open and there she was, the apple of my eye, looking absolutely gorgeous in a yellow dress, her long fair hair scraped back in a ponytail.

'Mummy, Mummy,' she yelled. 'Nanny said you have to get up. You're not allowed to go back to sleep because if you do you'll be in trouble.'

People have told me that Rosie is the image of her mother. And it was true up to a point. We both have blue eyes and hair the colour of wheat. Our noses are small and pointed, and we each have a slight lisp.

But Rosie has her father's facial bone structure and also his smile, which was one of the things I'd loved about him in the beginning. That was before I realised he used it as a distraction, a way to make me believe that he was a caring, faithful husband instead of a cheating scumbag.

9

'Hurry up, Mummy,' Rosie said excitedly. 'It's sunny and I want to go to the park.'

She stood next to the bed, pulling at the duvet, her big round eyes pleading with me to get up.

'Slow down, sweetheart,' I said. 'It's still really early and Mummy's got a headache.'

'I can kiss it better for you.'

The words out of my daughter's mouth never failed to lift my spirits. I put the mug back on the bedside table and reached over so that she could peck me on the forehead.

'I feel much better already,' I said.

Then I pulled her close to me and gave her a cuddle. She felt soft and warm and smelled of shower gel.

'Go and tell Nanny to make me some more coffee,' I said. 'I'll be out as soon as I've been to the loo.'

She skipped out of the room, repeating my words to herself so that she wouldn't forget them.

I then dragged myself out of bed, only to be confronted by my own reflection in the wardrobe mirror.

I usually wear silk pyjamas at night but I'd either forgotten to put them on or I just hadn't bothered. I couldn't remember which. Anyway, I was naked expect for my watch and a going-out necklace.

As always I cast a critical eye over my body. And as always I felt a pang of disappointment. Despite all the diets, gym sessions and yoga classes, I was still very much a work in progress. My breasts were not as firm as they used to be, my thighs were riddled with cellulite, and my tummy looked as though it was in the early stages of pregnancy.

But I did have my good points, thank God. My hair was full-bodied and shoulder-length and I never had to do much with it.

I was just over five seven in bare feet and had a face that most people considered attractive. In fact my ex went so far as to tell me that I reminded him of the actress Jennifer Lawrence. It gave my ego a huge boost up until the day I discovered that he was incapable of being truthful.

I shook my head, annoyed that I'd allowed that deceitful sod to invade my thoughts this early in the morning. But then it wasn't as though I could distance myself from him. For all his faults – and there were plenty of them – he adored Rosie and made a point of seeing her twice a week as part of the custody arrangement. It meant we remained in contact, and in all honesty it wasn't as bad now as it had been at the start. I was over the shock and humiliation of his betrayal, and all the feelings I'd had for him had evaporated.

I was now civil to him whenever we met and that made life easier all round. There were never any arguments over maintenance payments and he was usually willing to help out when I needed certain favours.

Naturally my mother hated him with a vengeance, and when he called at the house she made a point of retreating to her bedroom to avoid seeing him.

It wouldn't be an issue today because he'd taken Rosie out on Thursday and wasn't due to see her again until Wednesday, when he'd pick her up from the nursery.

Today it was my turn to spoil her – if I didn't have to go to work. And that was a bloody big if.

I turned away from the mirror, picked up my robe from the chair next to the bed and peered through the curtains. The bright sun made a change since we were in the middle of one of the wettest and coldest Novembers for years.

My bedroom was at the front of the house and the view was

11

of a row of almost identical terraced houses opposite. All of them were worth in excess of half a million pounds, which seemed extraordinary to me given that Peckham used to be one of the grimiest and most dangerous parts of south London. But having undergone massive regeneration and steady gentrification, the area was now considered a trendy place to live, attracting families and city workers alike.

For me Peckham was both familiar and convenient. The house was a short walk from the railway station and from there it was just a ten-minute train ride to London Bridge and the offices of the *The Post*, the evening newspaper that served the capital. I'd worked there for the past five years.

Peckham Rye Common was also close by and that was where I'd planned to take Rosie today. I really didn't want to disappoint her because Mum was right about me not spending enough quality time with her. I definitely needed to make more of an effort, put Rosie before everything else and stop jumping to the tune of the newsdesk.

I came to a decision suddenly. If the newsdesk asked me to go to work I'd tell them it wasn't possible. I'd say I'd already made plans and they couldn't be changed.

They'd no doubt be surprised because I loved the job and could usually be relied on to come in at short notice. But this time they'd just have to call up someone else, assuming they hadn't done so already.

'You took your time getting back to me,' Grant Scott said. 'I was about to get someone else to cover a story that we've just got wind of.'

'I'm afraid that's what you'll have to do, boss,' I said. 'It's my day off and I've made plans.'

'Well, I suggest you change them or else you're going to be sorely disappointed. This is huge.'

'That's what you always say when you're short of people.'

'I mean it this time, Beth. You've got first call on this because you're the paper's crime reporter. So I want you on it from the start. And trust me it's right up your street.'

Grant was *The Post*'s senior news editor and an expert in the art of manipulation. He was an old-school newspaperman who knew there was one sure way to get a reporter – any reporter – to do his bidding, and that was to dangle the carrot of a cracking yarn.

'So just out of curiosity what's the story?' I said.

I could imagine him smiling on the other end of the line, thinking he'd got me hooked and that all he had to do was reel me in. He'd been my mentor after all, helping nurture my career since I got the job at *The Post*. He was also the one who had nicknamed me The Ferret, because of my uncanny ability to ferret out stories.

Three years ago he appointed me to the position of the paper's first-ever female crime reporter. And in the pub afterwards he told me: 'You got the job because like me the news is embedded in your psyche, Beth. It's part of your DNA. You can't resist the excitement that comes from being the first to tell people what bad things are happening all around them. It's like the rush you get from a sniff of the white stuff.'

He'd been right, of course. From an early age I'd been fascinated by the news and how it was covered and disseminated. Before I left school I knew exactly what career path I wanted to follow. It wasn't easy, given my background, but I'd managed to pull it off, and like every other hack I knew I was now addicted to the chase.

'There's been a murder,' Grant was saying. 'And the victim is none other than Megan Fuller.'

It took a second for the name to register.

'Do you mean the actress?' I said.

'Yep, although as you know that's not her only claim to fame. As well as being a former TV soap star she was also the ex-wife of a well-known London gangster.'

'Christ,' I blurted. 'Danny Shapiro.'

'That's right,' Grant said, as though he'd scored a point. 'Danny fucking Shapiro – the villain with the film-star looks who took over a huge criminal empire after his notorious father got banged up.'

I felt a surge of adrenalin. Grant wasn't far wrong in saying the story was huge. Danny Shapiro was one of the country's highest-profile criminals. His gang operated south of the Thames and was involved in drug trafficking, prostitution, extortion, money laundering, and even kidnapping. He and Megan Fuller had been tabloid fodder throughout their three-year marriage which had ended in divorce fourteen months ago.

'Megan was found stabbed to death at her home in Balham earlier this morning,' Grant said. 'We had a tip from a paramedic who attended. So we've got the jump on everyone else.'

I was suddenly oblivious to the ache in my head as my mind filled with a flood of questions that I doubted Grant would know the answers to. I was certain the story would have created a buzz in the newsroom. The headline writers would already be focused on the paper's early edition front page, and the online team were probably about to publish something on the website. Then it'd be out there, leading to a full-blown media firestorm.

'So do you still want me to pass the story on to one of your colleagues?' Grant said. 'Only I can't piss around. We need to move on this.'

From where I stood in the kitchen I could see Rosie at the table in the adjoining dining room. She was busy drawing pictures on a pad with big colourful crayons. My mother sat next to her, but her eyes were on me and her brow was scrunched up in a frown. I could tell she knew what was coming.

I felt my resolve dissipate and the guilt rear up inside me again as I turned away from them and said into the phone, 'Okay, give me the details and Megan Fuller's address. I'll get right on it.'

'That's my girl,' Grant said. 'I knew you wouldn't disappoint me.'

2

Ethan Cain

The girl had said she was 18, but Ethan Cain wasn't sure he believed her. She looked younger. Much younger.

It hadn't stopped him spending the night with her, though. She was mature enough to know exactly how to please him.

Even if she was underage there was no danger of anyone in authority ever finding out. The girl would be too scared to let slip that she'd been shagged by a 34-year-old man at his flat in Wandsworth.

She was still asleep on the bed and she hadn't stirred when he'd got up just now to have a piss. It didn't surprise him. Last night she'd consumed copious amounts of vodka and had sniffed at least five lines of coke. So she'd probably be comatose for a while yet.

But that was okay because he wasn't in a hurry to get shot of her. It was Saturday and he didn't have to go to work. Besides, he was already aroused at the prospect of fucking her again, maybe a couple of times this morning if he could manage it.

After emerging from the en-suite bathroom, Cain sat naked in the armchair next to the bed and lit his first cigarette of the day. It was always the best, the most satisfying, and he savoured the acrid warmth that filled his throat.

He knew he wasn't a pretty sight. He looked far better with clothes on. At least they concealed his paunch and the man boobs that had begun sprouting up after he'd stopped working out. He wasn't grossly overweight, just bigger and softer than he wanted to be.

The girl, on the other hand, looked good enough to eat. The duvet had been pushed aside to reveal her lying spread-eagled on her back. It was all he could do not to get back on the bed and feast on her bare flesh.

She had lush black hair, small pert tits, and skin as smooth as porcelain. It struck him that she was a picture of innocence. This made him smile because she was far from innocent.

Ania Kolak – if that was her real name – was among the thousands of Eastern European sex workers who had poured into London in recent years. She was Polish and had told him that she hoped one day to embark on a career as an actress.

He'd heard it all before. Most of them believed that selling their bodies was a means to an end and that after a few years they'd have enough money saved to be able to fulfil their dreams. But in most cases that never happened. Instead they ended up as drug addicts or pathetic zombies drained of every last drop of self-respect.

Not that he gave a toss. As far as he was concerned it served them right. They didn't deserve his or anyone else's pity.

He did have some sympathy for those who were forced into sex slavery, though. Their plight was indeed tragic. But all the women and girls he'd been with had clearly become prostitutes out of choice. Many of them had told him they actually enjoyed being on the game. It meant they had enough cash to live well in one of the world's most expensive cities.

It still amazed him how much some of them earned. The high-class escorts who worked the West End often raked in thousands of pounds in a single night. Ania wasn't in that league, not yet anyway, and her fee for an entire night was five hundred pounds. Cain was just glad he didn't have to pay her and the others out of his own pocket. He would never have been able to afford it.

As it was he was lucky. The girls and drugs were the perks he enjoyed for being on Danny Shapiro's payroll. Danny, like his father before him, ran the biggest prostitution racket this side of the Thames. But it was only part of his empire, an empire that stretched across the whole of south London.

He was without doubt the shrewdest villain in the capital and the most feared. Even the Russians, who controlled the West End, and the Albanians, who ran most of north London, knew better than to try to muscle in on his territory. They did attempt it a couple of years ago and quickly came to regret it. Two of their top people were shot dead outside their homes in Kensington, and one of the casinos they operated up west was set on fire.

It was widely accepted that Danny was just as ruthless as his old man, Callum Shapiro, who was doing a twenty-five-year stretch for a raft of convictions including murder.

Cain's relationship with Danny was purely professional. He didn't actually like the man, let alone trust him. But the arrangement they had was mutually beneficial. And to be fair Danny had always treated him with a modicum of respect – unlike

Frankie Bishop, Danny's second-in-command and the gang's most brutal enforcer.

Bishop, a career criminal, had earned his ferocious reputation on the south coast where he was groomed by a gangster named Joe Strickland. He'd managed the security arrangements at Strickland's pubs and clubs in and around Southampton. One night he attacked a punter who ended up with a fractured skull and ruptured spleen. For that he went down for three years. While in prison he met a couple of Danny's lads and they urged him to move to London if he wanted to see more action and more money. So after his release he dropped in on Danny and offered his services, and Danny jumped at the chance to take him on.

It was Bishop who handed Cain his monthly cash retainer and supplied the girls and drugs. But dealing with him was never a pleasant experience. In the underworld he was known as 'The Nutter' because it was obvious to everyone that he was a grade-A psychopath. Still, Cain reckoned it was a small price to pay to indulge his passions for drugs, gambling, and sweet young things like Ania.

She was still out cold, her chest rising and falling with every breath. It occurred to him that he ought to take one of his little blue pills so that he could make the most of her before she left. It would take at least thirty minutes to kick in so he decided to wash it down with a cup of tea.

He crushed what was left of his fag in the ashtray on the floor and rummaged in the bedside drawer for a pill.

In the kitchen he opened the blinds and reached for the kettle to fill it with water. That was when he noticed his mobile phone on the worktop next to the sink.

As soon as he picked it up he saw that he had two unopened text messages and three missed calls.

'Shit.'

At some point last night he'd put the phone on silent and had forgotten to take it off. It had been careless of him. Downright stupid.

He checked the times of the messages and the calls. They had all come in during the past hour, which was a relief. He would say he was asleep in bed and hadn't heard it ringing.

It wasn't until he phoned the office that he discovered why they were anxious to reach him. It was bad news.

He wasn't going to have a day off, after all. And there would be no time for even a morning quickie with Ania.

Cain didn't know what to make of it. Megan Fuller had been murdered in her own home in Balham.

Jesus.

He had never met the woman but he knew all about her. She'd appeared in a soap that had aired on the BBC for about five years, playing the glamorous wife of a cantankerous factory owner. In real life she'd been married to Danny Shapiro, and by all accounts it had been a tumultuous relationship.

The word on the street was that she'd fallen on hard times since the Beeb dropped her from the soap over a year ago as part of a character shake-up. She'd been struggling to find other work ever since and had recently been threatening to write a tell-all book about her life.

Danny was among a number of people who were apparently not happy about it. He feared she might reveal a bit too much about their life together in order to secure a lucrative publishing contract.

As Cain stood under the shower, he realised that Danny would most likely be in the frame for her murder because the book thing meant that he had a motive. If so, then things could get tricky. He thought about phoning Danny to find out what he knew, if anything. But he decided against it. Maybe later when he had a better idea about what was going on.

After the shower, he towelled himself dry and had another go at waking Ania. She hadn't responded to the first attempt, but this time her eyes flickered open and she looked up at him.

'I said get your arse out of bed and get dressed,' he told her. 'Something's come up and I have to go out.'

She licked her lips and cleared her throat. 'Can't you just leave me here? I'm tired and I don't feel well.'

'Like I give a shit,' he said. 'Your clothes are over there. Put them on and scram. I've left a thirty-quid tip on the chair.'

Suddenly he was no longer interested in her. He was in such a hurry to get going he didn't even look at her as she got out of bed and sauntered naked into the bathroom to use the toilet.

By the time he'd put on his grey suit and a white shirt he was flustered. He didn't bother with a tie because he hated wearing them.

He told Ania she would have to have a shower when she got home and while she put on her clothes he called her a cab.

'Charge it to my account,' he told the operator. 'The name's Cain. Detective Inspector Ethan Cain.'

After hanging up he grabbed his wallet and warrant card from the dressing table and slipped them into his pocket. Then he checked himself in the mirror one last time and decided that nobody would guess he'd been up half the night shagging a teen prostitute and snorting coke. That was a relief. It meant he was ready to report for duty.

He checked his watch. Seven forty-five. Balham was only a couple of miles away and with luck he could be at Megan Fuller's house in less than half an hour, traffic permitting.

3

Danny Shapiro

'We're getting reports that the British actress Megan Fuller has been found dead at her home in south London. Police say she was stabbed late last night. Her body was discovered this morning. Scotland Yard has confirmed that Murder Squad detectives are at the scene. We'll bring you more when we have it.'

Those words from the BBC newsreader hit Danny Shapiro like a cattle prod. His eyes snapped open and he struggled to focus on the TV screen fixed to the wall in front of his bed.

For a few seconds it was just a blur, and by the time his vision cleared the newsreader was talking about something else. But the caption scrolling across the bottom of the screen told him that he hadn't been dreaming.

Breaking News: Soap star Megan Fuller found murdered in her home.

Danny sat bolt upright and shuddered from a fierce intake of breath. He had turned the telly on twenty minutes ago to help him shake off his slumber before getting up. Since then he'd been dozing on and off and hadn't taken any notice of it.

Now though he was wide awake and the morning news had his full attention.

Megan Fuller. His ex-wife. Murdered. Stabbed. In her own home.

Fuck.

Surely it can't be true, he told himself. It must be a ghastly mistake or some sick joke. After all, he was at her house last night and she had been very much alive. As spiteful and as mouthy as ever. They had argued and there'd been a shouting match. He remembered threatening her and recalled the fear on her face as she'd backed away from him in the kitchen.

She had really pissed him off with her crude ultimatum, and he'd told her that he wouldn't allow himself to be blackmailed. But she'd laughed in his face and had said he would have to pay up or suffer the consequences.

Afterwards he'd come straight home and had drunk himself into oblivion because he'd been so angry. That was why his head was bunged up now and there were things he couldn't remember: such as whether he'd given her a slap – or worse – before storming out. If he had then it would have been the first time. During their three years together he'd never once laid a hand on her, even though he'd come close to it on numerous occasions.

He was sure he would have held back last night too, whatever the extent of the provocation. But right now he couldn't be 100 per cent certain. He closed his eyes briefly, cast his mind back to last night, saw himself inside Megan's house, yelling at her, threatening her.

The picture kept fading, which came as no great surprise. Although he enjoyed the booze, he wasn't a heavy drinker, and when he did get rat-arsed he often suffered partial memory loss the morning after. Usually the memories surfaced eventually, but sometimes they didn't.

He was reminded of the time he got into an argument with a stranger who got lippy with him in a nightclub. The next morning he remembered the argument, but had no recollection of punching the bloke in the face and then stamping on his head. Luckily Frankie Bishop had been with him in the club and had told him what had happened.

'I wouldn't worry about it, boss,' Bishop had said. 'Most of us don't remember everything we do when we're hammered. And I reckon that's a good thing. It's just a shame we can't blank out some of the stuff we do when we're sober.'

But Danny *was* worried. Not knowing exactly what had happened last night sparked a twist of panic in his gut.

He opened his eyes, grabbed the TV remote from the bedside table, switched over to Sky News.

And there was Megan's face filling the screen, her eyes staring right at him. He felt the air lock in his chest and was gripped by a sudden anxiety.

It was a photograph he had seen hundreds of times before, one of the professional publicity shots distributed by the BBC. It showed Megan at her most stunning, before her life became a train wreck. Her long brown hair framed an oval face with soft, delicate features. Her smile was warm and engaging, and for a split second he remembered why he'd fallen in love with her in the first place.

His mind carried him back six years to the night they met. It was at a New Year's Eve bash in a club his father had just taken over in Camberwell. She'd come along with a group of luvvie friends from television and he'd been there with Bishop and some of the crew.

Danny had introduced himself and had given them two bottles of champagne on the house.

'It's my way of thanking you for coming to the club,' he'd said. 'I do hope it's the first of many visits.'

It was Megan who asked him to join them at their table to welcome in the New Year. And from that moment he was beguiled by her beauty and the fact that she was a celebrity.

At the stroke of midnight they kissed, and he would never forget how good it felt and how his heart raced. It was the start of a passionate relationship that most people – including his father – predicted wouldn't last. They weren't wrong.

Callum Shapiro never did like Megan, and he told Danny he was a moron for getting involved with someone in the public eye.

'Are you off your fucking trolley?' he said after Danny proposed and Megan accepted. 'You're a villain and you need to keep a low profile. You've let this celebrity thing go to your head and it's a big mistake. On top of that you and her are from entirely different worlds. She'll be trouble, son. You mark my words.'

But Danny didn't listen. He loved Megan and he enjoyed the thrill of being in the limelight and going to film premieres and celebrity parties. And he lapped up the attention and the way the tabloids described him as the playboy son of the reputed gangland boss Callum Shapiro.

Four months after he met Megan they got married on Danny's twenty-seventh birthday. Then two months after the wedding his father was arrested and the lawyers warned them he was facing a life sentence.

It fell on Danny to take the reins of the organisation, which made his life more complicated and put an enormous strain on the marriage from the start.

If Megan had conceived during that first year then maybe things would have been different. But she put her career before a family and at the same time Danny found that being the boss meant a bigger commitment than he'd been prepared for. So the odds were stacked against them from the beginning. It didn't help that Megan found it tough coping with pressure and suffered bouts of depression, which she blamed on a difficult childhood and low self-esteem.

'Miss Fuller was thirty-two and married for several years to Danny Shapiro, the man who has repeatedly denied any involvement in organised crime in London.'

Now his own face stared down at him from the TV screen as the newsreader relayed background information relevant to the story.

Danny's unease mounted as he watched and listened with a hawkish intensity.

'The couple split up three years ago and were divorced fourteen months ago. Shortly after that Miss Fuller was dropped by the BBC from the long-running soap. A close friend has told Sky News that this – coupled with mounting debts – caused her to become clinically depressed.'

Danny had known all about the state she got herself into. She'd phoned him often enough to tell him it was his fault for being a shit husband and cheating on her with a string of women. Out of guilt and pity he had given her a large sum of money as part of the divorce settlement, plus two properties – the house in Balham and the cottage in the New Forest.

But he'd refused to accept responsibility for the fact that she blew the money on high living and a business venture that went tits up. She'd been forced to remortgage the house and put the cottage on the market.

On the TV the newsreader was saying that Megan's body was discovered by her own father when he called at the house this morning.

'Mr Nigel Fuller apparently looked through the kitchen window when he got no response from ringing the front doorbell. He then saw his daughter's body lying on the kitchen floor.'

Danny's mind conjured up an image of the scene that would have confronted Nigel Fuller. It caused the muscles in his jaw to tense and brought a lump to his throat. It also made him realise that deep down he still had feelings for Megan despite the friction that had developed between them, and for that reason he was saddened by the manner of her death.

He started to go through the events leading up to last night again in his head. Megan had called him on his mobile while he was still at his office in Bermondsey. She'd wanted to give him the news that her agent had secured a publishing deal for her autobiography.

'So here's the thing, Danny Boy,' she'd said. 'If you want to stop me dishing the dirt about you and your business then you'd better sort out the money fast. Half a mil buys my silence.'

She'd severed the connection before he could respond. He'd still been fuming an hour later when he left the office with two minders and headed for a business meeting in Clapham, a short way from Balham.

The meeting was with a bunch of Turks who had opened up a new drugs supply route into the UK from Istanbul. Over a plentiful supply of booze they'd struck a good deal. The Turks had access to some high-quality coke and heroin, and they were now going to be one of the firm's main suppliers.

But as he left the meeting above a pub his thoughts had switched back to Megan. And because he'd been tanked up he'd decided to go to her house to confront her. In hindsight it had been a mistake to have sent the minders home, but he'd wanted to go alone and to have a brisk walk to clear his head.

Clapham was about a mile away and halfway there it had started to rain, a steady drizzle rather than a downpour. Luckily he hadn't been suited up. As usual he'd been wearing a fleece with a hood, his 'uniform of choice' that allowed him to take to the streets without being recognised. Even so by the time he got to Megan's house he was wet, miserable and fit to explode . . .

'A *police source has just confirmed that she may have been murdered by someone she let in – someone she might have known.*'

The newsreader's words seized Danny's attention again and pulled him back to the present. That was when alarm bells started going off inside his head, and he realised that he had a serious problem. It didn't matter that he was convinced he didn't kill Megan. Unless it was obvious to the cops who did then he was going to be their prime suspect.

They'd probably find out that she phoned him earlier in the day, even though he used an unregistered mobile. They would know he was worried about what she would write in her forthcoming book. They'd probably drum up CCTV footage of him walking from Clapham to Balham. And he couldn't be sure, of course, that he hadn't been seen entering or leaving the house.

Fuck.

His heart started booming in his ears and a hole opened up in his stomach. He told himself to stay calm, not to panic, but he had to fight back an urge to scream.

This was bad. Really bad. The cops would jump at the chance to pin Megan's murder on him, and once they discovered he'd been to the house they'd have him bang to rights.

Fuck.

What he needed was an alibi and he didn't have one. He also had no idea what to tell the Old Bill when they eventually turned up. He needed to think, to get his mind around the problem and see if he could find a way out.

A coffee would help, he decided, followed by a hot shower. He had to flush the booze and the sleep from his system so that he could start firing on all cylinders.

He threw back the duvet and swung his legs over the edge of the bed. At that moment the landline started ringing in the other room. His heart froze in his chest and his body flooded with adrenalin. Only a few people had the number to the house phone – his father, his lawyer, his accountant, and Frankie Bishop.

He had no idea which one of them it could be or whether he should answer it. He didn't want to speak to anyone until he knew what he was going to say, so he listened to the ringing for about thirty seconds. After it stopped he didn't move. He just sat there, his mind whirring, as he tried to think of a way to save himself.

4

Beth Chambers

The story broke even before I left the house. I saw Megan Fuller's picture on BBC News as I stepped out of the shower. By the time I was on my second mug of coffee they were saying she might have been murdered by someone she'd known. That didn't surprise me, since most murders are committed by friends or relatives of the victims.

'So is that why you have to go to work?' my mother said, flicking her head towards the TV.

'It's a big story, Mum,' I said. 'And as I happen to be the paper's crime reporter they expect me to cover it.'

'But it's the start of the weekend.'

I huffed out a breath. 'I know that, Mum, and I'm sorry. But I can't help it. I'll make it up to Rosie. I promise.'

She gave me one of her long, prickly looks so I kept my gaze firmly fixed on the screen and pretended not to notice.

I could see her out of the corner of my eye, standing in front of the sink with her hands on her hips. Not for the first time I realised that I would probably be just like her when I too was the

31

wrong side of sixty. I certainly had her temperament. We were both stubborn, strong-willed, opinionated.

Thankfully the physical resemblance was less apparent. She'd had a hard life and it showed in the lines that were etched into her face. What remained of her grey hair was thin and wispy, and the whites of her eyes were tinged with yellow.

As a younger woman, Peggy Chambers had been beautiful, and it was no wonder she'd had more than her fair share of male admirers. She was 28 when she gave birth to me. I had only a vague recollection of my father because he was only around for a short time. He popped in and out of my life when I was a small child. He brought me presents and sometimes put me on his lap and gave me a cuddle. But he never took me out or came to any of my birthday parties.

Mum told me it was because he was married and I was the result of an illicit affair. She also told me that he turned out to be a low-life shyster who couldn't be trusted. One day when I was 5 he just decided he didn't want to see her any more and stopped coming to the house.

I couldn't even picture him in my mind's eye, although occasionally a distant memory came to me at night. A tall man with a husky voice telling me that he loved me, and that I was the most beautiful girl in the world.

My mother fell in love again when I was 8 with a black man named Tony Hunter, who she met in the Nag's Head pub in Peckham. He got her pregnant and so they married.

Tony was good to both of us and he treated me like his own daughter. When my brother Michael was born, Tony promised me he would always be there for us. But he wasn't, and the years that followed Michael's birth were filled with tragedy and heartache.

That was why my mother was like she was: tough, assertive, and intolerant. It had been her way of coping with the cruel blows she'd suffered during her lifetime. And however much she annoyed me at times, I knew she would do anything for her daughter and granddaughter.

Rosie thought the world of her, so she hadn't thrown a hissy fit when I'd told her that Nanny would be taking her to the park because I had to go to work. I'd sweetened the pill by promising to bring her back a present.

On the TV they were now showing a photograph of Megan Fuller and Danny Shapiro together, and it drew my mother's attention back to the screen.

'Do you think he killed her?' she asked me.

'I have no idea,' I said. 'But it wouldn't surprise me. The guy's a notorious thug. Just like his dad was before he got sent down.'

I'd written countless stories about Danny Shapiro. I'd even tried to expose the inner workings of his organisation. But along with every other investigative journalist who'd tried I had barely been able to scratch the surface. The guy was more careful, and more insulated, than most other villains I'd come across, which was why the police had struggled to bring him down.

Shapiro was a known face in this area of London. It was part of his manor, and most people knew who he was and what he did. His father, Callum, had lived in Peckham back in the days when my mother ran a salad stall in Rye Lane. He and a few other south London villains were among her customers. Since then times had changed and so had the Lane. These days it had little to offer well-heeled villains, who preferred more upmarket shopping streets.

'So have you ever met him?' my mother said.

'Do you mean Shapiro?'

'Who else would I be talking about?'

I shrugged. 'Well, I've approached him twice for an interview. But each time he turned me down.'

'And what did you think of him?'

'He's a bit flash,' I said. 'He's a charmer, though, and good-looking to boot. I can see why Megan Fuller fell for him.'

My mother shook her head. 'You know what, Beth? That man sounds just like your stepdad. He was also handsome and charming and as crooked as they come.'

The thought made me shudder, but she was right. Tony had been a career criminal just like Danny Shapiro, which was why he was no longer with us.

And it was why our lives had been filled with so much drama and sadness.

Grant Scott had arranged for a taxi to pick me up outside the house. The driver honked his horn to let me know he had arrived.

I apologised again to Rosie for having to work and she gave me a kiss and told me not to forget her present.

'If you do you'll have me to answer to,' my mother said. But as she spoke she had a smile on her face and I knew she'd forgiven me, just as she always did. I hugged her and thanked her for taking Rosie to the park.

'I don't know what I would do without you, Mum,' I said. 'You're a gem.'

'And you're a right royal pain in the backside, Bethany Chambers,' she said. 'But I love you just the same.'

So all was well on the home front as I left the house.

I still felt guilty, though. It was always the same when I left Rosie at home and went to work, even though I knew I didn't really have a choice. After all, someone had to pay the bills. I found some comfort in the fact that I was luckier than most single mums. My own mother was there to help and I took home a good wage. According to the latest hot parenting book I was actually setting a good example for my child.

But that didn't mean I was able to shake off the brutal burden of so-called 'working mum's guilt'. It was going to plague me for years to come; of that I was certain.

It was chilly out and I was wearing my designer jeans, black T-shirt, and a thick fleece jacket. My hair was pulled back in a tight ponytail and I had sunglasses on my head.

I was carrying my favourite M&S leather shoulder bag containing my purse, iPad, phone, Olympus voice recorder, and small make-up bag. So I was back in reporter mode and ready to roll.

I gave the driver Megan Fuller's address and made myself comfortable on the back seat. Then as soon as we were moving I started making calls. The first was to the New Scotland Yard press office. I was well known to the team and they confirmed what I had already gleaned from the TV news. They also told me that the investigation would be run by Wandsworth CID based in Lavender Hill. The officers leading the inquiry were Detective Chief Inspector Jack Redwood, who I'd never met, and Detective Inspector Ethan Cain, the toerag who happened to be my ex-husband.

It didn't surprise me that Ethan had been assigned to the case because it was on his patch, and he was part of the murder team. It also didn't surprise me when he failed to answer his mobile. I knew it'd be because he either wasn't ready to talk to me or he was too busy. No matter, I thought. I'd call again later when he was bound to have more to tell me anyway.

The second call I made was to another contact inside

Wandsworth nick. He was a senior officer in the uniform division who'd been feeding me with information for years, despite the crackdown on the cosy relationship between the press and the police that followed the Leveson Inquiry. I referred to the officer as Doug, although that wasn't his real name. In fact I gave false names to all my police contacts because it meant there was less risk of them being outed.

Doug, who was well rewarded for his indiscretion, provided me with some useful off-the-record information.

'Word is the murder took place between half ten and midnight,' he said. 'Megan Fuller suffered a single stab wound to the throat and probably died instantly. There's no sign of a break-in, but neighbours have reported hearing raised voices around that time.'

'Is it true the body was discovered by her father?' I asked.

'Correct. He called at the house at just after seven this morning.'

'Have you got his contact details?'

'I only know that he lives in Lewisham. I'll have to text you the full address when I have it. But I do know he's still in Balham.'

'Where exactly?'

'He's at a neighbour's house. I'll try to find out which one and text that address to you as well.'

I hung up and looked out of the window, saw that it was shaping up to be a beautiful day. The puddles from last night's persistent rain were already slowly disappearing, and the sky was an insane shade of blue.

The streets of Peckham were teeming with life. Shops were opening and stalls were being set out. It could have been a scene from John Sullivan's classic TV sitcom *Only Fools and Horses*, which was set in Peckham but was actually filmed mostly in Bristol. The series followed lovable rogue Del Boy Trotter and his hapless brother Rodney, and it depicted Peckham as a place filled with harmless villains and wheeler-dealers, while making it appear overwhelmingly white and British.

In reality Peckham was one of London's most ethnically diverse districts, with a high percentage of the population being black African and Caribbean. Drugs, guns, knives, and street gangs continued to be a problem despite the regeneration. I'd lost count of the number of stories I'd written about crime in Peckham since I started out as a young reporter on the *South London Times*. Living and working in the community gave me a unique insight, as did the fact that I had experienced first-hand the consequences of endemic crime and violence.

At school I witnessed no fewer than four stabbings, and I once saw a boy of 12 shoot another boy dead in the playground with a gun stolen from his uncle. At the age of 15 I was attacked by three boys when I made the mistake of visiting a friend's flat on the notorious North Peckham Estate. I suffered a black eye, bruised ribs, and a fractured wrist. I only escaped being raped because someone raised the alarm and my assailants fled.

When I was 14 my stepfather Tony was shot dead while walking along a street in Tulse Hill. My brother Michael was 9 at the time and the loss of his father turned him against the world. He joined a febrile gang known as the Peckham Boys, and my mother and I eventually lost control of him.

After five years of running wild he himself was killed when a rival gang member smashed his skull with a machete in a dispute over drugs.

Some years later – in 2011 – I was in the thick of it again when the London riots spread to Peckham. I won't ever forget the fear I experienced while reporting from the front line as young men wearing hoods set fire to shops and cars and threatened anyone who got in their way.

The stories I filed during the riots earned me a journalism award and brought me to the attention of the national press. I then worked as a freelance journo for a spell and managed to come up with a string of exclusive stories about the crime scene south of the Thames.

By this time I had a large number of contacts within the police and underworld, and I'd built a reputation as a reliable reporter. This was despite the fact that I often sailed close to the wind by employing unethical methods to get a story. Like a lot of reporters I used to hack mobile phones and use unauthorised electronic surveillance to spy on people. I had also resorted to posing as a police officer to elicit information from those who wouldn't otherwise have parted with it.

It wasn't something I was particularly proud of, but then I took the view that the end justified the means.

For me the job wasn't just about chasing down juicy stories and seeing my name emblazoned beneath the headlines. There was actually more to it than that. Deep down I was motivated by a higher purpose, a compulsion to get at the truth even if it meant occasionally breaching the ethical boundaries. Nothing was more satisfying than exposing wrongdoers and causing criminals like Danny Shapiro to be brought to justice. Working as a crime reporter on *The Post* allowed me to do just that. The paper approached me after I started selling them stories, and within a couple of months Grant Scott decided to call me The Ferret.

'I can't help but admire you, Beth,' he told me. 'You unearth more exclusives than the rest of the team put together. And that's no mean achievement. I've never known anyone to be so passionate about their work. For the paper's sake I hope you never come off the boil.'

* * *

I had always considered Balham an upmarket version of Peckham. The streets were cleaner, the shops more varied, and the people seemed a lot friendlier. It also boasted an underground station, which Peckham lacked.

Megan Fuller's house was in Ramsden Road, one of the area's longest and smartest streets. The cabbie dropped me close to the scene of activity. A police cordon had been set up across the road and traffic was being diverted.

Four patrol cars were parked beyond the incident tape and two of them were displaying flashing blue lights. There were cops in high-vis jackets everywhere and the air was filled with police radio static.

I stood on the pavement for a few moments to get my bearings and decide how to approach things. The house was behind a high privet hedge. It was near the top end of the road and had an attractive red-brick Victorian façade.

The media scrum was just getting started. I spotted two reporters I recognised from the nationals and there was Billy Prior, the photographer from *The Post*. The TV crews hadn't yet arrived but they were no doubt on their way. Soon there'd be a crowd of us jostling for position as we sought to gather the facts.

The paper expected me to file copy as quickly as possible for both print and online editions of the paper. I was already in a position to freshen up the story with what Doug had told me, plus I could throw in colour about the crime scene and get a few quotes from shocked neighbours.

I made a quick note of what was going on. Police were searching gardens and drains. One officer was videoing the scene while another was taking photographs.

I moved right up to the incident tape. Asked a uniformed officer if the detectives in charge were prepared to provide us with an update.

'Not just yet,' he said, gesturing towards two figures standing on the path leading up to Megan's front door. 'As you can see they're tied up. But I've been told that a statement will be forthcoming within the hour. I know they're keen to make an appeal for information.'

I had assumed the pair were scene-of-crime officers. One of them was wearing a protective forensic suit and the other was slipping into one.

Now I recognised both of them. The guy already wearing the suit was DCI Jack Redwood. The other man was DI Ethan Cain, my ex, and it looked as though he had only just arrived.

Redwood was doing the talking and Ethan was listening. Both men wore solemn expressions.

When they disappeared into the house I turned my attention to a group of neighbours standing on the pavement across the road. Five minutes later I had elicited a few useful quotes from them. One woman told me she had known Megan Fuller well and had considered her a friend.

'This is terrible,' she said with tearful eyes. 'I can't believe it's happened.'

A man in his sixties who lived opposite said he'd seen Megan the previous morning as she'd walked home from a shopping trip to the Waitrose store at the end of the road.

'She smiled at me and asked how I was,' he said. 'She seemed in good spirits. Who the bloody hell could have done such a thing?'

That gave me enough to fire off my first piece of copy. I sent it via my iPad and included the quotes and the facts about how Megan had been stabbed and the estimated time of the murder.

Grant Scott called me straight back to say well done and to tell me to hang around.

'Just keep filing updates as and when you get them,' he said. 'We're pulling together a background piece on Megan at this end. I've got two people bashing the phones to get reactions. We've already got quotes from the BBC and a couple of her showbiz friends.'

'I read somewhere that she had a boyfriend,' I said. 'Took up with him after her divorce from Danny Shapiro.'

'Have you got a name?'

'I'm afraid not. See if you can dig it up. It's odds on the police will want to talk to both him and Shapiro.'

As soon as I hung up a text message came through on my phone. It was from Doug and he'd sent through the address in Lewisham of Megan's father. A minute later I received a second message. In this one Doug confirmed that Mr Fuller was still in Ramsden Road and he gave me the number of the house where he was being comforted by a neighbour.

5

Beth Chambers

Nigel Fuller was staying at a terraced house about fifty yards from his daughter's place. It was just outside the police cordon and I was surprised there were no uniforms standing out front.

I fully expected him to decline the opportunity to speak to the press but decided it was worth a try. As any reporter knows you can never be sure how loved ones will react when approached. Some consider it the ultimate intrusion. Others just slam the door in your face, or refuse to even answer it in the first place. But a sizable number do actually open up and perhaps even find it cathartic to talk about how shocked and grief-stricken they are.

I had to play this carefully. Mr Fuller might well still have been here because the detectives wanted to interview him again, in which case they wouldn't want me anywhere near him. But if I could persuade him to talk to me it would put me way ahead of the pack.

When a woman answered the door I knew it probably meant that there were no police officers inside. That was a result. She

42

was plump and middle-aged. She wasn't wearing any make-up, and her face was a grey, washed-out colour.

Before she could get a word out I flashed my press card and said, 'My name's Bethany Chambers and I'm a reporter with *The Post*. I've come to have a word with Mr Fuller.'

Her eyes narrowed and her expression became wary.

'How did you know he was here?'

'The police told me,' I said. 'They're keen to put out an appeal for information and they believe a quote from Megan's father would ensure it has maximum impact.'

Okay, that was stretching it, but it wasn't actually an outright lie since the cops would soon be using the media to reach out to the public anyway.

'Of course I'll understand if he's not up to it having gone through such a traumatic experience.'

'But I don't understand,' she replied. 'The detective told us not to talk to anyone. He said Nigel should wait here until he came back, and that a family liaison officer was on her way over. That's who I thought you were.'

'The thing is the sooner the appeal can go out the better,' I said. 'The police are desperate to contact anyone who might have seen or heard something last night.'

The woman bit down on her lower lip and looked back over her shoulder. I could tell she was anxious and confused. And I knew that if I didn't get over the threshold in the next few seconds I never would.

'Perhaps you should ask Mr Fuller,' I prompted. 'It might be something he wants to do. I promise I'll only ask a couple of questions.'

She was about to respond when a man appeared in the hallway behind her.

'Who is it, Martha?' he said.

The woman turned.

'It's a newspaper reporter. She wants—'

'The name's Bethany Chambers, sir,' I cut in. 'I'm with *The Post*. Are you Mr Fuller?'

He stepped forward and stood next to his neighbour in the doorway.

'I am,' he said. 'What is it you want?'

I cleared my throat and weighed my words before I spoke.

'Well, let me begin by saying that I'm truly sorry for your loss, Mr Fuller. What has happened to your daughter is truly shocking. We're now cooperating with the police to get as much publicity as possible. My paper is about to publish an appeal for information and it's been suggested by the police that you might like to include a few words about Megan.'

I had used the same spiel on numerous occasions before and it had worked about fifty per cent of the time. There was no easy way to approach a grieving relative, and it was always hard not to come across as insensitive, or even callous.

I studied the man as he thought about what to do. He was in his late fifties, and tall enough to look down his nose at me. His grey hair was cropped short, and his eyes were red and puffy.

After a few seconds he gave a stiff nod and said, 'Very well. You'd better come in.'

I followed him along the hall and Martha closed the door behind us. In the living room he sat on the sofa and gestured for me to sit on an armchair opposite. Martha asked me if I wanted a cup of tea; I declined, but she said she would put the kettle on anyway and left the room.

I took out my notebook and pen and rested them on my knee. Questions stormed into my mind, but I didn't want to rush things.

I was acutely aware of how upset Mr Fuller must be and that he might break down at any moment. Therefore I had to tread carefully.

I pulled in a heavy breath and said, 'Perhaps you could start by telling me what sort of person Megan was. Most people will only know her as Lisa Fawkes from the TV soap.'

His eyes grew sorrowful and the muscles in his jaw tensed.

'She was wonderful,' he said after a beat. 'She got on with most people and was very thoughtful.'

'I understand she'd been at a low ebb since losing her job with the BBC.'

'That's true. It came as a shock, and this last year in particular was hard for her. She was quite depressed. I think she found it hard to accept that her life had changed so much.'

'Were you close?'

He nodded. 'Of course, although I now regret the fact that we didn't see much of each other in recent years.'

'What about her mother, your wife?'

'Trisha passed away six years ago. Cancer. Megan was very much like her mother and we were both so proud of her.'

I felt a lump rise in my throat and had to pause before asking another question.

'Can you tell me what happened earlier this morning, Mr Fuller, when you arrived at Megan's house?'

He swallowed hard and looked beyond me at something that wasn't in the room.

'She asked me to come over because she wanted to talk to me,' he said. 'She knew that Amy and I were planning to visit Amy's son in Canterbury this afternoon.'

'Amy?'

'My fiancée. We're getting married next year.'

'I see. So you arrived at Megan's house about seven. Is that right?'

'Yes. But there was no answer when I rang the bell so I thought she must have overslept. I don't have a key so I went around the back to call up to her bedroom window. That's when I looked into the kitchen and saw her on the floor.'

'Then what did you do?'

'I smashed the door window with a rock from the garden and got inside. I thought she might still be alive even though there was a lot of blood. But when I knelt down beside her and saw the gash in her throat I realised that she wasn't.'

The tears he'd been holding back began to spill from the corners of his eyes and his face creased up. I could almost feel his pain and a cold flush went over my skin.

I gave him time to recover, then cleared my throat for the second time. 'When was the last time you spoke to Megan, Mr Fuller?'

He wiped his eyes on his sleeve and switched his gaze back to me.

'Yesterday evening,' he said, his voice cracking. 'She was upset. I didn't realise how upset until I got a text from her much later asking me to come over this morning. She must have sent it just before . . .'

He couldn't finish the sentence and my face grew hot as I watched him struggling to hold it together.

I leaned forward, elbows on knees. 'What was Megan upset about, Mr Fuller? Can you tell me that?'

His voice dropped to a hard-edged whisper, and anger suddenly blazed in his eyes.

'She was upset because of that gobshite Shapiro.'

'You mean Danny Shapiro, her ex-husband?'

'That's right. They'd had words again yesterday, but she said that this time he threatened to kill her because she was planning to include derogatory statements about him in her autobiography.'

I was taken aback by this bombshell revelation. Danny Shapiro had threatened to kill his wife only a short time before she was murdered. It was a dynamite piece of information even though we probably wouldn't be able to print it at this time for legal reasons.

'I assume you've told the police,' I said.

Nigel Fuller nodded. 'Absolutely. But they're not stupid. They must have guessed that he's the one who killed her. He hated Megan and he's been vile to her ever since she left him.'

'What was their reaction when you told them?'

'They said they'd talk to him right away. I'm hoping the bastard has already been arrested.'

I was still processing what I had just heard when the doorbell chimed. As Martha went to answer it I put my notebook and pen back in my bag and stood up. Instinct told me it'd be the police at the door and a few moments later I was proved right when one came into the living room.

'It's the family liaison officer, Nigel,' Martha said from behind her.

Her name was Lauren Tomlinson. Sergeant Lauren Tomlinson. The last time we'd met – about six months ago – she'd given me a bollocking for trying to gain access to the wife of a man who'd been shot dead in Greenwich.

'What the hell are you doing here?' she said to me before she had even introduced herself to Mr Fuller.

'I was actually just about to leave,' I said. 'Mr Fuller here was kind enough to grant me a short interview.'

'Did you get permission?'

'I didn't think I needed it. There were no officers outside when I arrived.'

Tomlinson was a tall woman with short dark hair and storm-grey eyes which stared at me accusingly. She clearly wasn't happy, and I could tell she was up for making an issue of it. But Nigel Fuller took the wind out of her sails by getting to his feet and saying, 'It's not a problem, Officer. I was happy to cooperate in the hope that an appeal for information will produce a result.'

Tomlinson masked her disappointment well by introducing herself to him and then offering to show me out.

'No need to bother,' I said. 'I know the way.'

I then turned back to Megan's father and offered my condolences again.

'It's impossible for me to imagine what you're going through,' I said. 'I'm confident though that whoever killed Megan will be brought to justice.'

My words ignited another blast of emotion in him. He dropped back onto the sofa and buried his face in his hands.

As I walked out of the room his shoulders were pumping up and down with his crying and I became aware of guilty feelings stirring inside me.

Sure, I'd got an exclusive interview and an explosive angle on the story. But the man's grief had dampened my enthusiasm and reminded me of what it was like to lose a loved one.

6

Ethan Cain

Detective Inspector Ethan Cain studied the body as dispassionately as he could. Even so the sight of it caused something to stir in the pit of his stomach.

Megan Fuller was still lying on the kitchen floor with a gaping hole in her throat. The blood that had spilled onto the lino was now dry, but some still glistened inside the wound and between her thin, purple lips which had been cut from a blow to the mouth. Her nose was broken and her pale, lifeless eyes stared unseeing at the ceiling.

She was wearing a navy-blue blouse and tight jeans. Her long brown hair was fanned out around her head and had soaked up some of the blood.

'The bloody shoe-prints belong to the father,' Detective Chief Inspector Redwood said. 'The poor sod will have to live with what he saw here for the rest of his life.'

Cain lifted his gaze from the floor to the back door, which stood open. Nigel Fuller had gained access by smashing one of the glass panels and reaching for the key left in the lock.

Any dad would have done the same in his position, Cain thought. After all, he must have believed there was a possibility that she was still alive. Trouble was he had contaminated the crime scene and they would never know for sure if he had inadvertently destroyed any crucial evidence.

'There's no other sign of a break-in,' Redwood said. 'So there's a good chance she let the killer in.'

Cain turned to his boss, who was standing in the doorway. Redwood was in his early forties, barrel-chested and broad-shouldered. Dark stubble bristled on his face and his eyes were bright blue and slightly bulging.

He was a hard-nosed individual with a short temper and a gruff voice. He didn't drink or smoke and rarely socialised with the team, preferring the gym to the pub.

As the senior investigating officer he was in charge of the investigation, and Cain knew he'd do a thorough job. Redwood was fairly new to the Met, having moved down from Manchester five months ago, and he'd brought with him an impressive reputation. Unlike Cain he still viewed police work as a worthwhile vocation rather than a relentless grind on behalf of an unappreciative public.

The gaffer was the kind of copper that Cain used to be before disillusionment set in and he was told he'd probably never be promoted beyond the rank of detective inspector within the Met. And long before he fell into the trap of wanting to spend more money than he earned.

'Megan suffered a single stab wound to the throat,' Redwood was saying. 'The doc says the blade must have been a minimum of fourteen millimetres long. It cut through the trachea and hit the cervical vertebrae. The killer then sliced downwards and ripped open the thyroid gland and the oesophagus. It's a safe bet the knife was taken from the block over there on the worktop.'

It was a six-knife block and one of them was missing. Cain had already been told that there was no sign of the murder weapon. Officers were searching the house, the front and back gardens, and the surrounding area, although in all likelihood the killer or killers had taken it with them when fleeing the scene.

'There are no signs of a struggle in any of the other rooms,' Redwood said. 'But it does appear as though the house has been searched. Drawers have been left open and the contents dropped on the floor. Having said that we don't know if anything has been stolen but this doesn't look like a burglary gone wrong to me.'

Redwood had had time to acquaint himself with the scene, having arrived an hour ago. Cain had been delayed by traffic hold-ups in Clapham. He needed to look around for himself and get a feel for the place.

'Come out into the back garden,' Redwood said. 'The SOCOs want to get back in here and I need to tell you and the others what else we've got.'

The others were detective constables Rachel Fisher and Toby Dean, who had also just arrived and were already waiting in the garden to be briefed.

They all stood on the patio, out of the way of the scene-of-crime officers who were dusting and swabbing every inch of the house.

Redwood pulled down the hood of his overall and took out his notebook. He began by telling them what they already knew – that the victim was 32-year-old Megan Fuller who lived alone in the house and was well known as a TV soap actress.

'Estimated time of death is between ten thirty and midnight last night,' he said. 'The neighbour to the right apparently heard raised voices around ten but no screams. The house doesn't have a video security system but there are some CCTV cameras around here so I want them checked.'

Cain was fairly certain that a person or car approaching the house would have been caught on camera at some point. He himself had turned into Ramsden Road from Balham High Road and had spotted at least two cameras at that junction alone. But last night it had rained so there was no guarantee that any footage would be useful.

'What does the father say?' Cain asked.

'I was just coming to that,' Redwood said. 'I've only had a brief conversation with him, but he's with one of the neighbours so we can talk to him again before he's taken home.'

'Did he tell you why he turned up here this morning?' Cain said.

Redwood nodded. 'Megan sent him a text last night at twenty past ten, which was presumably just before she was killed. Her phone was in the kitchen and I had a quick look before it was bagged up.' He lowered his eyes and read from his notes. 'She wrote, and I quote: "*Can you come over early tomorrow, Dad? Need to talk to you.*" He then replied that he'd be here about seven. Mr Fuller also says he had a conversation with her earlier in the evening during which she said she'd had a bust-up with her ex-husband Danny Shapiro and that Shapiro threatened to kill her.'

Cain felt a flash of heat in his chest. He had known it was only a matter of time before Danny came into the equation, but he hadn't expected this.

'I don't need to remind you who Danny Shapiro is,' Redwood went on. 'Or that he's more than capable of committing murder or getting one of his henchmen to do it for him. He's therefore our number one suspect. Megan's phone shows that she made a call earlier to an unregistered mobile number that's in her contacts under the name Danny. That's why a team should be descending on his flat in Bermondsey about now.'

'He probably won't be there, guv,' DC Fisher said. 'He hardly ever stays at the flat.'

'How do you know?'

'It's common knowledge, sir. Danny Shapiro spends most nights at a secret address. That's one of the reasons he's been dubbed Mr Paranoid.'

'This is news to me.'

'You would have found out eventually, boss.'

'Yeah, well, I obviously have a lot to learn about London's leading underworld faces.' He turned to Cain. 'Are you up to speed on Shapiro, Ethan?'

Cain shrugged. 'I know about as much as everyone else, guv. The guy doesn't trust anyone, apparently, and it's not hard to understand why. His father Callum was less careful and eventually paid the price. After months of covert surveillance the organised crime teams managed to gather enough evidence to take him down.

'Shortly after his son took charge of things a rival villain took a shot at him as he left his flat. The bullet missed but it convinced Shapiro that he wasn't safe there – or anywhere else that people knew about. The flat is still his formal address and he occasionally entertains and holds court there. But we've no idea where he lays his head most nights, except that it's somewhere in London.'

Redwood nodded several times as he mulled this over. Then he said, 'Well, Shapiro is not our only suspect. Megan has been phoning and texting someone named Sam on a fairly regular basis. I get the impression from the messages that he was her boyfriend up until a short time ago. But it seems they had a falling-out. He sent her a text three days ago in which he apologised for hitting her and promised not to do it again. She responded by saying it was over and that if he came to the house again she'd call the police.'

'He sounds promising,' Cain said.

Redwood nodded. 'We need to find out who this Sam is and where he was last night. We've got his number so it shouldn't be hard.'

Cain found himself hoping that Sam had murdered Megan and that they would quickly solve the case. The thought of having to pursue Danny Shapiro – the man he accepted regular bribes from – made his blood run cold. As long as Danny was in the frame his own duplicity was under threat of exposure.

The detectives then discussed possible motives for murder, one of which was the tell-all book that Megan had claimed she was writing. It was public knowledge because she'd mentioned it in several TV and newspaper interviews.

'I've asked the techies to look for notes and a manuscript,' Redwood said. 'It might be that the killer is someone who fears being featured in the book.'

Redwood asked DC Fisher to check Megan's bank accounts and phone records.

'There's been talk of her having money problems,' he said. 'If that's the case then I want to know the extent of it.'

After the briefing, Cain had a quick look around the house, careful not to get in the way of the forensic sweep.

It was much less impressive than he had expected. The furnishings were dated and it looked as though Megan hadn't been taking care of the place. The rooms were untidy and the stale smell of cigarettes hung in the air.

In the main bedroom the search teams discovered several wraps of cocaine and a leather pouch filled with cannabis. The drinks cabinet in the living room was stuffed with bottles of spirits, most of which were half empty. In the small study at the front of the house a SOCO found something significant after firing up Megan's laptop. Cain and Redwood responded to his request to go and check it out.

'I opened up her browser and then her Hotmail account,' the SOCO said. 'I immediately came across an email that I think you need to see.'

The email was from Megan to a Yahoo account in the name of Daniel Shapiro. When Cain read it a sliver of ice slid down his spine.

Don't make the mistake of ignoring me, Danny. A one-off payment is all I'm asking for. I know you can afford it. So if you fuck me about you'll seriously regret it.

'It's a clear motive for murder,' Redwood said. 'Shapiro was threatened by his ex-wife so he decided to sort her out.'

Cain felt obliged to play it down for Danny's sake.

'I'm not so sure, guv,' he said. 'From what I hear about Shapiro he's not stupid. I can't imagine he would kill her only days after that email was sent. He'd know how bad it would look.'

'She might have given him a deadline,' Redwood said. 'So he felt he didn't have a choice but to come here and make sure she didn't carry out her threat. Or perhaps he paid someone to do it for him.'

Cain felt a shiver of apprehension. He knew that what Redwood was saying made sense and that so far the evidence was pointing to Danny.

'How well do you know the guy, Ethan?' Redwood asked.

Cain shrugged. 'I've hauled him in a couple of times in connection with gangland killings but we've never been able to pin anything on him.'

Redwood narrowed his eyes in concentration as he turned something over in his mind. After a few moments, he said, 'I had dealings with a couple of the big-time villains in Manchester. It was always difficult because they're so well connected. I'm assuming that like them Shapiro has his fair share of friends in high places across London.'

'I reckon that goes without saying,' Cain said.

Redwood nodded. 'In that case we have to assume that he's got at least one or two of our colleagues in the Met on his books. Which means we have to play this close to our chests. I don't want him getting wind of evidence we need to keep to ourselves.'

Cain's stomach folded in on itself. He realised now that he was going to have to be ultra-careful. Redwood was clearly no novice when it came to dealing with criminals like Danny Shapiro who had heaps of cash and lots of clout.

He was aware that the tentacles of corruption reached into the guts of every force in the UK.

So he would know not to trust anyone – not even those officers who were working alongside him on the investigation.

7

Danny Shapiro

Danny tried to focus his mind as he showered and shaved. But it wasn't easy because of the rising sense of panic inside him. He was used to being in control, staying one step ahead of everyone else. Now he was on the back foot and struggling to see how he'd be able to convince the filth that he didn't kill his ex-wife.

There was no way he could admit to being in Megan's house last night, or that he had been anywhere near the area.

He'd been thinking about the CCTV cameras that would have picked him up during the walk from Clapham to Balham and felt sure the cops would struggle to identify him from any footage. It had been raining, after all, and he'd been wearing a hoody.

But even if he struck lucky there he still couldn't account for his movements. They would probably know by now that he hadn't spent the evening at the Bermondsey flat. The concierge would have confirmed that he hadn't been back there since Thursday. He couldn't even say he'd been here all evening – in the house that he actually considered his home and that precious few people knew existed.

A security camera on the front of the building and a CCTV camera on the street would have recorded him arriving back at about 11.30. That in itself would be another nail in his coffin.

What he needed was a cast-iron alibi and he didn't have one. There were any number of people working for him who could provide him with a false one, but he wasn't sure he had enough time to get it sorted. He'd first have to decide who he trusted, then find out what they were doing last night, before agreeing a story. Any mistakes on their part, any holes in the story, and the whole thing would come unstuck.

Bishop would have been the obvious choice, but Danny knew for a fact that his enforcer had spent the evening at their new club in Streatham.

Besides, as soon as he started asking people to give him an alibi they'd assume it was a sign of guilt and that he had killed Megan. He had been under pressure anyway to warn her off since she'd starting threatening to reveal details about the firm in her autobiography. Bishop and some of the other crew members had been concerned that she'd land them all in the shit.

Danny had tried to assure them that she was bluffing and knew very little about his business affairs. He'd nevertheless agreed to sort her out. But Megan had ignored his warnings, and even when he had offered her 100 grand 'for old times' sake' she had rejected it and continued to demand half a million.

Out of principle he would never have paid her that much, but he would probably have offered her another 100 k. If that still hadn't been enough to shut her up he wasn't sure what he'd have done. Now, of course, he didn't have to worry.

Not for the first time he wondered if she'd been telling the truth when she told him she had a publisher. For all he knew she wasn't even writing a book. Maybe it was just a desperate attempt to force him into giving her money.

He could feel the blood pulsing in his neck as he got dressed. Casual clothes as usual. Jeans, shirt, leather jacket. When he checked himself in the mirror he got a shock. His face was gaunt and pale, the lips set in a tight line.

He was pouring himself a cup of coffee when the landline phone rang for the second time that morning. After a brief hesitation he decided to answer it, and when he heard Bishop's voice the relief surged through him.

'Is that you, boss?'

'Who else would it be on this number?' Danny said.

'I called earlier and there was no answer. Wasn't sure if you were there.'

'I was in the shower.'

'Right. Well, I take it you've heard about Megan.'

'Of course. It's all over the fucking news.'

'At least she no longer poses a threat,' Bishop said. 'You want me to pass on a message to the lads?'

'Yeah. You can tell them I wasn't responsible. I haven't a fucking clue who topped her.'

''Course you haven't, boss. That goes without saying. But the Old Bill are looking for you anyway in case you don't know. I've just had a call from the office. They turned up there mob-handed about ten minutes ago and they've also been to your flat.'

'Well, I'll talk to them when I'm good and ready. Where are you?'

'On my way to the office. We were planning to have a team talk this morning or had you forgotten?'

'I hadn't forgotten,' Danny said. 'But I'll be late. I've got something to do first.'

'No problem. How do you feel about Megan?'

'I'm gutted. How do you think I feel? I was married to the woman for three years. And regardless of what a nuisance she's been since she left me, I wouldn't have wished this on her.'

'Yeah, I see what you mean.'

Danny wasn't surprised that Bishop appeared unmoved. The man didn't give a rat's arse about anyone. He'd known Megan for as long as Danny had and had been one of the few people who hadn't disapproved of the marriage. But even back then he wouldn't have shed a tear if she'd fallen under a bus. In fact he wouldn't have hesitated for a second if Danny had instructed him to push her under one.

That was the thing about Bishop. He had the perfect mind-set for the job he did. Granted, he was a psycho who relished hurting people. It was how he'd made a name for himself during his days in Southampton. And why the Old Bill there had been so glad to get shot of him. But he was also a fiercely loyal enforcer and committed *consigliere*. And when you ran an operation that meant you had to deal with the dregs of society he was the kind of person you wanted at your side.

'I take it you've got an alibi for last night, boss,' Bishop said.

'Naturally.'

'That's good, because you're gonna feel some heat over this. If there's anything you need me to do then let me know.'

Danny was tempted to seek his advice but decided it wouldn't be a good idea. Instead he told Bishop he would catch up with him later.

He replaced the receiver and drew in a breath. The house suddenly felt hot and airless.

He switched on the TV and watched the news again while drinking his coffee. Megan's murder was still the dominant story and reports were now coming live from the scene. No arrests had been made and it sounded like the police had no leads. That wasn't good. It meant that the problem wasn't going to go away anytime soon.

An alibi. He desperately needed one, and fast. But his options were dangerously limited. And he was running out of time.

As he paced the kitchen floor, his heart pounding, he found himself wishing he could just pick up the phone and call his father. Callum would know what to do, just like he always did.

But his dad was banged up because he'd been careless. And since the day of his arrest it had been up to Danny to sort out his own problems.

Danny had always admired his dad. Callum Shapiro had created a thriving business in one of the toughest parts of London.

He had been inspired by his boyhood heroes – Charlie and Eddie Richardson. The Richardson gang had reigned supreme over the south London manor during the Sixties. Their speciality was torture, including cutting off toes with bolt cutters, pulling out teeth with pliers, and nailing victims to the floor with six-inch nails.

The pair invested in scrap metal and fruit machines, businesses they used as fronts for racketeering, drug dealing, extortion, prostitution, stolen goods, and loan sharking.

Danny's father had met the brothers a couple of times and had employed their torture techniques on more than a few occasions.

Callum became a legend in his own right, and managed to do it without alienating most of the people on his south London patch. To many of them he was a larger-than-life benefactor, giving generous donations to local charities and causes, and protecting some of the most vulnerable against street scum who raped, mugged, and robbed – and in so doing gave all decent criminals a bad name.

Callum had modelled himself on the stereotypical Mafia gangster and had loved being referred to as the Godfather of south London. He would swan around in chauffeur-driven Mercs and wear ridiculously expensive Savile Row suits. Two burly bodyguards were never far behind, drawing attention and bolstering his ego.

Danny was born before his dad rose to prominence, back when Callum was making a name for himself in Peckham. He was married to Danny's mother Erica then and life was hard but good.

Erica tried to discourage Danny from going the way of his father, but it was a losing battle from the start. Callum used to say that he wanted to build an empire that his son would one day take over and so he started grooming Danny as soon as he reached his teens.

When Danny was mature enough to resist, saying he didn't want to follow a life of crime, there were ructions. Danny had his mother's support and would have dug his heels in if not for the fact that she died suddenly from a heart attack when he was 17.

Any thoughts of going to university or pursuing a proper career were put on hold so that he could be there for his father, who was overcome by grief. Callum had loved Erica with all his heart and it took him a long time to recover. He leaned on Danny for support and in the process Danny came to accept that his destiny was to be at his father's side.

Within a year of his mother's death, Danny was involved in the business, acting as an assistant manager at one of the clubs. Gradually he was given more responsibility and learned how to take care of himself.

In his private life Danny remained a free agent, enjoying the trappings of success and the steady stream of female companions that his good looks and notoriety attracted.

His dad eventually returned to his old self, thanks partly to an unlikely relationship with one of the prossies who worked in the lap-dance club they ran in Rotherhithe.

Tamara Roth, a striking redhead, was twenty years younger than Callum, and he became so besotted with her that he insisted she came off the game so that he could have her all to himself.

He paid off the mortgage on her house in Vauxhall and spoiled her rotten. When he was sent down she was devastated, and not just because she'd lost her sugar daddy. Danny suspected that she had probably come to love Callum as much as he'd loved her.

Tamara's face suddenly pushed itself into his thoughts. He hadn't seen her in months, even though the firm still made regular payments into her bank account as per his father's instructions.

He knew she was back in business, but working for herself this time, and turning tricks only for a few regular high-end clients. His father didn't know and she had asked Danny not to tell him.

Danny didn't blame her. She had a life to lead, after all, and nobody expected her to wait around for a man who was unlikely ever to leave prison.

Thinking about Tamara gave him an idea. She had said to him once that she would do anything for his father, and at the time he'd believed her. He wondered now if she could be persuaded to protect Callum's only son by lying for him.

He decided to find out because he realised he had nothing to lose. He looked up her number in his contacts book and called it. Thankfully she answered on the fourth ring and sounded surprised to discover it was him on the line.

'Oh, Danny, it's wonderful to hear from you. It's been too long, hon. But look, I've just heard about Megan on the news. I'm really sorry. I know you haven't been together for a while but it must still have come as a shock.'

'It did,' he said. 'I only just heard about it myself.'

'Well, if there's anything I can do for you, hon, you have only to ask. I still feel like I'm part of the family.'

'Actually there is something, Tamara,' he said. 'I need an alibi for last night, and I need it before I get stitched up for something I didn't do.'

8

Beth Chambers

I was now part of a raucous media circus. TV crews with their satellite trucks had turned up and the national press had gathered en masse.

We were being corralled behind a police barrier from where we could see the cops and forensic officers working the scene. Some officers were going door-to-door canvassing neighbours, while others were standing around with their arms folded, their expressions intense and stoic.

This was now the biggest show in town. The story had everything. A mysterious murder. A celebrity victim. A crime boss ex-husband who was among the suspects. It was the sort of thing that really got my juices flowing. It would also sell newspapers and lead to a boost in *The Post*'s circulation.

No wonder I could feel the adrenalin searing my senses. I was in my element and hoping – like the other reporters here – that there wouldn't be a quick resolution. It would be better for us if the story could be dragged out for at least a few days, or even weeks.

That would give us all time to dig up the dirt on Megan Fuller and her ex-husband. Once the police charged someone then reporting restrictions would kick in until the trial.

I'd already phoned over the quotes from Megan's father, and included a note about Danny Shapiro threatening Megan. The editor would have to talk to the lawyers to decide whether or not we could include it.

I wondered if his arrest was imminent. Or was Shapiro already in custody?

One thing I did know for certain was that I needed to find out as much as I could about the man. I'd written about him in the past but not at any great length. The stories had centred on his marriage to Megan, his father's imprisonment, and the attempt on his life when a rival Chechen gangster tried to shoot him in Bermondsey.

Since assuming control of the rackets in south London from his father he'd taken steps to lower his profile. He'd become paranoid apparently, fearful of being targeted again or of being entrapped by police surveillance. Megan's murder had thrust him right back into the limelight, along with his nefarious business activities.

'How's it going, Chambers?'

The voice made me turn and I found myself facing the diminutive figure of Steve Welland, *The Sun*'s chief crime reporter. He was in his fifties, with craggy features and unruly grey hair. He grinned at me and I saw that his nose and cheeks were red with broken capillaries.

Welland was a throwback to the days when it was common for Fleet Street reporters to abuse their expenses on a grand scale and take three-hour liquid lunches.

'It's going all right,' I said. 'What about you?'

He shrugged. 'I was in good spirits until just now when I heard that you'd managed to grab an interview with the victim's father, the man who discovered the body.'

'I had a stroke of luck,' I said. 'Got to him when no one was looking.'

'So where is he now?'

I grinned back at him. 'I'm afraid I've been sworn to secrecy.'

'Very funny.'

'Anyway he's been told not to speak to anyone else – especially any reporters from *The Sun*.'

He shook his head. 'How I long for the days when us lot used to share information.'

'That was way before my time, Steve.'

It was the usual friendly banter and it helped pass the time while we waited for something to happen. The rivalry between reporters was healthy, and it kept us on our toes. Sometimes I did swap information, but only when I knew I would get a tasty morsel in return. This time as far as I could see Welland had nothing to offer.

He was about to continue the conversation when we were both distracted by a sudden commotion. I looked towards the house and saw why everyone was excited.

Detectives Redwood and Cain had emerged from the house, having removed their forensic overalls. Now they were heading towards the media scrum in order to provide us with the promised update.

The two detectives stood side by side, and DCI Redwood was a good four inches taller than DI Cain.

Redwood was wearing a bespoke blue suit with white shirt and red tie. He looked smart and authoritative. I knew very little about him other than that he was a career copper who was fairly new to the Met. So far our paths had never crossed.

Cain, on the other hand, I knew only too well. He was wearing the beige linen suit he'd bought to take on our honeymoon. I found out later that it was chosen for him by a woman he'd been having an affair with at the time.

It was Redwood who started the ball rolling by making a brief statement during which he ran through the basic facts.

'Miss Megan Fuller was the victim of a savage knife attack,' he said. 'She was murdered last evening between ten thirty and midnight. We believe she was alone. I appeal to anyone who was in Ramsden Road at the time to come forward. It's possible you have vital information and you don't realise it.'

He confirmed that the killing had taken place in the kitchen and said it did not appear as though she had been a victim of robbery.

Having read the statement he invited questions and they came thick and fast.

Was Megan sexually assaulted?

Did she let her killer into the house?

Has the murder weapon been recovered?

Sweat beaded on Redwood's upper lip as he provided the answers, none of which came as a surprise to any of us.

As soon as I got a chance I raised my arm and shouted out, 'Is it true that Miss Fuller's ex-husband Danny Shapiro has been questioned?'

Redwood's head snapped towards me. The question had caught him by surprise.

He bunched his brows and said, 'We do intend to speak to Mr Shapiro along with a number of other people, but we haven't yet done so.'

'Does that mean he's a suspect?' I said.

I was close enough to see a nerve flutter at his temple.

'He's not a suspect at this stage,' he said. 'But we are hoping that he might be able to provide us with information about Miss Fuller.'

Redwood was turning away from me as I threw another question.

'Can you confirm that Mr Shapiro spoke to Miss Fuller by phone yesterday and that they had an argument? According to Mr Fuller, his daughter was threatened by Mr Shapiro.'

Redwood wasn't expecting that and he wasn't happy. His face tensed and for a moment he was lost for words.

Cain came to his rescue. He fixed me with an evaluating gaze and said, 'May I ask who told you that, Miss Chambers?'

That was when I realised that he and Redwood weren't aware that I'd interviewed Nigel Fuller.

'I spoke to Miss Fuller's father a few minutes ago,' I said. 'He told me about the phone call.'

'Well, we're still in the process of following up the information that Mr Fuller gave us,' Cain said. 'So I'm afraid I can't answer your question at this time, Miss Chambers.'

Cain gave me a knowing stare and the corners of his mouth twitched, hinting at a smile. But that was for the audience. I was willing to bet that inside he was fuming.

I transferred my gaze to Redwood and found it difficult to read the expression on his face. I could tell that his mind was racing, though, and I realised that someone was going to get a severe bollocking.

Redwood answered a few more questions and then called a halt to the briefing at the first opportunity.

I moved away from the crowd, powered up the iPad, and sent

some updated copy to the paper. I then took a call from Grant Scott, who said he had watched the briefing live on the TV news.

'You sure put them on the spot, Beth,' he said. 'They didn't look too pleased.'

'They'll get over it. So what now? I'm not sure how much more I can get from here. They'll soon be winding things down.'

'Then I think you should chase up Danny Shapiro. Maybe you can get a quote for the late edition. As far as I know he still hasn't been collared. I suggest you go to his office and see if he's there. I take it you know where it is.'

'Of course. I'm on my way.'

9

Danny Shapiro

Danny walked out of his mews house safe in the knowledge that the police weren't about to pounce on him. The very existence of the property was a closely guarded secret. It was his father who had advised him not to live on their south London manor.

'Don't make the same mistakes I did, son,' Callum told him. 'The Old Bill were able to follow my every move because I was careless and complacent. They bugged my home and my car, and wherever I went they had me on camera. I also made myself a target for my enemies.'

Danny took the advice on board but didn't act on it until that Chechen scumbag tried to shoot him over a territorial dispute. It was a wake-up call and it prompted Danny to reassess his lifestyle.

As a result he stopped using his own car, started using pay-as-you-go phones and wore a baseball cap or a hoody when he took to the streets. He also bought as much as he could with cash rather than with traceable credit cards.

The most significant decision he took was to move out of his luxury flat overlooking the Thames in Bermondsey. He never felt safe there anyway after the attempt on his life, and he was convinced the filth had it under surveillance.

There was no shortage of places for him to go since the firm had for years been investing in property across London. He settled on the mews house which had been purchased through an offshore company five years earlier with the proceeds from a major drugs deal. It had remained empty ever since, gathering dust and increasing in value.

There was nothing to link it to him or his father and because it was smack in the middle of the West End he considered it the ideal location.

In explaining the decision to his father, he'd said, 'It's in one of the busiest spots in the capital, Dad. The area's covered with CCTV cameras and teeming with tourists, and the streets are permanently gridlocked. I won't just be inconspicuous – I'll be fucking invisible.'

So far it had worked a treat. Most evenings he left the manor in a taxi or on a tube and disappeared into the bustle of the West End, making it impossible for anyone to follow him.

The house had four bedrooms, a garage that housed his rarely used BMW, and overlooked a small communal garden at the rear. It was located just off New Bond Street, within walking distance of Sotheby's and a range of designer shops from Burberry to Jimmy Choo.

The arrangement had its disadvantages, of course. He never took women back there and he sometimes wondered if it was worth all the hassle. Still, he couldn't deny that once he closed the door behind him he always felt safe and secure, knowing that no one knew where he was.

The flat in Bermondsey still had its uses. He stayed there

occasionally and it was great for parties and meetings. It was also where he took his women, usually prossies and one-night stands. But he knew he would have to have a rethink when and if he eventually entered into another long-term relationship.

As usual the area was heaving. Traffic was snarled up in New Bond Street so he walked up to Grosvenor Street to hail a black cab.

His progress would have been monitored by a whole bunch of security cameras but it didn't bother him because he'd be just another anonymous figure in the crowd. These days he preferred not to attract attention, which was why he dressed down and chose not to go everywhere with minders.

The years spent with Megan had turned him into the best-known villain in London. That hadn't been so bad when his father was running the show and he'd been able to concentrate on enjoying himself.

Now things were different. The onus of responsibility had made him appreciate just how vulnerable he was.

It had also made him realise that he couldn't trust anyone but himself.

Tamara lived in one of the residential streets bordering Vauxhall Park. As the taxi pulled up outside her house, Danny did a quick recce of the immediate area.

He couldn't see any street cameras and this came as a relief. It would make it harder for the cops to prove that he hadn't spent the previous evening here.

He still had to convince Tamara to provide him with an alibi, but he was hopeful because she hadn't turned him down on the phone. It would have been easy for her to do so and he would have understood.

She'd appeared sympathetic to his plight, and had said that she did not want to see him go to prison for something he hadn't done. But he reckoned it was probably the £50,000 bribe he offered her that had prompted her to tell him to come right over so that they could talk it through.

Hers was a modest terraced house with creeping ivy clinging to the brickwork. Danny's stomach was churning as he rang the bell. He had no back-up plan if she decided not to help him and he had no idea what he would do.

The filth were probably thinking he'd done a runner. He'd considered calling Ethan Cain, the firm's main man inside the Met, to find out what was going on, but had decided it should wait until after he'd sorted an alibi.

His empty stomach lurched when Tamara answered the door and ushered him quickly inside. The first thing she did when the door was closed was to give him a hug and the strong smell of her perfume made his eyes smart.

'Come into the kitchen,' she said. 'The kettle has just boiled.'

She was softly spoken and there was the subtle hint of an Irish accent in her voice.

The house interior was surprisingly old-fashioned, with chintzy curtains and wallpaper, and brightly coloured rugs on the floor.

In the kitchen Tamara told him to sit at a table while she poured the teas. A portable TV stood on the worktop and it was tuned into the news. An anchor was talking about the prime minister's latest pronouncement on welfare reform.

'Does your father know what's happening?' she asked over her shoulder.

'I don't know,' he said. 'I haven't heard from him.'

She turned and he watched her as she placed the mugs on the table. She was in her mid-forties but looked younger. Her eyes were dark, her lips full, and she had perfectly symmetrical features. There was a spray of faded freckles across the bridge of her nose, and her skin was clear and smooth with just a touch of foundation around the eyes.

She was wearing a grey sweatshirt and jeans, and her red hair hung loose about her shoulders. She sat down at the table and lit a cigarette, expelling the smoke in a long, thin stream.

'You look like you've got the world on your shoulders, Danny,' she said.

'Right now that's what it feels like. This has come out of the blue and I need to react to it.'

She leaned across the table and placed a hand over one of his.

'Before we talk about this I need you to do something for me, hon. I need you to look me in the eyes and tell me you didn't kill Megan. I'll know if you're lying.'

Danny straightened his back and thrust out his chin.

'I swear on my life that I didn't do it, Tamara. I've done some bad things in my time, but murdering a woman isn't one of them. It's not my style.'

'But you did go to Megan's house last night.'

'I did, and we argued like I told you on the phone. But she was alive when I left there.'

That at least was what he wanted to believe. The truth was there were still gaps in his memory. As hard as he tried he just couldn't remember how the argument with Megan had ended and what she'd been doing when he'd stormed out.

'The police are not going to believe me,' he said. 'If no one else is in the frame and I don't have an alibi then I'm toast.'

'So what makes you so sure that the police will believe me?'

'Why wouldn't they? It'll be hard, if not impossible, for them to prove that I wasn't here.'

'But I wasn't here myself, Danny. I told you that on the phone. I got home after midnight.'

'Did anyone see you?'

'I doubt it. The taxi dropped me right outside. I didn't notice anyone around. And the neighbours aren't particularly nosey.'

'So where had you been?'

Her face filled with colour and she flicked her head towards a calendar hanging from a hook on the wall behind her. It was too far away for Danny to see the words scrawled in the boxes.

'I spent the evening with a new client,' she said. 'I went to his place in Maida Vale at nine and left after midnight.'

'But that's not a problem,' Danny said. 'He never has to know what you've told the police. In fact no one has to know. As soon as you tell them that I was with you that'll be the end of the matter. And if anyone comes here asking you just stick to the story.'

She turned back to him, sucked in a breath, said, 'I wouldn't do it if I didn't believe you, Danny. Even for fifty thousand pounds. But I do believe you. So it follows that I can't stand by and let them fit you up. Your dad would never forgive me.'

'Does that mean . . .?'

She nodded. 'It means I'll tell the Old Bill that you were with me all evening and that you're often here. I'll say that between ten and midnight we were watching telly and drinking wine.'

Danny felt the knot in his chest loosen. 'I'll owe you big time, babe. And so will Dad. I'll make arrangements for the money to be sent wherever you want.'

'You and your father have done a lot for me, Danny. This is my way of paying you back.'

They spent the next half an hour agreeing the details of their story. They'd say he arrived early in the evening but that he couldn't recall the exact time because he'd been drinking. Then he stayed

76

overnight and heard about Megan's murder when he woke up this morning.

'We can get around the details by saying we were on the booze the entire time,' he said.

She gave a hesitant smile. 'So you're confident we can get away with it?'

'I'm positive. Trust me. It'll be fine.'

The TV news seized their attention suddenly. They were back to reporting on Megan's murder. Two detectives, one of them Ethan Cain, were standing before a crowd of reporters answering questions.

Danny felt his jaw set with tension when a woman asked them whether Megan's ex-husband had been questioned and if it was true he'd made threats against her. He recognised her straight away as Bethany Chambers, the crime reporter on *The Post*. She was well known on the manor, and not just because of her job. She was the stepdaughter of Tony Hunter, the blagger who was shot some years ago in Tulse Hill. How bloody ironic, he thought, that her job now was to report on such things.

He recalled meeting the cheeky cow a couple of times when she approached him for an interview. It occurred to him then, as it did now, that she was a ballsy bitch.

'*Can you confirm that Mr Shapiro spoke to Miss Fuller by phone yesterday and that they had an argument? According to Mr Fuller, his daughter was threatened by Mr Shapiro.*'

Danny's blood surged with a hot rush of anger. The fucking slag was trying to implicate him.

The anger mounted when she went on to say that Megan's father had told her about the phone call in an interview.

'Those fucking idiot coppers should have kept her away from him,' he blurted.

'Don't let it get to you, hon,' Tamara said. 'It would have come out sooner or later. And besides, it's common knowledge that you two were always arguing.'

Danny shook his head and the rage continued the burn inside him.

After a few seconds he switched on one of his three pay-as-you-go phones and tapped in a number he knew by heart. When DI Ethan Cain answered, he said, 'It's Danny Shapiro here, my friend. I just heard your lot are looking for me.'

10

Beth Chambers

I called up an Uber taxi and gave the driver the address of a well-known snooker club in south Bermondsey. It was from there that Danny Shapiro ran his operations, most of which were illicit.

On the way I did some research on Google. Unsurprisingly the search engine came up with thousands of hits going back years. *The Post*'s own archive was packed with stories about him, many with my by-line.

He hardly got a mention until after he married Megan Fuller, though. Before that it was his father who attracted the headlines. There were only a few photographs showing the pair of them together. The latest was taken just before the old man was arrested. The likeness was evident in their narrow faces and chiselled features.

One photo I came across I hadn't seen before. It must have come from a family album because it showed father and son posing under a tree. The boy looked about 5 and his dad was in his late twenties or early thirties. The caption beneath the picture said it had been taken on Peckham Rye Common.

There was no date, but it occurred to me that it was probably around the time that Callum was building his reputation as a hard man in Peckham. I wondered if that was also when he bought his salads from my mother's stall. She'd told me that he would often walk up Rye Lane on Saturdays as though he owned the place. I made a mental note to show her the photo. Then I came across dozens of other pictures showing Danny Shapiro and Megan together. It seemed to be a period in his life when he was actually courting publicity.

They were a glamorous couple – the soap star and the mobster. Or to be precise – the alleged mobster. It was a fact that despite everyone knowing what he did the police hadn't yet been able to prove it. His only criminal convictions were from years ago. He'd been put on probation for stealing a car and had done some community service after assaulting a pub bouncer in New Cross. But unlike his father he had never faced racketeering and murder charges.

Was that about to change? I wondered. Was Danny Shapiro about to get what was coming to him?

I couldn't help smiling at the thought that in the end most villains ended up in prison or dead at the hands of their enemies. It was certainly true of London's most notorious gangsters. The roll call was endless: Charlie and Eddie Richardson, Ronnie and Reggie Kray, George Cornell, Freddie Foreman, Jack 'The Hat' McVitie, 'Mad' Frankie Fraser, Callum Shapiro.

The list went on and I knew there was no way it would ever stop growing. Organised crime was as much a part of London as its multi-ethnic population. It would never be eradicated and would forever be a part of the capital's heritage – and its future.

* * *

The snooker club was just around the corner from Millwall Football Club's legendary stadium known as The Den.

My stepdad Tony used to take Michael to home matches there on Saturday afternoons and I went along a few times. I hated football but it was fun spending quality time with Tony and Michael.

It was before my little brother went off the rails and got sucked into the gang culture. Back then he was a delight to be with and I'd loved him dearly. We were unlikely siblings – me with my pale complexion and him with his coffee-coloured skin.

He was a happy boy with a pleasant demeanour and a disarming smile. I often wondered where he would be now if he hadn't died before his time. I liked to imagine him as a doctor or a lawyer, or perhaps even a Premier League soccer star.

My mother and I talked about him all the time, and when we did it was still hard not to cry.

According to various biographical snippets on the internet, Callum Shapiro had also been a Millwall supporter and a regular visitor to The Den. The snooker club had been one of his first investments and local legend had it that it was where he started selling drugs and dealing in stolen cars.

The members-only club was situated between an MOT centre and a confectionery wholesaler's. The cab dropped me outside and I asked the driver to wait. As soon as I stepped onto the pavement I was assaulted by the smell of exhaust fumes and rancid fat from the chip shop across the road.

The guy at the small reception desk looked like a Samurai wrestler with clothes on. He eyed me suspiciously and his brows almost came together.

'What can I do for you, love?' he said with a heavy, indeterminate accent. 'I take it you're not here to hit some balls about.'

'I have an appointment with Mr Shapiro,' I lied. 'The name's Bethany Chambers.'

It was all I could think to say to have any chance of gaining access. If Shapiro was on the premises – and not already in a police cell – then he might well agree to an interview. If not then there was just a possibility that one or more of his minions could be persuaded to talk to me, either on or off the record.

'Mr Shapiro ain't here,' the man said.

'Then where is he?'

'Are you with the police? Because they've already been here and checked the place over.'

'I'm not with the police,' I said.

'Then you can't come in. So bugger off.'

'If Mr Shapiro isn't here I'd like to speak to whoever is in charge.'

'Why?'

'That's my business. But I can tell you this. If you turn me away without checking you'll get in trouble. Do you want that?'

That gave him food for thought. He was just a lackey, after all, and the last thing he wanted was to get on the wrong side of the guys who ran this place.

After a couple of seconds of indecision he picked up the desk phone and spoke into it with his back to me. Then he gave a rigorous nod, replaced the receiver and said, 'Mr Bishop says you can go up to the office.'

Frankie 'The Nutter' Bishop. It had to be. He was Danny Shapiro's right-hand man and it was said that he went out of his way to live up to his reputation as a sociopath.

I mounted the stairs to what turned out to be a suite of offices above the snooker hall. A bloke in a black polo sweater was waiting for me. He was completely bald and had the build of a gorilla.

'Follow me,' he said.

I kept pace with him along a long corridor past several closed doors. The door at the end of the corridor stood open and the gorilla moved to one side and waved me in.

That was the precise moment when I realised I might be making a huge mistake. Not for the first time my eagerness to chase a story had blinded me to the risks. I was about to enter the inner sanctum of south London's most violent criminal gang. A voice in my head was telling me to turn around and walk away. But another voice told me to brazen it out.

'So what are you waiting for?' the gorilla said. 'Go in.'

I let out a breath I wasn't aware I'd been holding and entered the room. It was a large, airy room with a long mahogany table surrounded by about a dozen chairs. Five of the chairs were occupied by burly men in casual clothes. They were all leering at me like I'd walked in naked. Two other men were standing to my right next to what looked like a drinks cabinet. I was at once aware of a palpable air of menace.

My heart started pounding high up in my throat and I was sorely tempted to beat a retreat. But at that moment the man at the head of the table stood up and gave a twisted smile.

'It's good to see you in the flesh at last, Miss Chambers,' he said in a broad cockney accent. 'I'm Frankie Bishop and I have to say I'd willingly pay to give you one, as I'm sure would every man in this room.'

There were groans of agreement from the others and I felt my system flush with rage and indignation.

I was about to fire back an angry retort when the two men to my right lunged towards me. One seized my shoulder bag while the other grabbed my arms from behind and held me in a firm grip.

'What do you think you're doing?' I screamed. 'Let me go.'

'We need to be sure that you're not recording what goes on in this room,' Bishop said. 'It's just a precaution.'

The man with my bag emptied the contents on the floor. Then he picked up the phone and voice recorder and checked that they weren't recording.

'All clear,' he said as he set about putting everything back into the bag.

The other man now pushed me forward and onto one of the chairs. I wanted to resist but felt paralysed as raw fear flooded my body.

I sat there, trying to control my breathing, as Frankie Bishop lowered himself back onto his chair and stared at me.

He was a big, hard-looking bastard. His face was dimpled with small scars as if from terrible wounds. His nose was splayed and crooked, and his bulging biceps strained at the black T-shirt he was wearing. He had short cropped hair and eyes that were small and cold.

'I will say this for you, Chambers,' he said, dropping the Miss. 'You've got some front coming here and telling a big fat lie to get in. You never had any appointment with Danny. He never speaks to reporters as you well know.'

'I thought he might make an exception today,' I said with false bravado. 'In view of what's happened to his ex-wife.'

'Well, Danny's not here.'

'So where is he?'

He ignored the question. 'I don't think he'd be pleased to see you even if he was here. In fact I reckon he'd give you a slap for what you said to those coppers. We just watched it on the telly.'

'They were legitimate questions,' I said.

'Bollocks. You were trying to stir things up and get a reaction. Just like you always do. Ain't that why they call you The Ferret? You've been making a fucking nuisance of yourself around here for years.'

'How would you know?' I said. 'We've never met.'

He snorted out a laugh. 'I know a lot about you, Chambers. I knew that nigger who married your mother and I know the good-for-nothing prick who married you. I also know what happened to your turd-coloured brother.'

He paused to see if I'd react. When I didn't he carried on.

'The reason we've never met is because so far you haven't given us any grief and because Danny, bless him, is squeamish about hurting women. But it doesn't bother the rest of us. And that, my darling, is why I invited you upstairs. I want you to know that we won't stand for you sticking your nose in our business or in Danny's private life.'

I gritted my teeth and the rage simmered inside me.

'Is that a threat?' I said. 'Because if it is I'm sure the police will be happy to add it to the assault charge.'

'You haven't been assaulted.'

'When that man put his hands on me it was assault.'

Bishop laughed at that and so did the others. I felt a cold panic tighten in my chest as I watched Bishop stand up suddenly and walk around the table towards me.

When he reached me he pulled back his lips to reveal a set of off-colour teeth. And then he slapped me so hard across the face that I went flying off the chair and onto the floor.

'Now *that* was an assault, you stupid fucking bitch,' he yelled.

The pain was excruciating, and for a few moments I was too stunned to move. My cheek burned and my heart felt like it was about to crash out of my body.

'Get her up,' Bishop ordered, and two of the others took hold of my arms and hauled me to my feet.

'Before you start ranting on about calling the filth just ask yourself what the fuck they can do,' he said, his voice acidic. 'No one saw me lay a hand on you. In fact you came in here to attack me for no good reason. And these men will bear witness to that.'

I shook myself free and stared daggers at him. I wanted desperately to cry, but I fought against it because I didn't want to give him the satisfaction of seeing how hurt and scared I was.

'I'll make you regret this,' I said, and even to my own ears it sounded like an empty, pathetic threat.

'You're the one who'll regret it if you start sticking your nose where it doesn't belong,' he said.

'You don't scare me, Bishop.'

'That just shows what a fucking gobby little moron you are, Chambers. I have only to say the word and I can make you disappear.'

I felt a sudden breathlessness.

'You bastard,' I said.

He grinned. 'I'd like a pound for every time someone has called me that.'

I sucked in air through my teeth and reached for my bag, which had been placed on an empty chair. My hands were shaking uncontrollably.

'I'm going,' I said. 'Don't try to stop me.'

'I don't intend to. Just keep in mind what I told you. And don't think you're off limits because you're a reporter with lots of police contacts. That in itself makes you a piece of scum in our eyes.'

There was a burst of laughter around the room as I shuffled towards the door clutching my bag close. One of the men opened the door for me and I hurried through it and down the stairs.

I managed to hold back the tears and the vomit until I stepped onto the pavement. Then it all came out and I spewed up my guts in the road behind the waiting taxi.

As soon as I'd emptied the contents of my stomach the tears gushed out, and it was a full minute before I was able to tell the driver where to take me.

11

Ethan Cain

DCI Redwood hung up the phone and turned to Cain.

'You won't believe this,' he said. 'Danny Shapiro just turned up at the nick. He said he'd heard we were looking for him.'

Cain acted like he was surprised, but of course he wasn't. Just over half an hour had passed since Danny had called to tell him that he didn't murder Megan Fuller.

'I was nowhere near Balham last night,' he'd said. 'And I can prove it. I have a watertight alibi.'

Cain had told him to go straight to Wandsworth to hand himself in.

'I don't want anyone to know you phoned me directly,' Cain had said. 'It'll look suspicious.'

The two detectives were still in Ramsden Road gathering evidence and interviewing neighbours. Now Redwood was keen to get to the station to talk to Shapiro.

'Let's go see what the slippery bastard has to say for himself,' he said.

They left the SOCOs to continue their sweep of the house, but so far nothing of great significance had been found. They'd bagged and logged plenty of potential evidence – hairs, fibres, prints, the victim's personal stuff. But the killer, it seemed, had not left behind any obvious markers that would point the investigation in his or her direction.

They drove in separate cars back to Wandsworth and Cain was glad of that because it gave him a chance to gather his thoughts. He was worried about sitting in an interview room with both his boss and Danny Shapiro. It wouldn't be the first time he'd questioned Danny, but the huge conflict of interest always filled him with trepidation. It was like walking a tightrope between two contradictory parts of his life, the good and the bad. The part he was proud of, which included his lovely daughter, and the part that he was ashamed of. But that was how it was. He'd sold his soul to the devil a long time ago in return for cash, coke, and horny young tarts.

He hadn't always been a reckless thrill-seeker, or a victim of his own pathetic avarice. It seemed like not so long ago he was an idealistic copper who'd been blessed with good health and a promising future. Then a combination of factors contrived to bend his life out of shape.

It began with the realisation that his career had stalled and that his heart was no longer in it anyway. At the same time he sought to distract himself through gambling, mostly slot machines and the ponies. But that had just been the start of the slippery slope. It wasn't long before he was spending his winnings on drugs and whores.

He tried to sort himself out when it struck him that his behaviour posed a threat to his marriage. He went to Gamblers Anonymous and attempted to give up the drugs. But he'd left it too late and the walls of the hole he had dug himself crashed in on him.

Losses, debt and addiction drew him to Danny Shapiro's attention, which led to an offer from the firm that at the time was too good to refuse.

Luckily Danny didn't expect much in return for the money he gave him. The occasional tip-off about impending raids, the identity of police informants, the nod when the organised crime lot were mounting a major surveillance operation.

It assuaged Cain's guilt somewhat to know that he wasn't the only crooked copper inside the Met. There were dozens, and a few of them he knew about because they'd let it slip in unguarded moments or when they were pissed.

But it was nothing new. Police corruption was as old as the force itself, and the top brass had given up spending too much time and energy trying to root it out.

That didn't mean he could afford to be complacent, especially while working alongside Redwood. If he were to be exposed he'd face a long spell behind bars and then be at the mercy of some of the nuts he had put away.

So facing Danny Shapiro across an interview table was always going to give him cause for concern. And even more so on this occasion because he wasn't sure he'd believed Danny when he'd said he hadn't murdered his ex-wife.

At the nick they were told they couldn't talk to Danny immediately because he wanted his lawyer present and the guy hadn't yet arrived.

'In that case we'll brief the troops,' Redwood said. 'Let's get everyone together.'

An incident room had already been set up during the morning. It was now crammed with detectives, some of them tucking into sandwich lunches.

Cain hadn't eaten all day but he had no appetite. He settled instead for lukewarm black coffee from the machine.

Two large whiteboards had been placed at one end of the room and to these were attached photos of Megan Fuller and the crime scene.

'Okay, listen up, everyone,' Redwood said, positioning himself between the boards and clapping his hands to get their attention. 'We have developments to discuss and a murder to solve, so we need to get cracking.'

A hush descended on the room as Redwood began with a pointed reference to Beth Chambers.

'That woman put us in a difficult position today and I don't want it to happen again,' he said. 'The fact that she was able to talk to Nigel Fuller before we had finished interviewing him was a major cock-up on our part. We have to be more careful.'

He gave a little cough before continuing. 'I know most of you are acquainted with Beth Chambers because as well as a crime reporter she happens to be Detective Cain's former wife. But I don't want anyone to talk to her about this case. I'm happy to accept Ethan's assurance that he never discusses work with her. And I want the same assurance from the rest of you that you won't pass anything to Chambers or any other journalist.'

Redwood waited for everyone to respond by murmuring a yes or giving a nod. Then, having dealt with that issue, he went on to describe the scene in Megan's house for the benefit of those officers who hadn't been there. He pointed to the photos of the body and explained that she died from a single, vicious stab wound to the throat.

'There's no sign of the murder weapon,' he said. 'Forensic evidence taken from the scene is being processed and some of the CCTV footage from the area is being viewed. As you all know, the body was discovered by Megan's father. We've spoken to him briefly, but he's being brought back here to the station this afternoon to give us a full statement.

'The gist of it will be that Megan asked him to go to the house this morning so that she could talk to him. She was upset apparently and had told Mr Fuller that her ex-husband, one Danny Shapiro, had made threats against her during an argument over the phone earlier in the day.'

Everyone knew that Danny was waiting to be questioned. Word had spread like wildfire within seconds of him walking into the building.

'I'm anticipating that he'll claim he knows nothing about what happened in Ramsden Road,' Redwood said. 'But he's our prime suspect. For one thing it appears he had a motive, as we discovered from an email that Megan sent to him.'

Redwood picked up a black marker pen and using his notes he wrote the message Megan had sent to Danny on one of the whiteboards.

Don't make the mistake of ignoring me, Danny. A one-off payment is all I'm asking for. I know you can afford it. So if you fuck me about you'll seriously regret it.

'So there you have it,' Redwood said. 'Megan was trying to squeeze her ex for money. She was blackmailing him, probably threatening to reveal some of his secrets in her forthcoming book.'

Cain felt a spurt of anxiety. He had to admit it didn't look good for Danny. That email would almost certainly have provoked an angry response. Danny wasn't the kind of man to take such things lying down.

'However, despite the way it looks we need to keep an open

mind in respect of Danny Shapiro,' Redwood said. 'That's because he's not the only suspect. There's also a boyfriend who appears to have been dumped by Megan for slapping her around.'

He threw to DC Rachel Fisher, who had been tasked with looking into Megan's personal stuff, including her bank accounts and phone records.

Fisher was the youngest member of the team and one of the sharpest. She'd just returned from holiday and her face was tanned a rich shade of coffee.

'Megan's phone records show that she was in regular contact with a man named Sam Jones until recently,' she said. 'We've identified him from his mobile number and it turns out he has a criminal record for domestic violence against his former wife. He used to own a bar in Balham, which is presumably how they met. But it closed down a year ago and he was made bankrupt.

'I showed his photo to Megan's next-door neighbour and she confirmed that Jones used to be a regular visitor to the house. She also said they had frequent rows and that Megan told her two days ago that she'd dumped him.'

Fisher referred to the text Jones had sent to Megan apologising for hitting her.

'She sent one back saying it was over and warning him not to come to the house,' she said.

Fisher explained that Megan's bank account showed her to be massively overdrawn. Seven months ago she had remortgaged her house to pay off debts after losing her savings on a venture into the stock market.

'Do we know what that was all about?' Redwood asked.

'Only from what the neighbour told me,' she said. 'I haven't had time to confirm it. But it seems that her then boyfriend persuaded her to give him money which he used to buy some company shares that were meant to go through the roof. Instead the value of the shares nosedived and they lost the lot.'

'Which is probably why, out of desperation, Megan decided to put the screws on her ex-husband,' Redwood said. 'And that could have been another costly mistake on her part.'

Fisher said they were trying to track down Sam Jones. He had a flat in Tooting, but officers who had called there had reported back that he wasn't in. A neighbour said she'd seen him going out this morning. Plus, his mobile phone wasn't transmitting a signal so had probably been switched off.

'Keep trying,' Redwood said. 'We need to find this guy as a matter of urgency.'

DC Toby Dean, who had also been at the house, pointed out that the techies had examined Megan's laptop but hadn't so far found any document pertaining to the book she was supposed to have been writing.

'However, there are emails from her agent asking her why it was taking her so long to provide a synopsis,' he said.

'That might be because she hadn't actually got round to doing anything,' Cain chipped in. 'And perhaps she never intended to.'

Redwood frowned. 'What makes you say that?'

Cain rolled his shoulders. 'I just think it's possible she was bluffing about the book and it was an empty threat to extract money from Shapiro.'

'It's a thought,' Redwood said. 'We should check it out.'

The meeting carried on for another fifteen minutes, until word came that Shapiro's lawyer had arrived at the station.

But before going along to the interview room, Redwood and Cain were asked to go and look at several clips of CCTV footage that showed an individual who might have been Megan's killer.

They both entered the little viewing room hoping for a big break in the case. The officer who was going through the tapes that were so far in sat in front of a computer monitor.

'The house itself is in a CCTV black spot,' he said. 'But there are cameras at both ends of the street. This guy was caught entering from Balham High Road just before ten. He was then picked up retracing his steps thirty-five minutes later. He's caught on one other camera heading along the High Road towards Clapham before he disappears. It's possible he flagged down a cab or got into a car.'

The officer ran the clips, but what appeared on the screen was blurred and indistinct. The figure the officer was referring to couldn't be identified because he was wearing a hood and didn't once look at the camera.

For Cain it was a huge relief. The figure might well have been Danny, but it was impossible to tell for sure.

Redwood didn't bother to hide his disappointment.

'This is fucking useless,' he said. 'The only thing I'm pretty sure of is that we're looking at a man.'

'I've tried blowing up the image but it doesn't help,' the officer said. 'More tapes are due in soon so maybe we'll strike lucky then.'

Redwood turned to Cain. 'What do you reckon, Ethan? Could that guy be Danny Shapiro?'

Cain smacked his lips together as he stared at the moving footage. 'Actually I have my doubts, guv. From what I remember Shapiro has more of a swagger when he walks. And I can't see him wandering around that part of town without at least one bodyguard.'

He wasn't going to tell his boss that Danny preferred to go out without minders.

Redwood nodded. 'You've got a point there, except that if he was going to Megan's house to kill her he would have wanted to go by himself. Surely.'

Cain shrugged. 'I suppose so. But then it comes back to my point about him not being stupid. Why would he walk to the house and risk being caught on camera? It would have been much safer to go there in a vehicle that was stolen or couldn't be traced.'

As Redwood thought about it, Cain couldn't help wondering how many times in the coming hours and days he would try to point the investigation in the wrong direction or be forced to lie.

And whether the gaffer would eventually become suspicious.

12

Beth Chambers

The Post was part of a large media conglomerate that occupied a tall glass building close to London Bridge railway station, so it didn't take me long to get there in the taxi.

But I didn't go straight into the ultra-modern reception area. First I needed to go for a short walk because I felt all twisted up inside and my gut was still fighting waves of nausea.

What had happened had unsettled me, and I was struggling to regain my mental footing. It wasn't the first time I'd been attacked while pursuing a story, and I felt sure it wouldn't be the last. But what I'd experienced in that room above the snooker hall had been more vicious, and more scary, than anything I'd encountered before.

I couldn't get Bishop's face out of my mind, and his words sat cold inside me. I wasn't just badly shaken – I was also infused with a hot rage. The bastard had used threats and violence to try to stop me doing my job. Despite that I was determined not to bottle it. No way was I going to allow myself to be intimidated by that head case.

As I walked, I began to feel the tension leave my body and my heart regain its natural rhythm. Above me the sky shimmered in a cloudless sky and around me office workers and tourists went about their business.

Many of them would later be reading what I'd written when they picked up their free copies of *The Post* from stations, news-agents and street vendors. There was a much smaller print run on Saturdays because the commuters weren't pouring in and out of the capital. But the paper was still popular, partly because of the glossy entertainment supplement inside.

The story of Megan Fuller's murder would be another big draw because it broke too late for the morning tabloids. And as far as I was concerned it was my story, a story that I felt had the potential to get bigger and better, with lots of juicy angles.

So Frankie 'The Nutter' Bishop could shove his pathetic threats. I wasn't going to let him scare me into pulling back from what I did best – which was to ferret out the truth behind the headlines.

Before going upstairs to the newsroom I went to the ladies to empty my bladder and sort out my face. My mascara had run and my right cheek was still red from the slap. I applied some foundation and dragged a comb through my hair to make myself presentable again.

I'd phoned ahead so that Grant was expecting me. He was sitting at his usual place on the newsdesk, and around him about two dozen reporters were tapping away at their keyboards or speaking into phones.

Grant spotted me coming, got up and signalled for me to join him in his little glass-fronted office at one end of the room. He knew I'd had a rough ride at the snooker club but I hadn't given him the details.

'Take a seat,' he said as he stepped behind his desk. 'You look beat.'

Grant was a big, overweight man of 50 with folds of fat pouring out over his belt. His face was pockmarked with fading acne, some of which he tried to hide behind a neatly trimmed beard.

'You did some good work this morning, Beth,' he said. 'Especially getting the exclusive with the dad. We're still the only media outlet to have it.'

Praise from Grant was always appreciated. He was acknowledged as one of the best news editors in the business. His job was to source stories and coordinate the day-to-day operation of the news team. It was a tough task and he always pulled it off with style and charisma.

'So now tell me about the trouble you seem to have stirred up at Shapiro's place,' he said.

A shiver convulsed through me as I told him what had happened. His reaction was to blast out a loud stream of expletives and then reach for the phone on his desk to call the police.

'There's no point,' I said. 'I can't prove he hit me and there were other men there who will swear he didn't.'

'But we can't just leave it at that, Beth. I'm not happy that one of my reporters has been subjected to violent intimidation.'

'Well, it's happened, and when you're dealing with people like that the threat is always there.'

'At least you should let your police contacts know. Maybe there's something they can do without making it official.'

'Don't worry, I intend to. In the meantime we can't let it be a distraction. I'm sticking with the story and two fingers to Frankie Bishop.'

'That's exactly what I expected you to say, Beth. But I'm not sure it's a good idea. You've had a bad shock. You ought to go home for the rest of the day.'

My rational self told me he was talking sense, but we both knew it wasn't going to happen.

'I'm really all right now,' I said. 'Being threatened and attacked is an occupational hazard in this city. If I wasn't prepared to accept that I'd be writing about the arts instead of about crime.'

'That's not the point,' he said. 'If you were a guy I wouldn't be so—'

I held up my hand to stop him.

'Don't you fucking dare say you wouldn't be so concerned. It shouldn't make any difference and you bloody well know it.'

He realised he'd put his foot in it and blushed, which wasn't something he often did.

'Okay, point taken. I keep forgetting how sensitive you lot are.'

In some ways Grant was a dinosaur. To him there was still a gender divide in the newsroom and male reporters were better suited to a whole range of stories. He was on record as saying that he didn't believe women should report from the front line in war zones. Or that they should ever write about football, cricket and rugby.

I was sure he would never have appointed me as a staff crime reporter if I hadn't already proved myself.

He stretched his face into a smile and moved the subject back to the story itself.

'For your information there's been a development in the last fifteen minutes,' he said. 'Danny Shapiro has handed himself in at Lavender Hill. We were just tipped off.'

'Do you want me to write it up?'

'I've already added a line to the late edition. If you're determined to carry on working then I suggest you shoot over to Wandsworth and try to catch him when he comes out, assuming he does, of course.'

I picked up my bag and rose to my feet.

'And try not to upset him or anyone else,' Grant said. 'I really don't want anything bad to happen to my star reporter.'

13

Danny Shapiro

It was DCI Redwood who read out the pro-forma that preceded the interview.

Danny listened to what his rights and entitlements were and then turned to his lawyer and said, 'You got all that?'

Khalid Chandra nodded and tapped his teeth with his pen. He was a sinewy man in his forties, with sharp, narrow features and wiry black hair. His nose supported a pair of thick-rimmed glasses and he wore a smart blue suit.

He'd been acting on behalf of the firm since Danny sacked the brief who failed to keep his father out of prison.

Redwood named all of those present for the benefit of the tape. He had a deep northern accent and Danny got the impression that he was a tough, no-nonsense copper. The type it was best to steer clear of if at all possible.

As he spoke, Danny exchanged an uneasy glance with DI Cain, who looked as though he would rather have been anywhere but here. There were spots of sweat on his brow, and he kept drumming his fingers on the desktop. Danny wanted to tell him to relax and not to make it so bloody obvious that he was uncomfortable.

'Let me begin by thanking you for coming into the station,' Redwood said, his eyes fixed on Danny. 'As you probably know, we were trying to contact you all morning.'

'As a matter of fact my client had no idea what had happened until just before noon,' Chandra said. 'That's when he got out of bed and switched on the television.'

'Is that right?' Redwood said, his tone conveying a high level of scepticism. 'And there was me jumping to the conclusion that he would have known long before that.'

'I think we should cut to the chase, Inspector,' Chandra said. 'It'll save us all a lot of time and trouble. You obviously suspect my client of killing his ex-wife. But we're sorry to have to disappoint you. Mr Shapiro was somewhere else when the murder was committed. He was at the home of a young lady whose name and address I've given to the duty officer at the front desk.'

'And that's very useful, Mr Chandra,' Redwood said. 'It's being checked out as we speak.'

'Then I hope this won't take long since my client is a busy man and needs to get to work.'

Redwood cocked an eyebrow. 'So who is this woman, and what exactly is your relationship with her?'

Danny knew better than to lie at this point, especially to this motherfucker. It wouldn't take them long to establish that Tamara was a brass. In fact they probably already knew that. Her name was bound to be on the police database.

'Tamara Roth is a professional escort,' he said. 'We've known each other for a long time and she even went out with my father for a while. These last few years we've often spent time in each other's company.'

'And you paid her for sex?' Redwood said.

'Not at all,' Danny replied. 'We're friends. And that's all we are. There's no sex involved.'

Redwood gave a sardonic grin. 'You expect us to believe that?'

'Whether you believe it or not it's the truth.'

Redwood expelled a breath. 'So tell us what happened last night.'

Danny shrugged. 'I arrived at her house between about seven and nine. I can't remember the exact time because I'd had a bit to drink. I didn't leave there until this morning when I came here. And just for the record we slept in separate beds.'

Disbelief crossed Redwood's face like a shadow. 'Can anyone else support this alibi?'

'Don't see how. We were alone.'

'And how did you arrive at the house?'

'By minicab. I flagged one down in Bermondsey.'

'Can you remember where?'

Danny shrugged. 'Somewhere near our office. The exact location escapes me.'

Danny looked at Cain, who was nervously running a finger around the rim of a plastic cup. The detective was reluctant to make eye contact, and Danny could see that the tendons in his neck were so tight they looked ready to snap.

'Look, I didn't kill Megan,' he said. 'And I didn't pay anyone to do it for me. I won't deny she got on my nerves at times, but not enough to make me want to do something bad to her.'

Redwood chewed his tongue as he ruminated on this for a moment. 'Tell us about the argument you had on the phone with her earlier in the day,' he said. 'And about the threats you made against her.'

'I didn't make any threats.'

'She told her father that you did.'

'Is that so? Well, she was lying. She was always fucking lying.'

Danny could see that Redwood didn't believe him and he wondered if Cain also thought he'd killed Megan. He tried not to let the unease he felt show on his face, but it wasn't easy. The air in the room was loaded with tension, and a hard rock had settled at the bottom of his stomach.

'So what about the argument, Danny?' Redwood pressed.

Danny let his breath escape. 'It was nothing unusual. Megan has been trying to get money out of me for ages, as if she didn't get enough as part of the divorce settlement. But I refused to give her any more and she wasn't happy.'

'How much money are we talking about?'

'She wanted half a million quid. Her acting work had dried up and she'd got involved with some joker named Sam Jones who talked her into a bad investment.'

'Was she blackmailing you?'

'I suppose so. She was threatening to say things about me in a book she was supposedly writing on her life.'

'What kind of things?'

'Come on, Inspector,' Chandra broke in. 'My client has no intention of answering that question on the grounds that it might incriminate him.'

'I haven't a fucking clue what she was going to write,' Danny said. 'But I wasn't that bothered anyway and I told her so.'

Cain asked the next question, but not before clearing his throat. 'Have you any idea who would have wanted Megan dead?'

'If I knew that I'd tell you,' Danny said. 'Just because Megan and me weren't getting on it doesn't mean I didn't still have feelings for her. I loved her for a long time. What's happened is tragic and I would give anything to get my hands on the bastard who killed her.'

'Then why don't I get the impression that you're grieving?' Redwood said. 'In fact you don't even seem particularly upset.'

'I'm not one to show my feelings, Inspector. Never have been. If you'd been around this manor longer than you have then you'd know that.'

Redwood sat back in his chair and laced his fingers under his chin.

'We've seen the email she wrote to you, Danny,' Redwood said after a beat. 'The one in which she warned you that if you didn't give her money you'd regret it.'

Danny forced a mirthless smile. 'Megan had a vicious streak, Inspector. Most people didn't know about it. And when she suddenly found herself with no money, and no prospect of earning any, it brought out the worst in her.'

'So are you saying you didn't take the warning seriously?'

'Of course I didn't, and that wound her up even more.'

'She said in the email that she knew you could afford to give her the money. Is that true, Danny? Can you lay your hands on half a million just like that?'

Chandra started to object to the question, but Danny stopped him and said he was happy to answer it.

'I'm a successful businessman, Inspector. I own several clubs, a wholesale company and a snooker hall among other things. I'm also a landlord with a large number of properties to my name, both residential and commercial. So it follows that I have a few quid in the bank.'

'You forgot to mention the other stuff,' Redwood said. 'Like the drug dealing, the pimping, the loan sharking, the extortion . . .'

'That's enough,' Chandra said, slamming the side of his fist down on the table. 'My client has always denied any involvement in organised crime. And he's not here to be questioned about it yet again. So I would ask you to stick to the matter at hand, the murder of Megan Fuller.'

Chandra shot his cuff and consulted his watch.

'And I think it's time you told us why you've seen fit to point the finger at Mr Shapiro,' he continued. 'Is it based on evidence found at the scene?'

'The forensic evidence is still being processed.'

'Then of course you won't be surprised when Mr Shapiro's fingerprints and DNA turn up in the house as he did once own it and has been there on occasion since he and his wife split up three years ago.'

'We're aware of that,' Redwood said.

'So what else is there linking Mr Shapiro to the crime?'

Redwood shook his head and exhaled, the breath hissing between his lips. It was then that Danny realised that they had nothing on him. He felt sure that if they did then Redwood would have revealed it in order to regain the initiative.

Instead he asked Danny why he did not have a registered mobile phone.

'I prefer pay-as-you-go phones,' Danny said. 'It's safer and I don't have to worry about you lot listening into my conversations.'

'In that case how do people contact you?'

Danny shrugged. 'I give out numbers to those I want to hear from.'

'And I suppose that includes your old man, Callum.'

'Naturally. He takes a keen interest in my business.'

'I'm sure he does.'

Redwood then told Danny they were going to obtain a warrant to search his Bermondsey flat.

'But I gather you haven't been staying at the flat for a while,' he said. 'Care to tell me why?'

'I don't feel safe there,' Danny said. 'That's why I move from place to place.'

'But didn't you live there when you were married?'

Danny nodded. 'It was different then.'

'You mean you weren't running the firm so you didn't feel like you were a target.'

'No comment.'

Redwood grinned. 'So where do you spend most nights?'

'That's none of your business.'

'Well, I'm making it my business. And I don't understand why you're reluctant to tell me.'

Danny thought for a moment and then shrugged again.

'Okay. I rent out thirty properties. At any one time three or four are empty. I crash out in those sometimes or stay in hotels.'

'That's an odd thing to do for someone with so much money in the bank.'

'Not really. I don't want people to know where I live and what I'm doing.'

At this point Chandra intervened again. 'I'm sorry, Inspector, but this line of questioning is totally irrelevant. I insist you call a halt and either charge my client or let him go. And as for the search warrant you can forget it. Since you have no grounds I'll be entering a formal objection to the court.'

Just then someone knocked on the door to the interview room and pushed it open. A man in a suit poked his head in and asked if he could have a quick word. It was Cain who got up and left the room. Redwood carried on asking Danny questions about Megan and their marriage.

After a few minutes, Cain returned and whispered into

Redwood's ear. The latter's face clouded over and he fixed Danny with a contemptuous look.

'We've just heard back from the officers who went to interview Miss Roth,' he said. 'She confirmed your alibi just as we both knew she would.'

'I take it that my client is now free to go,' Chandra said.

Redwood nodded. 'He is for now, but I'm sure we'll want to talk to him again.'

Danny got to his feet and said to his lawyer, 'Let's get out of here. The rank smell of disappointment is making me feel sick.'

Danny heaved an almighty sigh of relief as he walked out of the interview room.

Redwood's parting shot didn't faze him. The cop was aggrieved because he'd been hoping that Megan's murder would be an open-and-shut case. And it might well have been if Tamara hadn't come through by providing him with an alibi.

He was 100 per cent confident that she wouldn't retract her story even under police pressure. That was why he'd put his trust in her rather than anyone else. She was dependable because she felt indebted to him and his father. And there was the money, of course.

But Danny wasn't going to just relax and assume that he was out of the woods. He now had time to make sure that the whole thing wouldn't suddenly unravel. He'd use his people in the Met – including Ethan Cain – to tell him exactly what was going on and whether there was any evidence that could undermine the alibi. Was there any incriminating CCTV footage, for instance? Were they going to carry out a sweep of all the cameras around Tamara's house in Vauxhall?

Danny was still worried that if Redwood believed him to be

guilty then he wouldn't pursue other suspects with anything like the degree of commitment and determination that was required. He'd seen that happen often enough. The cops decide who they think is guilty – however tenuous the evidence – and then close their minds to all other possibilities.

'Don't look so concerned, Danny,' Chandra said, slapping him on the back. 'They wouldn't be letting you leave the building if they thought they could pin it on you. And it's clear they would love to be able to.'

The lawyer knew better than to ask Danny if he was guilty or innocent. The man was paid to do his best for the firm whatever the circumstances. But Danny felt compelled to tell him that he didn't kill Megan.

'That's nice to know,' Chandra said. 'I didn't actually think you did.'

Danny was surprised to see a bunch of photographers and reporters on the pavement outside.

'My car's around the corner,' Chandra said. 'I'll give you a lift. And I suggest you don't say anything to the press.'

But just as they were moving away to the left someone shouted out his name and Danny snapped his head towards the voice.

A sudden jolt of alarm struck him when he saw that a man who had just got out of a black cab was striding purposefully towards him.

'Oh shit,' he said aloud to himself when it dawned on him that the man was Nigel Fuller, Megan's father.

He was wearing an anorak and had a face like thunder.

'Why the hell are they letting you go?' he yelled out.

Danny came to a stop and his heart took a leap. As Fuller closed in a camera flash went off nearby and Chandra grabbed his right arm. Danny realised what was about to happen and braced himself.

He couldn't afford to react or lose his temper, not with the press watching.

Fuller stepped right up to him and shoved him hard in the chest with his outstretched hand.

'You murdered my beautiful girl,' he screamed into his face. 'You stabbed her in the throat like she was some animal.'

Danny stood firm. He was rattled to the core but determined not to show it in front of the reporters and photographers who were desperate to see him react.

'You're wrong, Mr Fuller,' he said calmly. 'I had nothing to do with it. As I just explained to the police I was elsewhere when—'

'That's a fucking lie,' Fuller bellowed at the top of his voice. 'You're as guilty as sin. You told her you were going to hurt her.'

A uniformed police officer appeared suddenly and pulled Fuller away. At the same time Chandra yanked Danny in the other direction towards his car.

By now the press had closed in around them and Danny heard a woman's voice above all the others.

'Is it true, Mr Shapiro?' she shouted. 'Did you murder your ex-wife after making threats against her?'

Danny glanced back over his shoulder and realised who had fired the question even before he saw her face in the crowd.

Bethany Chambers.

The bitch was holding up what looked like a Dictaphone while struggling to keep up with him.

And that was when he did finally snap. He jerked his arm free of the lawyer's grip and spun round to face Chambers and the rest of the vultures.

'Let's get one thing straight,' he yelled. 'I had nothing to do with Megan's murder, despite what you just heard. I've told the

111

police and now I'm telling you that I was nowhere near Balham last night. And I've been able to prove it.'

He jabbed a rigid finger at Bethany Chambers, his mouth curling in disgust. She was standing only about six feet away from him and if they had been alone he would have smashed a fist into her face.

'And here's a warning for you especially, Miss Chambers. If you keep on repeating these provocative statements every chance you get then I'm going to sue you and your paper for defamation. You got that?'

He didn't wait for her to respond. Instead, he turned and let his lawyer lead him along the pavement to a black Mercedes that was parked at a meter. As soon as the door was closed behind him he squeezed his eyes shut and took a few deep breaths to try to calm down. But his adrenalin was through the roof and a fierce rage was heating up his blood.

He wanted desperately to vent his frustration, preferably on at least one of those bastards who were out to get him: Jack Redwood, Nigel Fuller, and Bethany Chambers.

But since that wasn't going to happen he decided that the next best thing was to imagine how he'd make them suffer if at some point in the future the opportunity presented itself.

14

Beth Chambers

Danny Shapiro's outburst took us all by surprise. But what made my heart lurch was the malevolent look in his eyes as he stabbed his finger at me. It made me realise why people were scared of him – and how he managed to command so much respect among the sadists and barbarians who populated the London underworld.

I wasn't sure how to react to the fact that he had recognised me. Was that from our brief encounters in the past? Or had he seen me on the television throwing questions at the two detectives outside Megan's house? I wondered also if Frankie Bishop had told him I'd been to the snooker club today and that was partly why he'd turned on me.

The guy was obviously feeling the pressure even though the cops had seen fit to let him go. It was no wonder Megan's dad was fuming. The poor guy had been ushered up the steps and into the station. A woman who had got out of the black cab with him had held back and was now talking to a couple of reporters.

'Nigel is still in a state of shock,' she was saying as I approached. 'He really can't be held responsible for his actions.'

The woman was fiftyish, slim and smartly dressed in a two-piece grey suit. In answer to a question, she identified herself as Amy Cassidy, Nigel Fuller's fiancée.

'Nigel was married to Megan's mother for a number of years,' she said. 'He told me that Megan desperately wanted to talk to him this morning and that she feared for her life. It's inconceivable that her ex-husband has been released. He's the man who put the fear of God into her and everyone knows he's a gangster.'

The woman began to cry as she shouldered her way through the crowd towards the entrance.

I dug in my jacket pocket for a business card as I pursued her up the steps.

'Please take this, Miss Cassidy,' I said, thrusting my hand towards her just as she reached the doors. 'It's my card. If you or Mr Fuller would like to do an interview at any point then please ring me.'

She glanced at me briefly and snatched the card. A second later she disappeared inside the station.

There was a coffee shop across the road and I went there to compose a short update on the story. There were no more print editions today but what I had just witnessed made good copy for the online pages, minus the libellous remarks from Amy Cassidy of course.

MEGAN MURDER INVESTIGATION

Detectives investigating the murder of soap star Megan Fuller questioned her ex-husband Danny Shapiro today. But he was released without charge after less than an hour. Outside the police station in Wandsworth he insisted he had nothing to do with his wife's murder. However, he was confronted by Miss Fuller's father who was enraged and had to be escorted away by police officers . . .

I phoned Grant Scott after filing the story and he told me to call it a day and go home.

'Try to forget what happened earlier,' he said. 'And take tomorrow off. We'll be across any major developments and I'll make sure the desk keeps you informed.'

'Stop fretting, Grant. You're beginning to sound like my mother. You should know me better than to think I'd allow the empty threats of some Neanderthal to affect my work.'

After hanging up, I decided it was time that I had a conversation with my ex. I'd been planning to do it later tonight, but in view of what had happened I felt the need to talk to him sooner rather than later. I called his mobile and he answered straight away.

'I wondered when I'd hear from you,' Ethan Cain said.

'Can you get away?'

'Not for at least an hour. Can't it wait?'

'No, it can't. Someone attacked and threatened me and I want to tell you about it.'

'Jesus. Are you okay?'

'Yes, but it shook me up.'

I heard him draw a breath. 'Very well. I can meet you at the usual place in about an hour. But I have to be careful for obvious reasons.'

The usual place was a pub in Camberwell. It suited me because I was suddenly gagging for a drink, something to take the edge off and help me to relax.

I still had half an hour to kill by the time I got to Camberwell so I headed for one of the pound shops. There I bought a couple of colouring books and a set of crayons for Rosie. She was really into drawing at the moment and it was something I liked to encourage.

To get to the Hornet's Nest pub I had to walk past King's College Hospital and seeing the place revived a few memories for me, some good, some bad. It was where I gave birth to Rosie and also where my brother Michael died from the terrible injuries inflicted by his attacker's machete.

King's was one of London's busiest hospitals and the emergency department dealt with victims of crime on a daily basis. Surrounding it were some of the capital's roughest and most dangerous areas, including Peckham, Brixton, and Walworth.

The Hornet's Nest was more upmarket than most of the pubs in Camberwell, and it had tables and chairs on a small terrace at the front. I got myself two large gin and tonics and drank one at the bar before taking the other outside.

It was a chilly end to the day but the air felt good – as did the gin. It was my favourite tipple, and I always felt the need to down a couple before meetings with my ex.

It wasn't that Ethan and I didn't get on these days. It was more to do with the shit from the past that I was always reminded of. Like finding out that he'd been spending our savings on prostitutes and gambling. And learning that he had a four-month affair with a colleague while I was pregnant.

It was hard to believe that when we met on a night out in Peckham – where he also lived at the time – I was instantly attracted to him. I was intoxicated by his smile, his sharp wit, the fact that his job meant he had lots of fascinating stories to tell. I thought I'd found the perfect man and was chuffed to bits when he proposed to me after I told him he'd got me pregnant.

It was good to begin with, but I soon came to realise that monogamy wasn't for him. He became restless, detached, and the longer it went on the harder it was to ignore my growing suspicions about what he was getting up to when he wasn't with me.

So I spied on him and soon found out about his affair and his sessions with prostitutes. There was a pile of evidence, from credit card statements to text messages on a mobile phone I never knew he had. When I confronted him he had no choice but to confess, and his only excuse was that he'd been stupid.

He promised me he would clean up his act and pleaded with me not to end the marriage. But my love for him was poisoned by his betrayal and I kicked the bastard out.

I spent months being swept along by a torrent of emotion until I finally came to terms with what had happened and managed to pull myself together. It helped that he stayed away from me and resigned himself to the fact that he'd fucked up and that I wasn't going to have him back.

The fact that he moved on so quickly with his life – or at least seemed to – made me realise that he couldn't have loved me as much as I'd loved him. And that if I hadn't fallen pregnant he probably wouldn't have proposed in the first place.

As usual when he finally turned up at the pub I wondered what I'd actually seen in him in the beginning. He hadn't changed much, but for me it was like seeing him through a different pair of eyes these days. He looked haggard now rather than handsome, and his face struck me as shifty rather than sensitive.

He paid the taxi driver and smiled when he saw me waiting for him. As he stepped onto the terrace I held up my glass.

'Mine's a G and T,' I said. 'Lots of ice and a slice of lemon.'

'Coming up,' he said. 'But I want to make it clear that I'm here because you sounded really worried on the phone. I'm not having you pumping me for information.'

'So what makes you think I'd do that?' I said, rolling out my bottom lip in an exaggerated pout.

'Because you're a devious little madam, Bethany Chambers.

And because I'm not so stupid I don't realise it's the only reason you ever want to see me.'

He was right on that score, of course. If Ethan Cain had been anything other than a fairly high-ranking detective in the Met he would have been no use to me.

And there would have been no need for us to have these clandestine meetings in a south London pub.

15

Beth Chambers

It was widely known in the Met that Cain was my ex-husband. But nobody knew that he was now one of my best contacts. We both encouraged the perception that we no longer had anything to do with each other, and that Ethan had only limited access to his daughter.

The truth was it suited us both to maintain contact. He got to see Rosie as often as he wanted, and in return I was able to pick his brains about what he and the other detectives working the patch were up to.

In this context it helped that Ethan was untroubled by conventional standards of morality. He was happy to betray any confidence as long as it didn't come back on him. And for my part I was happy to exploit what remained of our relationship because I felt he owed me after what he'd put me through.

Ethan returned to the table with my G and T and a pint for himself.

'Cheers,' he said, clinking his glass against mine.

Then he sat back, lit a cigarette and started polluting the

atmosphere. I noticed that he looked tired, and I wondered if it was because he'd been working hard or was struggling to keep pace with his latest bit of fluff.

'I was surprised to see you in Balham today,' he said, blowing jets of smoke out of his nostrils. 'Rosie told me you were taking her to the park.'

'That was the plan,' I said. 'But Megan Fuller's murder was too big a story to miss.'

'Was the little mite upset?'

'Not really. Mum took her and I've bought her some colouring books to make up for it.'

He grinned and it reminded me that his daughter meant a lot to him even though he'd been a shit husband and father.

'By the way, thanks for putting me on the spot with those questions,' he said. 'How the hell did you know where the father was? We didn't tell anyone.'

'A little birdy told me,' I said. 'But to be fair I went there expecting to find a uniform either outside or inside the house.'

'Yeah, it was careless, but we were spread too thin at the time and waiting for reinforcements. You had Redwood spitting blood.'

'Did you see what happened at the station after you let Shapiro walk?'

He shook his head. 'I heard about it. A case of bad timing.'

'So why did you release him, and after such a short time?'

He rolled his eyes. 'I should have known you were bullshitting me about being threatened by someone. You just wanted to meet up so you could find out what's going on.'

'That's not true actually. I *was* threatened and attacked by some hard arse who works for Shapiro. But I'll come on to that in a sec. First tell me why the bastard isn't locked up.'

120

He sipped at his beer and licked the froth from his top lip.

'He gave us an alibi that checks out. He wasn't in Balham last night.'

'So where was he?'

He twisted his lower lip, deciding whether to tell me. 'This is off the record, right. I don't want Redwood putting two and two together. He's already issued a warning to me and the rest of the team about talking to the press.'

'You know me better than that, Ethan. If you tell me it's not for publication then I won't write it up. I'm the honest one out of the two of us, don't forget.'

'Ouch,' he said, pulling a face.

He took another long drag on his fag and watching him inhale made me glad I gave up smoking as soon as I got pregnant. Before then I used to smoke at least fifteen a day.

'He was at some woman's house,' Ethan said. 'Claimed he spent the night there – but only as a friend apparently. That's despite the fact that she's a prossy.'

'And you believe him?'

He shrugged. 'It's a soft alibi, but if the woman sticks to her story and we can't prove she's lying there's not much we can do.'

'Is she known to the police?'

He shrugged. 'She's got form for soliciting, but nothing serious.'

I was about to ask him if she was one of the whores he'd been with but decided it was probably best not to.

'What's her name?' I asked. 'Perhaps I've heard of her.'

I didn't reckon for a moment that he would tell me, but he blurted it out without thinking.

'Tamara Roth,' he said. 'Lives in Vauxhall.'

When he realised his mistake he grimaced. 'Keep that to

yourself, for Christ's sake. I'll be put on the rack if it gets out that I told you.'

I grinned. 'That goes without saying. So it's still possible that Shapiro killed Megan even though he's put forward an alibi.'

His voice dropped, became even more conspiratorial. 'Redwood seems to think so, but Shapiro had an answer for everything. He confirmed that he argued with her over the phone yesterday but denies threatening her. What we do know is that she was trying to squeeze money out of him. She was in a financial shit hole and wanted him to give her half a million quid. She was threatening to say stuff about him in her autobiography if he didn't pay up.'

That was the upside about these meetings with Ethan. He was always so gloriously indiscreet. He went on to tell me about how unhelpful the CCTV footage had proved to be and how none of the neighbours had seen anything suspicious, although one had heard raised voices coming from the house.

He also mentioned Megan's boyfriend and the fact that she'd dumped him because he'd hit her.

'He's some bloke called Sam Jones,' he said. 'He has a conviction for domestic violence and it seems Megan got into serious debt because he gave her bad investment advice.'

'Have you talked to him?'

'Not yet. We don't know where he is.'

'So he could be the one who did her in?'

'That's right.'

Ethan finished off his beer, looked at his watch, said he had time for one more.

'I'll go and get us both another drink and then you can fill me in about what happened to you today. I can tell you're stressed out about it.'

My glass was empty by the time he came back with my fourth

G and T, but I still didn't feel tipsy, which was why I was able to talk him through what had happened at the snooker hall without stumbling over my words.

'I assume you're acquainted with Frankie Bishop,' I said.

A shadow passed over his face and he made a thoughtful noise in his throat.

'He's well known to us as Shapiro's enforcer. They don't call him The Nutter for nothing. I was told the police in Southampton held a party when he decided to move from there to London. It made a big difference to their workload. The guy's a nasty piece of work.'

'So I discovered.'

'You should have called us straight away, Beth.'

'And what would you have done?'

'Not much I suppose, seeing as his mates would have said you were lying.'

'That's exactly what I thought.'

'Well, if I were you I wouldn't go to that place again. Shapiro and his crew feel safe there. They think they can get away with anything.'

'So should I take Bishop's threat seriously?'

'You ought to take all threats seriously, Beth – for Rosie's sake if nothing else.'

His words sparked a frisson of guilt in me and I felt my shoulders sag.

'Tell you what I'll do,' he said. 'I'll get a message through to Bishop that I know what he did and that he shouldn't mess with you. How does that sound?'

'It sounds good, thanks. I appreciate it.'

He looked at his watch again. 'I'd better go. I'll walk up to the hospital to find a taxi. What about you?'

I held up my glass. 'I'll finish this and be off.'

We didn't kiss. We never did. That was how it was when we met up. There were boundaries that we both adhered to. For example, we never inquired into each other's private life. I had no wish to know what the dirty bugger was up to and I didn't want him to know that I still hadn't found anyone to replace him. We only ever talked about Rosie and whatever information I was aiming to elicit from him.

I rarely came away disappointed, though, and this evening was no exception. I had learned that DCI Redwood was sceptical about Danny Shapiro's alibi. And I'd been given a name.

Tamara Roth.

The woman Shapiro supposedly spent the night with. Tomorrow I'd try to find out where she lived and pay her a visit. I'd try to talk her into giving me an on-the-record interview.

At the same time I'd try to suss out whether or not she was telling the truth.

There was a bus stop close to the pub so I hopped on one and rode on the top deck to Peckham. It took just under fifteen minutes and I spent the time trying to shift my thoughts away from the events of the day.

The alcohol that was sloshing around inside me helped. I was more relaxed, in a better mood, and I couldn't wait to see my daughter.

Her usual bedtime was still an hour away and I was going to do some colouring with her. It was the least I could do after letting her down this morning.

Too often the job made me lose all sense of perspective, and I failed to prioritise the things that were most important to me. I kept telling myself that I was going to change but I honestly wondered if I ever would.

The bus dropped me at the bottom of Rye Lane so I walked from there. The street was still busy and many of the shops still open. On impulse I popped into a newsagent's and bought my mother a box of Ferrero Rocher, her favourite chocolates.

I called out as I let myself in the front door and Rosie came running into the hallway. My mother had already fed and bathed her, and she looked exceptionally cute in her new Cinderella pyjamas.

'Mummy, Mummy,' she cried out.

She was so excited to see me that she almost tripped over her own feet. I dropped my bag on the floor and swept her up in my arms, kissing her on both cheeks.

'And have you been a good girl for Nanny?' I asked her, and naturally the answer was yes. She'd been the *bestest girl* in the world, she said.

'Did you get me a present, Mummy?' she asked me.

I put her down and took the colouring books and crayons from my bag.

'There you go, sweetheart. I hope you like them.'

She gave a little giggle, then ran into the living room, a bound-less ball of kinetic energy.

My mother was bustling about in the kitchen.

'Hello, Mum,' I said, and handed her the chocolates. Her face lit up and she pecked me on the cheek.

'I made you a cottage pie,' she said. 'I'll put it in the oven. It won't take long to heat up.'

'That's great,' I said. 'I haven't eaten all day and I'm famished.'

'I saw you on the news. And it was weird watching Ethan answer your questions. He didn't look too happy about it and neither did that other detective.'

'Serves 'em right,' I said. 'They weren't as organised down there

125

as they should have been. But anyway I don't want to talk about work for the rest of the evening. Tell me about your day. Did you go to the park?'

'We did and Rosie thoroughly enjoyed herself. She's been a little darling as usual.'

My mother spoke as she put my dinner in the oven. She told me that after the park they had lunch and then spent the afternoon watching DVDs.

'She made me sit through *Shrek* again. That's the third time in a week. I really don't understand why she isn't fed up with it. I know I am.'

I laughed and then went upstairs to have a quick shower. Afterwards I snuggled into my robe, then came back downstairs for my dinner, which I ate on my lap in the living room so that I could watch Rosie do her colouring.

After I'd eaten I joined her on the floor and helped her colour in a couple of nasty-looking dragons while my mother watched the telly and stuffed her face with chocolates.

It felt good to chill out and relax after the day I'd had. And I was glad I was at last able to spend some quality time with my daughter. It was good for both of us. She got to have my undivided attention, and I got the chance to remind her that she was the most precious thing in the world to me. At one point I apologised again for not taking her to the park.

'That's all right, Mummy,' she said. 'Nanny says you have to go to work so that you can buy me things.'

My heart flipped and I had to force myself not to cry.

'Oh, sweetheart, that's a lovely thing to say. You deserve a big hug and a big wet kiss.'

I grabbed her before she could crawl away from me and held her in my arms as though my life depended on it.

I managed to plant half a dozen kisses on her cheeks before she wriggled free. Then it was back to the colouring, followed by a short game of hide-and-seek that left me positively breathless.

I let Rosie sit up until nine. By then she was exhausted and falling asleep in my arms.

When she was tucked up in bed I poured myself a glass of wine and joined Mum in the living room.

'The chocolates were delicious,' she said.

I shook my head and smiled at her. 'I can't believe you've eaten the whole box.'

'Why not? They're my favourites.'

I lost interest in the film we started watching and picked up my iPad to check my emails and *The Post*'s online site. When I saw my by-line on the front page I felt a flash of pride. The top of the story was exactly how I had written it, and they'd even inserted a stock photograph of me.

There were several other photographs relating to the story, including one taken by an agency photographer outside the police station in Wandsworth. It captured the moment when Danny Shapiro was confronted by Nigel Fuller and I could see myself in the background.

Another photo was of Amy Cassidy, Fuller's fiancée, talking to reporters. The caption underneath described her as a successful businesswoman. Out of curiosity I googled her and discovered that Miss Cassidy owned a chain of stores that sold wedding dresses. The forthcoming marriage to Fuller would be her second and she had two grown-up sons of her own.

Viewing all those photos reminded me of the one I'd come across this morning showing a young Danny Shapiro with his father on Peckham Rye Common. I'd saved it to my favourites so that I could show it to my mother. But as I was about to open the site she said something that totally threw me.

'I neglected to mention that someone phoned here earlier this evening asking for you. He wouldn't give his name but said he enjoyed meeting you at the snooker club.'

I froze and felt the hairs on the back of my neck quiver.

'So what were you doing in a snooker club?' my mother said.

I had to swallow to moisten my throat before responding. 'Oh, I went there to follow up a lead. I spoke to a couple of people.'

'Then do you know who the caller was? He sounded very polite. I wondered if he might have been someone who showed an interest in you.'

'I can't think who it might have been,' I lied. 'What else did he say?'

'Only that he's looking forward to seeing you again and if he has reason to come to Peckham he'll be sure to pop in.'

I was glad my mother's eyes stayed glued to the television because she would have seen the blood drain from my face. I didn't want her to know what Frankie Bishop had said and done to me, and the thought that he had phoned my home caused my skin to prickle with anxiety.

The rest of the evening was ruined. I couldn't concentrate on anything, and my thoughts became jumbled and dislocated. Even after I finally got into bed what my mother had said kept me awake. I lay supine on the mattress, staring into the darkness for what seemed like an eternity.

Try as I might I could not dismiss the gnawing fear growing at the back of my mind. The fear that Frankie Bishop had meant what he'd said and that they wouldn't stand for me sticking my nose in their business or Shapiro's private life.

I have only to say the word and I can make you disappear.

They were strong words, stark and unambiguous. And they served as a timely reminder that my job brought me into contact with some shockingly bad people; people who wouldn't think twice about committing an act of violence against a journalist.

Even if that journalist happened to be a mother with a young child.

16

Danny Shapiro

Danny rarely stayed in on a Saturday night. He would usually go to one of his clubs or pubs, pick up a bird, and end the evening at his flat in Bermondsey or at a hotel.

But tonight he was alone in the mews house off New Bond Street and he had already downed three whiskies.

He was in no mood for partying, and he did not want to be seen out enjoying himself only hours after his ex-wife was found murdered. He still felt cut up about that and he was annoyed that people were still pointing the finger at him.

After leaving the police station today he had gone straight to his office above the snooker club. It was obvious that a few of the lads thought he did it – or paid someone to do it – despite his denials.

'It's a good thing you have an alibi,' Bishop had said. 'Odds on you would have been fitted up otherwise.'

There was palpable relief among the crew that the Old Bill had let him go. He knew they liked having him as their boss, even though it had taken him a while to settle into the role.

He'd been nervous and unsure of himself at first, and his father had been a tough act to follow. So Danny had been forced to prove himself in order to win their respect and their loyalty. He had succeeded in this by demonstrating a level of ruthlessness that surprised and impressed even the most hardened members of the crew.

The first test of his ability came three months after Callum was jailed. A gang of Eastern Europeans tried to muscle in on the distribution of drugs to schools and colleges on the manor. When he told them to back off they ignored him, believing that with his father out of the way, Danny didn't have the balls for a turf war.

But he proved them wrong by kidnapping the gang's leader and his two bodyguards. He had them taken to a warehouse in Greenwich where they were tortured by Bishop until they agreed to up sticks and move out of London altogether.

It was a message to all those foreign outfits who thought the firm was dead. And it played well among his own people, especially those who had harboured reservations about his leadership credentials.

'After the police came here today we had a visit from that reporter with *The Post*,' Bishop had told him. 'I gave her a slap and warned her to stay away from us.'

At any other time Danny would have torn Bishop off a strip. It was never a good idea to threaten anyone but your rivals and people who owed you money. However he couldn't help smiling at the thought of Bethany Chambers being knocked off the chair. He was just sorry he hadn't been there to witness it.

He'd wanted to spend the evening by himself in order to reflect on everything that had happened. He was also expecting a call from his father, who had sent a message that he would phone the house around nine.

Callum would no doubt be worried about him and anxious to

know if he was okay. But he wasn't okay. Megan's murder had affected him more than he would have thought possible.

Memories of the good times they'd spent together kept pushing themselves to the forefront of his mind. Their wedding day, the honeymoon in Thailand, the celebrity parties, the cosy weekends at the cottage in the New Forest.

It wasn't as if she had been to blame for the break-up of their marriage. He was the one who'd been unable to keep his dick in his pants, the one who'd decided that holding on to the family firm was more important than holding on to his wife.

It was a shame that things had turned sour between them and that the last time they were together they'd had a blazing row.

When he closed his eyes he saw her face from last night, all twisted up in anger, spite spewing from her mouth. That he still couldn't remember how it had ended filled him with despair.

Had she pushed him too far? Had he lost control? Was that why his mind had blanked it out?

He was on his fifth whisky when his father rang. Strangely enough he still felt as sober as a judge.

Callum usually called about twice a week, using mobile phones that were smuggled into the prison. Rarely did he use prison phones for fear that they were bugged.

'Everyone is talking about Megan,' Callum said, his voice deep and gravelly.

'It wasn't me who killed her, Dad. But I swear that if the filth don't find out who did then I will.'

He couldn't bring himself to confess that he wasn't actually sure what had happened last night because the booze had created gaps in his memory. So he told him what he'd told Tamara – that he went to the house to confront Megan about the blackmail threat and then left after an argument. Next he explained how he had asked Tamara to give him an alibi and how she had saved his arse.

'Bless her,' Callum said. 'She's a doll. Please tell her that I'm as grateful as you are and that I miss her loads.'

'I will, Dad, but to be fair I've also said I'll pay her fifty grand.'

Callum laughed. 'Cheap at the price, son. You should also try to persuade her to go away for a bit. Book her on a cruise or send her to our place in Marbella. Just create some distance between her and the filth so they don't try to put pressure on her to change her story.'

'I'll give it a go, but I'm not sure she'll be up for it. Besides I don't think she'll let the bastards push her around.'

'It's worth a try, son. And my advice to you is to keep a low profile for a while. At the same time try to get as much intel as you can from your contacts in the Met so you can stay one step ahead of them.'

They then talked briefly about the business and about life in Belmarsh prison. It struck Danny that his father sounded different, but he couldn't put his finger on what it was. He asked him if he was feeling okay and Callum said he was fine. Danny suspected that there was more to it and that he was suffering from one of his frequent bouts of depression. After all, who wouldn't be depressed being banged up for twenty-five fucking years.

'Take care, Dad,' he said, before hanging up. 'And remember I'm always thinking about you.'

Danny had learned long ago that there was no point trying to encourage his father to cheer up. That served only to make him feel even worse about his situation.

Seated on the sofa in front of the television, Danny had a few more slugs of whisky before falling asleep.

* * *

133

He woke up in the early hours, snapping into consciousness from one of the most vivid dreams he had ever had.

Only it wasn't a dream, he quickly realised. It was a flashback to the night before – a series of images that had been dislodged from where they'd been concealed in his mind.

He sat bolt upright, knocking the half-empty bottle of whisky from his lap onto the floor.

The shock of what he'd seen tore through him like a bullet and goose bumps crawled up his arms. He held his breath and shut his eyes as more images floated before him and more memories snapped into place.

'That's it,' he screamed out. 'That's what happened.'

It all came back to him then in a burst of clarity, just as he had suspected it eventually would. He remembered everything that had gone on in Megan's house from the moment he entered it to the moment he left.

And the relief was almost palpable because he knew now that he didn't kill his ex-wife.

17

Beth Chambers

The next day, Sunday, the weather turned nasty again. A crack of thunder woke me from a fitful sleep, and when I got up to look out of the window a flash of lightning cut across the sky.

The rain was biblical, pounding the pavements and creating instant puddles in the road in front of the house.

I'd had a rough night, during which I'd been taunted by the faces and voices of two men – Danny Shapiro and Frankie Bishop. I'd thought about them and dreamed about them, and their threats were still resonating inside my head.

Bishop's warning to me to back off was the most chilling, especially as he had followed it up with a menacing call to the house. But Shapiro's threat to sue me had been delivered with just as much venom, and the look in his eyes had unnerved me.

It wasn't unusual for me to upset people. My job involved sticking my nose in other people's business, and rooting out the facts of a story even when the parties involved wanted to conceal them.

A year ago I was attacked by a Roma gipsy woman while

investigating a West End pickpocketing racket. She punched me twice in the face before chasing me down the street with a knife.

A few months after that I received a death threat while investigating the Russian mafia's dominance of organised crime in Soho. I'd ploughed on regardless and produced a centre-page spread that the editor had deemed worthy of a cash bonus. Needless to say I got to spend the money and did not end up in a ditch with my throat cut.

And therein lies the problem – having to decide whether or not to take a threat, any threat, seriously.

The problem had mushroomed in recent years with journalists among the most frequently targeted on social media. Sites like Twitter and Facebook had made it easy for internet trolls to intimidate and threaten and to do so with a degree of anonymity.

I was used to being abused and attacked via the web. One Twitter troll threatened to rape me for writing an opinion piece criticising an armed robber's early release from prison. Another said my home would be burned down for exposing a sex slavery scandal in west London.

Everything that had been thrown at me before today I'd taken in my stride. But for some reason Danny Shapiro and his psycho enforcer had made me feel particularly uneasy. His threats came as a salutary reminder that my single-minded determination to uncover the truth often exposed me – and by extension my family – to dangerous situations.

It was something my mother was acutely aware of and why she had accused me more than once of being reckless and selfish. Of course, she was absolutely right. But the brutal truth was that if I chose to be risk-averse I'd never be able to do my job. I'd have to give up chasing the bad guys.

So it was a true dilemma, and one I shared with most

investigative journalists and crime-busting police officers who had families to think of.

I looked at the bedside clock and saw that it was only 7 a.m. Mum and Rosie wouldn't be up for a while and I knew I'd never get back to sleep. I slipped on my robe and went into the kitchen to make a cup of tea.

I drank it at the breakfast bar while checking my emails. There was nothing worth reading except for a message from Trevor, my Friday night date. He wanted to know if I would go out with him again. But the thought of it made me cringe so I tried to let him down gently.

You're a great guy, Trev. But I don't think we're right for one another. Best of luck in the future.

That was what I liked about online dating. There was never any pressure to meet someone again. Just drop them an email or a text and move on to the next one. Simple and straightforward, but admittedly not always pain-free.

I then pulled up the online editions of the Sunday papers. All the tabloids were leading with Megan Fuller's murder, and I was pleased to see that none of them had anything we didn't have. They all carried the line that Danny Shapiro had been questioned and released. Two of the papers pointed out that detectives had ascertained that he was in another part of London at the time of the murder. There was no mention of Tamara Roth, which encouraged me to believe that if I could get her to talk it would be an exclusive angle for *The Post*.

A lot of column inches were devoted to Megan's marriage to Shapiro and to his alleged involvement in organised crime. The *Mail*'s crime reporter had written a well-researched piece about how Danny's father had built his south London criminal empire. The paper carried a photo of Callum standing outside one of his clubs. Dressed in a double-breasted suit and smoking a fat cigar, he reminded me of one of those legendary gangsters from America's prohibition era.

By contrast the post-divorce pictures of his son showed Danny casually dressed in jeans, T-shirts and jumpers. In several he wore a baseball cap that really didn't suit him but was probably meant to make him less conspicuous.

I was still wading through the papers when my mother came into the kitchen complaining that the rain against her bedroom window had woken her up. She was wrapped in her oversized dressing gown and wearing a hairnet.

'I'll make you a cuppa,' I said and as I put on the kettle she sat on the stool next to mine.

'Are you going to have to work today?' she asked me.

'Probably not,' I said. 'But it depends if there are any developments with the story. I suppose you know they questioned Megan's ex-husband and then let him go.'

'I saw it on the news.'

'Yeah, well between us the police aren't convinced he didn't do it. They think he may have come up with a dodgy alibi.'

'Can't say I'm surprised,' my mother said.

As I placed her tea on the breakfast bar I saw that she was looking down at my iPad which was displaying the front page of the *Sunday Mirror*. A photo of Megan and Shapiro together was spread across two columns.

'The bastard should be locked up along with his father,' she said through clenched teeth.

Her voice was pitched higher than usual and it took me by surprise.

'I'm sure you're not the only person who'll be thinking that this morning,' I said.

She stared at the photo and there was a hardness in her eyes that I hadn't seen before.

'It's not right, Beth,' she said. 'People like him never pay for their crimes. He'll have the police, judges, and local politicians in his pocket for sure. Just like his old man did.'

My mother never reacted strongly to anything in the news, but then this was the kind of story that stirred the emotions.

'Speaking of the father,' I said. 'I've got something to show you. I came across it yesterday.'

I picked up the iPad and opened the online page with the photo of Callum Shapiro and his son from years ago.

'I thought it might interest you,' I said. 'It was taken on the Common, probably around the time he was one of your customers on the stall.'

I handed the device over and she squinted at the photo.

After a moment, she said, 'That's just how I remember him. Callum bloody Shapiro. He tried to act like he was a kind-hearted family man when in reality he was a cruel, manipulative murderer.'

I was taken aback by the sharpness of her tone and the flush that suddenly burned across her cheeks.

'I know what he was like, Mum,' I said. 'It was common knowledge. But I didn't realise you had such a strong opinion of him. You've never mentioned it before.'

'That's because I've not had to think about him for a long time. Now everyone is talking about him again because of that murdering son of his.'

I reached over and put a hand on her arm. 'I still don't get it, Mum. Why does it bother you so much? Callum Shapiro never did you any harm, did he?'

She turned towards me then and there was a haunted look on

her face. She started to speak but the words seemed to get stuck in her throat.

'Jesus, Mum. What is it? What's wrong?'

Tears rose in her eyes, but she blinked them back. I had no idea what had got into her and it scared me.

'Come on, Mum,' I urged her. 'Spit it out. You're clearly upset and I want to know why.'

But she shook her head and tried to regain her composure.

'I'm sorry, Beth. I don't know what came over me. I'm just being silly.'

'Don't fib, Mum. I've never seen you like this. All this business with the Shapiros has got to you for some reason.'

'No, Beth. I'm just angry because it's not fair. It's not . . .'

What happened next completely threw me. My mother dissolved into tears, great racking sobs that made her body shake.

I was shocked, confused, momentarily lost for words. I hadn't seen Mum cry since Michael's funeral. Those, though, had been tears of sadness and loss. This was different. Something other than grief had brought it on; something from the past that was just as painful, though, and that she had bottled up for a very long time.

I put an arm around her shoulders, felt myself well up.

'Talk to me, Mum,' I said, my voice high and shrill. 'What in God's name is so upsetting for you?'

I pulled her close and held her tight until the tears subsided, which took longer than a minute. I could feel the heat rise from her body and the anguish in her sobs.

'Surely it can't be that bad,' I said. 'Otherwise you would have told me about it before now.'

She lifted her head and looked at me. Her eyes were red and tears slid down her cheeks.

'It's worse than bad, Beth,' she whispered. 'That's why I've kept it from you. I didn't want you to know.'

'Christ, Mum. You're scaring me. What is it you didn't want me to know?'

She picked up a tea towel and used it to wipe her eyes.

'I'm so sorry, Beth. That woman's murder, that photo – it's just brought it all back to me what that man did.'

My chest began to cramp and a bout of trembling gripped me.

'What man are you on about, Mum? And what the hell did he do?'

She stared right at me, her large wet eyes burning with intensity.

After a long, agonising moment, she said, 'It was Callum Shapiro. He did it. And he got away with it, Beth. Just like his bastard son will get away with it this time.'

I felt my brow furrow. 'I don't understand, Mum. What did Callum Shapiro get away with?'

As she spoke her face collapsed again and her voice broke into a sob.

'He killed Tony, Beth. He killed your stepfather. That's what he did, and it's why I hate him so much.'

18

Beth Chambers

My hands flew to my face in horror.

'It's true, Beth,' my mother said. 'I really thought it was best that you didn't know.'

The revelation that my stepfather had been one of Callum Shapiro's many victims hit me for six. I felt a cold numbness envelop me and a lump formed in my throat.

Surely it wasn't possible, I told myself. I'd been writing about the man for years. I'd covered his trial, watched the judge send him down for a quarter of a century.

How could my mother have harboured such a secret for so long? That was just one of the many questions that suddenly piled up inside my head.

'You should have told me, Mum,' I said. 'I can't believe you kept it from me for all these years.'

I was 14 when Tony was killed. At the time I was told only that a bad man had shot him, and I wasn't aware he was a criminal himself. It wasn't until afterwards that I discovered via the internet that he'd been a small-time villain who had been to prison as a young man after being convicted of robbing a jewellery shop.

His murder remained unsolved to this day. He was shot twice in the head after leaving a pub in Tulse Hill. The killer had never been identified and the motive had never been discovered.

'I didn't know at the time that Callum Shapiro got someone to carry out the killing,' my mother said. 'The rumours started to circulate a few years later and the last thing I wanted to do was bring it all up again. You had got over his death by then and I was terrified that if Michael found out he would have done something stupid.'

I had to concede that my mother had a point there. As young as he was Michael would probably have taken it upon himself to try to avenge his father's death.

I sat back on the stool and felt my eyes blur with tears. Now it was Mum's turn to console me. She reached out and squeezed my knee.

'It was never meant to come out, Beth. I won't forgive myself for losing control like that, and after all this time.'

I shook my head. 'I'm glad you did. But you can't just leave it at that. I need to know everything.'

As she spoke I struggled to hold it together against a whirlwind of emotions. Some of what she told me I already knew – that as a young man Tony had lived in Brixton where he'd been a member of the notorious Ghetto Guys, one of the most bellicose gangs in London. After serving time in prison he moved to Peckham and ran with a bunch of drug dealers and petty thieves.

'I met him soon after he moved here,' my mother said. 'I knew he was trouble and I should never have got involved with him. But as you know yourself, Beth, he was a charmer and such fun to be with. I fell head over heels in love with him even though I should have learned my lesson with your real father, who never did an honest day's work in his life.'

My mother explained that Tony and his pals eventually came to the attention of other gangs, including the Shapiros, because they started to expand their operations into Streatham, Brixton, and Stockwell.

'Callum was among those who warned them off,' she said. 'He actually threatened Tony in a club one night and Tony told him to sod off. Shortly after that two of Tony's people were badly beaten. I urged Tony to stop antagonising Shapiro and the other gangs and to go straight for the sake of you and Michael. Eventually that's what he decided to do. He took me out for dinner on my birthday and said we were going to move away from the area and he was going to get a job. Two nights later he was shot.'

I flashed on a memory – the police coming to our home to break the news and my mother collapsing in a heap on the floor.

'The police told me they had lots of suspects because Tony had lots of enemies,' she said. 'And I knew that to be true. But three years later someone who knew Tony told me about the rumours that Callum Shapiro was behind the shooting. I actually went to a pub he frequented and confronted him. He denied it, of course, but I could tell he was lying. So I went to the police, but they said there was no proof so nothing was done. I knew then that I would have to live with it and that I couldn't tell you or your brother.'

I realised then the extent of the burden my mother had carried for so many years. How painful it must have been to know – or at least to believe – that the man responsible for having Tony killed had got away with it.

'One of the happiest days of my life was when Callum Shapiro was sent to prison,' my mother said. 'You were still with Ethan at the time so you wouldn't have known that I bought myself a bottle of champagne to celebrate.'

It was all too much and it suddenly felt as though my brain had turned to mud. I leaned forward, hugged my mother, and kissed her on the cheek.

My heart was in free fall and I knew it was going to take a while for me to come to terms with what I had just been told.

I also knew that the name Shapiro would from now on arouse in me intense feelings of bitterness and antipathy.

19

Danny Shapiro

Danny hadn't been able to get back to sleep after waking in the early hours. He was too hyped up, having suddenly remembered everything that had happened at Megan's on Friday night.

The fragments of his memory that had been temporarily blacked out by alcohol had resurfaced and it had come as an immense relief to know that he hadn't killed Megan.

He had been going over it in his head now for something like five hours, and the more he thought about it the harder it was for him to accept that very soon after he left there she was stabbed to death.

Had the killer or killers watched him leave? Was it conceivable that they were in the house the whole time, listening to him and Megan shouting at each other?

He recalled her parting words now, hurled at him as she followed him down the hall to the front door.

'I'm desperate, Danny. I've got no money and I'm getting deeper into debt. I know enough about you and the business to fuck up your life if you don't come up with the cash.'

At the door he had been tempted to hit her just to shut her up.

Instead, he'd said, '*You've had enough from me, Megan. I'm not to blame for the state you're in. You need to sort yourself out and stop harassing me. Write your frigging book. I don't care.*'

'*For your information it's already written,*' she'd said as she wrenched open the front door. '*I'll give you a week to come up with the money or I'm sending it to the publishers. Then we'll see if you still don't care.*'

'*There's such a thing as the law of libel, Megan. So why would they publish shit about me? They'd know I'd sue them.*'

'*Yeah, well, I only have to stir things up enough to get the police interested. Plus, I've got lots of personal titbits that will embarrass the hell out of you. And what the publishers shy away from the papers will lap up. The tabloids have already put in bids for exclusive interviews. And on top of that there's the muck I can spread all over the internet.*'

'*You're lying, Megan.*'

'*Well, if that's what you think you're in for a shock. Now fuck off so that I can go to bed.*'

The fact that he'd got his memory back changed nothing in respect of his predicament. He knew the cops still fancied him for the murder and were sceptical of his alibi.

He was sure that Tamara wouldn't let him down, but all the same he hated having to rely on her. He checked the time. Nine o'clock. He had no idea if she'd be up, but he called her anyway.

She'd been up for ages, she said when she answered, and was now looking forward to a day with her feet up watching the telly.

'Same here,' Danny said. He then thanked her for helping him out and asked her how it had gone with the police.

'They were rude and arrogant and they made it clear that they

147

didn't believe me,' she said. 'But I insisted we spent the evening together and there was no way they could prove otherwise.'

'Well, they'll probably pester you again, along with the media. So just stick to the story.'

'Of course I will.'

'I spoke to my father last night. He wanted me to thank you on his behalf and to tell you that he misses you a lot.'

'And I miss him, Danny. I really do. We were good together in spite of the age difference.'

'I know you were, sweetheart. You made him very happy.'

'I'm glad. But the time we had was too brief.'

'At least you've got some good memories.'

'And I'm grateful for those,' she said.

He then told her what his father had said about her going away on a short holiday at the firm's expense.

'You really don't have to do that,' she said.

'I know we don't have to, but we want to. And it'll be on top of the fifty grand. There's the villa in Spain. I know Dad took you there a couple of times. Or what about a cruise? You could fly out tomorrow.'

'I need to give it some thought,' she said. 'I didn't expect this.'

'That's not a problem. Call me back later and we can sort it.'

After speaking to Tamara, Danny made himself some coffee and toast. He usually spent most Sundays at home because he invariably had a hangover. Thankfully he was feeling fine this morning despite putting away half a bottle of whisky last night.

There was no urgent business to attend to. Things were ticking over on all fronts and he'd be meeting Bishop later this evening to discuss what had to be done during the week ahead.

Until then he thought maybe he'd go for one of his walks

around the West End. Or perhaps visit the cinema, watch one of the new movies.

His life was very different these days to how it used to be, and there was no question he was lonely at times. He had no real friends, and the women who came and went only ever shared a bed with him.

Marriage had suited him, at least to begin with. But the mistake he'd made had been to try to have it all. His father had managed to pull it off, at least until the law caught up with him.

For years Callum had run his empire and held on to his marriage to Danny's mother, while having affairs on the side. But Danny wasn't made from the same mettle as his dad. He was sure he would have been happier without the power, wealth and notoriety. After all, this wasn't the life he chose for himself. It was thrust upon him at an early age because it was what his father had wanted. Sometimes it felt like he was serving his own life sentence. He knew he could never just jack it all in and walk away. Too many people depended on him, and those same people would turn on him if he suddenly left them in the lurch.

For guys like him who scaled the dizzy heights of organised crime there were usually only two ways out: in a prison van or in a coffin.

20

Beth Chambers

My mother and I would have wallowed in self-pity for hours if it hadn't been for Rosie. As soon as she was up she demanded our attention, and we both responded with alacrity.

I ran the bath while my mother prepared her breakfast. I was grateful for the distraction, and Rosie's laughter dispelled the gloom that had descended on the house like a big, dark cloud.

'Are we going out today, Mummy?' Rosie asked.

I pointed to the patio doors, through which we could see the rain lashing down onto the garden.

'I don't think so, sweetheart,' I said. 'The weather's really horrid.'

'Then will you do some colouring with me? Please!'

'Of course I will. But let's get you sorted first, eh?'

I bathed her and washed her hair and she splashed around so much I got a soaking. Then while Mum supervised her breakfast I went upstairs to get ready.

Before stepping in the shower I sat on the bed to reflect on my mother's shocking disclosure. Callum Shapiro had arranged for my stepfather to be murdered; at least that was what she believed. It was a dreadful, gut-churning thought and it was chewing me up inside.

It was irrelevant to her – and to me – that her conviction was based principally on rumours. While I knew only too well that guys like Callum Shapiro rarely left a trail of evidence in their wake, I also knew they took drastic steps to protect their business. And Tony and his crew had apparently posed a threat to that business by expanding their operations across south London.

It would have been a surprise to me if Shapiro or any of the other gang leaders had actually *failed* to retaliate.

I couldn't even begin to imagine how my mother must have suffered for all those years. The pain of losing her husband would have been compounded by what she'd subsequently learned. It must have hurt every time the Shapiros featured on the news – and every time I'd mentioned them, which had been quite often.

I felt that I needed to react in some way to what I'd been told, but I wasn't sure how. It was something I'd have to think about, analyse, stress over.

As I sat there staring at nothing in particular, my eyes were drawn to the bedraggled teddy bear sitting atop the chest of drawers. He was the last gift my real father had ever given to me and he had named him Olly. I'd treasured him for over twenty years, and he was still my most prized possession, even though he only had one eye and most of his fur had worn away.

He was a constant reminder to me of what might have been had my father not been married when my mother met him. Would she have been spared all the turmoil and heartache that had marred her life?

I was forever wishing he'd stayed around for longer so that I'd now have more than just a few vague memories of him. There was so much I'd never been told and probably a lot I'd forgotten. Had he really been as bad as my mother had always made out? *A shyster who never did an honest day's work in his life.* Surely she wouldn't have had him in our lives for so long if he'd been so terrible!

I resolved to confront my mother again, to plead with her to break her silence. If she could come clean about Shapiro after all this time then she could bloody well tell me what she'd been holding back about my father.

I didn't even know his name, for pity's sake. Or even if he was still alive. For too long I'd accepted her word for it that I was better off not knowing, whatever that meant.

But what had happened this morning had triggered in me a new determination. It was time to unravel *all* the secrets from my past and not just those that my mother saw fit to reveal.

I called the office after I'd showered and before I got dressed. Grant was on a day off so I spoke to the duty news editor, Evie Wren.

There was nothing new to report, except that Danny Shapiro had turned down an interview request made through his solicitor. His whereabouts were unknown, but the paparazzi were staking out his flat in Bermondsey.

'No one believes he's there,' Evie said. 'Still, they're hoping he'll turn up eventually.'

I told Evie I'd be at home for most of the day and to keep me updated on the Megan Fuller case and on any other breaking crime stories. The newsdesk would normally do that as a matter of course, but it didn't hurt to remind them.

I slipped on a light sweater and tracksuit bottoms and went downstairs make-up free.

My mother had made a toasted bacon sandwich – my favourite – and I was glad to see that she was having one too. Her eyes were still red and there were shadows beneath them.

I decided to wait until much later to broach the subject of my real father – and to tell her I'd come up with the idea of writing a feature on Tony's murder. I wasn't sure how she'd react to that, and I didn't want to risk sparking another flood of tears.

After breakfast I played with Rosie for an hour before I got to my laptop. I ran through the usual checklist first – emails, Facebook, *The Post*'s online site, the BBC News front page and finally my Twitter account.

Then I googled Tamara Roth. There were several women in the UK with that name, but I narrowed it down pretty quickly thanks to a newspaper story from several years ago.

It told how she had appeared in court at the then age of 23 charged with soliciting near her home in Vauxhall.

From there I managed to get her exact address and locate the website where she advertised herself as an escort. It included a small head-and-shoulders photo of a pretty red-headed woman in her thirties or forties. Then, to my astonishment, I came across several references to her in a couple of online news stories about Callum Shapiro.

'Jesus Christ,' I blurted out to myself, startling my mother, who was sitting across the room on the sofa helping Rosie do some colouring.

'What is it?' she asked me.

Excitement swelled in my stomach.

'Would you believe that the prostitute who's given Danny Shapiro his alibi for Friday night used to date his father?'

My mother's jaw dropped. 'Do you think the police know?'

'There's one way to find out,' I said, reaching for my phone.

I called Ethan, but it rang until his voicemail picked up. I left a message asking him to ring me back.

'I wouldn't get too worked up about it,' my mother said, having given it some thought. 'Danny Shapiro's lawyer will just say it's irrelevant and the police will probably be of the same opinion.'

'But surely it makes their story less believable.'

My mother shrugged. 'It doesn't matter. The only thing that counts is whether it can be proved that they're lying.'

She was right, of course, but it did nothing to stop the blood pumping supercharged through my veins.

I turned back to the laptop and carried on searching for information on Tamara Roth.

But within minutes I was in for another shock when the breaking-news app flashed up an alert on the top of the screen.

Police investigating the murder of soap actress Megan Fuller are questioning an unidentified man after swooping on a house in south London.

21

Ethan Cain

As soon as Sam Jones entered the interview room Cain took an instant dislike to him. The guy looked as though he was full of himself. He wore a soft plaid shirt and chinos, and walked with a pronounced swagger.

The duty solicitor trailed in behind him, a world-weary brief named Arnold Frobisher, who had been on the scene for as long as Cain could remember.

The pair sat down across the table from Cain and DCI Redwood. Jones was fortyish, of average height, with dark receding hair. He had dull, lacklustre eyes and a rosy drinker's hue on his cheeks.

Cain studied him with ill-concealed hostility. As a convicted wife-beater and murder suspect he felt it was no more than he deserved.

'For the record Mr Jones is here to assist our inquiries into the murder of his former girlfriend, Megan Fuller,' Redwood said. 'He's been informed that as part of the process we've applied for a warrant to search his flat and check his phone records.'

Frobisher leaned forward across the table and spoke, his voice a soft baritone.

'Also for the record my client has already stated that he knows nothing about Miss Fuller's death and has not seen her for several weeks.'

Frobisher was a small, scruffy man with beady eyes and a greyish pallor to his skin. But Cain knew that his appearance belied a shrewd analytical mind, and he was not to be underestimated.

Redwood opened a folder on his desk and shuffled some papers. Jones watched him. His mouth was set firm, expressing no obvious emotion. Then he placed his hands on the table as if he was about to push himself up. Cain noted the nicotine-stained fingers and chewed-to-the-quick nails.

He wondered what an attractive woman like Megan Fuller had seen in the guy and, for that matter, what she'd seen in Danny Shapiro. It occurred to him that she must have been a lamentable judge of character.

'The first thing I want to ask you, Mr Jones, is where you've been since yesterday morning,' Redwood said. 'We know you weren't at home because an officer was stationed outside your flat. And we know your phone was switched off because we tried calling you.'

'There's no mystery, Inspector,' Jones said. 'I spent yesterday and last night at my sister's house in Ramsgate. I forgot to take my phone with me and you couldn't get an answer because I'd also forgotten to charge it so the battery was flat.'

'Why did you go to your sister's place on the same day that Megan was found dead?'

Jones exhaled a long, slow breath. 'It was her birthday and I wanted to see her. I didn't know about Megan when I left the house in the morning to go to the train station. It wasn't until I got to my sister's that I found out.'

'I'm not sure how this is relevant, Inspector,' Frobisher said. 'It's my understanding that Miss Fuller was killed on Friday night.'

'I was coming to that,' Redwood said. He pursed his lips and his voice dropped an octave as he asked Jones where he was at that time.

'I was out on the lash with some mates,' Jones said. 'I've got their names and phone numbers if you want to verify it.'

'We certainly will want to,' Redwood said. 'So where were you?'

'A pub called the Flying Dutchman in Tooting. It's around the corner from my flat. They had an extension to mark the pub's fiftieth anniversary so I didn't get away until after one in the morning.'

'Will the landlord be able to confirm that you were there all evening?'

'Sure he will. His name's Terry Lee. Known him for years.'

Cain listened to Jones's answers with mounting irritation. If the alibi was genuine then they were back to square one and Redwood would want to shift the focus back onto Danny. It wasn't what Cain wanted, though. So long as Danny was in the frame then his own position was compromised. At some point Danny would start calling in favours and that would get very tricky indeed.

'Tell us about Megan,' Redwood said. 'Starting with why you broke up.'

Jones threw a glance at his lawyer, probably expecting him to say he didn't have to answer. But Frobisher merely nodded without making eye contact.

'Let me make it easy for you,' Redwood said. 'We've seen the last text message you sent to Megan apologising for hitting her. If that's why she dumped you then just say so.'

Cain was pleased to see that Jones didn't look so smug now, and a thin sheen of perspiration had gathered on his forehead.

'It was only a slap,' he said, as if that were permissible. 'She kept going on about the money she lost on the shares and acting like it was all my fault. But I was in just as much shit as she was. I don't have a job or any savings. So I got angry and snapped.'

'But what she said was true, wasn't it?' Cain said. 'Didn't you persuade her to buy the shares because you were expecting to make a quick buck?'

'She didn't need much persuading,' Jones said. 'She was up for it, but when it went wrong she got in a panic.'

'So you hit her,' Redwood said. 'Just like you used to hit your wife.'

As expected Frobisher intervened, telling his client not to respond to the question. But he did.

'Look, for your information I regretted what happened,' Jones said. 'I went too far and shouldn't have lost my temper. That's why I apologised. I wanted us to get back together. I missed her and I loved her.'

'You had a funny way of showing it,' Redwood said.

'Yeah, I know. It was the first time I'd got physical with her. It's a problem I have and it's why I went on an anger management course a while ago. But I never go completely over the top. I know when to stop.'

'Which is your way of saying you were happy to slap Megan around but would have drawn the line at stabbing her in the throat.'

'I'm not a murderer, Inspector. And when you talk to my mates you'll know I couldn't have killed Megan because I was with them when it happened.'

Redwood consulted his notes and then asked Jones if he

knew about the autobiography that Megan was supposedly working on.

'I knew about it because it was my idea,' he said.

'Care to explain that?'

Jones shrugged. 'It was after things went belly-up with the shares and Megan realised she was skint. We were discussing ways to raise some money and I asked her why she didn't write a book like a lot of other celebrities. Well, she thought about it for a couple of days and then said it would take too long but she'd come up with a way to make a ton of money by pretending to write one.'

'But she told her agent that she *was* going to.'

'She also told that to an interviewer on a TV chat show,' Jones said. 'It was never her intention though. It was just part of her plan to convince her ex-husband that she was going to reveal things about him that he wouldn't want to be made public.'

'A crude attempt at blackmail you mean?' Cain said.

'Exactly. I told her it was bloody risky, but she set her mind on seeing it through.'

'So she confronted Shapiro and demanded money from him?' Redwood said.

'That's right. She felt sure he'd stump up the cash rather than have his secrets revealed in a book. But his initial reaction was to tell her to piss off. She continued to threaten him anyway. That was another reason why we argued. I thought it was stupid to push someone like Shapiro, not to mention fucking dangerous. But she kept saying he'd see sense eventually.'

'Yet instead he called her bluff.'

'Well, that was the position just before she ended it with me. Even so she still believed she could persuade him to cough up. In fact she was so convinced her plan was a good one that she said she was going to target someone else with the same blackmail threat.'

The two detectives shared a look and Redwood said, 'Did she tell you who it was?'

Jones shook his head. 'I didn't bother to ask. But I assumed it must be someone else she knew who has a bunch of secrets.'

22

Ethan Cain

Cain and Redwood questioned Jones for another twenty minutes. But he continued to insist that he didn't know who else had been targeted for blackmail by Megan Fuller.

'I can only repeat what she told me,' he said. 'And I believed her. She really thought she was onto a good little earner.'

Jones was told he would have to stay at the nick until his alibi had been checked out. Frobisher objected, but Jones waved a hand and said he didn't mind.

Back in the incident room Redwood called the team together to brief them. Before speaking he removed his jacket and loosened his tie. There was sweat under his armpits and Cain could tell he was feeling the pressure.

'According to Megan's former boyfriend Danny Shapiro may not be the only person she was threatening to expose in her fantasy book,' Redwood said, his voice high and clipped. 'That means whoever it was also had a motive for wanting to see her dead. So we need to identify this person. The trouble is we don't have a name and we don't know if it's a man or a woman.'

He told a couple of detectives to go to the Flying Dutchman pub in Tooting to establish whether or not Jones's alibi was kosher. Another was assigned the task of overseeing the search of his flat once the warrant had been activated.

'And let's chase his phone records,' he said. 'I want a list of all his calls and messages.'

Cain knew it was a long shot, but it got everyone excited because they needed a break in the case. About thirty-six hours had passed since Megan had been murdered and they were struggling.

They had knocked on every door and questioned every witness and passer-by within a half-mile radius of Ramsden Road. They'd drawn a blank on CCTV footage and now the two main suspects had produced alibis.

It wasn't the best start to a murder investigation.

After the briefing, Cain went to his desk where he remembered he'd left his mobile phone. He noticed he had two missed calls from Beth. She had left a message asking him to ring her back and he guessed she wanted to know who they were questioning.

Sam Jones's name hadn't yet been released and the media were screaming for information. But he had no intention of phoning Beth back from the office. There were too many people around.

Besides, there was a cardboard box next to his desk containing some of Megan Fuller's personal effects. The Exhibits Team had logged them all and now he wanted to go through the things.

His lungs were calling out for nicotine as he sat down. There was no time to go outside for a smoke, which was how he usually tried to combat pressure when it started building up inside him, so he slipped a piece of gum into his mouth.

The fact that he was in a difficult position was stressing him out. Soon Danny would call up asking where they were with the investigation. He'd then demand that steps be taken to ensure that his alibi held firm and that any other incriminating evidence be destroyed or discredited. He'd done it before and Cain had sorted things out for him. But this time it wouldn't be so easy. Any attempt to shift the investigation away from Danny, or to cover up evidence, was going to be monumentally risky.

He saw Redwood approaching him so he picked up the cardboard box and started placing items from it on his desk.

'I'm going back to Ramsden Road,' Redwood said when he reached him. 'The residents have organised a meeting in the church hall and they want us to update them on progress. I'll use it to appeal for more information. Meanwhile, the post-mortem on Megan is scheduled for two o'clock. I'd like you to attend.'

'I'll go as soon as I've finished sifting through this lot,' Cain said.

Redwood started to turn away, but then stopped and leaned forward, resting a hand on Cain's desk.

'Is everything okay, Ethan?' he asked.

Cain swallowed. 'Of course, guv. Why wouldn't it be?'

Redwood moved his shoulders. 'I'm getting the impression that you're not fully engaged with the case. I wondered if you've got something on your mind that's a distraction.'

'I can't think what's given you that idea, sir.'

'Well, for starters you left it to me to ask all the questions in the interview with Shapiro. You actually appeared to be ill at ease. Like you would rather have been somewhere else.'

Cain felt his throat dry up and a chill spread across his body.

'I can assure you I wasn't, guv,' he said. 'You were asking all the relevant questions so I just thought I would leave you to it.'

Redwood rolled out his bottom lip as he thought about it.

'I will admit to being a bit under the weather,' Cain got in quickly. 'I've felt tired and lethargic for a few days. Maybe that's what you've picked up on.'

Redwood removed his hand from the desk and stood up straight.

'Well, that's okay then. I'm relieved it's nothing more serious. But are you sure you don't need to take time off?'

Cain nodded. 'I'm sure. I'm actually feeling much better than I did yesterday.'

'Good. The last thing I want is to lose any of my top people.'

Redwood looked at his watch and said, 'I'd better make tracks. Don't forget to go along to the PM.'

'I won't, guv.'

As Redwood walked away, Cain slumped back in the chair, his nerves as taut as violin strings.

He was furious with himself for having made it obvious that he'd been uneasy during the interview with Shapiro. How could he have been so stupid?

It was more than a little disconcerting that Redwood had seen fit to raise it. He just had to hope that the man did not progress from being merely curious to suspicious.

Cain turned his attention back to the stuff on his desk, which included personal letters, a Samsung tablet, a bunch of small diaries, several photo albums, a scrapbook of newspaper cuttings charting Megan's career, and a leather business-card wallet.

Cain wasn't sure how useful any of it would be, but sometimes a victim's belongings threw up a nugget of information that propelled a case forward.

In any investigation it was all about clues and evidence and piecing together the threads. So far they weren't having much success. They could point the finger at any number of individuals, but proving they did it was another matter.

There were three photo albums. One was devoted to family and childhood pictures and featured Megan's father and late mother. Another chronicled Megan and Danny's life together as a married couple, and the third was filled with wedding photos.

Cain had seen some of the wedding pics before because they'd appeared in newspapers and magazines. It was at a time when Danny never shied away from publicity. They were a glamorous couple and they were smiling happily in all the photos. Danny's father, Callum, appeared in a few of the group pictures, but he wasn't smiling. In fact he looked positively miserable.

He sifted through the personal letters next. There were a couple of dozen, but they were mostly to and from her agent and various BBC producers and were of little interest.

Next up were her diaries. These went back ten years, but were mostly filled with appointments and birthday reminders. Megan hadn't been one to record her observations on life or what she did each day. Over the last year the entries had petered out as her work dried up, along with invitations to celebrity events.

But something did catch Cain's eye. After her marriage broke up three years ago it seemed that Megan started having regular appointments with a psychiatrist named Drew Bellamy. Cain made a note of his name but then found his business card among those in the leather wallet. He had an office in Kensington and his private mobile number was scrawled on the back of the card.

Cain rang it, but there was no answer so he left a message. He then rang the office number and a recorded voice told him that Mr Bellamy would be in the office again on Monday morning.

The fact that Megan was seeing a shrink wasn't so unusual in itself, but it was possible she'd told the guy something that would be relevant to the investigation. Perhaps she had even revealed to him the identities of her other blackmail victims. And since she was dead there was no reason he shouldn't be able to disclose the details of those monthly sessions.

Cain put everything back into the cardboard box except for Bellamy's card, which he dropped into his pocket, and tapped a reminder into his phone to chase Bellamy up.

Then he got up and set off for the mortuary.

23

Beth Chambers

By late afternoon I was restless. Rosie had lost interest in playing with me and wanted to do her own thing. And my mother had withdrawn into herself, jolted by what she had revealed to me about Tony's murder. She'd hardly moved from the sofa all day, just watching TV between naps.

But I hadn't been able to relax. My mind was a riot of conflicting thoughts and emotions, and I was tearing my hair out trying to rumble who the police were questioning in connection with Megan's murder.

Ethan hadn't yet returned my call, and the Scotland Yard press office was keeping a lid on the name for now. My other Met contacts were either saying they didn't know or weren't even answering their phones.

That was how it went sometimes. The police decided to keep schtum about someone they had in custody because they didn't want the media to descend on their home or approach their family. Knowing that didn't make me feel any less frustrated now. I needed to do something other than stomp around the house with my head buried in my iPad.

It was still chucking it down outside so a leisurely walk wasn't an option. And I couldn't concentrate on the television.

It was four o'clock when my mother finally perked up and announced that she was going to make Rosie's dinner.

'Then afterwards we can watch a movie together,' she told her.

Rosie stopped playing with her doll's house and beamed a smile at her.

'I want to watch *Shrek*, Nanny,' she said. 'Please can I watch *Shrek*?'

My mother laughed. 'Of course you can, sweetie. You've been a really good girl today.'

I followed Mum into the kitchen and asked her if she was all right.

'I am now,' she said. 'I've just been feeling a little shell-shocked and sorry for myself. What about you? Are you all right or are you really upset after what I told you?'

'You've given me a lot to think about,' I said. 'But that's okay. I'm just a bit hyper right now.'

'And bored by the look of it. Beth, if there's something you feel you need to do then just go and do it.'

'But it's Sunday. And I said I wouldn't work today.'

'Well, in the circumstances I really won't mind if you feel the need to pop out for a bit.'

'What about Rosie?'

My mother grinned and glanced over at my daughter.

'To be honest I don't think she'll even notice that you're gone.'

It didn't take me long to get ready. I slapped on some foundation, a touch of eyeshadow, and a swipe of pinkish lipstick. I brushed my hair and let it hang loose, then put on a light sweater and jeans. Over the top I slipped on a shiny black raincoat.

Mum and Rosie were already into *Shrek* by the time I left the house and climbed into a taxi that I'd booked through the paper's account. I'd never owned a car because in London there was really no point. It was too easy to get around using cabs or public transport.

I told the driver where to go and felt the familiar buzz of excitement that came from not knowing what would happen when I got there.

A few minutes into the journey my mobile rang, and I snatched it out of my bag. Ethan's name showed up in the caller ID.

'I'm returning your call,' he said. 'Sorry it's taken so long.'

'I was beginning to think you were blanking me.'

'I was busy at the station. I don't want anyone to know you're calling me there.'

'Sorry about that. There are a few things I need to tell you and one thing I'd like you to tell me.'

'Let me guess,' he said. 'You want to know who we've hauled in for questioning.'

'Right in one, and if you give me a name I'll say lots of nice things about you to your daughter.'

'And if I don't?'

'Then I'll just tell her the truth about her dad and I'm sure you don't want that.'

He chuckled. 'Do you always have to act as though you're the most unscrupulous hack in London?'

'Of course I do,' I said. 'I have a fearsome reputation to maintain. Now I'm in a hurry so are you going to cough up or what?'

He sighed heavily into the phone. 'It's Sam Jones, Megan's

169

ex-boyfriend. But he claims he didn't do it and we're in the process of checking out his alibi. He says he was at a pub with friends.'

'Is that where you're going now – to the pub to check it?'

'No. I'm just leaving the mortuary. I had the pleasure of attending the PM on Megan.'

'Anything suspicious come out of it?'

'Nothing at all. She died as a result of the knife wound to the throat. No drugs in her system and no signs of sexual assault. And there was no skin from an assailant under her fingernails.'

'Anything I can use to move the story along, apart from the boyfriend?'

'Not right now. So what is it you want to tell me?'

I started with Danny Shapiro's alibi and expected him to be surprised when I told him that Tamara Roth used to go out with Danny's father Callum.

'We already know that,' he said. 'He volunteered the information himself during the interview and said he'd known her for years.'

'But surely it casts doubt over what he's told you.'

'Not at all. They say they were together when Megan was murdered. We have no evidence to suggest they're lying. The fact that she had a fling with Shapiro senior isn't really relevant.'

'But—'

'Forget it, Beth. It's nothing to get excited about. Now what else do you want to tell me?'

I told him what my mother had said about Tony's murder. He listened without interrupting, then said, 'Well, if you're hoping the Met will reopen the case based on rumours that were circulating years ago you're going to be disappointed. It may or may not be true, but without any new evidence nothing will happen, especially since the bastard is inside anyway.'

It was more or less what I had expected him to say.

'That's why I'm thinking of reviving the story with a feature in *The Post*,' I said. 'I can mention the rumours and maybe it will generate a fresh wave of interest.'

'That's a crazy idea. It'll just piss a lot of people off, including Callum and his son.'

'So what? If he did kill Tony then he shouldn't be allowed to get away with it.'

'It's a big fucking if, Beth. And even if it could be proved nothing much will come of it. The guy's already doing life.'

He was telling me something I didn't want to hear so I changed the subject and told him about Frankie Bishop calling the house.

'How can you be sure it was him?' he said.

'Oh, come on, Ethan. Who else would it have been?'

'Okay. I'll grant you that. It sounds like something he'd do.'

'You make it seem as though it's not a big deal.'

'In all honesty I can't imagine he'd be stupid enough to take it any further. Danny Shapiro wouldn't let him. It'd be more trouble for them than it's worth.'

'I hope you're right,' I said. 'But if I hear from him again I'm going to make an official complaint.'

'I'm sure you won't have to,' he said. 'And anyway I told you I'll ensure that he's made aware that we're across it.'

I thanked him again before hanging up, but for some reason I wasn't convinced he was going to do anything about Frankie Bishop.

I was still fifteen minutes away from Tamara's home in Vauxhall and I used the time to phone *The Post*'s newsroom and tell them that it was Megan's ex-boyfriend who was being questioned about her murder.

They said they would update the online pages straight away, and this cheered me up because it meant we were still ahead of the competition on the story.

24

Beth Chambers

The rain had stopped by the time I got to Tamara's house in Vauxhall. But there was no break in the clouds which hung dark and heavy above the city.

It was an unassuming terraced property with an ivy-covered façade and a tiny front garden facing the park.

I got the cabbie to wait until I knew if it had been a wasted journey. If Tamara refused to talk to me then I was planning to go straight home. But if I could get her to do a short interview it would be yet another mini exclusive for *The Post*.

It took her a long time to respond to the bell and I thought she might not be home. When she finally did answer the door I was ready with a big, bright smile.

'Hi there,' I said. 'You must be Miss Roth.'

She smiled back. 'That's right. How can I help you?'

She was casually dressed in a white cotton blouse and short grey skirt, and she held a mug of something in one hand.

'My name's Bethany Chambers,' I said. 'I'm a journalist with

The Post and I wondered if I could have a quick word about Danny Shapiro.'

Her eyes narrowed and she instinctively took a step back.

'Forget it,' she said bluntly and started to close the door.

'Look, please don't be alarmed,' I said quickly. 'I'm actually trying to help Danny, and I'm sure he'll be keen for me to talk to you, if not now then later.'

She hesitated and the door stopped moving.

'What do you mean by that?' she said.

'As you know, Danny has told the police that he was with you on Friday night when his ex-wife was murdered,' I said. 'But they don't believe him.' The lie that came next I'd made up in the cab. 'Then this afternoon they gave an off-the-record briefing to several newspapers during which they said they believed his alibi to be false.'

'But it isn't false. He's told them the truth. He was here with me.'

'And as far as we're concerned that's what the public needs to know,' I said. 'It's the only way to stop all the wild speculation on the internet and social media. Even though the police haven't arrested Danny most people are assuming he did it.'

I could see from her face that she was wrestling with indecision.

'We think it's only fair that the truth is put out there,' I said. 'All you have to do is tell me in your own words where Danny was on Friday evening and we can then make it clear in tomorrow's paper that he's an innocent man. I'm sure that's what you both want.'

She let go of the door and pushed her fringe away from her eyes.

'I'm really not sure,' she said. 'I'd have to ask Danny.'

Not a good idea, I thought.

'Why don't you let me in and we can talk it through first,' I said. 'And then if you still have reservations I'll go and leave you in peace.'

I knew that if I could just get inside I'd be halfway home. But as I watched her mull it over I realised it could go either way.

'I suppose that's fair enough,' she said after a few long seconds. 'Come in.'

I indicated to the taxi driver that he could go and stepped into the house. It was cosy, but dated, and there was a strong smell of cigarettes.

I followed her along the hall to the kitchen and she waved me into a chair while she remained standing. I sat down without bothering to take off my coat.

'Do you have any identification?' she asked.

I showed her my press pass and also gave her one of my cards.

'Weren't you on the news today?' she said. 'I'm sure I saw you on the television.'

I nodded. 'I went to Megan's house, and I was also at the police station when they let Danny go.'

'I don't know why they don't believe us,' she said. 'Why would I lie for him if there was a possibility he'd committed a murder?'

'Well, as I understand it the police are sceptical because you dated Danny's father, Callum.'

She bit down on her bottom lip as she thought about it and I took the opportunity to study her. She was in her forties and quite pretty, with healthy-looking skin and huge, dark eyes. She was slim, but endowed in all the right places, her breasts full and weighty. It struck me that she had a lot to offer the men who paid to bed her.

'Me and Callum were an item a long time ago,' she said. 'After he went to prison Danny stayed in touch with me. There's nothing wrong with that.'

'So are you and Danny a couple?'

She shook her head. 'Not in that sense. We meet up from time to time.'

'Is he one of your clients?'

'No. He's a friend. A close one.'

'So he doesn't pay you to be with him.'

She eyed me suspiciously, then reached for a mobile phone that was lying on the worktop.

'I'm not comfortable with this conversation,' she said. 'I don't think I should say any more until I speak to Danny.'

'I'm sure he wouldn't mind, Miss Roth. You're only telling me what you've already told the police.'

'I know, but I still think Danny should be made aware that you're here. It'll just take a second.'

She tapped at her phone and turned away from me as she put it to her ear.

I puffed out my cheeks because I just knew that once she spoke to Shapiro I'd be out the door. Still, I hadn't done too badly. Tamara had already given me enough for a couple of good quotes to freshen up the story.

I looked around me. The room was large and bright, with beige walls and grey appliances, including a tall old-fashioned fridge-freezer. On one wall there was a clock shaped like a frying pan and on the other hung a calendar with a picture of a castle above the monthly planner. I noticed that a lot of the boxes for November had been written in with a black marker pen.

'He's not picking up,' Tamara said, turning back to me. 'So I think perhaps you should go.'

I remained sitting and said, 'Did Danny tell you not to talk to the press, Miss Roth?'

'No, but I don't think he would like the idea.'

'Why not? You're only confirming what he said to the police. All I want to do is make people aware that he was here with you at the time of the killing.'

'I've already told you that,' she said. 'He was here from early Friday evening until late on Saturday morning. And that was when he found out what had happened.'

'So what would you like to say to those people who claim you're lying?'

She looked shocked, but before she could produce a furious retort her phone rang. She grabbed it from the worktop and this time she stepped into the hallway as she started talking to whoever was on the other end.

For no particular reason my eyes drifted to the wall calendar. Idle curiosity prompted me to lean forward and look at the notes she'd made in the monthly planner.

About half the boxes contained men's names and appointment times. Some had phone numbers and London addresses.

At first I didn't see what was staring me right in the face. In fact it was several seconds before I realised that on the day of Megan's murder, 17 November, Tamara had penned in an appointment for someone named Peter Kline.

There was an address in Maida Vale and beneath it were scrawled the words: *New client.*

But what really caused my heart to speed up was the appointment time. It was nine o'clock in the evening.

The same time that Tamara was supposed to have been here at home with Danny Shapiro.

*   *   *

177

I reacted swiftly to what I'd seen by whipping my phone out of my bag and taking a picture of the calendar. I was returning it to the bag just as Tamara stepped back into the kitchen.

She looked furious, and her features were set hard.

'Danny wants to talk to you,' she snapped, thrusting her phone towards me.

I stood up, held out my hand, felt a hot flush spread over my body.

'Afterwards I want you to go,' she added.

I took the phone, which was warm and moist, and spoke into it. 'Bethany Chambers here.'

There was a short delay before he responded, and when he did his voice was full of bitterness and scorn.

'Listen to me, you fucking parasite. I'm sick of you turning up everywhere and stirring things. There's only so much of it I'll take. Do you understand?'

An uneasy knot formed in my stomach, and my first instinct was to switch the phone off. But a primal rage seized control of me and I said, 'No, I don't understand, Mr Shapiro. I'm a reporter and I'm just doing my job. If you've got nothing to hide then what are you so worried about?'

'Leave it out, Chambers. You're trying to use Megan's murder to find out what you can about me and my businesses. That's out of order and you know it.'

'You're part of the story whether you like it or not, Mr Shapiro. So is Miss Roth.'

'You have no right to harass her, Chambers. And what goes on between me and her is none of your fucking business.'

'If it's relevant to the story then it *is* my business.'

He gave a laugh, harsh and abrasive. 'Frankie told me you were a gobby cow and he was spot on. But let me give you a word of warning, Chambers. The slap he gave you is nothing compared with what will happen if you carry on pissing me off.'

I felt my temper spark at the same time as a voice in my head started screaming for me to see sense and stop antagonising him. But I'd never been able to keep a lid on my emotions, especially when challenged by bullies and hypocrites.

So I blew into the phone, loud enough for him to hear. 'I'm used to idle threats from self-important wankers, Mr Shapiro. If I were to let them get to me I wouldn't be able to do my job.'

'You won't be able to do your job anyway if something bad happens to you.'

'You really are a chip off the old block, aren't you?' I said with all the contempt I could muster. 'I'm willing to bet that your psycho father said much the same thing to my stepdad before he had him shot dead.'

'What are you on about?'

I felt my insides contract as the voice in my head became more strident, urging me to shut up.

'Don't pretend you don't know about Tony Hunter,' I said. 'He was my stepdad and I loved him. But I just found out that your old man had him murdered. And believe me I'm going to go all out to make sure people know about it.'

I was on a reckless roll now and about to accuse him of killing his ex-wife. But suddenly Tamara snatched the phone from my hand and started screaming at me.

'Get out of my house, you mad bitch. How dare you say that about Callum?'

'Because it's the truth,' I yelled back. 'And since you used to shag the murdering old bastard you probably knew all about it.'

She lunged forward and grabbed my arm. 'Go. Now. Before I call the police and have you arrested.'

She started pushing me towards the hallway and I could see the tears gathering in her eyes.

'You won't call the police, Miss Roth,' I said. 'The last thing you want is for me to tell them that you're lying about the alibi.'

She lost it then just as I was approaching the front door. She gave me a hard slap to the back of the head and it almost made me lose my balance. As I spun round to face her she hit out again, but this time her open hand struck my shoulder.

'I won't have you accusing me of being a liar,' she screamed at me. 'Who the fucking hell do you think you are?'

I raised my arms in a defensive gesture, expecting her to take another swipe. But she stood in front of me, her lips pulled back in an angry snarl, sparks igniting in her eyes.

My breathing wheezed in my chest and a fiery rage balled in my stomach. I braced myself for another slap, ready to retaliate this time. Instead, her eyes swept over my face, full of contempt, and she raised her arm to point a finger at me.

'You deserved that, you bitch. And if I ever see you again you'll get more of the same.'

She reached for the handle and threw the door open. 'Now go crawl under your rock. And stop winding people up just so that you can sell a few more newspapers.'

Every nerve in my body was vibrating, and an intense heat radiated from my brow. A part of me wanted to stand firm and have it out with her, tell her that I knew she was covering for a man who had murdered his ex-wife. Yet I realised there was nothing to be gained by refusing to go. With emotions running this high there was a risk that one or both of us would push things too far.

She moved aside and gave me a look that could have melted ice. A red mist clouded my vision suddenly so I fought back the urge to lash out and stepped through the door.

As she slammed it shut behind me I walked away from the house as fast as I could, my head down, my heart slamming inside my chest.

I wanted to cry – but not until I was far enough away so that Tamara Roth wouldn't see me.

I got as far as the end of the street before I started shedding tears of anger and frustration. Meanwhile I carried on walking so that I could put as much distance as possible between myself and Shapiro's prostitute friend.

I could hear the blood hissing in my ears, and my legs felt like they had lead weights attached to them.

I couldn't believe I had been physically attacked twice in as many days. It had to be a record. The back of my head still hurt and my body felt like it was on fire.

Even so I was glad that I hadn't hit her back. It might have made me feel better, but it would have been grossly unprofessional. As it was I knew I had to accept some responsibility for what had happened. The situation had got out of hand because I had refused to let Danny Shapiro intimidate me. But then I had every right to tell him what I thought of him, and what I thought of his father.

I stopped walking and took a tissue from my pocket to wipe my eyes. An elderly man passing with his dog stopped to ask me if I was all right. I told him I was and then moved off again so that he couldn't ask me any more questions.

My mind was reeling under a jumble of thoughts and questions. Had I gone too far with Shapiro? Should I be worried about how he might respond? What was I going to do with the information I had come by?

I spotted a pub up ahead and realised I could do with a drink to help me calm down. It was almost empty inside so I was served straight away. A large G and T went down a treat. I sat in a booth with a second glass and drank it slowly as the rush of adrenalin started to wane.

I took out my mobile, opened up the photo I'd taken of the calendar on the kitchen wall.

17 November. Peter Kline. An address in Maida Vale. A nine o'clock appointment.

This was what had prompted me to tell Tamara Roth that she and Shapiro were lying about Friday night. Of course, I couldn't be sure that they were. Maybe she hadn't kept the appointment. Maybe she had cancelled it so that she could spend the evening with Shapiro.

I had to find out before I got too excited. And the only way to do that was to pay Mr Peter Kline a visit.

25

Beth Chambers

Maida Vale is a part of west London famous for its tree-lined streets and pretty canals.

My Uber taxi driver entered the address I'd taken from the calendar into his sat nav and it took us twenty minutes to get there from Vauxhall.

Peter Kline lived in an affluent area known as Little Venice, a beauty spot with boutique shops, trendy restaurants, and colourful houseboats. His whitewashed semi overlooked the Regent's Canal and that told me he must be minted. There was an integral garage with a silver-grey Lexus parked on the short driveway. It was a highly desirable location and a huge step up from our road in Peckham.

I got the driver to drop me fifty yards beyond the house because I needed more time to decide how to approach Mr Kline. I knew nothing about the man except that he was into prostitutes. But that didn't mean he lived alone. He could well be married with a wife and kids and the whole family might now be at home having dinner or watching television.

So I had to know what I'd say if a woman or child answered the door. And if Kline himself answered it how was I going to get him to tell me if he had or hadn't spent Friday evening in the company of Tamara Roth?

If I introduced myself as a reporter from *The Post* I fully expected him to tell me to bugger off rather than disclose his dirty little secret. It was a scenario I'd encountered many times during my journalistic career. I'd usually managed to rise to the challenge by resorting to devious and totally unethical practices.

It didn't take me long to decide that if ever there was a time when the end justified the means then this was it. After all, it was more than just a news story to me now – I was playing detective and there was a strong possibility that I was about to unearth evidence to prove that the well-known London gangster Danny Shapiro had given police a false alibi. It would almost certainly lead to his arrest for his ex-wife's murder. It would also provide my paper with a major exclusive.

But that was jumping the gun. First I had to overcome a very significant obstacle by getting Peter Kline to open up to me.

After pacing up and down the street for ten minutes I came to the conclusion that I would have to pretend I was someone I wasn't. If I then discovered that Tamara had been here on Friday I'd call Ethan to tip him off and wait for events to unfold.

There was a serious downside to this approach, however; I wouldn't be able to take credit for uncovering the lie.

That was because I was going to break the law in a bid to get Peter Kline to talk to me.

I'd impersonated a police officer several times in the past and had got away with it. In the ruthless world of tabloid journalism it's not an uncommon practice, especially among investigative reporters who resort to it when they can't extract information through legitimate means.

It's a risky business, though, and not for the faint-hearted. The courts can impose a heavy fine or even a prison sentence. But I had never let that stop me. In fact I carry a fake Metropolitan Police warrant card in a concealed sleeve in my purse. It identifies me as DC Karen Smith. I bought it on the internet, and it's an obvious forgery to anyone who's familiar with the real McCoy. Luckily most people aren't, so when I hold it up they rarely ask to have a close look.

Still, I wasn't going to take any chances with Peter Kline, just in case he was a copper himself, so before calling at the house I used my phone to see if I could find him online. And I was in luck.

A Peter J. Kline who resided in Little Venice came up through Google and on LinkedIn. Turned out he was an investment analyst for a private equity firm in the City. According to his online profile he was aged 37 and single. His photograph showed a bespectacled man with a narrow face and a neat goatee.

Buoyed by this information, I went to his house. I rang the bell and waited. If someone other than Kline answered I was going to say that I was calling at all the homes in the street to advise them to be extra vigilant following a spate of burglaries in the area.

I didn't have to worry because when the door opened it was Kline who was standing there. He looked exactly like he did in his profile picture. Thin face. Glasses. Trim goatee.

He was wearing an open-necked shirt and neatly pressed trousers and was a good six feet tall.

'Mr Kline?' I said.

A polite smile. 'Yes, that's me.'

I flashed the phoney warrant card, holding it up for just a second.

'I'm Detective Constable Karen Smith. Met police. I wonder if I could have a word.'

He frowned. 'What about?'

'It might be advisable to talk inside, sir. Are you alone?'

'Yes, but this sounds serious.'

'I can assure you that you're not in any trouble, Mr Kline. I'm just hoping that you can help us with our inquiries in respect of another individual.'

His face creased with genuine bewilderment. 'You had better come in then.'

I felt a rush of nerves as I entered the house because now I was committed, and if I slipped up things could go horribly wrong.

Kline steered me into a living room which had pale walls and modern leather furniture. I could tell a lot of money had been spent on it.

He stood with his back to a large fireplace. 'So how can I help you?'

'We're gathering information on a woman I believe you're acquainted with, Mr Kline. Her name is Tamara Roth.'

His eyes grew large, like those of a startled animal.

'What makes you think I know her?' he said.

'Well, we understand you engaged her services as an escort and she paid you a home visit.'

I took out my phone. It was already cued up on the online photo of Tamara from her website.

'Take a look at her picture. It'll help jog your memory.'

He glanced at it briefly and I saw a flash of recognition in his eyes.

'We need to know if that woman spent Friday evening here with you, Mr Kline,' I said.

He wet his upper lip with his tongue and swallowed. 'Why do you want to know? Has she done something wrong?'

'I can't discuss that with you right now, I'm afraid. But it's very important that you confirm whether or not she was here with you.'

'Has she told you that she was?'

'Indeed she has. But we want to know if she's telling the truth.'

His face was full of anxiety and he suddenly didn't seem to know what to do with his hands.

'There's no need to be embarrassed, sir,' I said. 'Please just answer the question. Tamara was either here on Friday or she wasn't. That's all I'm asking, and I promise there will be no comeback on you.'

He pushed out a sigh and seemed to visibly relax. 'Yes, she was here. It was the first time. A friend recommended her.'

Bingo!

I let out a trembling breath and felt every muscle in my body go stiff.

'Look, I don't normally entertain those women—'

'That doesn't matter, Mr Kline,' I interrupted him. 'What you do with your time is your business. Please tell me what time she arrived here and when she left. Be as accurate as possible.'

He didn't have to think about it.

'She turned up just after nine and then left shortly after midnight,' he said.

'Are you sure?'

'Of course I am.'

I could barely contain my excitement. Posing as a detective had paid off, and I now had proof that Shapiro had lied when he said he was with Tamara when Megan Fuller was murdered.

Jesus.

'That's all I need to know, Mr Kline,' I said. 'You've been most helpful. I'll ask you not to contact Miss Roth about this and another officer will be in touch again to get a formal statement. But that's just a formality.'

He was clearly relieved, as well as curious, as he walked me to the door.

As I was stepping outside, he said, 'Can you leave me one of your cards Constable? Just in case I have to contact you again.'

Instinctively I reached into my bag for my business cards, the ones emblazoned with *The Post*'s logo and the words: Bethany Chambers – Crime Reporter.

But I realised my mistake in the nick of time.

'I've just remembered I've run out,' I said. 'But I shouldn't worry, Mr Kline. I very much doubt you'll find it necessary to speak to me again.'

26

Ethan Cain

Cain arrived at the house in Bermondsey just before 8 p.m. It was a run-down mid-terrace property in a grim street close to Southwark Park. Whenever Danny Shapiro wanted to talk to him face to face this was where the meeting took place.

Other coppers on the firm's payroll also came here, and the house – one of many Danny owned in the city – was kept empty for that very purpose.

Cain hated being summoned like he was just another of Danny's minions. And what really grated was that the calls always came from that prick Frankie Bishop.

'Danny needs to see you,' he'd said without preamble. 'So drop whatever you're doing and get your arse over to the usual place.'

Cain hadn't bothered to ask what it was about. That was bloody obvious. Danny would want to be briefed on how the investigation was coming along, and Cain knew he would have to tell him because he had no choice. The firm had him by the bollocks. Since the moment he took that first backhander four years ago he'd been forced to do their bidding.

189

He had no one to blame but himself. It was what he'd signed up for. Every young whore he'd fucked and every line of coke he'd snorted had got him deeper into their debt.

It was Frankie Bishop who answered the door. Just the sight of him made Cain's flesh crawl. The man was built like a brick shithouse, with a face that was ravaged by scars and an ugly, shapeless nose.

He treated Cain to his trademark shark's smile. 'Hello, Detective. How's it hanging, my old mate?'

'Same as ever,' Cain responded as he stepped inside.

'That's great. Little Ania told me you gave her a good seeing-to the other night. Just let me know when you want her over again and I'll arrange it.'

'Thanks, Frankie. I'll do that.'

'And if you're interested we've got a new bird on the books. Name's Chloe. She's seventeen with huge tits and a mouth that was made for sucking.'

'I'm always interested in someone new, Frankie,' Cain said. 'But I'm not sure that now is the right time to talk about it.'

'Yeah, you're right,' Bishop said. 'Best to get the serious stuff out of the way first.'

Cain felt a ripple of unease as he walked along the hall and into the living room. The house was filled with cheap furniture and a stale, unlived-in smell permeated the air.

Danny was sitting in one of the armchairs. He was wearing a leather jacket, jeans, and a baseball cap that sat high up on his head.

'Good to see you, Ethan,' he said. 'Thanks for coming at short notice. I know you're a busy man.'

'It was no problem.'

Danny cracked out a thin smile, revealing a set of unnaturally white teeth.

'Take a seat, mate,' he said. 'Relax.'

Cain sat down on the other armchair and tried to act like he wasn't uncomfortable.

'I was going to give you a ring later,' he said. 'Bring you up to date with the investigation.'

'This will save you the price of a phone call then,' Danny said. 'And anyway you know I don't like to conduct any business over the blower unless I really have to.'

Bishop moved across the room and stood behind Danny with his back against the wall. An image of the bastard smacking Beth flashed unbidden into his mind and sent a chill through his body. No way was he going to raise it as an issue now. He'd just tell Beth that he had.

'It's not just the investigation I want to talk to you about, Ethan,' Danny said. 'It's that fucking ex-missus of yours. She needs to be reined in. And I want you to sort it. I know you're still in touch with her because of the kid.'

Cain forced a grin. 'But we hardly ever talk, and besides there's not much I can do about her. She's been giving us some grief too. But as a reporter it's her job to make a nuisance of herself.'

'This time it's different. She's making me nervous.'

'Well, you needn't be. As far as I know she doesn't have anything on you or the firm.'

'Yeah, well that doesn't mean she won't turn something up if she keeps on digging. And that's what she appears to be doing. She's like a dog with a bone. Are you aware that the bitch has been to see Tamara Roth this evening to ask her about my alibi? How the fuck did she even know about her?'

'I didn't tell her if that's what you think.'

'I'm not saying you did, mate. I don't think you're that fucking stupid. But someone on your team must have.'

'I can't imagine who.'

'I spoke to her on the phone while she was there,' Danny said. 'She got lippy with me, for fuck's sake. And get this. She's threatening to stir up shit on my dad.'

Cain felt his stomach twist and drop. He didn't dare let on that he already knew about that.

'She reckons that Callum had her stepfather shot,' Danny said. 'Christ only knows who's told her that, but I know for a fact that it's not true. Tony Hunter was a thorn in my old man's side for a while back then but the guy was taken out by the Russians.'

'I wouldn't know about that, Danny. But I don't see how it will give you a problem.'

'Well, I don't want the bitch sniffing around and drawing attention to me and the firm.'

'And you expect me to put the frighteners on her? Is that it?'

Danny nodded. 'Exactly. Do it in an official capacity if you think that's the best way. Warn her she'll be done for harassment or something. Just get her off my back.'

'I'm not sure I can . . .'

Danny's expression darkened, and his voice suddenly became harsh and unpleasant.

'You'll do as you're fucking told, Ethan. It's time you earned your keep. For too long you've been getting more out of this arrangement than you've been putting in. You've fucked your way through most of our girls and given us shit-all in return. So now I expect you to sort Chambers out because if you don't then we will.'

'Come off it, Danny. There's no need for that.'

Danny shook his head and his voice rose to an acute pitch.

'You don't seem to get it, mate. The bitch is out to cause trouble and from what I'm led to believe she's bloody good at it. Ain't that why they call her The Ferret? Because she doesn't stop digging until she finds what's she's looking for. And it's not as if she works in isolation. She has a frigging media conglomerate backing her up.'

Cain felt his throat catch and a wave of impotent rage swept through him. Danny had never spoken to him like this before and he was shocked. He was also terrified at the prospect of trying to persuade Beth to back away from the story. She wasn't stupid. She'd know or suspect that someone was pulling his strings.

'Just do it, Ethan,' Danny said. 'If she tells you to fuck off then so be it. But at least you will have proved to me that you're still on board with the firm.'

Bishop spoke up for the first time, his tone mocking. 'We'll make a point of showing our gratitude, old mate. I'll set up a threesome with Ania and Chloe and throw in a bucketful of coke.'

Cain felt totally humiliated, and wondered how the hell it had come to this. He was a detective inspector in the Met, for pity's sake, and yet he was letting some deranged thug treat him like a mug.

'I'll see what I can do,' he said. 'But I can't promise she'll even listen to anything I have to say.'

'Just try,' Danny said. 'Make it clear to her that she's playing a dangerous game. And you can also tell her that I don't like being threatened.'

Cain twisted his lower jaw and gave a slow nod.

'So that's settled then,' Danny said. 'Now tell me about the investigation.'

Cain wiped his mouth with the back of his hand and felt a weary resignation. As he spoke he tried not to think about

Redwood and the rest of the team and how he was being disloyal to them.

'There's not much to tell,' he said. 'There's no useful forensic evidence from Megan's house and we haven't been able to identify anyone from the CCTV footage because it was dark and raining. The only possible suspect was wearing a hoody. We're still talking to Megan's friends and contacts and we're hoping to persuade her father to front a press conference and make an appeal.'

'What about that prick of a boyfriend? Didn't you pull him in today?'

'We did, but his alibi checks out. He was in a pub with friends when Megan was murdered. The landlord confirmed it for us this afternoon.'

'You're sure it's genuine?'

'Seems to be. We're going to trawl through the pub's CCTV footage just to be sure.'

'And that's all you've got?'

'Well, the only other thing is something the boyfriend told us. He said that Megan was trying to blackmail at least one other person as well as you.'

'Did he say who it was?'

'She didn't tell him. That's the problem. Have you got any ideas?'

Danny shook his head. 'I haven't a clue. Could be anyone.'

Cain's phone rang then, making him jump. He was going to leave it, but Danny said, 'You should take it. I assume you're still on duty.'

Cain took it from his inside pocket, saw Beth's name on the screen.

'It's Bethany,' he said, and felt a sudden rush of heat to his head.

Danny leaned forward. 'Then see what the fuck she's got to say.'

Cain pressed the accept call icon. 'Hi, Beth. What's up?'

As he listened to what she had to say he could feel his own body temperature rocketing.

'Text me the name and address,' he said. 'We'll check it out.'

And then: 'That was a stupid thing to do, Beth. What the hell were you thinking?'

He told her to leave it with him and to go home.

'Don't speak to anyone about this,' he said. 'And that includes the paper. Right? Good. I'll call you tomorrow.'

Cain severed the connection and looked at Danny. 'You've got a problem. And it's a big one.'

A deep furrow entrenched itself in Danny's brow. 'What kind of problem?'

Cain took a breath before responding.

'Bethany Chambers has just found out that you've been lying, Danny. You weren't with Tamara Roth when Megan was killed, and Beth says she can prove it.'

27

Danny Shapiro

An expression of alarm passed over Danny's face. He took a shivering breath and exhaled before responding to what Cain had told him.

'Don't keep me in frigging suspense. What did she say?'

Cain's face was grave and Danny felt a sick feeling wash through him.

'She reckons Tamara was with a client all Friday evening and not with you,' Cain said. 'The client's name is Peter Kline. He's single and lives alone in Maida Vale. Beth's just been to see him and he told her that Tamara was at his house from nine until after midnight.'

'I don't get it,' Danny said. 'Why would he confide in a reporter?'

'Beth didn't tell him she was a reporter. She posed as a police officer, a detective. So he opened up to her.'

'And she went to this bloke's house after leaving Tamara's? Is that what she said?'

Cain nodded. 'But Tamara didn't tell her about him. Beth spotted a calendar on the kitchen wall while she was there. Last

Friday had an appointment against it – Peter Kline, with his address and phone number. Beth took a picture of it while Tamara was on the phone to you. She then checked it out.'

Danny felt something cold move over his skin. He remembered what Tamara had said about seeing a new client in Maida Vale. He even recalled how she had gestured towards the calendar when she'd said it.

Shit.

'But how she found out isn't the point, Danny,' Cain said. 'The point is you lied about it.'

Bishop stepped forward and lowered himself into the second armchair.

'Does this mean you did kill Megan, boss?' he said.

Danny shot him a sharp look. 'I told you I didn't kill her and I meant it. So get that into your thick fucking skull.'

'Then you need to explain yourself, Danny,' Cain said. 'If you really didn't do it then why fabricate an alibi?'

Danny got up and started pacing the floor, his mind in over-drive. The air was suddenly heavy around him. Claustrophobic. He could feel the weight of it, warm against his face.

The other two stayed silent, waiting for him to speak. Waiting for him to explain himself.

What a right bloody mess!

His mind suddenly conjured up an image of Bethany Chambers. Then saliva pooled in his mouth as he thought about what he would like to do to the interfering bitch.

'You need to be honest with us, boss,' Bishop said. 'Otherwise we can't help.'

Danny stopped pacing and looked from Bishop to Cain. He nodded. Mustered a weak smile. Then he flopped back down in the armchair and said, 'I went to the house on Friday night just before ten to see Megan. We argued over what she was threatening to do to me. But I didn't touch her. When I left there she was alive. That's the God's honest truth.'

Danny paused, cast his eyes towards the ceiling. His breath hissed fast and shallow through his nostrils.

'I heard what had happened to Megan when I woke up yesterday morning,' he said. 'I knew that I'd be in the frame and that if I didn't have a plausible alibi I'd be collared for it. So I went to Tamara and got her to say that I was at her place.'

He lowered his eyes, stared at Cain, who was watching him open-mouthed.

'I had to do it, Ethan. I couldn't bank on your lot finding the real killer. And it would have been fine if not for Chambers.'

Danny blew out a lungful of air. Having come clean he now had to turn his thoughts to what to do next.

Bishop was one step ahead of him.

'We can sort this, boss,' he said. 'We just have to make sure that this bloke Kline doesn't tell anyone else. Without him Chambers doesn't have a story and the filth can't prove you weren't with Tamara.'

'That's how I see it, Frankie,' Danny said. 'We have to take him out. It's the only way to contain this.'

Cain began shaking his head, his face white. 'I can't believe what I'm hearing here. In case you guys haven't noticed there's a detective in the room.'

'That's right,' Danny snapped back. 'A detective who works for me. Which means I'll expect you to help put things right.'

Cain leapt to his feet, his body trembling. 'You can't be serious. It's bad enough that I now know you lied about the alibi. But I am not going to be part of a fucking cover-up that involves killing an innocent man.'

Bishop shot up and grabbed Cain's suit jacket by the lapels, shoving him back into the chair. He leaned over him, spit bubbling at the corners of his mouth.

'You seem to be forgetting that you're a bent copper and we own you,' he shouted. 'When we tell you to jump, you jump. When we tell you to get your hands dirty we don't expect you to suddenly develop a conscience.'

'Frankie's right, Ethan,' Danny said, his voice lower, more controlled. 'You've been on the firm's payroll for four years now. You owe us big time.'

Danny watched as the detective's anxiety flared into blind panic.

'This will be a step too far, Danny,' he said. 'You really can't expect me to go along with it. I'm paid to tip you off, give you the names of informants, smooth things over. Not to help you kill someone.'

'You're paid to follow orders, Ethan. Like all the other coppers we've taken into the fold and looked after.'

Beads of sweat appeared on Cain's forehead. Danny could sense the cogs in his brain turning, desperately trying to find a way out of the situation he'd got himself into.

After some lip-chewing, the detective said, 'Okay, I get it. You want me to turn a blind eye so I will. When I walk out of here I'll pretend that this didn't happen. I'll tell Beth that I've not been able to contact Peter Kline. That he must have gone away somewhere. She'll suspect that something has happened to him but she won't know for sure. And she'll never be able to prove anything.'

'That's good, Ethan,' Danny said. 'You're coming round. But it's not enough.'

'What? Why?'

'Because Frankie here is going to drop in on Mr Kline tonight and I want you to go with him.'

'You're joking.'

'I'm afraid not, mate, for two reasons. The guy is unlikely to open his door after dark to someone who looks like Frankie. But he will open it if you flash your warrant card. You just get Frankie inside and he'll do the rest.'

Cain stared at Danny, mortified.

'The other reason I want you to go along is so that you'll then be in this up to your neck like I am,' Danny said. 'That means I seriously doubt you will ever contemplate succumbing to a guilty conscience.'

Cain wiped the sweat from his brow with the back of his hand. 'And what if I refuse? What happens then?'

Danny always came to these meetings prepared, just in case any of his crooked coppers thought too much was being asked of them. He reached into his inside pocket and brought out a small computer flash drive.

'Here's a little present for you,' he said, tossing it to Cain who just managed to catch it. 'On that thing is enough incriminating evidence to put you away for years. There are several audio tapes of you tipping us off about stuff over the phone. There's video of you counting out money you've just been given, plus footage of you screwing a bird who happens to be under the age of consent. There are also shots of you sniffing coke off a whore's belly while slagging off your superiors.'

Danny paused to let it sink in. This wasn't something he enjoyed doing, although it wasn't the first time he'd had to do it. But then these scumbags sometimes needed to be put in their place and reminded that they couldn't just pick and choose what jobs they did for the firm.

'I've got a few more copies of that,' Danny said. 'And I'm assuming you don't want me to send them to Scotland Yard and the Sunday papers.'

Cain's eyes darted fearfully around the room, as though looking for a way out. When they settled back on Danny his lips parted and three words came tumbling out.

'You fucking cunt.'

Danny responded with a low-voltage smile.

'I've never pretended to be anything else, Ethan. I thought you would have known that by now.'

28

Beth Chambers

I was high on adrenalin as I rode home in a taxi. I was dying to call the paper to tell them what I'd discovered but I'd promised Ethan that I wouldn't.

That was fair enough, I supposed. It was up to him now to visit Peter Kline, or send one of his officers to do so. I was hoping he'd go himself so that when Kline mentioned having already spoken to a female detective alarm bells wouldn't start going off.

I couldn't help feeling pleased with myself. Impersonating a copper had been the right call. No way would Kline have talked to me otherwise about inviting a prostitute into his home. Sure, I'd reinforced my credentials as a totally unethical journalist and risk-taker, but at least I'd got another result. I had succeeded where the real coppers had failed, and it was going to lead to the downfall of that wife-murdering gangster, Danny Shapiro.

I was itching to start writing the story of his arrest, the first of many relating to this horrible business. The formal charge against him would follow, then the crown court trial.

I'd pull together different strands and angles for *The Post*. How

Shapiro's incarceration would impact on his firm's reign of terror across south London. How his father had arranged for Tony Hunter to be shot. The truth behind Megan Fuller's downfall. A profile piece on Shapiro himself, the cold-blooded killer with the playboy lifestyle who married an actress – and then stabbed her to death.

It was a story dripping with blood, pathos, drama. A tale of intrigue, violence, tragedy. The papers would gorge on it, and the TV news channels would produce spin-off documentaries.

For me it would also be a personal success story, a vindication of my dubious methods and a reward for my dogged perseverance.

And something more.

It would be sweet revenge for what Callum Shapiro did to my beloved stepdad.

I got home just before ten. Rosie was in bed, of course, but my mother was still in the living room where she'd fallen asleep in front of the television.

I woke her gently and thought she'd go straight up to her room like she always did. But instead she decided she wanted a mug of hot chocolate.

'I'll make it for you,' I said. 'And I'm sorry that I didn't get back sooner. Was my baby okay?'

'Good as gold, apart from the verbal diarrhoea.'

In the kitchen I put the kettle on while she took her blood pressure tablets and various others.

I was bursting to share my news with her, so when she asked me what I'd been up to I told her everything – except the bit about posing as a police officer. She didn't have to know that I didn't always operate within the law.

'So you've done Ethan Cain's job for him,' she said. 'How did he react?'

'He seemed a little subdued if I'm honest.'

'That's probably because you've shown him up for the useless cretin that he is.'

My mother wasn't one to miss any opportunity to slag off my ex-husband.

'Anyway, he's going to follow it up,' I said. 'So by this time tomorrow Danny Shapiro should be in custody and facing a murder charge.'

A grin tugged at my mother's mouth. 'Not before time. You did well, Beth, and I'm proud of you. I hope it gives you some satisfaction after what I told you today about his father.'

'It does. And more so because of the way he threatened me on the phone. He tried to scare me, Mum.'

'Well, he'll be in no position to carry out any threats against anyone if he's locked up, Beth. He'll have more important things on his plate.'

I spooned Mum's chocolate into the mug and poured hot water on top. I was hoping she might stay downstairs for a while as I was too excited to turn in. But she decided to take the chocolate up to bed because she was tired and cold.

I kissed her goodnight and watched her climb the stairs. I was in no mood for a hot drink so I poured myself a glass of wine from the fridge. Then I sat at the breakfast bar, switched on the telly, and savoured the feeling as the cool, sweet nectar washed its way through my gullet.

My heart was racing in anticipation of what lay ahead. I was still in pole position on the Shapiro story, with the inside track on developments and access to some colourful background material through my mother.

For a crime reporter it didn't get much better. It was the kind of thing that made us tick and fuelled our passion for the job.

I reached for the remote and switched channels on the TV so I could watch the ten o'clock news, see what they were doing with the story.

That was when I got a sudden reality check, a reminder that in the cut-throat world of daily news it was impossible to stay ahead all of the time.

The Beeb was running an exclusive interview with Sam Jones, Megan Fuller's former boyfriend, who had been released from police custody a couple of hours ago after being questioned about her murder. A middle-aged guy, he looked tired and dishevelled.

'The police were wrong to treat me as a suspect,' he said to the reporter. 'As I've explained to them I was with friends in another part of London when it happened.'

He then went on to say that although he and Megan had recently split up, he still loved her and was devastated by her death.

As I watched him speak I felt there was something disingenuous about his manner. It was like he was reading from a pre-prepared script and acting up for the camera.

He described Megan as beautiful, talented and kind-hearted. Then he vehemently denied the rumours that he had been abusive towards her.

'I would never have laid so much as a finger on that woman,' he said.

He was lying about that for sure and I could see it in his eyes. But it was true that he hadn't killed Megan. He couldn't have. For one thing he had what appeared to be a firm alibi.

And for another his name wasn't Danny Shapiro.

29

Ethan Cain

They travelled in Cain's car to Maida Vale. The detective sat behind the wheel, but he struggled to concentrate on his driving. His skin was clammy with dread and panic filled his chest, pressing hard against his lungs.

Frankie Bishop sat next to him, an imposing presence who seemed perfectly calm even though he was on his way to commit a murder.

Murder.

Oh, God.

It felt to Cain like he was in a bad dream, unable to extract himself. Danny Shapiro's words, the overt threats, echoed in his mind, chilling his blood.

This should not be happening, he told himself. How in God's name did I get myself in such a mess?

He felt there was nothing he could do but acquiesce to their demands. Not unless he was prepared to be outed as a corrupt copper and face the awful consequences.

And he wasn't.

He couldn't face the prospect of losing his job and going to prison. The Met would make an example of him and behind bars his life wouldn't be worth living. He had no choice, therefore, but to see this thing through, to allow whatever shreds of dignity and self-respect he had left to slip away with the blood of a stranger who had done nothing wrong. The guilt and shame would come later. Right now it was fear that was thundering through his system making it hard to breathe.

'Don't look so worried,' Bishop said. 'With luck it'll all be over in a little while and you'll be on your way home. Then just push it to the back of your mind. That's what I do.'

'I'm not like you,' Cain said.

'Oh, we're not that different. If we were we wouldn't be together now and on our way to do a job for our paymaster.'

'But I shouldn't be here,' Cain said. 'Danny should be clearing up his own fucking mess.'

'He employs people like us to do it for him.'

'Well, it's not right and it's not fair.'

Bishop laughed, and it made Cain want to take his hands off the wheel and hit him.

'Do you even believe he's telling the truth now when he says he didn't top Megan?' Cain said.

Bishop nodded. 'Sure I do. I didn't think he did it to start with. It's not his way and he rarely loses his temper. If he'd wanted her out of the way he would have got me or someone else to do it for him.'

Cain pressed his lips together, shook his head. He couldn't believe he was having this conversation.

'Megan was a nuisance and she was making mischief,' Bishop said. 'Me and the lads told Danny that he needed to make sure she didn't say anything to jeopardise the firm. But he kept telling us we didn't have to worry because she was only pretending she knew about stuff when she didn't.'

'So what was she like?'

Bishop thought about it before answering.

'She was a decent bird with a nice face and a great body,' he said. 'But she was also demanding, moody and hard to please. A right handful in other words. It always seemed to me that there was a lot she didn't reveal about herself. Like she was hiding a secret she couldn't even share with her husband.'

'I didn't realise you knew her that well,' Cain said. 'I always thought Danny led what amounted to two separate lives. That he went to a lot of trouble not to expose his wife to his work and his business associates.'

'He did, but I met her enough times. I sometimes acted as her minder.'

'How did you get on with her?'

Bishop started to answer the question, but then seemed to change his mind and instead said, 'Look, I don't want to talk about Megan. It's a distraction. Let's be quiet and focus on the job at hand.'

It struck Cain as an odd response. Almost as though the question had touched a nerve.

At any other time it would have aroused his curiosity, but at this moment he had something more pressing on his mind.

There was a faint drizzle in the air when they got to Maida Vale.

'This is good,' Bishop said. 'There'll be fewer people around.'

He told Cain to park up well short of Maida Avenue.

'We'll leave the car here,' he said. 'Don't want to chance it being picked up on CCTV.'

208

Cain could feel the dread inching up his spine as they walked side by side towards Peter Kline's canal-side home. His heart pounded in his chest like a trapped animal and his throat was suddenly so dry he couldn't swallow.

'So just remember how this will go down,' Bishop told him. 'We're gonna be faced with one of two scenarios. The first is he's got someone in the house with him. If that's the case then you say we're following up a conversation he had earlier with one of our colleagues. At the same time I'll suss out the situation and decide how best to handle it.

'If, as we expect, he's alone then we don't piss about. I'll do what needs to be done. If he has his own car then I'll make use of that to take his body away. If there's no car then I'll make a call and arrange for one of the lads to come over with a vehicle that can't be traced to us. If all goes to plan then this bloke's disappearance will be a mystery to everyone, including your lot.'

Bishop made it seem so simple, Cain thought. But that was obviously because he had done this sort of thing many times before. He was the firm's most notorious enforcer after all. Frankie 'The Nutter' Bishop – one of the most violent villains in the whole of London.

'This is the house,' Bishop said, and the sight of the whitewashed façade made Cain feel nauseous and dizzy.

There was a fraction of a second when he was tempted to swallow it and take flight. To leg it away from here and go and confess all to his colleagues. But it passed as Bishop nudged him through the open gate.

They both noted the Lexus on the driveway and the fact that there were lights on inside the house.

As Bishop rang the bell Cain looked around. There were no

neighbours in sight and no people walking along the street. But that didn't help settle his nerves. His mind felt as though it was ready to explode.

The door opened on a chain and a man peered out at them.

Cain already had his warrant card out and he held it up. 'Are you Mr Peter Kline?'

The man nodded. 'Is this about Tamara? A police officer was here earlier.'

'We're aware of that, Mr Kline. This is a follow-up. We just have to ask you a couple more questions.'

'But can't it wait? I was just about to go to bed. I've got a busy day at the office tomorrow.'

'It'll take just a few minutes, Mr Kline,' Bishop chipped in. 'And we wouldn't be bothering you at this hour if it wasn't important.'

Kline issued a deep, audible sigh, then removed the chain and pulled open the door.

'Are you by yourself, sir?' Bishop asked him.

'I am as a matter of fact. Come in.'

He gestured for his two visitors to follow him through to the living room. But as soon as they stepped into it, Bishop whipped a length of nylon rope from his pocket and pounced on Kline from behind, pulling the rope tight around the man's throat.

Kline's instinctive reaction was to claw at the rope with both hands. Then panic seized him and he started thrashing his body from side to side with such force that Bishop was shoved against a bookshelf, causing him to relax his grip.

Kline then managed to get his fingers under the rope and at the same time throw his head back into his attacker's face.

The blow struck Bishop on the chin, sending him staggering backwards across the room.

'You fucker,' Bishop roared as he struggled to stay on his feet.

Kline spun round and found himself face to face with Cain, who was blocking the doorway.

'Please let me go,' he yelled, his eyes wild and desperate.

But the detective hesitated for only a split second. Then as Kline rushed towards him he decided he was in too deep now to allow the man to escape.

So he stepped aside, making Kline think he was letting him go. Just as Kline passed through the doorway, he stuck out his right foot and tripped him up, sending him flying across the hallway and into the wall.

That was all Cain had to do because Bishop was on Kline in a millisecond, dropping himself onto the man's back.

'This time you won't wriggle out of it,' Bishop seethed.

Having retrieved the nylon rope, Bishop placed it around his victim's throat again. Then his mouth curled into an ugly snarl as he pulled on it as hard as he could. It took him less than a minute to squeeze the life out of Peter Kline and it was obvious to Cain that the bastard took great pleasure in it.

The detective didn't move, just stared in slack-jawed disbelief. He felt tears push against his eyes and he had to force himself to gulp air into his heaving lungs.

'Go find the car keys,' Bishop said, his voice unaffected by what he had just done.

Cain was frozen to the spot, his head pulsing like an infection.

'For fuck's sake I'll do it myself,' Bishop said as he got up and started searching the house.

The sudden silence roared in Cain's ears, and he realised that what he had just seen and done would change his life forever. The shame barrelled through him and he felt an overwhelming urge to be sick. He probably would have thrown up if Bishop hadn't suddenly reappeared with a set of keys.

'I've found them,' he said. 'I've also found a door into the garage. We'll take the body out that way and put it in the Lexus. There's less chance of being seen.'

Cain managed to hold it together for the next five minutes. That was how long it took them to carry Kline's body through the garage and put it into the boot of the Lexus.

It was a ghastly ordeal and throughout it Cain's mind spun in circles and his heart hammered in his chest.

He stood just inside the front door while Bishop turned off the lights and checked that they wouldn't be leaving behind any evidence of their presence.

'I'll take off in the Lexus,' he said. 'You get your car and go home. Forget this ever happened.'

Like it would be that easy, Cain thought, as he stepped outside into the night and walked away as fast as he could.

The first thing Cain did when he got home was to dash into the toilet and be sick. Some of the vomit missed the pan and sprayed on his shoes and trousers.

After emptying his guts, he stripped down to his underpants. Then he fired down a large brandy and snorted a few lines of coke.

He felt wretched, and the guilt started stalking him like a black shadow. He wanted to roll up and die, but he knew he wasn't going to be that lucky. Instead he would have to live with what he had seen and done tonight.

He poured another brandy, lit a cigarette. He kept hearing Kline's voice in his head as the poor bastard begged them to let him go. And he kept seeing the brutal expression on Bishop's face as he committed cold-blooded murder.

Cain sat on the sofa without moving for a good hour, tormented by his thoughts and the loud beating of his own heart.

Then he remembered the flash drive that Danny had given him. He fired up his laptop and plugged it in.

It was as bad as Danny had warned him it would be. The sound bites from various phone conversations made him flinch. But what really turned his stomach was the video sequence of him shagging a girl whose name he remembered as Nicole. It was about eight months ago at a West End hotel that the firm had paid for. He wondered if the little whore had known that the session was being recorded on a hidden video camera. Was that why she had made a point of telling him several times that she was three months away from her sixteenth birthday?

Oh, Christ!

He'd been fucked over good and proper. Entrapped like the gullible pillock he was.

He switched off the laptop and switched on the CD player, turning up the music to try to drown out his own thoughts.

Another drink. Another cigarette. Another line of coke. His senses becoming more confused and distorted.

He sat down, shoved the heels of his hands into his eyes.

And started to cry for the first time in as long as he could remember.

30

Beth Chambers

Monday morning. I was up at the crack of dawn, having slept for about five hours.

Quick shower. Quick dry. I could feel the restless energy burning through me as I got dressed and went downstairs. Mum was already up and she had a mug of tea waiting for me.

'How did you sleep?' she asked.

'Like a log.'

'I'll put some toast on. Don't want you going to work on an empty stomach.'

She said more or less the same thing every weekday morning. But I didn't mind. It was kind of sweet.

I switched on the TV news. The Shapiro story had been relegated to third place on Sky, pushed down the running order by another mass shooting in the States and the shock resignation of a Labour MP.

When they came to it they had nothing new to report except that Sam Jones, Megan's ex-boyfriend, had been released without charge.

I waited until seven to call Ethan because I felt sure he'd be up by then. But there was no answer.

Damn it.

I was desperate to know if he had acted on the information I'd given him. If so, then why hadn't he called me or sent a text message? And if not, then why was he dragging his heels?

It was a dramatic development after all; a major turning point in the investigation. Surely Peter Kline should have been interviewed by now and Danny Shapiro pulled in for further questioning.

'You need to be patient,' my mother said, after I told her why I was tense and frustrated. 'They're probably waiting until this morning to put the wheels in motion.'

I wasn't convinced so I called the press office at New Scotland Yard, asked them if there had been any developments overnight. They said there hadn't, and I was in no position to contradict them.

I ate the toast as I moved about the house getting myself sorted. My mother was planning to take Rosie to the nursery and then go shopping, so I gave her some cash.

'Anything special you want me to get you?' she asked and I said there wasn't.

We were back into the weekly routine, which worked well for both of us. My mother felt she had a purpose in life and didn't have to spend most of her time alone. And I got to continue doing the job I loved and didn't have to fork out a fortune for childminders.

It wasn't an ideal situation and lacked the one ingredient that would have made my life complete: a man. Still, until I found that elusive Mr Right – or he found me – it would have to suffice.

Rosie called out while I was drinking my second cup of tea. I brought her downstairs and spent ten minutes making a fuss of her.

'Have a great time at the nursery, sweetheart,' I said. 'Mummy's going to miss you very much. But I'll be home before you go to bed.' *Hopefully.*

As I left the house I tried calling Ethan again, but there was still no answer so I left a message.

They were forecasting a dry but cloudy day. Though it was cold outside the air felt soft. I took the train from Peckham to London Bridge and was in the office by 9.15. The morning meeting, chaired by Grant Scott, was due to get under way at half past.

I used the time before then to try to reach Ethan. When he failed to answer his mobile I called the number I'd been given for the incident room in Wandsworth, only to be told that he was out of the office.

At the meeting Grant asked what they could expect from me today on the Megan Fuller murder. I couldn't be totally honest with the team about the story that was about to break because of the method I'd used to uncover it. I didn't want to follow in the footsteps of Arnie Wilson, an investigative reporter sacked by *The Post* two years ago – for posing as a police officer!

So I said that one of my police contacts had told me there was going to be a major development later in the day.

'I've arranged to meet him this morning,' I lied.

'Sounds promising,' Grant said. 'The Met are also planning to hold a press conference at which Megan's father might make an appeal. I'd like you to go along and cover it.'

'Will do, boss,' I said.

After the meeting, I retreated to my desk and tried yet again to contact Ethan. No answer. Now I was beginning to fear that something wasn't right. I could feel it in the pulse of my blood.

Was the bugger purposely avoiding me because he hadn't yet

done anything about the Peter Kline revelation? Or was he part of a team of officers that was in the process of swooping on the homes of Danny Shapiro and Tamara Roth?

Either way I needed to know, if only to stop me worrying that another reporter would be tipped off about it. That had to be a distinct possibility if Ethan had already shared the information with DCI Redwood and the rest of his team.

What a disaster it'd be if someone else was able to claim credit for what was my bloody exclusive!

Given how I had come by the information my options were limited. But I did think of one way to find out if anything was happening and that was to phone Peter Kline himself.

I pulled up the photo I'd taken of Tamara's calendar. What appeared to be Kline's mobile number was written on it along with his name and address.

I called the number but it rang out. I then looked him up again on LinkedIn and made a note of the investment company he worked for in the City. A few seconds later I had the company's phone number. When I got through to the switchboard I asked for Peter Kline and was put through to the office he worked in.

'I understand you're inquiring after Mr Kline,' said the woman who answered. 'If it's to do with anything he's working on then perhaps I can help.'

'It's a personal matter actually,' I said. 'I tried his mobile but he's not answering.'

'Oh, I see. Well, we've also tried to contact him on his phone without success. He's not at home either.'

'So you don't know where he is?'

'I'm afraid we don't, which is very strange because he was due in this morning at seven for an important meeting.'

'Is it unusual for him not to turn up on time?'

'Absolutely. And if he was going to be late we'd expect him to call to let us know.'

'Is it possible he's had an accident?' I asked.

A pause, then: 'Look, can you tell me what your relationship is with Peter, I mean Mr Kline? I think I should know who I'm talking to.'

'I'm just a friend,' I said. 'We live close to each other in Little Venice. I was ringing to invite him to our place for drinks.'

'Well, in that case might I suggest that you call back later? Hopefully we'll know by then what's happened to him.'

'Have you thought about contacting the police?' I said.

'No, not at the moment. We don't want to overreact since there's probably an innocent explanation.'

Innocent explanation! I wasn't so sure. It seemed too much of a coincidence that he should fail to arrive at work the morning after I'd paid him a visit.

A tiny alarm started ringing somewhere deep inside me. I felt I should do something but I wasn't sure what. I didn't really know the man and could never admit to meeting him while posing as a detective.

I told myself to calm down. He'd only been missing for about three hours. Anything could have happened. He might have decided on the spur of the moment to take the day off. He might have overslept. Or maybe he had gone for an early-morning bonk with another prostitute and had lost track of time.

Would Ethan know where he is? I wondered. Was it conceivable the police had taken him into protective custody for his own safety?

I tried reaching Ethan yet again, on his mobile and at the nick. Still no response.

I then called Doug, my other police contact at Wandsworth. I gave him Peter Kline's name, but didn't tell him who he was. He said he had never heard of the man and as far as he knew nobody was being held in protective custody.

'As for DI Cain, I understand he's over in Lewisham, trying to persuade Megan Fuller's father to appear at this afternoon's press conference,' he said.

I thanked him, and as soon as I came off the phone Grant asked me to write a piece for the next edition of the paper, even if there was nothing new.

I cobbled something together using quotes from the press office and filler material from the wires. There was so much more that I wanted to put in but couldn't.

After filing the copy, I phoned Kline's office again and this time a man answered and told me that he still hadn't turned up.

It wasn't meant to have been like this. By now I should have been breaking the story of Shapiro's arrest. Instead I was struggling to suppress a growing panic, and hoping to God that no harm had come to Peter Kline because of what I had done.

31

Ethan Cain

Cain had spent the best part of an hour at Nigel Fuller's house in Lewisham. DCI Redwood had told him to go there to find out more about his daughter Megan.

Cain's brief was also to convince Mr Fuller that it would be a good idea to attend this afternoon's press conference and appeal for help in finding Megan's killer.

To begin with he refused because he was still furious that Danny Shapiro had been released without charge.

'He's the ultimate Teflon man,' he said. 'Nothing ever sticks to him.'

Eventually, though, he'd seen the sense in helping with the investigation and had agreed to attend the press conference. He asked if his fiancée Amy Cassidy could accompany him and Cain had said it wasn't a problem.

To the detective's surprise she revealed that she had never met Megan. It turned out that Mr Fuller and his daughter had had very little contact in recent years.

'She was always too busy to come over,' he said. 'But now I

bitterly regret not making more of an effort myself to stay in touch. Sadly that's how it is with a lot of families.'

Mr Fuller had little to add to what he'd already told the police.

Before leaving the house the couple told Cain that they had pushed back the date of their wedding by six months.

'It's the least we can do,' Mr Fuller said. 'A small gesture of respect for Megan.'

Back in the car Cain fired up a cigarette and sat for a while to get his thoughts together. His head was fogged up and he felt bleary-eyed through lack of sleep.

He was also suffering from the effects of too much brandy and cocaine. Not to mention the weight of guilt that was draped around his shoulders like a heavy chain.

What he had witnessed last night was still chewing at his heart. He saw the whole thing being played out in his mind's eye every time he closed his eyes. For the first time in his life he felt utterly ashamed of himself.

He had never pretended to be a good man. He had lost his moral compass back in the mists of time. Greed, temptation and a warped sense of entitlement had influenced his journey through life and shaped him into the unprincipled person he'd become. A corrupt copper, a cheating husband. And now he was something far worse.

Last night he'd been an accessory in the cold-blooded murder of an innocent man. That made him as guilty and as contemptible as Frankie Bishop.

He dragged heavily on his cigarette and snapped his thoughts back to the present. He knew that he had to somehow pull himself together and climb out of the pit of despair before he lost himself in it completely.

221

He retrieved his phone from his pocket and took it off silent mode. He had a bunch of missed calls, all but one from Beth.

Drew Bellamy, Megan's psychiatrist, had responded to the message he'd left the previous evening. However it was his secretary who answered. She explained that her boss was in the States and was due to fly home tonight.

'He's been attending a conference in Houston,' she said. 'He's catching a plane this evening and should arrive back in the UK tomorrow morning. Can you tell me what it's about?'

'It's concerning one of his patients,' Cain said. 'Megan Fuller.'

'Oh dear, I heard about that. It's so awful. But I'm not sure Mr Bellamy even knows about it yet.'

'Well, I need to talk to him as soon as possible about the treatment Miss Fuller was having since it might have a bearing on the case. Can I reach him on his mobile?'

'Possibly, but I can tell you that he won't provide you with information over the phone. You'd need to speak to him face to face and he'd have to verify your credentials.'

'In that case can you get him to ring me as soon as he's back tomorrow and I'll come to your office?'

'Of course, Inspector.'

Cain put in a call to Redwood to update him. He made sure he sounded upbeat and excited.

'I've managed to talk Megan's father into coming along to the presser, guv,' he said. 'He wasn't keen to start with, but he's now prepared to make an appeal.'

'Well done,' Redwood said. 'Did he tell you anything new about his daughter?'

'Not really. Seems they didn't see much of each other and he feels guilty about that.'

'Okay, Ethan. Where are you now?'

'About to leave Lewisham and head back to the station.'

'Make it snappy then and I'll get the team together for a briefing.'

Cain hung up, relieved that the gaffer hadn't harked back to the awkward conversation they'd had earlier.

Cain wanted to put off ringing Beth, but decided it would be a bad idea. She was obviously working herself into a frenzy because he hadn't already been in touch. He had been putting it off because the thought of lying to her filled him with a billowing sense of dread.

He'd already rehearsed in his head what he was going to say to her, but he just knew it was going to make her angry as well as deeply suspicious.

A vein in his neck started to throb as he speed-dialled her number. She answered after the first ring.

'About bloody time,' she said. 'I've been trying to get you all morning.'

'I've been up to my neck in it. And, believe it or not, Beth Chambers is not my number one priority.'

'Is that right, even though I've managed to solve your case for you?'

'Well, that's the thing, Beth. You haven't. Not yet anyway.'

'Are you telling me that you haven't spoken to Peter Kline or Shapiro?'

'There's no point speaking to Shapiro until we've got a statement from Mr Kline. And we don't have one because I've not been able to contact him.'

'So you don't know where he is?'

'No, I don't. Earlier this morning I went to the address you gave me. He wasn't in, but a neighbour told me he went out in his car late last night and hasn't returned. I also contacted his office and they say he hasn't shown up for work.'

'Then where the hell is he?'

'How should I know? Maybe you said something to scare him off.'

'Don't be ridiculous.'

'Well, it seems odd that he took off shortly after you dropped in on him pretending to be a detective.'

'It doesn't make sense,' she said. 'When he told me about Tamara going to his house he didn't seem overly perturbed about it.'

'Okay, so maybe it's got nothing to do with you. Maybe he'd been planning to drive off somewhere before you even arrived at his house.'

'That wasn't the impression I got.'

Beth fell silent for a couple of seconds, and when she next spoke her voice was more urgent.

'Who did you tell about this after I called you last night, Ethan?'

'Nobody. Why?'

'Are you sure? Only what if Shapiro found out?'

'Now you're the one being ridiculous. I haven't told a soul about it yet. Not even Redwood. I wanted to check it out myself first.'

Lying to Beth had come easily to him during their marriage. But now he was having to force the words out past a knot in his throat. At the same time it felt like his lungs were burning oxygen and his palms were leaking hot sweat.

'So what are you going to do about it?' Beth said.

A fierce anger rose up in him. He wanted to tell her to fuck off. That she was to blame for what had happened. That Peter Kline would still be alive if she hadn't poked her nose where it didn't belong.

224

Instead he held it all in and said, 'Look, I have to be careful how I play this. If I raise the alarm now then Redwood will want to know what Peter Kline has got to do with anything. And I can't tell him without dropping you in it.'

'Surely doing nothing is not an option, Ethan.'

'I realise that. But it's not as if the guy's been kidnapped or anything. He drove off under his own steam and he could turn up at any minute.'

'Yeah, I suppose. It seems odd to me though.'

'You need to relax, Beth. I'll check on him throughout the day. I can't do more than that. There are other things I need to be following up.'

'What about Tamara? Shouldn't you be talking to her again? Ask her about the note on her calendar. Tell her you know she was in Maida Vale on Friday night.'

'All in good time, Beth,' Cain said. 'First we need to hear from Peter Kline. If we question her about the appointment now there's nothing to stop her saying she cancelled it in favour of a date with Shapiro, which may well have been the case.'

'Okay, I see what you mean,' Beth said. 'But promise me you'll keep me in the loop. This is my story, Ethan.'

'Of course I promise. And meanwhile don't you do anything more to wind up Shapiro and his thugs. At least for now.'

'Do they know I told you what Frankie Bishop did to me?'

'They do, but I've not had any feedback so just be careful. These people are dangerous, Beth, and you really don't want them on your case.'

She had more questions for him but he told her he didn't have time to answer them. She was in mid-sentence when he ended the call.

The conversation had drained him mentally. He now felt even

more tired and fractious. He was also struck by the unsettling realisation that Beth wasn't going to respond to any threats or warnings from him or anyone else.

This was going to put her on a collision course with a man who would have no qualms about having her killed.

32

Beth Chambers

Ethan's reaction to Peter Kline's disappearance left me confused. Why was he not more concerned? Why was he not doing more to find out if something had happened to the man?

I could appreciate that my posing as a copper was an issue for him. But surely the problem could easily be overcome. There were any number of ways to skirt around my involvement and the truth about how he'd discovered that Shapiro had lied about his alibi. He could say he'd received an anonymous tip-off, or been given Kline's name by an underworld contact.

So why was he holding back, especially with a press conference looming? The timing couldn't be more perfect. The Met could flag it up by saying there was going to be a major announcement – and then I could break the story a couple of hours before.

The Post *can reveal that events in the Megan Fuller case have taken a surprise turn. Danny Shapiro, her former husband and an alleged gangland figure, has been arrested. A Scotland*

Yard source has told this reporter that new evidence has come to light blah, blah, blah . . .

That was the story I should have been writing. Instead we were going to be carrying a rehash of the facts without telling our readers anything new. It was so bloody frustrating.

I let out a sigh of exasperation. I should have been on a high now but I felt unsettled and deflated.

On impulse, I called Kline's company again and got the same woman I had spoken to earlier. No, she said a little frostily, Peter still hadn't arrived at the office and they hadn't heard from him. And yes, they were becoming increasingly concerned.

I asked her if she could give me the names and contact details of any of Peter's friends or relatives, but she said that was out of the question. She did say, however, that his parents lived in Spain and were retired and he had a sister in Cornwall.

'We've spoken to the parents and the sister,' the woman said. 'And they have no idea why he can't be contacted.'

I then spent half an hour ringing round all the main London hospitals to check if a man named Peter Kline had been admitted. But that drew a blank. There had apparently been no fatal accidents in the capital since yesterday afternoon.

That did it. I decided I couldn't just sit on my arse waiting for something to happen. What if he didn't turn up at all today? Or tomorrow? Or the next day?

A shudder of unease ran through me as I tried to work out what to do. The press conference wasn't due to take place until five o'clock. That gave me ample time to get out there and try to make sense of what was going on. But where to start? That was the question.

There was no point rushing out of the office with no idea where I was going and who I was going to speak to.

Then suddenly the answer came to me. I'd start in the obvious place – Peter Kline's house in Maida Vale. Maybe I'd get lucky and one of his neighbours would be able to offer up a clue to his whereabouts.

I told Grant I was going to meet a contact and that I would call in if I came up with a new line on the story.

That was the good thing about being a specialist reporter. You were left to your own devices most of the time. The newsdesk was happy to let you get on with it so long as you came up with the goods on a regular basis. And I did.

The sky was still a grey blanket over the city and there was a lot of moisture in the air. Despite what the weather forecasters had said I was pretty sure it was going to rain again.

I jumped into a cab outside the building and told the driver to take me to Little Venice. I wasn't wildly optimistic about what I would achieve when I got there. But at least I was being proactive.

My thoughts were all over the place, though, and a cold weight had settled in my chest. I kept seeing Peter Kline's face in my head and going over the conversation we'd had. It had been very short, and he hadn't said anything to suggest that he was going to perform a vanishing act soon after I'd left his house.

That worried me because according to his work colleagues it wasn't something he usually did. It was out of character. He wasn't the type of person to fail to turn up for a business meeting without giving an explanation.

So where had he driven to last night and why had he dropped off the radar this morning? These were questions I was desperate to know the answers to, if only for my own peace of mind.

33

Ethan Cain

Cain was in for a surprise when he got back to the incident room. There had been a development, and as DCI Redwood briefed him he let his breath out in a low whistle.

It was the CCTV footage from the Flying Dutchman pub in Tooting, where Sam Jones had spent Friday evening. The disc had arrived a short time ago and an officer had just finished viewing it.

It confirmed that Megan's ex-boyfriend had been telling the truth about going there for a drink with his mates to celebrate the pub's fiftieth anniversary, and that he left there just after one in the morning.

But it seemed he had neglected to mention that he'd popped out during the evening for about an hour.

Cain went with Redwood to view the footage and there was no mistake. Sam Jones could be seen arriving at the pub at just after seven. He was clearly visible on the camera covering the public bar as he drank and laughed with his friends.

Another camera covering the pub's exterior then picked him

up stepping out of the main door at 10 p.m. He walked out of shot and did not return until 11 p.m. He then stayed knocking back pints until the pub closed after one in the morning.

'I'm having him brought back in,' Redwood said. 'He could have walked from the pub to Ramsden Road in about fifteen minutes. By car it would have taken him just a few minutes.'

'What about CCTV cameras between Balham and Tooting?' Cain said.

'We're checking them now.'

There followed a team briefing at which Redwood told the troops about Jones.

'It doesn't mean he's our killer,' he said. 'But he'd better have a bloody good explanation.'

Cain then announced that Nigel Fuller had agreed to attend this afternoon's press conference. He also told the team that he'd left a message with Megan's psychiatrist, Drew Bellamy, and was contacted by his secretary.

'He's flying back from the States so I won't be meeting him until tomorrow,' he said. 'His secretary says he won't divulge information about his patients over the phone.'

'That's about par for the course with those blokes,' Redwood said. 'Anything else, Ethan?'

Yes, sir. There's actually plenty more to report. I've found out that Danny Shapiro has lied to us. He did not spend Friday evening with his prostitute friend. Oh, and the man who the woman was actually with was murdered last night by Shapiro's mad enforcer Frankie Bishop. And I happened to be there to witness the whole thing . . .

That was what he should have been saying, but instead he swallowed back the bile that was forcing its way into his mouth and said, 'There's nothing else, guv.'

He felt a knot twist in his gut as he walked back to his desk. It was as though the full enormity of what he had done had only just hit him. His body was steaming under his clothes as he sat down, and when he reached for his computer mouse he realised his hand was shaking.

Cain was yanked out of his self-destructive reverie when DC Rachel Fisher dumped a thick wad of documents on his desk.

'I was told to give these to you, guv,' she said. 'They're Megan Fuller's old phone records going back five years. I've gone through them and checked out most of the numbers.'

'Anything interesting?' he asked.

'Not in the recent past. Most of the ingoing and outgoing calls were between her and Sam Jones. Others were to and from Danny Shapiro, her agent and her stepfather. But going back further I did come across a bunch of calls and text messages which reveal that Megan had an affair while married to Shapiro.'

'Really?'

'Yep. And it seems to have carried on for a while after she and Shapiro separated three years ago. I've listed all the calls and text messages on a separate sheet, along with the name of her lover.'

'Is the guy known to us?'

She grinned. 'He is, guv. And you're in for a surprise when you see who it is.'

With that she turned around and walked away. Cain frowned as he reached for the documents, but before he could read any of them Redwood came up to his desk to tell him that officers were bringing Sam Jones back to the station.

'He'll be here in fifteen minutes,' Redwood said. 'I want you with me in the interview room.'

'No problem. I'll be there.'

Cain decided to grab a coffee first. He left Megan's phone records unread on his desk and walked over to the vending machine.

He wasn't sure what to make of the Sam Jones development. Did he lie during the first interview or did he genuinely forget that he left the pub for an hour – giving him plenty of time to go to Megan's house and kill her?

If that was what happened then it meant that Danny was telling the truth. It also meant that he wouldn't have needed to concoct an alibi, and that Peter Kline would not have had to die.

Cain shook his head and gulped down some more coffee as he returned to his desk.

There was just too much to think about. Too much to process. It felt like his mind was coming apart.

He sat back down at his desk, finished off his coffee and decided to get another one. But first he pulled Megan's phone records towards him and glanced at the note that Rachel had put on the top of the pile.

When he saw the name of the man Megan supposedly had an affair with he felt his heart bang in his throat.

'Fuck me,' he said aloud to himself. 'I don't believe it.'

It was yet another shock to the system. Another thing for him to think about.

Another development that was going to have serious repercussions.

34

Beth Chambers

When I got to Maida Vale the first thing I did was go to Peter Kline's house. There was no car on the driveway, and when I rang the bell there was no answer.

I pushed open the letterbox and shouted through it. Then I tried the side gate. It wasn't locked so I opened it and went through to the back. From the rear patio I could see into the living room and kitchen. They were both empty.

'Excuse me. Are you looking for Peter?'

The voice from behind startled me. I spun round, saw a man peering over the fence from the neighbouring garden. He was in his sixties with a bald head and dark glasses.

I felt a thud of dread in my gut as I walked towards him, but then I relaxed when he smiled at me.

'Yes, I am actually,' I said. 'I'm a friend and I expected him to be in this morning. That's why I took the liberty of coming round the back when he didn't answer the door.'

'Well, I hate to disappoint you, young lady, but he's out.'

'I don't suppose you have any idea where he is?'

'He should be at work, but I gather he didn't show up.'

'How do you know that?'

'There was a man here about half an hour ago.'

'Was he a police officer?'

He furrowed his brow at me. 'Heavens, no. He was one of Peter's work colleagues. I saw him out front when he arrived in his car. I told him I hadn't seen Peter this morning and he gave me his card.'

So Kline's colleagues were getting seriously worried. Why else would they dispatch someone to see if he was still at home? Surely it was only a matter of time now before they raised the alarm and reported him missing.

'Why did you ask if he was a police officer?' the neighbour said. 'Is Peter in some kind of trouble?'

I shook my head. 'Not at all. It's just that he seems to have gone missing.'

His eyebrows shot up. 'My God. That's awful.'

'He's probably perfectly okay,' I said quickly. 'The problem is he's not answering his phone. Apparently one of his neighbours said he went out in his car late last night.'

'Well, it wasn't me. I was in bed before eight. And I haven't seen him since the day before yesterday.'

I took out my notepad and jotted down my mobile number.

'Would you mind giving me a call if he turns up? My name's Bethany. Peter and I have known each other for years.'

I didn't give him my card because I didn't want him to know that I was a reporter. He took the note and promised to call me.

I went back out front and made a beeline for the house on the other side of Kline's. Just as I stepped onto the empty driveway the front door opened and a woman and a small boy emerged.

She didn't notice me walking towards her until she'd closed

the door behind her and taken the boy's hand. I smiled at her and she responded with a hesitant smile of her own. I guessed she was somewhere in her late thirties and the boy was about 6 or 7.

'I'm going to the shops,' she said. 'So if you're a Jehovah's Witness or a sales rep I'm really not interested.'

I stopped just in front of her and shook my head. 'I'm not a cold caller. I'm a friend of your next-door neighbour Peter Kline, and I'm trying to find out where he is.'

Her eyes narrowed slightly. 'Oh, well, I expect he's gone to work.'

'Actually he didn't turn up at the office this morning and nobody can contact him.'

'I think you might find that he spent the night away from home.'

'Why do you say that?'

She shrugged. 'My husband and I heard him drive off last night quite late. And this morning when I looked outside his car wasn't there.'

'What time was that?'

'About half five. We're always up early, you see.'

'Can you remember what time he went out last night?'

'Not exactly. Must have been about eleven. It was shortly after he had visitors.'

My heart fluttered in my chest. 'How do you know he had visitors?'

'Because I was closing the curtains before getting into bed. I looked out of the window to see if it was still raining. That's when I saw two men walking up Peter's driveway.'

'Did you see their faces?'

'No, I didn't. It was too dark.'

'But you're sure they were men?'

'As sure as I can be. But to be honest I didn't pay them much attention.'

'One last question,' I said. 'Have you spoken to any police officers this morning?'

Her eyes narrowed even further. 'Of course not. Look, who exactly are you and what's going on?'

'The truth is I don't know,' I said. 'But I'm determined to find out.'

I came away from Peter Kline's house with the blood thundering in my ears. I knew now that I had been right to be concerned and suspicious. Something bad had happened to him. I was sure of it.

Following my visit last night two men had arrived at his home and soon after his car was driven away. Now he was missing and I couldn't help wondering if it was down to me.

Was it possible that someone had followed me from Tamara Roth's house in Vauxhall to Maida Vale? Or did Kline call Tamara after I'd left to warn her that the police had been round asking questions? If so, then she would have got straight onto Danny Shapiro to tell him that his alibi was about to be blown apart. And Shapiro might have instructed two of his thugs to make sure that Kline told nobody else.

I felt my knees weaken as I hurried along the street with the canal on my right. Tremors ran through me and the pit of my stomach turned icy.

At the end of the avenue I stood on the bridge that crossed the canal and took out my phone. I had to tell Ethan what I'd found out. It was time he took Peter Kline's disappearance more seriously.

As soon as he answered I spluttered out what I wanted to say, tripping over my words. So he got me to repeat myself, and after I'd finished he was silent for so long I thought we'd been disconnected.

'Are you still there, Ethan?'

'Of course.'

'Well then, don't you think it's time you launched a full-blown search for Peter Kline? He might well have been kidnapped – or worse.'

'You're jumping to conclusions, Beth. There's no evidence to suggest that the two men who called at his house last night were up to no good. They might have been a couple of mates.'

'You don't really believe that, do you?'

'I honestly don't know what to believe, Beth. But what I do know is that you should remember that you're a reporter and not a detective. We don't need you to do our job for us.'

I felt myself recoil at his words and a flash of anger tore through me.

'Jesus, Ethan. What the fuck has got into you? It's obvious that something's not right and that Peter Kline's life could be in danger. He's the one person who can prove that Danny Shapiro lied about his alibi. And he's gone missing.'

'And I've told you I'm looking into it.'

'Is that right? Then how come you didn't speak to his next-door neighbours when you came to Maida Vale this morning?'

'I did speak to a neighbour. That's how I found out that he drove off in his car last night.'

'Well, I don't know who you spoke to because those on either side of him said they haven't spoken to the police.'

His tone grew sharper. 'I didn't say I spoke to any particular neighbour, Beth. And I don't see why I have to explain myself to you anyway.'

I was on the verge of losing my temper with him and I didn't want to. Instead I took a deep breath and closed my eyes, pressing my fingers into the sockets.

'You need to trust me, Beth,' he said. 'I am looking into this and now you've told me about the two men I'll put more effort into it.'

I opened my eyes, stared up at a sky streaked with ragged strips of cloud.

'The thing is there's been another development,' he added. 'And I've been focused on that since I got back.'

'What's happened?' I said.

'It's Megan's ex-boyfriend. Sam Jones. We're bringing him back in because there's a hole in his alibi. It looks like he could be our murderer.'

This came as a shock, and I wasn't sure what to make of it. If it was true then I was way off course. But I found it impossible to believe.

'Tell me what you know,' I said.

He gave me the details and insisted I wasn't to run the story just yet. I said I wouldn't if he promised that I'd be the first to know if Jones was charged. He agreed and then said he had to go because Jones had just arrived at the station.

There was more I wanted to ask him but didn't get the chance. I was left feeling totally confused about what he'd told me.

How could the police possibly think that Sam Jones had killed Megan? Danny Shapiro was the man responsible. That was why he got Tamara Roth to lie for him and why he was so keen to silence me.

I glanced at my watch. It was coming up to midday. I decided to look for a café so that I could have a coffee and a think. There were quite a few in the area so it didn't take me long to find one.

Over a double espresso I took out my pen and pad and jotted down some notes, along with a list of questions. But it didn't make things any clearer when I read it all back and asked myself the questions out loud.

Was Megan murdered by her ex-boyfriend or her ex-husband?

If it wasn't Shapiro then why did he concoct an alibi?

And why had Peter Kline disappeared? Had he been seized from his home so that he wouldn't be able to tell the police that Tamara Roth was with him on Friday evening?

I rubbed my face, my eyes. Trying to think, to concentrate. Nursing the questions in my head until it felt like my brain was overloaded.

By the time I'd finished my third espresso I'd convinced myself that I should trust my own instincts, and they were telling me that Shapiro was Megan's killer. Not Sam Jones.

To me the evidence against him was overwhelming. Megan had told her father that Shapiro had threatened her. It was a fact that she'd been trying to blackmail him. Therefore there was a strong motive. He was doing all he could to stop me pursuing the story with my usual vigour. And he'd gone to the trouble of making up an alibi.

It should have been enough to convict the bastard. But it was obvious to me that the police were allowing themselves to be distracted, which made me feel like the onus was on me to find a way of exposing Shapiro's lie for what it was and to get the cops to take Peter Kline's disappearance more seriously.

It took a few more minutes of careful consideration before I came up with an idea. It was one that was sure to piss Ethan off, but that was the least of my worries.

I left the café and went in search of a public phone box. The first one I came across wasn't suitable because it was within sight of

240

a CCTV camera. If the call I was intending to make was traced then I didn't want anyone knowing it was me who made it.

The second phone box was in a side street set back from the canal and there were no cameras in sight. I slipped inside and a few moments later I was through to the murder incident room in Wandsworth.

I put a tissue over the mouthpiece to help disguise my voice and spoke with a forced cockney accent.

'I'm calling with information about a man who's been abducted by two men from his home in Little Venice, London,' I said. 'His name is Peter Kline and his home is on Maida Avenue. He hasn't been seen since last night.'

The person on the other end of the line tried to interrupt me but I continued talking.

'This is not a crank call. I'm telling you because I happen to know that Mr Kline has information that will prove Danny Shapiro's alibi for Friday evening is false. He was not in Vauxhall with a prostitute as he claims.'

I then abruptly hung up and stepped back out onto the street.

My insides were churning, and I had to tell myself that I'd done the right thing. If nothing else, at least the search for Peter Kline should now begin in earnest.

35

Danny Shapiro

Danny was in a bad mood and had been all day. It was because he hated having the blood of an innocent man on his hands.

Over the years he had instructed his people to carry out a total of three murders. He himself had ended the lives of two men, both of them rivals who'd wanted to kill him.

But all of those killings had been gang-related. The victims had deserved to die. In contrast Peter Kline, the investment analyst who worked in the City, had done nothing wrong. The poor sod was just a victim of circumstance; and that preyed on Danny's conscience.

But there was no way they could have allowed him to live, not after his little chat with Bethany Chambers.

Bishop had told Danny that the hit had gone smoothly and that DI Ethan Cain had played his part, just as Danny had known he would. There was only one thing the detective cared about and that was himself. The thought of being found out and going to prison would have scared him witless.

After leaving Maida Vale, Bishop had driven to a building site in Streatham owned by the firm and had dumped the body in the foundations of a block of flats. Peter Kline was now encased in concrete and within six months there'd be around a hundred people living on top of him. His Lexus car had been dropped off at the firm's scrapyard in Kennington where by now it would be just a mangled wreck.

They had such things down to a fine art, so they didn't have to worry about anyone finding out what had happened to the man.

Despite that, Danny still couldn't relax. As he stood at his office window above the snooker hall, he had a feeling that it wasn't over by a long shot. Things had almost come unstuck because Chambers had spotted the calendar on Tamara's kitchen wall. It was only through a stroke of luck that the Old Bill hadn't seen it when they'd called at the house. According to Tamara they'd spent all their time talking to her in the living room and hadn't ventured into the kitchen. But it had been a close call and was a prime example of how easily things could go wrong.

Tamara had been shocked when he'd told her and had since destroyed the calendar. He'd also had to tell her that Kline had been dealt with, but she understood why and didn't ask for details.

That bitch of a reporter Bethany Chambers still worried him, however. He'd been making inquiries about her and what he'd found out made him uneasy. The moniker someone had given her was well deserved. The Ferret. Hardly flattering, but an apt description of how she operated.

She was the girl from Peckham who had done good. In that sense he and she were alike. Both brought up in the same rough manor and both now at the top of their respective fields. It was a quirky fact that almost made him smile. But not quite.

Bethany Chambers was one of those tenacious reporters who were infused with a sense of purpose. Within the Met she was liked and disliked in equal measure. It was clear that she had a lot of police contacts – and that in itself made her dangerous.

Across the newspaper industry she was well respected even though it was rumoured that she often stepped over the ethical line. Danny had already discovered for himself that she wasn't shy when it came to breaking the law. It took a lot of front for a journalist to pose as a copper in this day and age. Despite himself, he had to admit that he had a grudging respect for her.

The thing that bothered him wasn't that she was good at her job. It was that she was too bloody good. Plus, she didn't scare easily, unlike most of her contemporaries, especially the female reporters. He wasn't the first villain to have threatened her. She'd even stood her ground against the Russian mafia, for Christ's sake. He'd heard on the grapevine how much she'd pissed those guys off. Yet it hadn't stopped her writing about their operations in Soho.

The thought of having to use brute force to get her off his back did not appeal to him, so he was hoping that her ex-husband would make her see sense. If not, then he might have to get Bishop to rough her up a bit.

The call from Ethan Cain did nothing to improve Danny's mood. It came just as he was winding up a meeting with the crew and was thinking about retreating to his West End bolt hole.

He had asked Cain to provide him with an update before the press conference so that he would know beforehand what was going to come out.

'There's stuff you need to know, Danny,' Cain said, his voice fretful.

Danny responded as he stepped out of the meeting room and back into his office.

'Does that mean you've got a confession out of that tosser Sam Jones?'

Danny had heard that Megan's ex-boyfriend had been hauled in again for questioning and he'd been praying the bastard would be nailed for her murder.

'No such luck,' Cain said. 'He's still denying it. And we still haven't got enough evidence to charge him.'

'But you told me his alibi didn't stack up.'

'It's certainly not rock solid. He left the boozer he was drinking in for about an hour around the time that Megan was killed. But he claims he went home to get some money because he ran out of cash. He lives just round the corner from the pub and so far we can't prove that he's not telling the truth. We're checking CCTV cameras as we speak but unless we can pick him up on one in Balham a charge won't stick.'

Danny screwed up his eyes in despair and swallowed the phlegm that had gathered at the back of his throat.

'So what other joyous news have you got for me, Ethan?'

'There was an anonymous call to the incident room a while ago,' Cain said. 'It was a woman and it must have been Bethany.'

'What makes you say that?'

'Because she rang me from Maida Vale earlier to say she'd spoken to Kline's neighbours. One of them told her she saw two men walking up the driveway last night before Kline's car was driven away. It's convinced her he was abducted.'

'Holy fuck. Frankie told me nobody saw the pair of you.'

'Well, he was wrong.'

'So why did she call in anonymously? I don't get it.'

'She's convinced Kline was kidnapped and she thinks we should be doing more to find him. I told her to leave it with me and to stop playing detective, but she's impatient to move things along quickly without implicating herself.'

'What exactly did she say when she rang in?'

'She gave Kline's name and said he'd been abducted from his home in Maida Vale by two men. She also suggested that Kline was snatched because he can prove that you weren't at Tamara Roth's house on Friday night.'

'Oh, for fuck's sake. So how have your lot reacted?'

'A missing person investigation has been launched and a forensic team has been sent to Kline's house. My boss wants us to find out everything we can about the guy and that means pulling up his phone records. They're bound to link him to Tamara so you'd better mark her card about that. And if by chance she told him in a text that she'd be at his place on Friday she needs to say she cancelled the appointment to be with you.'

Danny felt the blood stir in his veins. 'This is a fucking shit storm, Ethan. You were supposed to muzzle Chambers.'

'I've tried. But Beth is a law unto herself. There's only so much I can do and I can't guarantee that she won't make things more difficult for both of us.'

'Then I suppose it's up to me to sort her out.'

'You can't hurt her, Danny. She's too high-profile and too well connected.'

'Bollocks. She's another tabloid tart who likes to see her name in print. And from what I hear she's got plenty of enemies.'

'That's not the point. You can't just go around having people killed because—'

'I didn't say I was going to have her killed, Ethan. I'll just make sure she's taken out of the equation until this shit storm blows over.'

246

'But that's not—'

'Shut up, Ethan. I don't give a frigging fart if she's your ex-wife and you've got a kid between you. As far as I'm concerned she's a threat to us. If she keeps beavering away there's a chance she'll turn up something else that your lot have missed. And then we'll all be in a hole.'

'So what are you going to do?'

'It's best you don't know. Just do your job and find out who murdered Megan. It wasn't me so it's either Sam Jones or someone else who had a grudge against her. Find that scumbag and our problems go away.'

'We're doing our best,' Cain said.

'Yeah, well, your best is not fucking good enough. In fact it's time I got my own people to have a look at whatever you've got, including all the info on Sam Jones and the forensic reports.'

'That's not possible, Danny.'

'Bullshit. You've done it before. It's all on your computer. Just attach the main documents and statements to an email and send them to an address that I'll give you.'

'You've got to be joking. This case is different. It'd be too risky and would leave a trail.'

'Then dump it onto a flash drive. And do it right away. I want it this afternoon.'

'I can't do that,' Cain said. 'I'm snowed under here and we'll soon be staging the press conference.'

'That's not happening until five. So you've got plenty of time to nip out before then. I'll send Frankie over to meet you near the nick and he can pick it up.'

'It's really not a good idea, Danny. I can drop it off later tonight. I need to talk to you anyway about something.'

'I'm not sure where I'll be later,' Danny said. 'And I want to know what the fuck is going on asap.'

Cain was silent for a few beats. 'I'll do what I can,' he said. 'But I'm not happy about it.'

'Well, that's too bad. I'll tell Frankie you'll meet him between four and four thirty somewhere within walking distance of the station. Text him with a location as soon as you can.'

Cain had more to say, but Danny hung up and cut him off mid-sentence. He then called Frankie Bishop into his office.

'I've got a couple of jobs for you,' he told his enforcer. 'I want you to meet up with Cain and collect something from him. He'll text you the location.'

'No problem. What's the other thing?'

'Beth Chambers,' Danny said. 'It's time we sorted her out.'

36

Beth Chambers

I was going to be a bit early for the press conference at Lavender Hill. My taxi driver was an old hand and knew how to avoid the worst of the south London traffic.

As we approached Wandsworth my ears were buzzing with excitement. I told myself over and over that I had done the right thing in making the anonymous call. Someone had to make the coppers see sense. I was convinced that Ethan and his team were being sidetracked and I couldn't just ignore my fears for Peter Kline, or the disturbing thought that I'd been indirectly responsible for whatever had happened to him.

I wanted with all my heart to learn that he was okay, that he hadn't been kidnapped or murdered, that the two men who had turned up at his house last night were indeed his mates and not Danny Shapiro's goons.

The trouble was I just could not bring myself to believe it. Instead I was in the grip of a deep and unrelenting sense of foreboding.

'Where shall I drop you, miss?' the cabbie said.

The police station was just up ahead. I could see a television crew on the pavement out front, a suited reporter speaking into a camera.

'This'll be fine,' I said. 'Just park on the left.'

He pulled over to the kerb and as I leaned forward to hand him the fare I happened to glance through the windscreen and spot a familiar face. It was Ethan, and he was hurrying down the station steps with his phone clamped to his ear.

'Keep the change,' I said to the driver and got quickly out of the taxi.

I raised my hand and called to Ethan, hoping to seize his attention. But he didn't look my way or break stride as he dashed across the road at the traffic lights.

I stood watching him, wondering where he was going in such a hurry just before the start of the press conference. I half expected him to pop into the coffee shop just across the street or to nip into the off-licence next door for a packet of cigarettes.

But once across the road he moved west along Lavender Hill. I called his name again but he didn't hear me above the din of the traffic.

It was then that I noticed he was carrying a large buff-coloured envelope in his free hand and that he kept looking furtively behind him.

My curiosity suddenly got the better of me and I decided to follow him. I stayed on this side of the road, knowing there was little chance of him seeing me through the heavy traffic.

He walked for about two hundred yards and then turned into a street between two estate agents. I didn't want to lose him so I waited for an opening in the slow-moving traffic and crossed the road.

I looked up at the street sign: Altenburg Gardens, and below it was an arrow pointing to a Catholic church.

I was about to turn into the street when it struck me that I ought to peer around the corner first. I was glad I did because Ethan was standing not twenty yards away talking to a man who was leaning on the open door of a parked Audi.

I watched as Ethan handed him the envelope he'd been carrying. A few words were exchanged before Ethan turned and walked back the way he'd come.

I had to duck quickly through the open doors of the estate agent's on my left to avoid being seen. Not so quickly though that I didn't get to see the face of the man he'd had his brief encounter with.

It was Frankie Bishop.

Through the estate agent's window I saw Ethan turn into Lavender Hill and head back towards the station.

I held my breath as blood roared in my head. I could not believe what I had just witnessed. My ex-husband passed an envelope to the man who had threatened me. The same man who was known to be a sadistic killer.

It had been a clandestine meeting, of that I had no doubt. And it had probably been hurriedly arranged, which was why Ethan had rushed here from the station.

'Are you looking for a property, madam?'

A smartly dressed woman appeared at my side suddenly and it made me jump. I couldn't respond because my throat felt like it was in a tight noose. Instead I ignored her and stepped swiftly out onto the pavement.

Glancing to my left I saw that Frankie Bishop had driven off with whatever Ethan had given him. My stomach spasmed as I let go of the air held in my lungs.

There was only one way to interpret what had just happened and it made me want to chase after Ethan and attack him in the street. The cheating dirtbag was in cahoots with Danny Shapiro. He was a crooked cop on the gangster's payroll. Why else would he have met with Frankie Bishop?

It made sense to me suddenly why his response to what I'd found out had been so muted. He had probably known all along that Shapiro's alibi was a false one. That was why he wasn't keen to make a big thing of Peter Kline's disappearance.

I bit my lip, hard enough for it to hurt and felt the rush of a thousand memories swirl around me. Ethan's lies, his betrayal, his duplicity. He was a man with little or no conscience.

I replayed in my head the conversations I'd had with him over the past couple of days. He'd been open about the investigation and I hadn't got the impression that he was holding anything back from me. But I had detected a change in his tone after I'd told him about Peter Kline.

He should have been wild with excitement, yet instead had told me to keep it to myself.

'You need to trust me, Beth.'

Of course I should have known better than to think I could ever really trust the man. And I should certainly have known, or at least suspected, that someone so lacking in morals could not possibly walk a straight line as a police officer.

On the way back to the station I had to fight against the impulse to call the office and tell Grant Scott that one of the lead detectives in the hunt for Megan Fuller's killer was a bent cop on Danny Shapiro's payroll.

What stopped me was the thought that whatever Ethan had done he was still Rosie's dad. I just couldn't do it, at least not until I'd confronted him and given him the chance to explain himself.

I didn't think for a single moment that he'd have a legitimate excuse for what had just transpired but I reckoned it was only fair that I heard what he had to say.

I got back to the station half an hour before the press conference was due to start. Reporters and camera crews had gathered and were being marshalled into a conference room that had been set up with chairs and a long desk at one end. There was no sign of Ethan so I assumed he'd returned to the incident room.

I considered waiting until after the presser to confront him, but I was too wound up and wanted to get it over with. I called him on his mobile and when he answered I told him I was downstairs and that I needed to have a private conversation with him.

'It has to be now,' I said. 'I've got something important to tell you.'

He wasn't keen, but after a long pause he agreed.

'There's a meeting room on the ground floor,' he said. 'I'll get someone to take you there. Wait in reception and don't for fuck's sake let on to anyone else.'

I was approached in the reception area by a young female officer in uniform who led me along a corridor to a small room with a table and four chairs. Ethan was sitting on one of the chairs and the moment the door was closed behind me, he said, 'Before you start I want you to know that I'm mightily pissed off with you, Beth.'

The tone of his voice added fuel to the fire that was raging inside me.

'Why is that, Ethan?' I said as calmly as I could.

'Because I know it was you who made that anonymous call. It couldn't have been anyone else.'

'Really?'

'I can't believe you did it after you promised to hold fire on Peter Kline's disappearance.'

'I made no such promise,' I said. 'I did promise you that I wouldn't run the line about Sam Jones and I didn't.'

'So why did you go and make that bloody call?'

'Isn't it obvious? The guy's gone missing and you don't seem to be in a hurry to do anything about it.'

'That's not fair. I made it clear to you that I was working on it.'

'Yes, you did, but there was no sense of urgency. You acted like it was no big deal and it is. That's why I went back to Kline's house. I felt that something needed to be done. And it's lucky I did because otherwise we still wouldn't know about those two mystery men. At least now we know he almost certainly didn't just go for a joyride last night. Something must have happened to him.'

'Maybe you're right. But the way you've gone about it is stupid. I just hope you don't come to regret it.'

'Why would I?'

'Because this way all kinds of questions are going to be asked and it might not be easy to cover up the fact that you posed as a police officer. That's a serious crime, in case you've forgotten.'

'You and Peter Kline are the only two people who know about that, so I don't see why it should get out – unless you're planning on grassing me up.'

He gave a long, theatrical sigh.

'This is just typical of you, Beth. As soon as you pick up the scent of a story you're like a dog straining at the leash. You go at it without thinking it through and in so doing you upset and irritate a lot of people.'

254

'Does that include Danny Shapiro as well as you, Ethan?' I said.

'You know it does. We've talked about that already and I told you that you need to be careful where he's concerned. The man's violent and dangerous. And if he comes to regard you as a threat he'll do whatever it takes to shut you up.'

'And I don't suppose you'll lift a finger to stop him, will you, Ethan?'

'What's that supposed to mean?'

'Oh, come on,' I said, raising my voice. 'I wasn't born yesterday. You should have been ecstatic when I told you I had proof that Danny Shapiro's alibi was false. But you weren't. And I reckon it's because you wanted to play it down in order to give Shapiro time to sort himself out.'

'That's bollocks.'

I stabbed a finger at him as the anger boiled over inside me. 'Kline disappeared after I told you I'd been to see him. A strange coincidence if you ask me. Did you tell Shapiro? Is that what happened? And did Shapiro then do something to him?'

His expression was one of shock and outrage.

'This is unbelievable,' he said. 'Are you actually suggesting that I answer to Danny Shapiro? Because if you are you couldn't be more wrong.'

'Don't fucking lie to me, Ethan. I know you're in bed with him. And even for you that's a new low, given that he poses a serious threat to both me and your own daughter.'

'Bloody hell, Beth. What's got into you? You're insane to even think that.'

'Am I, Ethan? Am I really?'

'Of course you are. You need to calm down. You're talking crap.'

He took a step towards me and reached for my shoulder, but

I knocked his hand away and then slapped his face as hard as I could.

'You treacherous, fucking scumbag,' I screamed at him. 'I know you're lying because I just saw you with Frankie Bishop. I followed you from here because I was curious. You gave him an envelope and I'll bet there was something inside it that he wasn't meant to have.'

He just stood there, mouth open, the colour leaving his face like cola from a bottle.

'How long, Ethan?' I said. 'How long have you been on the bloody take?'

He shook his head. 'You've got it wrong, Beth. It's not that. It's not what you think.'

'Don't insult my intelligence,' I said. 'I saw you with my own eyes. And it's all clear to me now. I feel like such an idiot because I should have realised what was going on.'

He was sweating profusely and it confirmed to me that I wasn't accusing him of something that he hadn't done. The guilt was writ large on his face, like a mask of shame.

When he started to speak, I raised a hand to stop him.

'Don't say another word, Ethan. Not unless you're going to break the habit of a lifetime and tell me the truth. I want to know exactly what it is you gave to Bishop and I also want to know what's happened to Peter Kline.'

I held his stricken gaze for a couple of seconds, and when he stayed silent the urge to swing a punch at him was strong, even though I knew it would serve no useful purpose.

'You make me sick to the stomach,' I fumed. 'I fucking hate you.'

Then I pushed him out of the way and let myself out of the room.

* * *

The press conference was late starting because the unmarked police car that was sent to pick up Nigel Fuller got stuck in rush-hour traffic. But that suited me because I needed to calm down and get my mind back on track.

After leaving Ethan I went to the loo to splash cold water on my face and regain my equilibrium. Then I made a conscious effort to compartmentalise what I'd discovered so that I could do my job. It proved far from easy.

And it got much harder when the conference got started and Ethan appeared. He walked to the front of the room where he sat next to DCI Redwood and Megan's father.

I forced myself to concentrate on Nigel Fuller. His face had become even more sallow and drawn since Saturday when he had confronted Shapiro in front of the police station. Grief had etched its way into his features and sucked the life out of him.

His appearance here would make all the difference, which was why the police had wanted him to come along. The distraught relative or loved one of a victim turned an otherwise mundane press conference into a media event.

Nigel Fuller's emotional appeal would be carried on the evening news bulletins, and his face would be splattered across the front pages in the morning. It would help maintain public interest in the story and hopefully generate a flood of calls to the incident room.

I took my notebook from my bag and rested it on my thigh as DCI Redwood introduced himself. The buzz of conversation around me died down and a couple of camera flashes went off.

'With me to answer the questions about the investigation into Megan Fuller's murder is Detective Inspector Ethan Cain,' Redwood said.

I noticed then that Ethan was staring at me. He was obviously worried that I might stand up and denounce him. As I stared back at him I began to tremble with a flood of emotions, so after a few seconds I had to wrest my gaze away and look again at Redwood, who was in full flow.

'We've called this press conference in order to make a fresh appeal for information,' he was saying. 'Whoever killed Megan is still out there. Based on what evidence we have we believe the person responsible is a man who may or may not have known his victim. At this point I would like to pre-empt at least one of your questions and state that Megan's ex-husband Daniel Shapiro is not a suspect.'

A great torrent of anger and guilt welled up inside me. I wanted to cry out, to tell everyone in the room that Shapiro had lied and that one of the detectives working on the case was corrupt. Naturally I bottled it. But I told myself that it was only for the time being. What I'd found out today had strengthened my resolve. I was more determined than ever to uncover the truth about Megan's murder. If my ex got caught up in the fallout then he had no one to blame but himself.

DCI Redwood was now explaining to his audience that Megan's stepfather wanted to make a direct appeal to the public and all attention switched to Nigel Fuller.

I could see sweat glistening on the poor man's forehead. His face was like a sheet of wax, and as he read from a pre-prepared statement, his voice sounded unnatural and slow.

'I believe – as do the police – that someone somewhere must know who killed my Megan,' he said. 'Whoever it is would have returned home late on Friday night. He might well have had blood on his clothes or been in an agitated state. If you know, or suspect, an individual, then please, I beg you to contact the police with the information. Megan was a treasure and she did not deserve to die in the way she did.'

His words cut through me and went to the core of my being. My breath caught and a hard knot tightened in my throat.

I turned to Ethan again and willed him to look at me. I wanted him to see the rage in my eyes. But his gaze was directed at the ceiling.

Mr Fuller's face strained with the effort of speaking, and he seemed mightily relieved when he finished his statement. Redwood explained that Mr Fuller would not be taking questions but he and DI Cain would.

That was my cue to leap to my feet and get in first.

'Bethany Chambers with *The Post*,' I said, then directed my first question at Redwood. 'Is it true that you've again been questioning Megan's ex-boyfriend, Sam Jones?'

Ethan's eyes locked on mine. He swallowed and wet his upper lip with his tongue.

'Mr Jones has indeed been interviewed again,' Redwood said. 'He's among a number of people who are helping us with our inquiries.'

I stayed on my feet and raised a finger in the air. 'I have a second question, Detective. Is it also true that you're now following a new line of inquiry involving a man named Peter Kline who has disappeared from his home in Maida Vale?'

The question took everyone by surprise, and a low murmur rippled through the room.

'I'll answer the question as best I can, Miss Chambers,' Redwood said, his voice low and steady. 'But I'm afraid there's not a great deal I can say about it at this stage. Mr Kline is an investment analyst who works in the City. We're anxious to contact him because he did not turn up for work at his office this morning.'

'So what's your interest in him, Inspector?' I said. 'Is he perhaps a suspect or a witness?'

Redwood shook his head. 'Mr Kline is most definitely not a suspect. His name cropped up today in relation to a specific aspect of the case, the details of which I'm afraid I can't go into.'

It got everyone excited and over the next few minutes they tried to extract the details with a flurry of follow-up questions.

It gave me enormous satisfaction because at least now Peter Kline was at the forefront of their minds. That had to be a significant step towards both finding the man and uncovering the truth about Danny Shapiro's alibi.

The press conference only lasted another half-hour because the police didn't really have much to say. The aim had been to keep the momentum going by using Nigel Fuller to grab some headlines, and they had probably succeeded in doing that. It would have helped too that the mystery man Peter Kline had been lobbed into the mix.

As we were all piling out of the room my mobile vibrated with an incoming text message. It was from Ethan.

We need to talk, Beth. Come for a drink. And please don't go and do something stupid.

I wanted to talk to him again to find out the answers to a barrage of questions. But not right now. I simply didn't trust myself not to hurt him.

So I typed a two-word reply to his text.

Fuck off.

Outside on the street Nigel Fuller was giving a one-to-one interview to a TV news crew. I stood behind them so that I could hear what was being said. But at the same time I spotted Fuller's fiancée, Amy Cassidy, standing next to an unmarked police car that was parked at the kerb waiting to take them home.

I made a quick calculation that a few quotes from her would add a bit more colour to the story. She was wearing a dark knee-length overcoat and her hair was held back on one side by a tortoiseshell clip. I introduced myself and was surprised that she remembered me from Saturday.

'You gave me your card,' she said. 'And I know you interviewed Nigel on Saturday morning in Ramsden Road.'

'That's right,' I said. 'How is he coping?'

'Not very well if I'm being honest. I didn't think he would come here today after they decided that Danny Shapiro was no longer a suspect. Nigel was convinced that he killed Megan. But the police have told us the man was with someone miles away when it happened. So perhaps he is innocent after all.'

The guilt hit me like a raging tsunami and it was all I could do not to blurt out what I knew. I looked away from her so that she couldn't see the shame on my face.

'We've postponed our wedding for at least six months,' she said. 'It's hard to get your mind around such things when something like this happens.'

She seemed happy to continue talking to me, but it didn't feel right. My throat had run dry and the guilt had enveloped me. I felt sure that if I didn't walk away I'd lose the plot.

So I thanked Amy Cassidy and wished her well. I then called the office as I headed along the street while looking out for a taxi. The newsdesk wanted me to file copy for the online edition of *The Post*, and I told them to expect it within the next ten minutes.

The roads were gridlocked and all the taxis I saw were taken. Instead I dropped into the first pub I came to, ordered a G and T, and then sat in a booth to type a story into my iPad. It took longer than it should have because my mind kept switching back to Ethan and what I was going to do with what I now knew. Each sentence seemed to take an age to construct.

There were dramatic developments today in the hunt for the killer of Megan Fuller. The soap star's ex-boyfriend was questioned for the second time. Police have also linked the murder to a man who has disappeared from his London home. Meanwhile, Miss Fuller's grief-stricken father made an emotional appeal at a press conference this afternoon . . .

After I'd sent it I phoned my mother to tell her that I would hopefully be home in about an hour.

'Shall I keep Rosie up?' she said.

'If that's okay. I'd like to read her a story.'

'She'll like that. I'll make sure she's ready for bed.'

Back outside I gave up on the taxis and headed in the direction of Clapham Junction railway station. From there it was a fifteen-minute train journey to Peckham.

On the way I would try to work out what to do next and decide whether it was time to stop all contact between my daughter and her wretched father.

37

Danny Shapiro

Danny got home in time to watch live coverage of the press conference on television. A reporter standing outside the station linked into several video clips.

The first showed Megan's father appealing for help from the public. The second showed Beth Chambers tossing Peter Kline's name into the proceedings like it was an incendiary device.

Now everyone knew that Kline was missing and that he was linked in some way to Megan's murder. It seemed to Danny that Chambers had succeeded in doing what she had set out to do. The bitch had drawn attention to Kline and questions would now be asked.

But Danny was comforted by two thoughts: the man from Maida Vale had taken his secret to his grave. And within hours Beth Chambers would be in no condition to do her job.

He was still disturbed by how quickly things had spiralled out of control. It had been a big mistake to rush over to Megan's house on Friday night in a fit of pique. He should have ignored her threats. But then how could he possibly have known that someone else would drop in on her a short time later – someone whose intention was to give her more than just a bollocking.

He wanted more than ever to find out the identity of the killer, and with the documents Cain had provided perhaps his own team would hit upon something the Old Bill had missed. If Sam Jones wasn't the killer then who the hell could it have been? He found it hard to believe that the police weren't able to track down the other person or persons she'd supposedly been blackmailing. Surely, he thought, there would be pointers to one or more of them on her phone or computer.

He padded softly across the room to his well-stocked drinks cabinet, intending to pour himself a large whisky. But before he got there his phone rang. He guessed it'd be his father and he was right.

'Thought I'd check to see how you're doing, son,' Callum said.

The sound of his father's voice lifted him, and he was reminded of how much he missed the old duffer.

'Well, you'll be glad to know that business in booming in all areas, Dad,' he said. 'The deal with the Turks is going through and today I saw the accounts for the clubs. Turns out October was our best month so far this year.'

Callum tutted. 'That's not what I'm interested in, you wally. I want to know how you're coping with the other thing. I gather there's a lot going on.'

Danny pushed out a sigh. 'How much do you know?'

'Only what's been on the news, but I assume they've only got half the story.'

'You're not wrong there, Dad.'

'So who the fuck is this Peter Kline bloke? I just watched Beth Chambers bring up his name at the police press conference. Looked like everyone was suddenly a bit uncomfortable.'

Danny hesitated. He had promised Tamara that he wouldn't tell Callum that she was back on the game. But how else could he explain Peter Kline's involvement?

'You know how much I hate it when you hold things back from me, son,' Callum said. 'So don't even think about it.'

Danny told him everything. How Tamara had actually been at Kline's house on Friday night. How Beth Chambers had spotted the scribbled note on Tamara's calendar. How she had then gone to see Kline posing as a copper. And how he had told her that Tamara spent Friday evening in his bed.

'I was in a room with Ethan Cain when she phoned him,' Danny said. 'She urged him to get a statement from the guy and then to arrest Tamara and me so that she could be first with the story. That's why I had to act quickly to stop it happening.'

He explained how he'd sent Ethan along with Bishop to Kline's house and how nobody would ever find out what had happened to the man.

'It's a mess, Dad,' he said. 'And look, I didn't want to have to tell you that Tamara is back doing the business. She didn't want you to know.'

'I'm not stupid, son. I knew she'd be whoring again. It's all she knows and I don't have a problem with it. I'm more concerned about this other stuff. You need to make sure it ain't gonna blow up in your face.'

'I'm on top of it, Dad. As I see it Chambers poses the biggest problem. So I'm sorting her out.'

'How?'

'I told Frankie to send some lads over to Peckham to give her a good hiding. She can't create problems for us if she's in hospital for a couple of months.'

Callum's reaction to this was to release a loud gasp. Then when he spoke his voice appeared to be on the edge of panic.

'Jesus, son. When are they supposed to be making a move on her?'

'Sometime this evening. It might even be happening now. Why?'

'Because you have to stop them,' he said.

'But that's not—'

'Don't fuck around,' he yelled. 'Just do it. That's not the way to handle Beth Chambers.'

'It's the only way, Dad. She doesn't respond to threats.'

Callum's tone pitched up another notch. 'And you really think that beating her up will put her out of the game? If you do then you're a fucking moron.'

Callum sounded like he had lapsed into a state of raw shock. He started breathing into the phone like an exhausted runner, and Danny could hear the phlegm gathering in his chest.

'Call the attack dogs off, Danny. Before they turn a problem into a major fucking crisis.'

Danny was totally confused. He had never known his father to get so worked up over something as trivial as giving someone a going-over. Here was a man who over the years had killed and maimed dozens of people, most of them with his bare hands.

'I'm not asking you son,' Callum snarled. 'I'm frigging telling you not to harm that woman.'

'I hear what you're saying, Dad, but you're not making any sense. Why are you so rattled? Is there something you're not telling me?'

Callum drew a screech of breath and then fell silent. Danny pictured him in his tiny prison cell, a man forced to live in the past, a man who liked to think he still called the shots.

'This is *my* problem,' Danny said. 'If you don't want me to sort it my way then you'd better tell me why. Or so help me I'm hanging up.'

A pause ensued. Then Callum made a lot of noise clearing his throat before saying, 'Okay, son. But you'd better brace yourself because you're not going to like what you're about to hear.'

38

Beth Chambers

I had the strangest feeling that someone was watching me. I'd just got off the train at Peckham Rye station and was standing inside the entrance sheltering from the rain. From here it was only a ten-minute walk home, but I didn't have a brolly and had no wish to get drenched.

Along with about a dozen other people I was waiting for the rain to ease off, hoping it was just a passing shower. For some reason I was convinced that one or more of them was checking me out, sizing me up, maybe even trying to make eye contact.

The group around me were an equal mix of men and women, mostly young to middle-aged. I stood huddled in my coat, casually turning to look at their faces. They all seemed pretty ordinary and most were preoccupied with their own thoughts while staring out into the rain.

But one man had his eyes on me. He was wearing a leather jacket and jeans and must have been about my age. When he saw that I'd spotted him, he smiled and that was when I realised that he was quite good-looking in a rough-and-ready sort of way. Definitely my type, I thought.

Why can't I meet someone like you on the dating sites?

It was easy to smile back because I felt flattered and I knew that in a moment we'd be going our separate ways and so there was no reason not to acknowledge him.

Another time, another place, and I would have been happy for him to strike up a conversation, just like they do in those romantic films when it leads to the altar. But this wasn't the time or the place. I was in a hurry to get home to my daughter and too many negative thoughts were spinning around inside my head, including what I was going to do with the knowledge that DI Ethan Cain was on Shapiro's payroll. So I turned away in case my smile prompted the guy to come over and try his luck.

As soon as I did I saw that the rain had suddenly died to a drizzle and I decided to go for it. It wouldn't matter if I got a bit wet since I was planning to have a bath and wash my hair anyway.

I did up all the buttons on my coat, turned up the collar, and stepped out from the cover of the station.

I went to the right and came out on Blenheim Grove. Rye Lane with all its shops and stalls was to the left. I went the other way and walked past All Saints Church, my heels clicking on the pavement.

Walking through Peckham in the dark is never a pleasant experience, even this early in the evening. You can't help being reminded that the area is considered one of the most dangerous in London. Poverty, ethnic tensions, and a thriving gang culture deter a lot of people from walking the streets by themselves.

Two years ago I had my bag snatched by a couple of black youths and six months later I witnessed a mugging quite close to here. Even so I was determined not to let such isolated incidents turn me into a quivering wreck.

Blenheim Grove was empty as I hurried past a row of small industrial units on my right. An MOT centre, a cash and carry warehouse, an auto repair shop. They all appeared to be closed.

I was about to cross over the road in order to take a left at the next corner when I heard what sounded like my name being called out. I stopped abruptly and turned around, just as a stiff breeze pushed the rain against my face.

'It's me, Bethany,' the voice said. 'I knew you didn't recognise me back there.'

Under the sombre sodium glow of the streetlamp I saw the guy in the leather jacket walking towards me. I frowned because I was sure I'd never seen him before today. But it wouldn't have been the first time that my memory had failed me.

I narrowed my eyes to slits, and as he drew close I tried to place him.

'Long time no see, Bethany,' he said, smiling at me.

Bethany? Who did I know who called me that instead of just Beth?

What happened next took me completely by surprise. While all my attention was focused on Mr Leather Jacket, someone else grabbed me from behind. Before I could cry out a hand was clamped over my mouth and an arm was wrapped around my throat.

I was yanked backwards and dragged through an open gate into one of the units.

As I tried to struggle free my bag fell to the pavement and I saw Leather Jacket pick it up and then check to see if anyone was watching.

I realised then that I'd been ambushed by him and an

accomplice. My heart gave a frightened beat and the fear spread through me like a raging virus.

My attacker's hand pressed harder against my mouth, and I could feel the sharp edges of his fingernails digging into my skin.

Oh my God.

'Take her into the workshop and don't let her scream,' Leather Jacket said in a voice that was loud and hoarse.

I was hauled unceremoniously between a couple of stripped-down cars as the gate was pulled shut behind me. I grabbed hold of the arm around my throat and tried to pull it away with all the force of desperation. But it was locked tight and I wasn't strong enough to budge it.

I was pulled out of the rain and into a grimy workshop where the air had a stale, lifeless quality. A naked bulb suspended from the ceiling softened the darkness.

The terror rushed through my body and I felt the panic crushing my chest, making it hard for me to breathe through my nose.

Leather Jacket's face suddenly filled my vision. He was standing right in front of me, and the smile I had seen earlier was back on his face, only now it was far from pleasant.

'Time for the fun to begin,' he sneered.

Several things happened at once. His accomplice let go of me, and my breath was released in a loud, violent gasp. Then Leather Jacket swung a punch hard into my ribs and I fell over, whimpering like a beaten dog.

I rolled onto my back on the filthy floor and let out a horrified grunt. Looking up I saw both men staring down at me. Leather Jacket's accomplice was squat and heavy-set, with a square jaw and shaved head. His expression was cold and menacing.

'Don't hurt me,' I pleaded and my voice did not sound like my own. 'There's money and stuff in my bag. Just take it and go. Please.'

Leather Jacket leaned forward, seized the front of my coat and pulled me back up. Then he slammed me against a wall and I felt it shudder. I opened my mouth to scream but it got stuck in my throat.

The other guy then gave me a fierce slap around the face that I didn't see coming. The pain was tempered by fear and adrenalin, but the force of it sent me staggering sideways into a shelf full of spare motor parts that tumbled to the floor around me.

I just about managed to stay on my feet, although my eyes started drifting in and out of focus.

'W . . . why are you doing this?' I yelled, and the words rasped in my throat. 'Who are you?'

'We're your worst nightmare, Bethany Chambers,' Leather Jacket said. 'And we're going to make you pay for whatever you've done wrong.'

Whatever I've done wrong! What in God's name did he mean by that?

I squeezed my eyes shut and mouthed a silent prayer. I felt paralysed by shock and the dread of what was to come. They were going to beat me up and rape me. I was sure of it. But even as this thought exploded in my head I knew that there had to be a more compelling motive behind this madness. I wasn't the victim of a random street attack. These bastards knew who I was. Knew my name. They'd followed me. Ambushed me. And now they were going to punish me for some perceived wrongdoing.

Danny Shapiro's name leaped into my mind. He was behind this. Had to be.

'Open your fucking eyes, woman.'

I did as I was told. It was the other man who had spoken, his voice pure south London.

My muscles went rigid when I saw that he was unbuckling his belt.

'You've got a choice, love,' he said, a manic grin on his face. 'If you keep still and let me get my end away, we won't damage your face. You'll get to keep your good looks and we'll just break a few bones.'

I recoiled almost as if he had hit me again.

'Please tell me you're not serious,' I screamed at him. 'This can't be happening.'

His jeans dropped to his ankles and he barked out a laugh.

'There's no point me wasting a golden opportunity, love. You're a tasty bit of crumpet and I ain't had a poke in weeks.'

I shot a glance at Leather Jacket, who was standing to one side with his arms folded across his chest.

'Did Danny Shapiro send you?' I said. 'Is that what this is all about?'

He shrugged. 'I don't know anyone named Shapiro.'

I felt the bottom drop out of my stomach and my chest started pumping for oxygen.

'Now take your coat off, turn around and bend over the table that's behind you,' the other man said. 'I'll do the rest.'

I didn't move. I couldn't. My muscles seized up and my limbs turned to jelly. But my heart continued to thrash around in my chest as he stepped out of his jeans and kicked them away from him.

He was just over an arm's-length away from me so when he lashed out with his fist it landed smack in the middle of my stomach. I doubled over, grunting as the air went out of my lungs.

'We ain't got all night, bitch,' he steamed. 'So be sensible and do as I say or so help me I'll make sure that even your own kid won't recognise you.'

The thought of Rosie waiting at home for me was like a bolt of electricity. It fired up my anger and released the invisible grip on my body.

And it prompted me to charge forward like a raging bull and straight into the bastard. He was caught unawares and lost his balance. We both went crashing onto the floor and I laid into him like someone possessed. I managed to smash my head against the bridge of his nose and he roared in pain. Then I shoved my knee into his groin and felt a shiver of satisfaction when he cried out again.

Immediately Leather Jacket was pulling me off him by the hair and throwing me across the floor. My head struck the side of a wooden workbench and the pain ripped through me.

Before I could recover he was standing over me and threatening to 'kick the shit' out of me. I braced myself by curling up like a hedgehog. But once his mate was back on his feet the first thing he did was force me onto my back and tell me that he was going to make me wish I had never been born.

'We're gonna fuck you good and proper,' Leather Jacket said. 'And after that we're gonna see to it that you end up in hospital with a body so broken you'll be stuck there for months.'

Leather Jacket's mate started to take off his pants and I felt a corkscrew twist in my gut.

Then the sound of a phone ringing stopped him and he looked up and pinned back his shoulders.

It was Leather Jacket's phone, and as he snatched it from his inside pocket he threw out a heavy sigh.

'Shit,' he said when he peered at the caller ID. 'I have to take this.'

He stepped across the room to answer the phone and his mate started swearing.

I lay there gasping for breath, the blood throbbing in my temples, while they put raping me on hold. It was surreal. Horrendous. Unbelievable.

I tried to get up but the shaven-headed perv put his shoe on my chest to stop me moving. He pressed down hard enough to make me squeal.

I rolled my head from side to side, looking for something within reach that I might be able to use as a weapon. There was nothing and I felt a crushing despair wash over me.

Leather Jacket ended his phone conversation and stepped back into my line of sight.

'Put your jeans back on,' he ordered his mate. 'We have to go.'

The other man took his shoe off my chest and grimaced.

'Are you crazy? What are you on about?'

'There's been a change of plan. So just do it.'

'Jesus, man. We haven't—'

'And we're not going to. So get a move on.'

'What about her?'

'We're leaving her here.'

I couldn't believe what I was hearing and I thought for a second that it was a wind-up, until the look of anger and disappointment on the other guy's face made me realise that this was really happening.

'You're one seriously lucky bitch,' he said to me as he pulled on his jeans. 'But it don't mean I won't get to have another crack at another time.'

The two men then hurried out of the workshop leaving me lying on the floor.

Every imaginable emotion began to churn inside me. Anger, fear, panic, relief . . .

I struggled to my feet and stood staring at the doorway for a good minute, expecting them to return to finish what they had started.

When I realised they weren't coming back I broke down in a paroxysm of tears.

39

Beth Chambers

I staggered outside, crying and clutching my stomach. The rain and cold air felt good against my face, which was burning up.

To my relief I found my bag on the ground just inside the entrance to the unit. I picked it up, plunged my hand inside and discovered that my attackers hadn't taken anything. Clearly theft hadn't been their motive.

Their intention had been to hurt and scare me, and I was willing to bet that Shapiro had paid them to do so. But then why had they suddenly fled before seeing it through? And who had Leather Jacket taken a call from?

I pulled out my phone as I stepped cautiously through the open gate onto the pavement. The street was still deserted. No sign of Leather Jacket and his mate, thank God.

I stood there on the pavement, clutching my phone and not knowing what to do with it. I was still in shock, shaking all over, feeling light-headed and dizzy.

Suddenly a bolt of nausea hit me, and I couldn't hold back the vomit that burst out of my mouth and into the gutter.

I wiped my mouth with a tissue and straightened up. My eyes were swimming with tears and it was hard to see the keys on my phone. But after a while I managed to tap out 999.

'I need the police,' I said in answer to the operator's question. 'I've been attacked.'

I gave them my name and location and told them my attackers had run off. And no, I didn't need an ambulance.

'Just stay where you are then, Miss Chambers. The police will be with you in a few minutes.'

I didn't want to stop there. I wanted to go home. But I knew that I had to hang on so that I could explain to the cops exactly what had happened.

I had the presence of mind to ring home and tell Mum I was going to be late. I didn't tell her why, though, and before she could ask I hung up.

The urge to break down in tears again right there in the street was almost unbearable, but I resisted. I was gradually regaining control of my senses, and as I did so a rush of thoughts and questions left me breathless.

Who were those men? Why did they target me? How did they know how to find me? Did one or both of them follow me from Clapham Junction? Or had they been waiting at the station along the road?

The police, when they arrived, had a bunch of other questions for me. I sat in the back of a patrol car to answer them and I was struck by the fact that it didn't seem to them like a huge deal. Was that because I hadn't been raped or badly beaten? Or was it because my bag hadn't been stolen?

A couple of detectives arrived. A man and a woman. I didn't know them, but they said they had heard of me. They made me go through it all again. This time I went into more detail. Told them what Leather Jacket had said to me.

278

We're going to make you pay for whatever you've done wrong.

No, I didn't know what he'd meant by that but I told them that I'd been threatened by Danny Shapiro, and that I was sure he was behind it.

'Are you prepared to make an official complaint about that, Miss Chambers?' the female detective asked me. She was plump and in her forties, with a face that seemed strangely out of balance.

'Is there any point?' I said. 'He'll only deny it and you'll never be able to prove it.'

I then went back into the workshop with the detectives and explained what had happened and where. They asked me if the men had touched anything, and I answered truthfully that I couldn't remember.

'And you're sure that you didn't know either of these men?' she asked.

'I'm positive,' I said. 'The one in the leather jacket pretended to know me to get my attention on the street.'

'So have you any idea what made them halt the attack on you and run away?'

I told her that I didn't, and I could see that she wasn't sure what to make of it. I couldn't blame her for that. I didn't know what to make of it myself.

The detectives made notes and took all my details but it was obvious to me that they would not be putting too much effort into finding the two men who had attacked me.

'We'll circulate their descriptions and check CCTV cameras around here, including those covering the station.'

I was asked again if I wanted to go to the hospital to be checked over but I said it would be a waste of time. I wasn't seriously hurt. My left cheek was sore and my stomach ached, but it could have been much worse.

They gave me a lift home and said they'd be in touch. I thought it unlikely that I'd hear from them again. Before the night was out they would no doubt be dealing with victims who were in a much worse state than I was.

My mother was looking out of the front window when the police car pulled up in front of the house. It was nine o'clock so I was hoping that she had already put Rosie to bed. I'd been wrestling with how much to tell Mum and how much to hold back. Before walking through the front door I decided to tell her I'd been the victim of a random attack.

I thought I'd be able to stick with that as I ran through what had happened. When the tears came again, though, my resolve began to slide into the insanity that was engulfing me.

I couldn't hold back. I told her about the threats from Shapiro and his enforcer, Frankie Bishop, and then about Tamara Roth and Peter Kline, and how I'd found out that Ethan was on Shapiro's payroll.

She struggled to take it all in and her hands balled into fists as she listened. She then spent the rest of the evening fretting over me and threatening to murder Danny Shapiro.

'You need to calm down, Mum,' I said. 'It's not good for your blood pressure. In any case I can't be sure he was behind it.'

A long hot bath helped to ease the soreness out of my muscles and made me feel half human again.

Meanwhile my mind continued to seethe with vivid images from inside that workshop, and with the thought of what would have happened to me if Leather Jacket's phone hadn't gone off when it did.

When I finally went to bed I curled myself into a ball, knees up to my chest. Yet I couldn't sleep. I rewound the whole awful experience in my head and played it from every angle.

It was as clear as a printed page that my attackers had been acting on orders.

We're going to make you pay for whatever you've done wrong.

And:

You'll get to keep your good looks and we'll just break a few bones.

Those statements were surely an obvious indication that they'd been told to give me a beating and that they didn't really know why. Raping me had been their own idea, an opportunity too good to miss.

I knew in my heart that Danny Shapiro had sent them. Who else could it have been? It was his way of stopping me from working up the story and revealing what I knew.

I let out a long, dramatic breath and reached for the phone on the bedside table. It was late, but I was certain he'd be up, either off his head on coke or screwing some whore.

'Hello, Beth,' Ethan said when he answered. 'I didn't expect to hear from you tonight.'

He sounded wide awake and coherent.

'Of course you didn't,' I said. 'You thought I'd be in hospital.'

'What?'

'Don't what me, Ethan. I was attacked by two men in the street on the way home from the press conference.'

'Jesus. Are you all right?'

'No, I'm not all right. And don't pretend you didn't know it was going to happen. They were sent by your friend Danny Shapiro.'

'I swear I knew nothing about it, Beth.'

'Well, I don't believe you.'

'Look, just forget about that for a second and tell me what happened. Please. How bad was it and did you call the police?'

'Of course I called them,' I said. 'But I don't believe for one minute that they'll find the fuckers.'

'So what did they do to you?'

'Why don't you ask Shapiro? He'll know. That's why I'm calling. I want you to tell him from me that if his aim was to scare me into dropping the story then it hasn't worked. In fact I'm now going to double my efforts to make sure the truth about his alibi gets out. And then . . .'

A sob reared up in my throat suddenly and I couldn't finish the rest of what I wanted to say, so I ended the call and switched off my phone.

My heart was thumping in my chest, and hot tears of rage were streaming down my cheeks.

I was glad I'd made the call, though. I'd needed to get it off my chest now, tonight, as I knew that in the cold light of day I might chicken out.

I could already hear a tiny voice in my head telling me that I should throw in the towel – because the next time Shapiro's thugs came for me I probably wouldn't get to walk away in one piece.

40

Ethan Cain

Cain poured himself a large brandy in the hope that it would help to get him through the night. Beth's call had given him something else to feel guilty about, on top of the fact that she had seen him with Frankie Bishop. That alone was enough to get him royally fucked. He just had to hope that she kept it to herself, at least until he had a chance to talk to her.

Meanwhile, this whole wretched business was getting messier and more dangerous by the minute. It was also making him feel increasingly vulnerable and powerless, and he had no control over the events that were impacting on his life.

This attack on Beth was yet another shocking development. It didn't sound like she had been seriously hurt and that was a relief. But was that because Danny had told his goons just to put the frighteners on her? Would he get them to put her in hospital next time?

Cain looked at his watch. It was midnight and he decided it was too late to call Danny to confront him. He'd arranged to see him tomorrow anyway so he would raise it then.

Nevertheless he was eager to know more about the attack on Beth so he called CID in Peckham. He managed to speak to one of the detectives who attended the scene and she filled him in. But what she told him left him confused. It didn't make sense that the two attackers had suddenly fled after one of them received a phone call. What in Christ's name was all that about?

Cain paced the floor of his living room, his nerves shrieking in spite of the brandy. A feeling of despair clawed at him as he tried to focus his mind on what he should do. It wasn't only Beth he had to worry about. The investigation into Peter Kline's disappearance was now well under way. His house had been searched and his neighbours questioned. Luckily only one of them had seen the two men walking up his driveway and she hadn't been able to give a detailed description. But maybe someone else would come forward, someone who could ID him and Frankie Bishop. Then he really would be up shit creek.

41

Beth Chambers

I woke up in a spasm of panic. My eyes were wet and I realised I must have been crying in my sleep.

A peek at the clock on the bedside table told me it was 5 a.m., which meant I'd only slept for about two hours.

It had been a hot and horrible night. I hadn't been able to stop thinking about what had happened to me, and when I did drop off my two attackers appeared in a nightmare.

I could already feel the anxiety stirring in my gut so I was forced to remind myself that I'd actually had a lucky escape. I could have been waking up in hospital having been gang-raped and badly disfigured. That was the thought I had to cling to. The positive spin. It was the only thing I could use to resist the pull of a dark depression.

I decided to have a shower before going downstairs in the hope that it would make me feel better. It did, but only a little. One of the detectives had warned me that the shock would take several days at least to leave my system, and I could well believe that.

To my surprise my mother was already up, hunched over a

mug of tea at the breakfast bar. She hadn't got much sleep either, and she looked terrible. She was obviously badly shaken and worried about me, and I was beginning to wish that I hadn't told her the whole story.

'I can't believe you're going to work,' she said. 'You should stay at home. You can't possibly be in the right frame of mind to do your job.'

'I've got to, Mum,' I said. 'I can't sit here all day feeling sorry for myself. I think it's best to carry on as though it didn't happen.'

'But it did happen, Beth, and you can't just shrug it off. What if it happens again and the next time they really hurt you?'

'I can't let the fear of that stop me doing what I do, Mum.'

'You're not thinking straight, my love. And you're not thinking about Rosie. Being a mother comes before being a reporter.'

'So what are you saying – that I should stop chasing the story and keep quiet?'

'That's part of it,' she said. 'But you need to reveal the truth about Ethan as well. He can't be allowed to get away with it just because he's Rosie's father. He's as bad as the rest of them and you have no idea if he'll do something despicable to stop you talking.'

'He wouldn't hurt me, Mum.'

'You can't be sure of that, Beth, and you know it.'

My mother's words really hit home. Their impact was almost physical. I tried to take a breath, but it was as if the air in the room had vanished.

She had made me realise that I hadn't fully considered the likely consequences of taking on Shapiro and his notorious firm. The collateral damage could be considerable, especially now that I knew Ethan was working with the enemy. I'd been so obsessed with pursuing the story that I hadn't given enough thought to my own daughter. That was unforgivable and I felt ashamed of myself.

The guilt expanded in my chest when Rosie got up and I held her in my arms.

'I get it, Mum,' I said. 'You're right. I've been selfish. This little pumpkin should come first.'

I thought about it on the train to London Bridge, and by the time I got to the office I had it all worked out. I knew exactly what I was going to say to Grant Scott and then to the police. I'd reveal what Peter Kline had told me but I wouldn't say I'd posed as a police officer. And I'd own up to making the anonymous call.

The trouble was I didn't get to say any of it because Grant spoke first when I entered the newsroom, and what he told me changed everything in an instant.

'I've been trying to contact you, Beth,' he said, his voice shrill with excitement. 'Why haven't you been answering your phone?'

I took my mobile from my bag, saw there were two missed calls.

'Sorry,' I said. 'I've been in another world this morning. Didn't hear it ring. Why? Is there a problem?'

He held up a sheet of paper. 'We just received this from Callum Shapiro's lawyer. He asked us to pass it to you when you turned up. Apparently he rang your home number but your mother said you'd left for work.'

'What is it?'

'It's a prison visiting order. The old gangster wants you to go and see him.'

42

Beth Chambers

To say that I was stunned would be a huge understatement. I was absolutely thunderstruck.

Callum Shapiro had languished in prison for almost six years. And now all of a sudden he wanted me to drop by for a chat. Jesus.

'His lawyer says it'll be a personal visit and the Ministry of Justice is insisting you won't be there as a journalist,' Grant said. 'You'll have to sign a document agreeing not to make public any aspects of the conversation, which is a damn shame as far as I'm concerned.'

I was confused, intrigued, gobsmacked. What the hell was Shapiro going to say when I sat across a table from him in the visitors' hall at Belmarsh?

'Have you got any idea what it's about?' Grant said.

I shook my head. 'Not a clue. I've never been in contact with the man.'

'But you've written a lot about him and his son.'

'Of course. And I could understand it if he wanted to arrange for me to do an interview. But a personal visit! I don't get it.'

He handed me the visiting order. I scanned it quickly and said, 'This is for this morning. Ten o'clock.'

'So I noticed. He's obviously very anxious to meet you.'

'Has this been planned? I mean, it can take ages for these things to be set up.'

'I asked the lawyer about that. He said Shapiro's request was a spur-of-the-moment thing and has been fast-tracked. Apparently the old geezer still has a few influential friends on the outside and strings were pulled.'

'This is weird. I'm not even sure I should go.'

'Well, if I were you, I wouldn't pass up the chance to speak to him. Whatever he wants to tell you it's bound to be worth hearing in your capacity as a crime reporter, even if you have to keep it to yourself.'

I came close to telling him then about the attack on me and about the threats from Shapiro's son. But I didn't. It would take too long, and be a distraction.

'So you don't mind if I go?' I said.

'Don't be daft. I've already arranged for a taxi to take you. It's downstairs waiting.'

Some of Britain's most dangerous criminals are held in Belmarsh prison, a bleak and oppressive place in Woolwich, south-east London.

A ball of heat was building up in my chest as I sat in the back of the taxi taking me there. I still found it hard to believe that this was actually happening. I was going to meet the notorious underworld legend Callum Shapiro, the man who, according to my mother, had arranged for someone to murder my own stepfather.

I had mixed feelings about meeting him. On the one hand I was giddy with excitement and my curiosity desperately needed sating.

On the other hand, I knew it was going to be an emotional experience. And I was probably going to find it hard to rein in my anger.

Already a thousand questions were buzzing around in my head like bees in a jar. But would he answer them? Would I even be allowed to ask them?

I just couldn't fathom why I'd been effectively summoned to the prison. I could only surmise that he wanted to get something off his chest – and that it related in some way to the events of the past few days.

43

Beth Chambers

I joined a bunch of other visitors going through the security checks at the prison. The X-ray machine, the metal detectors, the pat-down.

My bag was put into a locker and I was taken to one side and asked to sign a document agreeing not to write about my conversation with Callum Shapiro. This was no great surprise since it was hellishly difficult for journalists to arrange face-to-face interviews with inmates, especially Category A ones like Shapiro.

Eventually I was allowed through to the visitors' hall and directed towards a table with two chairs facing each other. A minute later the prisoners started to trundle in and I felt my stomach tying itself in knots.

I suddenly thought about my mother and wondered if I should have called to tell her that I was coming here. Would Shapiro's lawyer have identified himself and explained why he was trying to reach me? Probably not, since I hadn't received a call from her. And if I had told her perhaps she would have tried to talk me out of coming.

I looked around at the other visitors. Most of them were women who were here to see their husbands, sons and boyfriends. I doubted that any of them were as nervous as I was. They knew why they were here and what to expect. I didn't.

I recognised Callum Shapiro the moment he entered the room. He recognised me too. His face slid into a half-smile as he walked towards me.

My first impression was that he looked old and withered, a shadow of the man I'd watched for weeks in the dock at the Old Bailey. He was no longer tall and stocky. Now he was thin, emaciated almost, and he walked with a stoop.

When he reached me he stood for a moment looking down, his colourless eyes seemingly searching my face for something. I stared back, conscious of the lump in my throat.

His shirt was open at the neck and his sleeves were rolled up, revealing dark tattoos scrawled on his arms. His white hair was long and pushed back behind his ears.

'Hello, Miss Chambers,' he said, his voice as scratchy as a seventy-eight flat disc record. 'I'd like to thank you for coming.'

My body went rigid as a board and I felt a chill run up my spine.

'So what's this about?' I said, trying not to sound at all friendly.

He pulled out the chair, sat down, seemed perfectly relaxed. Unlike me.

He leaned forward on the table, made a tent with his fingers. His heavily wrinkled face was so pale it was almost transparent.

'I must say you're a very attractive young lady, Miss Chambers. Or may I call you Bethany?'

His mouth split into an easy smile, showing tobacco-stained teeth.

I sat there in a state of pure, simple shock, wondering what the hell this was all about.

'I don't care what you call me,' I said. 'So long as you get to the point quickly and tell me why I'm here.'

'All in good time,' he said. 'First I want you to know that I really do appreciate you coming at such short notice. I had to pull in some favours to make it happen so quickly.'

'I guessed that. But why the sudden urge to meet me? You must know from your son that I'm not one of your biggest fans.'

'I wouldn't expect you to be. I'm not the sort of person people look up to and idolise. At least not these days I'm not.'

'You can say that again.'

His smile widened as he studied me from beneath his big, bushy eyebrows.

I wasn't sure what to make of him. He certainly wasn't what I had expected. I'd imagined a large, threatening figure with dark, impenetrable eyes and a hard face: in other words a cold-blooded monster.

Instead it was like sitting with a weak old man in a care home. Was he really the same ruthless villain who had terrorised south London for so many years? The same man believed responsible for so many murders? It hardly seemed possible.

He sat back in his chair, looked around as though to make sure that nobody was listening. The table to our left was empty. The one to our right was occupied by a young Asian man and a woman who was probably his mother.

'I suggest you get on with it, Mr Shapiro,' I said. 'I want you to tell me why you invited me here.'

He leaned forward again and his face slipped into a grimace.

'I asked you here, Bethany, because there are things I need to say to you before it's too late.'

'What things?'

'Well, first off you have to promise me that you won't repeat any of what I'm about to tell you.'

I shook my head. 'No promises.'

'Then I'll just deny I said it.'

'That's up to you.'

He shrugged, and then to my surprise carried on, seemingly undeterred. He spoke slowly, measuring his words.

'I'll start with my son, Danny,' he said. 'I want you to know that despite what you think he did not murder his ex-wife. Believe me, I would know if he had.'

'Then you must also know that he gave a false alibi. And that your ex-lover Tamara Roth is covering for him.'

Shapiro nodded. 'Of course I know that. But he had no choice. You see, he did drop in on Megan on Friday evening, because he wanted to talk to her about her threats to blackmail him. He didn't harm her, though, and when he left to go home she was very much alive. But the next morning when he heard what had happened he panicked because he had no alibi and he knew he'd be stitched up by the police if they didn't find the real killer. So he got Tamara to help him.'

I shook my head again. 'I find that very hard to believe. And even if it were true I can't think why you would tell me.'

'I'm telling you because you seem to be on a mission to get my son convicted of a crime he didn't commit.'

I had to laugh. 'Is that why you got me here – to plead your son's case for him?'

'It's partly the reason.'

'Well, you've wasted your time and mine. And for your information, I'll be informing the police of what you've told me.'

'I think you might change your mind after you hear the rest of what I've got to say.'

'Is that because you're going to threaten me?' I said. 'Because in case you haven't heard I've already been threatened by your son, and he even sent two men to beat me up.'

'Ah, but they didn't go through with it, did they?' he said.

I felt a rush of blood to my head. 'You know about that?'

He nodded. 'I phoned Danny last night. He told me that he'd arranged for you to be roughed up to make sure you couldn't pursue the story. It was a stupid move and I told him to call the lads off. I gather the message got through just in time.'

I was too shocked to react. So that was why the two men had run off!

I felt the weight of my jaw on my chest, and I had to swallow to clear the lump in my throat.

'You probably think I'm insane to be telling you this stuff,' he said. 'But there is a method to my madness. You see I reckon this situation is now dangerously out of control, and unless you and Danny declare a truce I fear you'll destroy each other. I can't let that happen for both your sakes.'

'This surely has to be a joke,' I said. 'I mean, why would you care what happens to me? And you can forget about a truce between me and your maniac son. I'm a journalist, not a rival gangster.'

For several seconds his eyes drilled into mine, unblinking. Then he cleared his throat. 'I'm going to pass on a secret to you that I'd always intended to take to my grave. But in the circumstances I think you need to know because I believe it will make a difference to how you and Danny feel about each other. And I hope you'll then decide to use your journalistic skills to help him rather than hurt him.'

Unbelievable. As far as I was concerned the conversation had now gone from the slightly bizarre to the totally ridiculous.

'I think that being in prison has turned you into a raving lunatic, Mr Shapiro. Why would I even contemplate helping your son after what he's done to me?'

Shapiro blew out his cheeks and brought his eyebrows together. 'For the simple reason that he's your half-brother, Bethany. And I'm sure you wouldn't want to see him end up in here for the next twenty-odd years.'

I gulped a breath and felt my eyeballs pop out on stalks.

'That's right, my love,' Shapiro said, leaning halfway across the table towards me. 'It means I'm your daddy. Your real daddy. And I can't tell you how good it is to see you again after all this time.'

44

Danny Shapiro

Danny was the first to arrive at the house in Bermondsey. Frankie and Ethan Cain had let him know by text that they were on their way.

He was curious to know why the copper had asked for the meet. Cain hadn't wanted to say over the phone, and Danny was hoping that it wasn't more bad news. He was still feeling traumatised by what his father had told him last night. He had a half-sister, for Christ's sake. None other than Bethany fucking Chambers. Christ.

He'd spent a sleepless night trying to get his head around it and he still couldn't. All these years and he didn't know. All these years Callum had kept it from him.

He had known about the old man's affairs, of course. And he'd heard rumours that he had fathered an illegitimate child. But Callum had always denied them, and there was never any evidence to the contrary.

The affair with Peggy Chambers had apparently lasted almost six years and began when Danny was just three. It ended when

Bethany was five because Danny's mother found out and Callum was forced to choose.

Danny tried to cast his mind back to that period. Had his father said or done anything to suggest that he had a secret love child and that she lived just down the road in Peckham?

It was too long ago to remember. And it wasn't as if he saw much of his dad in those days. He was always off doing business somewhere and trying to stay one step ahead of the law.

'In the end I couldn't leave your mother,' Callum had said. 'So we ended the relationship and I walked away. Peggy and I agreed to go our separate ways and I'd have no contact with Bethany. I did help financially until she remarried. It was the least I could do.'

Danny knew that the secret would probably never have come out if his half-sister had been anyone other than Bethany Chambers.

'I'm telling you because I can't let you hurt her, Danny,' Callum had said. 'I would never forgive myself.'

And then the old man had dropped another bomb. He was going to confess all to Chambers as well in the hope he could persuade her to turn a blind eye to what she'd found out. Danny had lost his temper then, yelling down the phone that it would be a huge mistake. But Callum had insisted that he was going to do it and would be inviting her to the prison today.

'Nothing good can come of it,' Danny had told him.

'I think you're wrong, son. I think if you both know the truth it'll stop this thing ending badly.'

'It's under control, Dad. I've told you. She doesn't have the evidence to bring me down.'

'Maybe she doesn't have it yet, son. But that doesn't mean she won't get it.'

Danny had continued to put up a fierce argument, but his father had made up his mind and there was no budging him. It got to the point where Danny was about to hang up out of sheer bloody frustration.

That was when his father said, 'There's something else you need to know, Danny boy. It'll help explain why I'm determined to do this.'

He then made his son privy to yet another secret. A secret that was just as momentous, and just as difficult to come to terms with.

It was thanks to Danny's father that Beth Chambers wasn't in the hospital. After their conversation on the phone last night, Danny had called Frankie Bishop, who in turn had phoned the two lads tasked with giving her a hiding. Bishop had phoned back later to say that he had got to them just in time.

'She was slapped around a bit, but no serious harm was done to her,' Bishop had said.

Danny hadn't told Bishop why he'd had a change of heart, but it was the first thing Bishop asked when he arrived at the house.

'It's been bugging me all night, boss. I thought you wanted the bitch out of the picture for a while.'

Danny had thought long and hard about how much of what his father had told him he should share. It was a difficult one because he didn't want people to know and yet it was bound to get out eventually once Chambers herself knew.

He'd decided to tell Bishop about Chambers being his half-sister. For the time being he was going to keep his father's other secret to himself.

Bishop was floored by the news, but it actually made him laugh.

'That's the weirdest thing I've heard in years, boss. You and the gobby reporter have the same father. Fuck me, you couldn't make it up.'

'It's not funny, Frankie. The bitch is out to screw me, and my dad says I've got to be nice to her.'

Bishop couldn't stop smiling. 'Well, he's right, ain't he, boss? Beth Chambers is family now. And you've always moaned about not having a family. As she's your little sister you'll be expected to look out for her.'

Danny was furious with Bishop for acting like it was a joke. 'This is serious shit, Frankie. It's not something to be laughed at.'

'Oh, come on, boss. It doesn't have to be the end of life as you know it. Besides, it's her I feel sorry for. The poor cow won't be dancing a jig to the news that Danny Shapiro, hotshot London gangster, is her older brother.'

Danny felt a wave of anger course through his body, and Frankie would have felt the full force of it if it hadn't been for the sound of the doorbell.

'That'll be Cain,' Danny said through gritted teeth. 'Let him in and not a word about this other business.'

Cain was wearing the same suit he'd had on the day before and was looking pretty rough. There were dark half-moons under his eyes and his complexion had a sickly hue.

'So what's up, Ethan?' Danny said, looking at his watch. 'I've got a lot on this morning so I hope this is not a waste of my time.'

Cain poked a thumb at Bishop. 'I said I needed to talk to you in private, Danny. What I have to say is for your ears only.'

'Don't be a twat, Ethan. I've got no secrets from Frankie. So just tell me what's got you all excited.'

Cain looked at Bishop, who crossed his arms and gave a wry smile. Then he turned back to Danny, shrugged his shoulders, and took several sheets of folded-up paper from his inside pocket.

300

'I want you to see these,' he said, handing them to Danny.

'What are they?'

'They're extracts from Megan's phone records going back five years. I've highlighted a particular phone number and the name of the person it belongs to. I've also listed some of the text messages that passed between that person and Megan. They clearly reveal that she was having an affair while married to you.'

Danny glanced down at the top page, noted the name that was printed in bold black letters and felt the air lock in his chest.

'The guy was listed on Megan's old phone as BF,' Cain said.

As Danny read speedily through the typed-up text messages a sick feeling washed through him.

Megan: *Hi, babe. Filming's due to finish early. Fancy meeting up for a quickie before I go home?*

BF: *Sure thing. My place at 4. Let yourself in.*

Megan: *Danny's gone to see old man at Belmarsh. Can you come over?*

BF: *'Course. But you need to be careful. If Danny finds out I'm a dead man.*

Megan: *He won't find out, babe. He's too busy playing at being Al Capone.*

BF: *I've still got a stiffy from last night. You are a dirty bitch.*

Danny felt a cry in his throat but he refused to let it out. Instead he dropped Megan's phone records onto the floor and as he stared across the room, his eyes sparkled like flames.

Bishop stared back. He had unfolded his arms and they now hung stiffly at his sides. His fists were clenched. His eyes were huge and anxious. And a muscle twitched in his neck.

His guilty posture added to the weight of evidence against him as far as Danny was concerned. The back-to-front initials on the text messages. The familiar mobile phone number. The memory of how he had always been one of the few people to say nice things about Megan.

Now Danny understood why. The bastard had been screwing her.

'I trusted you, Frankie,' he said, stepping towards him. 'And you betrayed me.'

Bishop held up his hands. 'Look, boss. You can't believe—'

'What can't I believe, Frankie? The evidence of my own fucking eyes.' He pointed to the sheets of paper on the floor. 'It's all there in black and white. The phone calls. The text messages. Are you actually going to deny that you were fucking Megan behind my back?'

Bishop drew a hand across his forehead and through his hair. Danny could see he was struggling to find something to say that would defuse the situation.

'It was a long time ago, boss,' he said. 'At the time you were shagging around yourself. Megan knew it. So why does it have to be a huge deal now?'

Danny's eyes blazed with a ferocious fury. He switched his gaze to Cain. The detective blinked warily and swallowed.

'You hear that, Ethan?' Danny said. 'The two-faced cunt doesn't think there's any reason for me to get upset.'

Danny was beside himself. Each intake of breath felt sharp in his lungs. He got to within a couple of feet of Bishop and stabbed an accusing finger at him.

'I took you on when you came out of prison, you slag. I can't believe that was how you decided to pay me back.'

Bishop took a step back, palms out.

'It's all in the past and trust me it didn't mean anything.'

It was like throwing petrol onto a raging fire. Danny gave a loud roar and charged. He seized Bishop by the throat and pushed him back against the wall, before smashing his forehead into his mouth. The contact was solid and full of pent-up emotion.

Bishop yelled in pain and grabbed Danny's arms. But Danny held on and rammed his knee into the other man's pubic bone.

Bishop was by far the bigger and stronger of the two, and he used his weight to pull Danny sideways. They both hit the deck with a loud thud and Danny lost his grip on Bishop's throat. They rolled across the floor as one, hands, elbows, feet bumping into the furniture and walls.

Danny managed to drive two punches into his opponent's stomach but they lacked power because he was too close. He then made the mistake of trying to poke his fingers into Bishop's right eye. He left himself open and Bishop punished him by shoving the heel of his hand against his chin.

Danny's teeth smashed together and a white-hot pain exploded in his head. His body went limp with shock, and Bishop seized the opportunity to struggle to his feet.

'Stay down, Danny,' he shouted. 'I don't want to have to hurt you.'

But Danny was enveloped in a red mist. Through it he could see Megan and Bishop having sex on the marital bed. His wife and 'The Nutter'. Both of them laughing at him. Taking the piss. Betraying his trust. It was something he could never forget or forgive, no matter that it was a long time ago.

Anger poured through his veins like liquid fire as he stared at Bishop. In a straight fight he knew he was no match for the burly psycho, but Danny didn't let that stop him as he dragged himself up.

'Let's talk, boss,' Bishop said, spitting blood through his teeth. 'Please. This ain't necessary.'

Danny took no notice. He lunged forward, fists flying. Bishop was ready for him and wheeled away, then swung a right hook that caught Danny on the left temple.

The blow sent him crashing into the wall where his elbow dented the plasterboard. Somehow he stayed on his feet, twisted his body, and threw himself at Bishop again.

This time the big man kicked out, catching Danny's ankle, hard enough to unbalance him. Danny managed to grab hold of Bishop's jacket and pull him down with him. They landed on top of a glass coffee table that shattered beneath them.

Bishop was the first to gain the initiative by throwing himself across Danny's stomach, pinning him to the floor.

'There's only so much shit I'll take from you,' he shrieked as he aimed his fist at Danny's face.

Danny turned his head so the blow made contact with his cheekbone.

Bishop raised his arm again, ready to deliver another punch, but that was when Cain joined in the fray. The detective seized Bishop in a headlock and snapped his body backwards.

Danny gasped as the pressure left his stomach and he wasted no time getting up. Cain still had a firm hold on Bishop, who was thrashing about like a shark out of water.

Danny showed no mercy. He went for Bishop like he was a punch bag. Several hard blows to the face. Then the stomach. Then the face again.

Cain released his grip and Bishop collapsed on the floor. Danny delivered a sharp kick to his chest and then another to the back of his head.

'That's enough,' Cain yelled. 'You don't want to kill the fucker here.'

He pulled Danny away, and Bishop rolled onto his side, blood-stained spittle drooling from his mouth.

'You're finished, you bastard.' Danny spat the words at him. 'I never want to see your arse again around here.'

Bishop may have taken a severe beating but he still wasn't out for the count. He pushed himself up, wiped a sleeve across his mouth, stared at Danny.

'You can't do this,' he said. 'You owe me. I've served you well. I've got a stake in the business.'

Danny shook his head. 'I don't owe you a thing. You came to me with nothing and I looked after you. And then you showed your appreciation by banging my wife.'

Bishop started to speak, but Danny raised a hand to stop him.

'Don't even bother. I don't want to hear it. I just want you gone.'

Bishop groaned out loud as he rose steadily from the floor. But he had to put his hand against the wall for a couple of seconds to hold himself firm.

'Don't think I'm just gonna let you do this to me,' he said. 'You haven't seen the last of me.' Then he turned to Cain. 'And neither have you, copper. I'm gonna make you regret what you did.'

Danny pointed a trembling finger at him.

'If you know what's good for you you'll fuck off back to Southampton. You're not welcome on this manor and if I see you again I'll finish what I started. So just count yourself lucky and piss off.'

Danny braced himself in case Bishop had another pop. Instead Bishop gave a slow shake of his head and decided the odds were stacked against him.

Danny watched him move towards the door and realised that he was going to have to take the man out, otherwise he was crazy enough to come back seeking revenge. This wasn't the right time or place, though. It'd be too messy. The neighbours had probably heard the racket and they might have seen the three of them arriving. He would look to sort it before the day was out.

The front door slammed shut and Danny breathed a sigh of relief. He turned to Cain, who had dropped onto the sofa and was breathing heavily through his mouth.

'Thanks for stepping in there, Ethan. I'm not as handy with my fists as I used to be.'

Cain shrugged. 'No problem. He's not the easiest of opponents.'

'You're right about that. I can see why you didn't want to talk to me in front of him. It was bound to kick off.'

'Actually, Danny, the business about the affair was only part of it,' Cain said. 'There was something else I wanted to flag up and I can do it now that he's gone.'

Danny sat on the armchair, his mind in utter disarray.

'So fire away,' he said. 'What is it?'

The detective lit up a cigarette before responding, drawing the smoke deep into his lungs.

'Those messages relating to the affair were on Megan's old phone,' he said. 'But Frankie's mobile number also showed up on the one she's been using for the past year. However, they only called each other twice in all that time and it was just two weeks ago.'

Danny inclined his head thoughtfully. 'Are you saying you think they might have got back together?'

Cain shook his head. 'Not at all. What I'm thinking is that she might well have called him to ask for money in return for her silence over the affair.'

'So he could have been targeted just like I was?'

Cain nodded. 'And it follows that he could also be the person who killed her. But if I go after him there's no telling what he'll say about us. Right now I'm the only one on the team who's put it together. I think it's best that it stays that way.'

45

Beth Chambers

It took Callum Shapiro fifteen minutes to tell me his story. I listened without interrupting, entranced by what he had to say.

About meeting my mother on the salad stall where she worked back then. About the start of the affair. Her getting pregnant. Me being born.

For almost six years he was unfaithful to his wife, Danny's late mother. And for five years he was the man I called daddy, who popped into our house when he could, which wasn't very often. And then his wife found out and gave him an ultimatum.

'It can't be true,' I said when he finally stopped talking and waited for me to respond.

Or was it that I just didn't want it to be?

'I'm sorry, Bethany,' he said. 'But it *is* the truth, however unpalatable that may be. You and your mum meant the world to me, but so did my wife and son. I had to choose and I did. It wasn't easy and I've often thought I made the wrong choice.'

My thoughts raced, my mind felt numb. For a few seconds I was lost somewhere deep inside myself. I could feel a pulse pounding in my head, a cold sweat breaking out on my forehead.

'The last time I saw you I gave you a present,' he said, his voice breaking through the turmoil in my head. 'I named him Olly because Oliver is my middle name.'

My heart began to hammer then and I had to take a breath to slow it down.

Olly. My God.

There was only one way he could have known about my precious, bedraggled little teddy.

'You were never supposed to find out, Beth,' he said. 'That was the deal your mother and I struck when I ended it. Please tell her from me that I'm sorry. But I had to tell both you and Danny. It was the only way to sort this mess and get you to stop gunning for each other.'

My eyes brimmed with tears and I blinked them away. My internal voice clicked in, filling my head with questions, igniting an emotional whirlwind that paralysed my senses.

I looked around, thinking everyone would be staring at me. But they weren't. They were engrossed in their own conspiratorial conversations. Talking about their own fractured lives. Not caring that my own life had been turned on its head.

Then again, why would anyone care except me? I was the one who had to live with the pain and shame of being the illegitimate sprog of Callum Shapiro, the man who'd made a living out of murder, robbery and extortion. The man who'd paid someone to shoot Tony Hunter.

'You killed my stepfather,' I blurted out.

A shake of the head. 'No, Beth, I didn't. I would never have done that to you – or Peggy.'

'But she says you did.'

'Well, it's not true, Beth. It hurt me that I couldn't convince her of that when she came to see me. I swore blind that I didn't do it. But she believed the rumours and I think it was partly because she wanted to hate me for leaving her.'

'So are you going to deny that you warned him off and threatened him?'

'No, because when I did that it was for his own good. Tony Hunter was treading on too many toes. Upsetting too many faces. I told him and his crew that they were being too ambitious. But they wouldn't listen. They wanted to break into the big time. It got to the point where something had to be done. I told my lot to lay off Tony but I didn't tell them why. And I never had to explain myself because the Russians took him out.'

There suddenly didn't seem to be enough air in the room to breathe. He had given me another thought to grapple with; another decision to make as to whether I believed him.

'I won't deny that I killed people, Beth,' he said. 'And I got my guys to carry out killings on my behalf. That's why I'm in here. But I promise you that your stepfather was not one of my victims. I knew him and believe it or not I liked him. We actually had a drink one time and he told me about you. How great you were and how much he loved your mum. He was a good man and that gave me comfort. So there was no fucking way I would have had him shot.'

Neither of us spoke for several seconds. I tried to run it all through my head and make sense of what I'd been told, but there was too much to process. Too much to accept.

My mind drifted through memories. I remembered the tall man with the husky voice who used to bring me presents and tell me that he loved me. I remembered the times I'd pressed my mother to tell me more about him, when she would only say that it was best I didn't know.

310

Now I knew why she'd kept the truth from me. She was ravaged by guilt and shame. Hadn't wanted me to know that I'd come from the sperm of an infamous gangster.

'What did Peggy say about me?' Shapiro said as if reading my mind. 'I'm sure you asked her a lot of questions over the years.'

I noticed suddenly that his eyes were awash with unshed tears and it gave me quite a shock.

I shifted my gaze away from them and said, 'She told me that I was the result of an illicit affair with a married man. She said you just walked out one day and never came back. She would never tell me who you were and not in my wildest dreams would I have guessed it was you.'

'Are you disappointed, Beth?'

I lifted my eyes back to his face, saw what looked like a mixture of pain and regret etched into his features.

'I'm gutted, to be honest,' I said. 'But I'm glad I know. And I'm glad you stopped coming to see me when you did. I hate to think what my life would have been like if my mum had stayed with you. I'd have probably ended up like your son.'

He sighed hard through his nose, and when he next spoke his voice sounded pathetic and threadbare.

'Danny really ain't as bad as you think. I brought him into the firm against his mother's wishes. He didn't want to be like me but I didn't give him a choice. That's why I'm asking you not to stir things up with what you know. The alibi he's given is the only thing that's stopping the police stitching him up for murder. He's got himself into a real pickle, but he shouldn't go down for something he didn't do.'

'That's his own fault,' I said. 'I shouldn't have to compromise myself or withhold information to help him out.'

'You'd be helping yourself too, Beth. And your family. If you

311

leave Danny alone then he'll leave you alone. No more threats and unpleasant surprises.'

I shook my head. 'This is blackmail. And I don't see any reason why I should go along with it.'

'He's your half-brother, Beth.'

'So you say. But I don't think I'll ever be able to see him that way.'

'Then do it for me?'

I gave him a disdainful look. 'Now you're going from the sublime to the ridiculous. You abandoned me and my mother when I was five years old. Now you want me to do you a favour. Don't you think that's a bit much?'

He gnawed at his bottom lip for a few moments and seemed to come to a decision. Leaning forward across the table again, his watery eyes were determined to hold mine.

'Then look at it this way, Beth,' he said. 'You'll be fulfilling your father's dying wish. You see, I have bowel cancer and they've given me six months to live.'

46

Ethan Cain

After leaving the house in Bermondsey, Cain headed back to the incident room. His mind was racing, buzzing, throbbing. The brawl with Frankie Bishop had shaken him up, as had 'The Nutter's threat to get his own back.

He felt like he was caught up in a never-ending nightmare. It had been bad enough worrying about what Beth was going to do with what she had found out about him. Now he had fallen foul of a genuine psychopath. A man he'd seen commit a brutal murder like it was as easy as swatting a fly.

Best-case scenario now would be for Danny to have Bishop killed. Otherwise the guy was a loose cannon. If he was hauled in and questioned about Megan's murder there'd be nothing to stop him blabbing. And if he was allowed to walk away then he posed a serious threat to everyone.

Cain wished now that he'd refused to tell Danny about Megan's affair in front of Bishop. But Danny had insisted, and deep down Cain had got a sadistic pleasure from putting Bishop on the spot. It was like payback for all the times Bishop had teased and humiliated him about the drugs and young prossies.

Nevertheless it was a cheap thrill that had been over in the blink of an eye. It would have been much smarter to have told Danny in private so that he could have confronted Bishop and got rid of him at the same time and in the same place.

Now the bastard was out there having been cast adrift by the firm. He was angry and unpredictable, and literally spitting blood.

He would also be plotting his revenge. Of that Cain had no doubt.

As soon as Cain got back to the incident room, DCI Redwood called him into his office.

'Sit down, Ethan,' he said. 'I need to ask you some questions about your ex-wife.'

Cain felt the blood stir in his veins as he folded himself into the chair facing his boss.

'What do you want to know, guv?'

'You can start by telling me when you last saw her.'

Cain chose not to mention the meeting he'd had with her before the press conference and he hoped to God that Redwood didn't know about it.

'I saw her a few days ago when I picked up my daughter. You know about the access arrangement.'

'I do. But I take it you've spoken to Chambers on the phone since then.'

A sixth sense told Cain to beware of falling into a trap.

'As a matter of fact she called me last night, guv.'

Redwood nodded and Cain realised that the bastard already knew that. He'd been trying to catch him out.

'I assume this was after she was mugged near her home in Peckham.'

Cain forced a frown. 'How did you know?'

'I saw an overnight report,' Redwood said. 'Made some inquiries and discovered that you rang Peckham CID late last night to ask about it.'

'I see. Well, she was pretty cut up. She wanted to talk to someone about it.'

Redwood pinched the bridge of his nose. 'She told the officer who dealt with it that she had no idea who attacked her. Is that what she told you?'

'Pretty much.'

'But did she also mention that Danny Shapiro had made threats against her earlier?'

Cain's throat felt dry and constricted, but he tried desperately not to show his nerves by swallowing.

'She did mention that and I assured her we'd look into it.'

'So when were you going to tell me, Ethan?'

It sounded more like an accusation than a question.

'This morning, guv. But I've only just got in.'

'That's right. Remind me where you've been.'

'I rang in with a message. Woke up with a migraine and couldn't get out of bed until the tablets kicked in.'

Redwood pursed his lips. 'I didn't get the message.'

Cain could feel his armpits getting damp with sweat, and a tight coil of panic was twisting in his gut. The boss was suspicious of him for some reason. He couldn't have made it more bloody obvious.

'Anyway, back to Bethany Chambers,' Redwood said. 'I want you to tell me if you've given her any information off the record about the case.'

'Of course not, guv. I would never do that. And I gave you my word.'

'So you didn't tell her that Tamara Roth was providing Shapiro with an alibi?'

'No, I didn't.'

'Well, someone did. And you're the most likely suspect for obvious reasons, Ethan.'

Cain felt his eyes bulge. 'I resent that, guv. I told you before that I've always been careful about what I say to her. I'm not stupid.'

'Then how come she seems to know more about what's fucking going on than we do?'

'What makes you say that?'

'For one thing, she's got on the wrong side of Danny Shapiro and we can't discount the possibility that he sent those two men to rough her up as a warning. It's also bloody obvious that she must have been the anonymous caller who told us about Peter Kline and linked him to Shapiro. That's how she knew to pose the question at the press conference.'

'I asked her about that, guv. She said she herself received an anonymous phone call.'

'Maybe she was lying. Maybe she found something out that she's not prepared to share with us.'

'I doubt that, guv. I can't imagine she'd hold anything back. She'd be well aware of the consequences and she wouldn't want to risk it.'

'Perhaps you don't know her as well as you think, Ethan. There's something going on that we're not privy to. Something between Chambers and the Shapiros.'

'I think you're probably jumping to conclusions there, guv.'

'Is that right? Then how do you explain the fact that she's been to Belmarsh this morning for a cosy chat with Danny Shapiro's old man, Callum?'

Cain's stomach did a flip. 'I can't explain it, guv,' he said. 'I had no idea.'

'Are you sure about that, Ethan?' Redwood said. 'Are you seriously telling me that you didn't know?'

'That's exactly what I'm telling you, guv. It's news to me. In fact I'm probably the last person she'd confide in about that.'

Redwood didn't seem convinced. 'For your information, I took a call from a contact at the prison half an hour ago. Chambers had just left. She was with Shapiro for almost an hour.'

'Did she interview him for *The Post*?'

'Apparently not. He sent her a visiting order out of the blue. Used his contacts to get it fast-tracked. It was authorised as a private visit.'

Cain was confused. Why the bleeding hell had Callum wanted to see Beth? And why hadn't Danny told him about the visit? Surely he must have known.

'It's time we had a word with Bethany Chambers,' Redwood said. 'Find out what Callum wanted and what she knows about the Peter Kline business.'

'Why don't you let me talk to her, guv?' Cain said. 'If we make it official she's bound to get on her high horse. And it's odds on she'll turn up with a lawyer from the paper and we'll get nothing out of her.'

Redwood mulled this over for a few seconds, his bottom lip caught between his teeth.

Then he shook his head. 'We'll do it together, Ethan. It's not that I don't trust you, but I think I need to be there when we put her on the spot. However, I will leave it to you to arrange for her to come in.'

*   *   *

317

Cain hurried back to his desk, grabbed his cigarettes and went outside for a smoke. It was a relief to feel the cold, sobering air against his sweat-soaked face.

But there was no relief from the panic that was starting to consume him. He felt like he was in the deep end and drowning. On top of everything else he now had the gaffer on his back, and that wasn't good.

There was no knowing where it would lead if Redwood questioned Beth. What would she tell him, for Christ's sake? Would she go so far as to reveal that he had given an envelope to Frankie Bishop and that he worked for Shapiro?

Cain eyed his watch. Saw it was almost twelve. Decided to give her a call. But it rang through to voicemail.

Is she not picking up because she knows it's me? he wondered.

He tried *The Post*, got through to the newsroom and was told she was out of the office.

Fuck.

He flicked his half-smoked fag into the road and lit another. Then he phoned the pay-as-you-go number he had for Danny. The call was answered on the second ring.

'I was about to give *you* a buzz,' Danny said.

'I hope you were going to tell me why Beth has been to Belmarsh to see your old man,' Cain said.

Awkward silence. Then: 'I can't go into that over the phone.'

'Yeah, well, that's not good enough, Danny. I've been ordered to find out. And my boss also wants to know if Beth's got other information that she's not sharing about you and Peter Kline.'

'Keep calm, Ethan. She may well know the truth but she can't prove it if Kline stays missing and Tamara sticks to her story.'

'But you can't be sure that Tamara will if Redwood puts her under pressure.'

'Don't you worry about Tamara,' Danny said. 'She's solid. And I'm hoping that Chambers will be less inclined to land me in it after her chat with my dad.'

'How'd you mean?'

'I'll tell you when I see you. But look, I was about to call you because I've found out that Frankie Bishop couldn't have killed Megan.'

'Are you sure?'

'A hundred per cent. I remembered that on Friday night he was covering for me at the opening of our new club in Streatham. I checked with the manager. He says that Frankie was there from nine right through to two in the morning. I even got him to check the security tapes and Frankie is clearly visible around the time she was murdered.'

'Well, that's one bit of good news, I suppose. Means I won't have to cover it up. Have you decided what to do about him?'

'Let's just say that by tonight he won't be a problem for us.'

'Good.'

'Meanwhile, let me get back to you about Beth Chambers. I need to speak to my father to see how he got on. I'll call you later.'

Danny hung up and Cain had a sudden urge to throw his phone against the nearest wall. Instead, he took a long, meaningful puff on his cigarette and tried to take control of his thoughts. There were too many of them and they were messing up his head.

He craved a line of coke and a couple of stiff brandies. Something to relieve the pressure. But he was on duty and under suspicion and he couldn't risk it. So he brooded for a bit, feeling sorry for himself, then decided that the best way to cope with the stress was to concentrate on the investigation. On finding Megan Fuller's killer.

He finished his cigarette and went back inside. He was just in time for the midday briefing, where it was clear from the various reports that they were no nearer to solving the crime.

Redwood told the troops about Beth's visit to Belmarsh and about her being attacked. And he said that they would be speaking to her. He added that there was still no sign of Peter Kline and no forensic evidence at his house to suggest what had happened to him. They were still waiting for his phone records to come in.

Just as the meeting ended, Cain's phone rang. It was Drew Bellamy, the psychiatrist who'd been treating Megan.

'I got your message, Inspector,' he said, and sounded out of breath. 'I've just landed at Heathrow and should be back in my office in just over an hour. Can you meet me there?'

'That's very kind of you, Mr Bellamy. But I don't want to waste your time or mine. So perhaps you could just tell me over the phone if you think it'll be worth my while talking to you about Megan and her treatment.'

'In actual fact I do, Inspector,' Bellamy said. 'You see, I didn't know about her death until I read about it on the plane. And it strikes me that you need to know the reason Miss Fuller was such a troubled individual. I think it could have a bearing on the case.'

'Really? In what way?'

'Well, I think there's a strong possibility that it might lead you to the person who killed her.'

47

Beth Chambers

I was still walking aimlessly through the streets of south-east London as I had been for the past two hours since leaving Belmarsh prison.

My eyes were swollen and moist from where I'd been crying hot, silent tears. I'd received calls on my mobile from Grant, Ethan and my mother, but I hadn't bothered to answer them. To Grant I'd simply replied with a text message saying I wasn't well and needed to take the rest of the day off. I didn't want to tell him why I felt so dreadful and I wasn't sure I would ever be able to.

The conversation with Callum Shapiro had shaken me to the core. I kept playing it in my head, and it made me oblivious to the cold and the traffic and the groaning of my empty stomach.

About twenty-four hours ago I'd discovered that the father of my child was a corrupt cop. Now I was expected to accept that Callum Shapiro was my father and Danny Shapiro was my half-brother? It was a dreadful thought and it was going to impact on every aspect of my life, from my job to my relationship with my mother. And God forbid that Rosie would ever have to know the identity of her grandfather.

I kept shaking my head, telling myself it couldn't be true. How could I possibly be connected by blood to two such reprehensible characters?

I was reminded of all the terrible things Callum had done. The stuff that had come out at his trial. The murders. The scams. The suffering of his victims.

I'd spent years writing about both the father and the son. I'd investigated their illicit operations in the hope of uncovering evidence that could be splashed across the front page of *The Post* before being handed over to the police.

Now I had to try and come to terms with the fact that I was part of their blood family.

Jesus!

I felt a strange mixture of emotions, from shock to regret to a profound sadness. But above all I was possessed by an anger that was so intense it gave rise to a pain in my chest.

I felt the need to take it out on someone. To let them know that my life had been twisted violently out of shape through no fault of my own.

And I knew who that someone should be: the person who was ultimately responsible for unleashing these demons from the past.

My mother.

It's about seven miles from Woolwich to Peckham, but it took me over three hours to get there because I didn't walk in a straight line. In fact at one point I realised I was heading in entirely the wrong direction.

When I finally got home my mother was relieved to see me

because Grant Scott had phoned to check if I was okay. He'd told her I'd sent him a text to say I was unwell.

'He also told me where you'd been,' she said, her expression grave.

I took off my coat and poured myself a large glass of wine. My hands were shaking and it was an effort to control my temper.

'Where's Rosie?' I said through tight lips.

'She's upstairs having a nap.'

We both sat at the kitchen table, each of us waiting for the other to say something. For a while the only sound was the tick and creak of the radiator.

'The man who rang this morning asking for you didn't tell me what it was about,' she said. 'I gather from your boss that he was Callum Shapiro's lawyer.'

I nodded. 'That's right. He sent me a visiting order because he wanted to see me.'

I gulped at my wine, felt my chest heaving up and down. My mother's eyes were fixed on me, her pupils wide and dark, her face one big question mark.

'What did he say to you, Beth?' she asked.

I kept her waiting. Was it a childish form of punishment on my part? Maybe.

Eventually I put the glass down and said, 'He told me everything, Mum. That he's my real father and that his son is my half-brother.'

'And you believed him?'

That was when I let rip.

'Of course I fucking believed him,' I screamed at her. 'He told me about Olly. He remembered that it was the last thing he gave me.'

A small, startled cry flew from her mouth and her face seemed to fold in on itself.

'I can't believe you kept it from me for all these years,' I yelled. 'How could you have done that? It's not as if their names never came up. I've talked about them to you more times than I can remember. I covered Callum's trial, for heaven's sake.'

Her face turned ashen and her eyes dropped.

'He promised me he would never tell you,' she said. 'I didn't want you to know. I wanted to protect you.'

'But I'm twenty-nine, Mum. I had a right to know who my real father was.'

'And what good would it have done, eh? Your life would have been blighted. You would never have been the success that you are.'

'That's not the point.'

'It was to me. I did what I thought was best.'

'Did Tony know?'

She shook her head. 'I didn't tell him. There was never any need to.'

'But you must have known that it would eventually come out.'

'I hoped it wouldn't. I prayed it wouldn't. And the fact that you now know won't make your life any better or easier. In fact it's bound to have the opposite effect.'

I drew a breath and squeezed my eyes shut. It felt like they were burning at the edges.

'Why did Callum tell you, Beth?' she asked, her voice a hollow rasp. 'And why now after all these years?'

I took a couple of deep breaths to calm myself. I felt bad suddenly for shouting and was determined not to lose control.

I told her what Callum had said about Danny and I declaring a truce. And that he felt the only way to stop us destroying each other was to tell us we were half-brother and -sister.

As she listened, tears sparkled in her eyes, and I felt the anger that had built up inside me start to recede.

'He told me that he wasn't responsible for what happened to Tony,' I said. 'He insists the Russians killed him.'

'He's lying, Beth. I know he did it.'

'But you can't be sure,' I said. 'Maybe you just wanted to believe the rumours because of what he did to you.'

She flinched at that and her gaze hardened.

'You don't know what he's like, Beth. He lies. He manipulates. And it's not something he'd admit to you anyway, is it?'

'I think he was telling the truth,' I said.

She was angry now. Defensive.

'Rubbish,' she cried out. 'He just wants to get inside your head. It's what the bastard does.'

I felt my hackles rise. I was the one who was supposed to be angry. The one who had something to be angry about.

'You'd be a fool to be taken in by him,' she said. 'I'm convinced he had Tony killed. It wouldn't have mattered to him that you and I would suffer. With Callum it was all about taking care of his other family.'

She stared at me, judgement in her eyes, and her reaction ignited a sudden rush of fury in me.

'So come on then,' she said, her tone more strident. 'What else did he say? What other bullshit came out of his gob?'

I'd had enough. I stood up abruptly and said, 'He told me to let you know that he's sorry he didn't stay with you back then.'

'Is that right? Well, I'm pretty sure that's another lie.'

'Then I doubt you'll believe the last thing he told me before I left him,' I said. 'He told me he has bowel cancer and that he'll probably be dead within six months.'

Her expression changed then and her eyes went wide with shock. I instinctively wanted to reach out to her, to cry into her shoulder and let her cry into mine. But I couldn't bring myself to do it. There were too many conflicting emotions churning inside me.

'I'm going to the pub,' I said. 'I need a drink.'

I left her sitting there, and as I stepped out of the front door I wondered if she was happy or sad to know that the man she had loved all those years ago had only a few months to live.

I went to the nearest pub, an insalubrious establishment that I had never set foot in before. There were only a few other customers, old men hunched over their drinks or staring goggle-eyed at the big TV above the bar.

I bought myself a large gin and tonic with a whisky chaser, then settled down at a corner table away from everyone else.

I knocked back the whisky and sat there deep in melancholy thought. Everything felt out of sync and I had a splitting headache. There was just too much to take in. I was feeling completely overwhelmed.

I downed the first G and T, got another. But I knew that on an empty stomach it'd hit me hard, so I ordered a cheese sandwich and a bag of crisps.

I could still hear Callum Shapiro's voice in my head and I reckoned I would for days to come. I also knew that at some point I would have to respond to what I'd been told. Should I tell someone or should I refuse to accept it and get on with my life as though nothing had changed? I also wondered if I should pass on what I'd learned to the police. Or should I do what he'd asked and pull back from doing anything that might harm his son?

My mind was in chaos and I desperately wanted to wake up and find that it was all a horrible dream.

Someone turned up the volume on the television and it grabbed my attention. It was the five o'clock news on Sky and they had a new line on the Megan Fuller story. It was another interview with the former boyfriend, Sam Jones.

He was again being forced to defend himself against claims that he'd been physically violent towards Megan during their time together. Some of her friends had taken to social media to say they'd witnessed him bullying her and one was alleging she was told by Megan that he'd hit her on a couple of occasions.

The claims had gone viral and had prompted Jones to issue a statement rebutting them. As I watched him squirming on the screen I wondered if he had indeed killed her. There was definitely something dodgy and unpleasant about the man. But then the same could be said for Danny Shapiro. And despite what Callum had told me I still found it hard to believe that his son – my half-brother – had absolutely nothing to do with Megan's death.

48

Ethan Cain

Cain's thoughts were racing when he left Drew Bellamy's office in Kensington.

The conversation with Megan Fuller's shrink had focused his mind and got him excited. He was shocked and dismayed by what had been revealed to him, and he could see why Bellamy had been keen to pass the information on and why he'd felt it was a potential lead for the police.

So Cain wasn't going to hold back on acting on it. Checks needed to be carried out and urgent inquiries made.

Outside on the street he struck up a fag and called the incident room. He asked to speak to DC Fisher.

'I need you to chase up a vehicle registration and some CCTV footage for me, Rachel,' he said.

He gave her an address and said he wanted her to check all the road cameras within a quarter-mile radius of the property.

'Go back to Friday evening between about nine and midnight,' he said. 'See if the car shows up at any point.'

DC Fisher said she'd get right onto it.

'Keep it to yourself for now, Rachel,' he said. 'I don't want the others to get worked up if it turns out to be nothing.'

'Are you coming back to the office, guv?'

'Of course. I'll be about an hour.'

He wanted to have a walk to clear his head first. Maybe grab a bite to eat and something to drink. He was feeling even more wired and jumpy now, and he needed to give himself some time to think and settle his nerves.

He snuck into a pub just off Kensington High Street and ordered pie and chips. He didn't really have an appetite, but he felt the need to fuel his body. He also treated himself to a pint of lager.

He was still waiting for the food to arrive when he took a call on his mobile from Danny.

'I'm ringing to tell you to keep your eyes peeled for Frankie Bishop, Ethan,' he said. 'I sent a guy over to his place in Camberwell. He was supposed to wait for him to show up and put a bullet in his head. But Bishop spotted the guy in his car. He overpowered him and sliced his face up with a knife and told him to deliver a message to me.'

'Holy fuck. What was the message?'

'He said he's planning a nasty surprise for you and me and that we'll know about it before the end of the day.'

Cain didn't get to finish his pint or his pie and chips. He left the pub and flagged down a taxi. He decided the safest place for him to be during the coming hours was inside the incident room in Wandsworth.

49

Beth Chambers

I was about to order up another G and T when I got a text from Mum. She wanted me to go home because Rosie wasn't feeling well and she wasn't sure whether to phone the doctor.

By this time the food and drink had taken the edge off my headache and eased the tension inside me. I felt slightly better and more able to keep the negative thoughts at bay.

As I hurried out of the pub my only concern was for Rosie. I didn't bother to call Mum to find out what was wrong because the pub was only a five-minute walk from the house, and I was sure it wouldn't be anything serious otherwise my mother wouldn't have just sent a text.

Still, it enabled me to put things into perspective and to remember that the most important thing in my life was my daughter. Not Callum Shapiro. Or my job. Or my hitherto secret past.

Rosie's well-being was all that mattered at the end of the day and I told myself I should never forget that.

Two things struck me as odd when I got home. There was a

white Transit van that I hadn't seen before parked outside the house and our front door was open a few inches. But because I was in a hurry I didn't give either too much thought. I just stepped into the house, closed the door behind me, called out as I rushed through to the kitchen.

I saw my mother first. Sitting on a chair that had been placed in the middle of the room, with Rosie curled up on her lap.

Behind her, with his back to the sink, stood a man I recognised instantly as Frankie Bishop.

He had a malicious grin on his face and was pointing a revolver at my mother's head.

The scene filled me with abject terror. My mouth gaped open and every muscle in my body shut down.

'Don't scream or make me do anything to pull the trigger,' Bishop said.

My mother's face was rigid with fear, her eyes as wide as saucers. I couldn't see Rosie's face, because it was buried in the folds of my mother's cardigan. But I could hear her sobbing, and it made me want to dash across the room and grab her.

'If you do as I say then no harm will come to them,' Bishop said to me. 'Your daughter is fine by the way. Just upset. I got your mum to send you that text to get you here.'

I swallowed and felt the saliva slide down my throat. My legs were threatening to collapse under me, and I started to shake all over.

Bishop stepped out from behind my mother. I noticed then that his face had taken a beating recently. His top lip was red and swollen and there was a dark bruise under his left eye.

He shifted the gun so it pointed at me. His stance was tense, full of aggression.

331

'You and me are going for a ride, Chambers,' he said. 'The van outside is mine. In a minute you'll go and get in the back. If you don't then I'll take it out on your kid first and then your mother.'

'Please don't hurt them,' I begged him.

'Then make sure you cooperate and don't make a fuss.'

My chest tightened and I started to feel faint. 'What's this about? Why are you here?'

He expelled a puff of air. 'Your half-brother and me had a fall-out. Now he's out to get me and the prick thinks I'll just let him. But I don't intend to. And I'm not going to disappear without a proper payoff. That's where you come in.'

I shook my head. 'I don't believe it. You're taking me as a hostage? Is that it? Because if it is it won't work. Danny Shapiro won't try to get me back.'

'We'll see about that. Don't forget you're part of the Shapiro family now. And they look after their own.'

I looked at my mother. Her nostrils flared as tears trickled down her cheeks.

'I'll do whatever you want,' I said. 'Just don't hurt them.'

Rosie twisted herself out of my mother's grip. She tried to break free and come to me. But my mother held on to her and Rosie started to cry.

'Then go straight outside,' Bishop said. 'The back of the van is unlocked. Get in and wait for me. If you run I'll crush your daughter's skull with the gun. Now drop your bag on the floor.'

He nudged the side of my mother's head with the gun. 'And listen to me, old lady. When we've gone you'll do absolutely nothing. If you call the police I'll kill your daughter. Understood?'

My mother nodded and Bishop turned back to me. I thought fleetingly about charging him but realised it wasn't worth the risk. We were all completely at his mercy.

He came up to me then and turned me so I was facing away from him. Then he searched my pockets to satisfy himself that they were empty.

'I'll be watching from the window,' he said. 'Disappoint me and everyone suffers. Now go.'

My heart was in my mouth as I rushed out of the room and out of the house. The rear door of the van was unlocked just as Bishop had said it would be. I pulled it open and before climbing in I looked back and saw him standing at the window.

I knew I had no choice but to follow his instructions. As I hauled myself up and inside, a spasm of absolute terror sped through my body.

The back of the van was spacious, but half of it was filled with cardboard boxes and plastic bags packed with everything from books to clothes.

When I pulled the door shut behind me the darkness was as thick as oil.

A few seconds later I heard a key being turned in the lock. And then the engine was switched on and the van started to move.

I sat on the cold, hard floor and prayed that I'd see my family again.

50

Danny Shapiro

Danny had spread the word among the crew that Frankie Bishop had gone rogue. And he marked the cards of those he suspected of having split loyalties. He told them that anyone caught offering support to Bishop would suffer the same fate that would eventually be meted out to him.

Danny made no mention of what it was all about and hopefully the lads would never have to know about Bishop's affair with Megan, although he couldn't be sure they didn't know already.

Some would probably think he had overreacted by kicking Bishop out of the firm. To Danny, however, it was the ultimate betrayal and something he couldn't countenance. He would never be able to trust the man again and he'd forever wonder what other strokes the bastard had pulled over the years.

But he had definitely created a problem for himself by acting so decisively in telling Bishop to fuck off. The guy was now a serious threat. He was a psycho who was more dangerous than any man Danny had ever known.

That was why he'd come back to his West End retreat the first chance he got. It was safer than surrounding himself with a posse of minders. From here he could make calls and coordinate efforts to track Bishop down. He could also try to relax and work out how he was going to seize back control of his life. Because right now it felt like he'd lost it.

He still couldn't be sure if the truth would get out, or if his father had managed to persuade Beth Chambers to back off. Now he had this business with Bishop to contend with, the man he had trusted for years but who had taken the piss on a grand scale.

And if that wasn't enough hassle there was the startling revelation from his old man about Beth Chambers and about the cancer that was slowly killing him.

Danny couldn't remember a time when he'd had to deal with so much crap at once. Or when his mind had been battered by so many shocks, one after the other. It was sapping his strength, clouding his judgement. Doing his fucking head in.

A drink. That was what he needed. What he always needed when he felt the pressure grinding him down. He poured a large, neat whisky into a tumbler and closed his eyes with the first swallow.

Just then his mobile rang. He was expecting a call from his father and he was anxious to know how Chambers had reacted to the news that she was his daughter.

But it wasn't Callum, and a shiver danced over Danny's shoulders when he saw Bishop's name in the display window.

As soon as he accepted the call, Bishop spoke.

'You're making too many bad mistakes, Danny. You shouldn't have kicked off like you did over that slut Megan. And you shouldn't have sent that twat to get rid of me.'

'The biggest mistake I made was to trust you,' Danny said. 'You're a two-timing piece of shit.'

'I admit I shouldn't have got involved with Megan. But believe me, she did all the running. She was gagging for it back then because you were ignoring her.'

Danny felt the veins in his temples start to pulse. 'I'm going to make you pay for that, Frankie.'

'No, you're not. What you're going to do is pay me what you owe me for everything I've done for you. No way am I walking away with sod all.'

'Dream on, you cunt.'

Bishop grunted out a bitter laugh. 'Let's stop the name-calling and get right to the point, eh? In a few minutes I'm going to text you the number of an offshore bank account. And then you're going to transfer one million pounds into it by midnight tonight. Don't try to fob me off by saying you can't lay your hands on that amount of wonga. I know for a fact that you have at least two bank accounts, each with five mil in.'

'You're even crazier than I thought you were,' Danny said. 'Why would I even think of giving you a single penny?'

'Because if you don't I'm going to kill your half-sister,' he said. 'She's with me now and I reckon you can call it a classic hostage situation. If the money's not wired to the account by the deadline then she dies. That won't be the end of it either. After that you'll have to pay me two million to stop me coming after you. So I suggest you save yourself a heap of money and act fast.'

'How do I know you have her?'

'Because when I hang up I'm going to send you a photo.'

'And what makes you think I give a shit about what happens to her? In fact you'll be doing me a favour by killing her.'

He laughed again. 'Don't take me for a fool, Danny. Things have changed on that front. Your old man would never forgive you if you let his daughter die. And I'd make sure he found out.'

Bishop hung up then and Danny remained rooted to the spot in the middle of his living room, despair gnawing at his mind and body.

A few moments passed and then a text message came through on Danny's phone. It contained bank account details.

Seconds later came another text, this one with a photo attached.

Danny opened it. The picture showed a woman cowering in the corner of what looked like the back of a van. There was no mistaking it was Beth Chambers. And the terrified expression on her face told its own story.

51

Ethan Cain

Cain was in the incident room when he took the call from Danny on his mobile. It was just after eight and most of the detectives had left.

But Cain was in no hurry to go home. He was too busy staying safe and following up what he regarded as the most promising lead so far in the hunt for Megan Fuller's killer.

'I need your help,' Danny said. 'So drop whatever you're doing and listen up.'

Danny went on to say that Frankie Bishop had kidnapped Beth and was demanding a million pounds by midnight. Before Cain could ask the obvious question, Danny explained why Bishop felt that he could use Beth as a hostage.

'She's my half-sister, Ethan,' he said. 'Which makes her Callum's daughter. I only found out last night. Anyway, Callum's just been on the phone. He wants me to do whatever it takes to get her back safely.'

Cain was speechless. He sat with the phone pressed against his ear, mouth agape, head on fire.

'Don't even try to get your mind around it now,' Danny said. 'There's no time. I have to find out where that mad bastard has taken her.'

Cain struggled to find his voice and when he did it sounded weak and barely audible.

'What do you want me to do?' he said.

'For starters try to get a fix on their mobile phones. You've got Frankie's number. He called about ten minutes ago, so there's still a chance it's switched on and transmitting a signal. I would have rung you before now but my dad phoned.'

'Leave it with me,' Cain said. 'I'll see what I can do.'

'Ring me when you have something.'

'Sure, but before we hang up I need to ask you a question.'

'Go on then.'

'If you don't find them before midnight are you going to transfer the money to his account?'

He heard Danny sigh. 'I probably would if I thought he'd let her go. But I really don't think he can afford to if he wants to be free to spend it.'

The first thing Cain did was to call Beth's mobile number. It rang for a bit and when a woman's voice answered his heart jumped because he thought it was her and that Danny had got it wrong. But he realised instantly that it wasn't Beth.

'Is that you, Peggy?' he said. 'This is Ethan. I need to talk to Beth.'

Long pause, then: 'She's not here.'

Peggy was scared. He could tell that from her shaky voice.

'Okay, Peggy,' he said. 'I'm well aware that something is up. So tell me if you know where she is and if she's all right.'

'He told me not to talk to the police,' she said. 'He said he'd kill her if I did.'

'I'm not calling in an official capacity, Peggy. But I need you to tell me what you know.'

Another long pause, then when she spoke again her voice was tearful.

'A man came here a short time ago,' she said. 'He had a gun. He threatened me and Rosie. Then he took Beth away in a white van and warned me not to talk to anyone.'

'Did he hurt you?'

'No, but I think he's going to hurt Beth.'

'Right. Well, the man who's taken her used to work for Danny Shapiro. He's demanding a ransom for Beth and Danny has asked me to help find her. Did the man say where he was going?'

'No.'

'Did you see the registration number of the van?'

'No.'

'Very well, Peggy. Just sit tight and I'll get back to you when I have some news. Is Rosie okay?'

'She's curled up on the sofa. She doesn't realise what's happened but she's very upset.'

'Take good care of her and I'll phone you back.'

As he ended the call, DC Fisher approached him and said, 'I've found something, guv, and I think you need to see it.'

'What is it?' he said, distracted.

'We got a result on that address and car you asked me to check out. Turns out there's a CCTV camera at the end of the road. The recorded feed from Friday night has been patched through and I just viewed the tape.'

'And?'

'The car is seen driving away from the house at nine thirty and returning at eleven forty-five.'

'Blimey.'

'Do you want to come and have a look?'

'Not right now, Rachel. I've got to make a couple of calls. But I'd like you to see if you can track the car from there. I want to know if it went anywhere near Ramsden Road in Balham.'

'Those wheels are already in motion, guv.'

'Good. And one other thing. I think you should alert the DCI. I know he's on his way home, but he'll want to be in on this. Tell him I think we should apply for a warrant to search the house.'

Cain knew that he should have made that call himself, but Beth was his priority now. So for the next fifteen minutes he sat at his desk and stayed on the phone.

That was how long it took to get the information he needed from the network service provider. As soon as he had it he phoned Danny.

'Beth doesn't have her mobile with her,' Cain said. 'And Bishop has switched his off. According to the location history the last call he made was earlier this evening from the Fleet services on the M3 motorway.'

'In that case I bet he's heading for his old stomping ground of Southampton,' Danny said. 'I know he still has a place down there but I don't have an address.'

'What are you going to do, Danny?'

'Drive there myself, and while I'm doing that I need you to find out where they are.'

'That might not be possible.'

'I know, but you have to try.'

'Have you got someone to check his flat?'

'Yeah, but he's cleared it out. He lived there alone and it's one of our properties so he's never paid rent. According to the lads all his personal stuff has gone.'

'What about the van he's using? Is it his own?'

341

'Not as far as I know. He drives an Audi and that's still parked outside his flat apparently. My guess is he's either borrowed the van or hired it to take away his stuff. Try the rental companies or one of those car-sharing clubs. There are a few around Camberwell.'

'I'll do what I can, Danny. But you have to understand there's only so much I can achieve on my own.'

'I know, Ethan, but neither of us can afford to make this official. If your lot get involved we'll be drawn into a mess we can't get out of.'

52

Beth Chambers

The van was on the road for two and a half hours according to my watch. It stopped once and Bishop opened the door so that he could take a photo of me on his phone.

Now the engine was turned off and I guessed we'd arrived at our destination, wherever that was.

The fear and dread grew inside me, and the blood thundered in my ears. I had no idea what was going to happen. The only certainty was that my life hung in the balance.

The doors were pulled open and Bishop was standing there. He said, 'Welcome to Southampton. Now get out.'

Why Southampton? I wondered. And then I remembered reading somewhere that he used to be based down here before moving to London to join Shapiro's firm.

I stepped down onto the gravel driveway of a large detached house.

He immediately grabbed my arm in a vice-like grip.

'The only way you'll survive this is to behave yourself,' he said. 'If you scream or try to run away I'll hurt you bad.'

I believed him. There was violence in his eyes, and I sensed that he wouldn't need much of an excuse to lay into me.

'What is this place?' I asked, looking up at the two-storey house that looked like it needed some work done to it.

'I bought it a few years ago,' he said. 'Time to sell up, I reckon.'

He pulled me roughly towards the front door. I looked around, tried to separate the shapes from the darkness. The property was screened by a high hedge, beyond which I could see the lights of other houses. So it wasn't a rural setting. We were probably in a suburb of Southampton. It was a place I didn't know at all well, having only been here a couple of times, once to board a ferry to take me to the Isle of Wight music festival.

Bishop pushed me to one side and used a key to open the door. Once inside, he turned on the hall light and led me through the house. Dust sheets covered what little furniture there was. The wooden floors desperately needed treating and the air felt cold and damp.

He led me through to the kitchen where he made me sit in a high-backed chair. Then he produced two zip-ties from his pocket. One he used to secure my hands behind my back and the other to attach my right foot to the chair leg.

My chest was tight and burning and I had to fight a rising panic. I wanted to scream and shout and launch myself at my captor. But I knew it wouldn't do me any good because he'd be able to neutralise me in seconds. I was no match when it came to physical strength.

I watched him looking through the kitchen cupboards, probably checking to see if there was anything to eat or drink.

'What are you expecting to get from Danny Shapiro?' I said.

He stopped what he was doing, turned, gave me a steady look.

'Money,' he said. 'And lots of it. I need it to start a new life away from this stinking country.'

'And if he doesn't come through with it?'

A grim smile touched his lips. 'Then you can kiss goodbye to life, Chambers. He has until midnight to wire the money to my account. If he doesn't then he'll discover that I mean business.'

'So you'll kill me?'

'If I have to, yeah. And you've probably guessed it's not something I'll find too difficult.'

The taste of vomit rose in my throat and my lungs started pumping for air.

'No need to panic,' he said. 'I'm confident he'll pay up. His dad will make him.'

'I don't understand,' I said. 'You were his main man. His enforcer.'

'That was until he found out I'd been poking his wife.'

'My God. Is that why he killed her?'

'He didn't kill her,' Bishop said. 'If he'd wanted her dead then he would have got me to do it. I didn't kill her either – even though she tried to blackmail me too by threatening to tell Danny about the affair I had with her years ago.'

'But he found out anyway?'

'That's right. Though not from her. She backed down after I threatened to cripple her. No, it was that slimy ex of yours who told Danny after he got access to her phone records.'

'Ethan!'

'That's right. It amazes me what a bird like you saw in that creep.'

I didn't say anything, just sat there feeling the cold finger of fear dragging along my spine.

'You do know he's as bent as a nine-bob note, don't you?' he said. 'He's been on the payroll for years. In return for helping the firm he gets to satisfy his passions for young tarts and cocaine.'

He was only confirming what I already knew. But I didn't want to hear it. Not now, not here.

'I feel sorry for your kid,' he said. 'It's not fair on her having a shit like him for a father.'

'He's not all bad,' I said, surprising myself by defending him.

'Yeah, well, you don't know the half of it,' he said, his eyes ablaze suddenly. 'You think you're so fucking clever while all the time you're just as gullible as the rest of them.'

'What do you mean?'

He took a step towards me, his arms splayed aggressively.

'The Peter Kline thing, for example. You confronted him, didn't you? Told him you'd found out that Danny's alibi was a fake one. Well, that was when Danny decided that Kline had to be put out of the picture. So I went to his house. And guess who was with me when I did the deed.'

I just stared at him as the adrenalin crashed through my bloodstream.

'That's right, Chambers,' he said. 'Your ex-husband. The detective. He saw me strangle the poor fucker with a piece of nylon rope.'

Two men, the neighbour had said. Two men seen walking up to the house in the dark.

'But he won't get away scot-free if it's any consolation,' Bishop said. 'His colleagues at the Yard will soon receive a computer flash drive in the post with my compliments. On it is enough evidence to get him banged up for years.'

A cold sweat trickled down my spine and I felt a crushing heat in my chest. It wasn't just because of what he'd said about Ethan, although that was bad enough.

It was because by telling me about Peter Kline I couldn't believe he would ever let me go, even if he did extract money from Danny Shapiro.

53

Ethan Cain

Cain couldn't shake Beth from his thoughts. He was terrified of what Frankie Bishop would do to her.

He had seen first-hand what the man was capable of and he had heard the stories. A couple of the young girls the firm had sent to his flat had told him how brutal Bishop had been towards them. One said he'd raped her and another that he'd crushed a lighted cigarette on the back of her neck because she refused to go with a client who was into rough sex.

Cain didn't want anything to happen to Beth. He still had feelings for her and she was the mother of his child.

He was already finding it hard to live with himself after the things he'd done. But if Beth was killed or seriously hurt the guilt would surely suffocate him. He was both appalled and amazed at how the drama had played out. Only yesterday Danny Shapiro had been making all kinds of threats against Beth. Now he was desperate to save her life because she was his half-sister! What's more, the man who had abducted her was Frankie Bishop, who for years had been the firm's most trusted enforcer.

Cain was going to do all he could to find her, although it wasn't going to be a doddle with so much else going on.

Through his own initiative the murder inquiry had been ramped up a gear and he was beginning to believe they were closing in on the real killer. He was seriously tempted to walk away from it and tell Redwood that he had another migraine. But that would mean leaving the incident room and make it harder to find Beth. At least here he had access to all the police resources.

He was already making use of them. Calls had been made and wheels were turning. He had been onto Southampton CID and they were searching their files for information on Frankie Bishop. They'd told him that when Bishop lived in the city he had rented a flat near the football stadium, but there were rumours that when he came out of prison he'd bought a property in the area before moving to London. That was all they were though. Rumours.

Cain was now busy calling round the rental firms and car-sharing clubs. Identifying the van offered the best chance of locating it, through either the number plate recognition network or GPS.

But he was wasting his time if Bishop had borrowed the van from someone or had stolen it.

He made a note on his pad to check to see if any white Transit vans had been nicked in London since this morning. This would be another shot in the dark because it sometimes took owners days to discover that their vehicles were missing.

Cain kept looking at his watch and wondering how far Danny had got. It was about a two-hour drive to Southampton in light traffic. But it was a huge city with a population of over 250,000. Danny had no hope of finding Beth without knowing where to look.

'Get off the bloody phone, Ethan. We need to get moving on this.'

Redwood's voice startled him. He hung up midway through a conversation with the manager of a car-sharing club and turned towards his boss who was standing behind him.

'What did you say, guv?' he asked.

The DCI was in a state of high excitement. 'I said we need to move. Fisher just went back over the CCTV footage we already had in from Balham on Friday night. And your hunch was right. The car she was looking for is on there. It drove along Balham High Road just before the murder. We didn't spot it before because we weren't looking for it.'

'Christ.'

Redwood beamed a smile. 'Looks like the bastard has been lying to us all along. If it hadn't been for Megan's shrink we'd be none the wiser.'

'So what now, guv?' Cain said.

'We're about to get a warrant to search his home. We'll bring him in and put him through the wringer. Put your coat on and let's get going.'

Cain's mobile phone rang as he stood up. It was on his desk so he recognised the number. It was one of the car hire firms ringing him back.

Did that mean they'd got a result on the van?

'Don't even think about answering that,' Redwood warned him. 'There's no time. Whatever it is will have to wait.'

54

Danny Shapiro

Before leaving the house, Danny armed himself with the revolver
he kept in the safe. It was a Glock that had belonged to his father.
He'd used it only once before and just having it on him made
him nervous.

Once he was clear of London, he thundered down the M3 in
his BMW 5 Series. The motorway would take him through
southern England all the way to Southampton. What he would
do when he got there remained to be seen. It would depend on
what Cain was able to come up with, and whether Bishop had
actually travelled to the city. After all, it was just an assumption
that he had. Maybe he'd called from the Fleet services because
he'd known that Danny would get Cain to triangulate the signal.
It could have been a ploy to make Danny think they'd travelled
south when in fact they'd gone in a different direction.

Danny knew that Bishop shouldn't be underestimated. He was
a thug and a nut job. But he wasn't stupid. In fact like all psycho-
paths he was cunning and shrewd, which was why he'd been such
an asset to the firm.

Danny had never really liked Bishop, but then he didn't like any of the men who worked for him. Bishop was the worst of a bad bunch of villains and scoundrels, the type of guys he would have steered clear of if he'd followed an honest path in life.

He wondered what Megan had seen in him. Was it just that she'd fancied a bit of rough? Sex with a man who probably scared her if truth be told? Or was it more than that? Had she actually had feelings for him?

Danny remembered now that they had spent quite a bit of time alone together, when Bishop had acted as her bodyguard on shopping trips and functions that Danny couldn't get to. He wondered how many times they'd sneaked off to hotels or to his flat to have sex.

'I never did trust that demented fucker,' his father had said after Danny told him earlier what was happening. 'He made my flesh crawl whenever I looked at him.'

It was Callum who had pleaded with Danny to do whatever it took to save Beth Chambers.

'Even if it means paying the bastard off,' he'd said. 'Whether you like it or not she's my daughter and I don't want to go to my grave knowing we abandoned her to that lunatic.'

Danny had promised Callum that he would do what he could and he'd meant it. His father had been wrong to have kept things from him all these years, but he still loved the man.

And if Callum did only have six more months to live then it was probably the last thing that Danny would ever be able to do for him.

Danny had considered getting a team of tooled-up lads to follow him to Southampton. He only hadn't because he feared it would turn out to be a wild goose chase.

He was approaching the city now and he still hadn't heard

from Cain. That could only mean he'd had no success in finding out where Bishop had gone.

Years ago Danny would have been able to call on the local firms for help. Since then the faces he'd known had either died or retired. These days the foreign gangs were running things. The Poles and Asians dominated the drugs trade and other rackets all along the south coast, and Danny had had very little to do with them.

So as he pulled off the motorway and entered Southampton he was at a loss and wondered if he had made a mistake by coming down here without really thinking.

He was no stranger to the city, and knew his way around. He'd owned a cottage in the nearby New Forest where he and Megan had spent quite a few weekends. They had come into the city centre to shop and visit the casinos.

Tonight the city was cold and relatively quiet. The rain had held off and the moon sat full in a cloudless sky.

Danny drove around for a bit and called Cain a couple of times, but all he got was a recorded message.

He was feeling pissed off and anxious, and beginning to believe that in the end he'd be forced to wire the money to Bishop's offshore account even though there was no guarantee he would let Beth go.

He decided to stop for a drink and headed for the waterfront and a hotel he knew close to the docks. It was almost eleven when he pulled into the car park. One hour to midnight and Bishop's deadline.

His mouth felt dry and pasty and he was looking forward to something strong and cold at the bar. He was just about to get out of the car when his mobile rang. It was Cain.

'What the fuck has taken you so long to get back to me?' he said.

Cain's voice was so low he could barely hear him.

'Listen, Danny. I've been tied up and couldn't use my phone. But I've just managed to talk to a car hire firm in Camberwell. They rented out a white Transit van to one Frankie Bishop.'

'Jesus, Ethan. You did good.'

'Not only that. The vehicle's equipped with a GPS tracker and they've given me its exact location.'

55

Beth Chambers

I watched Frankie Bishop as he paced up and down the kitchen. He was restless and angry, and he kept looking at his watch.

He had also placed two mobile phones on the kitchen table. Only one of them was switched on; this he kept checking, presumably to find out if Shapiro had sent the money to his account.

'What time is it?' I said.

He looked at me with chilling coldness and I noticed that the wound to his mouth had opened up slightly and a small drop of blood was poised to spill out.

'It's just gone eleven,' he said. 'Your brother is cutting it fine.'

My brother! Jesus. If it hadn't been so scary it would have been funny. This time yesterday I didn't have a brother – or rather a half-brother – and now my life was in his hands. But even though I kept telling myself to have faith, I just didn't believe he would come to my rescue. There was no good reason why he should. He must still view me as a threat despite Callum's crude attempt at bringing about a 'truce'.

And what Bishop had told me had made me even more of a

threat. I now knew that Shapiro had got Bishop to kill Peter Kline in order to protect himself. I also knew that he had got my ex-husband – a serving police officer in the Met – to go along for the ride.

So I couldn't imagine why he wouldn't prefer to see me dead. At least then he wouldn't have to worry about me going to the police and turning it all into a front-page story for *The Post*.

The clock was ticking and the fear was thick inside me. I was shivering and sobbing uncontrollably.

Bishop was ignoring me now. It was as though I wasn't in the room with him. He continued to walk around, his attention switching between his phone and his watch.

I'd given up begging him to let me go because he had threatened to put duct tape over my mouth if I didn't shut up. Instead I focused on praying he'd let me live for Rosie's sake. I was growing increasingly fearful that I would never see my beloved daughter again. It would be left to my mother to bring her up. I wouldn't see her in a school uniform or a wedding dress. I wouldn't be there to protect her in a world that was becoming more dangerous by the day. And it was all my fault. I had pushed things too far, taken too many risks, ignored all the warnings.

I tried to blink away the tears, but they kept on coming, along with waves of nausea. My mind was spinning with things I wanted to say but what was the point in saying them since no one was listening?

Bishop stepped in front of me suddenly, his damaged lips twisted into a predatory smile.

'It's looking to me as though your new brother has decided you're not worth a million quid,' he said.

A million! It sounded like a ridiculous amount of money to

demand. Was any life worth that? I wasn't sure. Then again my head was in no fit state to dwell on it.

'It's not too late,' I said, my voice distorted by the sobs that racked my body. 'Please let me go back to my family.'

Something dark crept into his eyes and the veins in his neck stood to attention.

'You're mistaking me for someone who gives a shit,' he said. 'Ain't you ever wondered why they call me "The Nutter"?'

I lost all hope then and the breath rushed out of me. I shut my eyes. Tried to force my mind back into the past, to before my life was torn apart. Instead I found myself staring into the future. At Rosie's tear-soaked face. At a headstone with my name on it. At my own obituary on an inside page of *The Post*.

These images twisted me up inside and made me feel like I was going to faint.

Then something happened that pulled me back from the brink. It was a sound.

The sound of a doorbell ringing.

56

Danny Shapiro

It was ten minutes to midnight when Danny rang the bell to the house that he assumed was owned by Frankie Bishop. There was a white Transit van on the gravel driveway and lights on in a couple of the downstairs rooms.

It had taken him over forty minutes to find the place because he had made a couple of wrong turns. He'd parked outside on the road in a position where the BMW couldn't be seen from the two-storey property. There were houses on either side separated by tall hedges.

Before approaching the front door he'd had to quickly decide how he was going to play it. With no time to call for help, he had no option but to go it alone and hope that Beth Chambers was not only inside but also still alive.

He'd crept around the outside of the house to get his bearings and to find out what he was up against. At the back he'd been able to peer into the kitchen through a narrow gap in the venetian blinds. That was when he'd seen them both: Beth tied to a chair and Bishop standing next to her with his back to the window.

Beth had looked to be in a bad way, her body rigid, her face teary and swollen.

His first instinct had been to throw open the back door and storm into the kitchen, catching Bishop off guard. But when he'd gently moved the door handle he'd discovered it was locked. He then considered shooting Bishop through the window, but he was moving around and the risk of hitting Beth was too great.

It had made him realise that with time running out there was only one way to gain access to the house and that was through the front door.

As he waited for Bishop to answer it he had no way of knowing how the bastard was going to react. The only thing he was certain of was that he was about to put his life on the line for a woman who had been trying to get him arrested. If that wasn't the height of madness then he didn't know what was.

He stood back so that Bishop would have a clear view of him through the peephole. The Glock was in his back pocket and he was poised to reach for it at the first opportunity.

'Open up, Frankie,' he shouted. 'It's me, Danny. And I'm by myself.'

Bishop was quick to respond by shouting out. 'There's no way you would have come here without arming yourself, Danny. So take out whatever weapon you've got and drop it behind you. And don't fuck me around by saying you're not tooled up.'

Danny took out the Glock, held it up, threw it onto the driveway.

'Now hold up your hands,' Bishop demanded.

Danny did as he was told and the door was wrenched open. There Bishop stood with a revolver in his hand, probably the one he had taken from the shooter Danny had sent to kill him.

'How the fuck did you find this place?' he demanded to know, his eyes ablaze with violent fury.

'With Cain's help,' Danny said. 'There's a GPS tracker in the van.'

Bishop shook his head. 'I should have thought of that. And I'm sure I would have if I hadn't been in such a fucking hurry.'

He looked beyond Danny, his eyes searching the darkness.

'I came alone,' Danny said. 'Didn't have the location until a few minutes ago. Let me in and we can talk.'

'I tried to talk earlier,' Bishop said. 'But we moved way beyond that when you sent that amateur prat to kill me.'

'So what do you expect me to do then, Frankie? Go back to London?'

Bishop thought about it for all of ten seconds. Then he waved Danny inside.

'Go through to the kitchen,' he said.

When Beth Chambers saw him her jaw dropped and she squinted through tear-filled eyes.

'My God,' she shrieked.

Her face was ghostly white and her body was shaking violently. Danny actually felt sorry for her and this surprised him.

'How touching,' Bishop said. 'A family fucking reunion.'

He pushed the muzzle of the gun into Danny's back and told him to move towards where Beth was tied to the chair.

'There are only a couple of minutes to go to the deadline, Danny,' he said. 'When I last checked you still hadn't wired over the money.'

'Did you really expect me to?'

'Well, if you don't, this little lady dies on the stroke of midnight.'

Danny shook his head. 'You were never going to let her go and we both know it. No matter how much money I gave you.'

Bishop bared his teeth and raised the gun, pointing it at Beth.

'So you won't mind if I blow her fucking head off?'

'I don't think you're that stupid, Frankie,' Danny said. 'For one thing the neighbours would call the filth and for another you'd lose the only bit of leverage you've got.'

That gave Bishop something to think about and hesitation flashed in his eyes.

Danny turned to Beth and said, 'Are you all right?'

She looked up at him, and for the first time he saw something of his father in her face. They had the same square jawline and high cheekbones; the same generous lips.

'I've been better,' she said, then frowned. 'Why did you come here?'

He shrugged. 'Callum told me to. He's suddenly come over all concerned about the daughter he never told me about.'

'That's enough,' Bishop broke in. Then to Danny, he said, 'You being here changes nothing. I still want the money. It's a small price to pay to get rid of me.'

Danny's mind was racing. He didn't have a plan so he needed to buy some time to come up with one. As things stood he didn't stand a chance of getting the drop on Bishop. They were too far apart and Bishop would be ready to respond to any sudden movement.

Danny looked around the kitchen. 'I knew you had a place down this way, but I didn't realise it was so big.'

'We all need a bolthole, Danny. Somewhere to go when shit happens. You have yours and this is mine.'

'I think it's pretty good,' Danny said. 'Worth a few quid, I reckon.'

'Yeah, well, I don't give a damn what you think. All I care about is getting the money I'm due. So use your phone now to get it transferred to the account I gave you. Then I'll leave you both here and fuck off. And if you can't persuade the bitch not to go to the Old Bill then that's your problem. I'll be long gone by then.'

Danny stared into Bishop's eyes and wondered if he could trust him. Suddenly the money wasn't an issue. A million quid didn't seem a lot if it meant that nobody died and Bishop walked away. It wasn't as if he would even miss it since it was just sitting there in one of the firm's offshore bank accounts.

But would Bishop keep his word? Or would he kill one or both of them once the money was transferred?

All the years they had worked together counted for nothing now, Danny realised. What they had done to each other had made them enemies. There was no going back to how it was because the damage was done. There was no more trust between them.

'Be sensible, Danny,' Bishop said. 'One way or another I'll get you to move the cash. You know what I'm capable of. If you want blood and tears then try dicking me around.'

Danny looked at Beth. Her eyes were full of anguish, her breath shallow and rapid.

His father's words echoed in his head: *Do whatever it takes to save her, son.*

He realised then that only one course of action lay open to him. If he and Beth were going to survive this then transferring the money would be a huge mistake. Instead he would have to somehow take Bishop down. There was no way he could trust the man to stick to his end of the bargain. He feared that once Bishop had the money he'd make them suffer for what had happened to him. And Danny knew that he'd take great pleasure in it too.

Hurting people was his raison d'être. He had told Danny once that he preferred it to sex.

'So what's it to be, Danny?' Bishop said. 'Are we going to do this or what?'

Danny sucked in his top lip and nodded. 'You haven't given me any choice. I'll transfer the money as long as you just go and I never have to see you again.'

'It's a deal,' Bishop said.

That was the easy part, Danny thought. Now he had to work out how to disarm the man.

'There's one problem,' he said. 'I left my phone on the hands-free mount in the car.'

Bishop's eyes narrowed. 'That sounds like bullshit to me.'

'Well, it's not. I need to go and get it. You can come with me or trust me to go by myself. The car's parked on the road.'

'Take off your jacket and throw it over here,' Bishop snapped. 'I should have searched it before now anyway.'

Danny cursed under his breath. His intention had been to get Bishop to accompany him outside where he'd hoped to be able to turn things around. Now Bishop was about to discover that Danny's phone was in the inside pocket of his leather jacket.

He took it off anyway, playing for time again, and then on impulse decided that this was probably the only opportunity he was going to get to make his move.

Bishop was standing about eight feet away from him and he was holding out his free hand.

But Danny took aim at the other hand – the one that held the gun – and then lobbed the jacket as hard as he could. At the same time he let out a howling shout and threw himself forward.

363

It was a bold but clumsy move. The jacket did catch Bishop by surprise as it struck his hand.

And it did prompt him to swear out loud.

But it didn't stop him pulling the trigger before Danny reached him.

57

Beth Chambers

The sound of the shot was actually muffled by the jacket that landed on top of the gun. It was loud enough to blast my eardrums but I doubted that the neighbours would have heard it.

The bullet must have missed Danny's head by a whisker as he charged into Frankie Bishop. It ended up crashing into the fridge door on the other side of the room.

The gun fell onto the kitchen tiles as the two men slammed against the back door.

I watched in horrified disbelief while trying desperately to shake myself free of the chair. But the zip-ties were pulled tight and were cutting into my wrists and ankle.

A cry erupted from Danny's mouth as he took a savage punch to the side of his head. He dropped onto one knee and Bishop kicked him in the back, sending him flying forward onto his face.

'This time you ain't got Cain to save your fucking arse,' Bishop bellowed.

He stamped on Danny's head and then stepped over him to pick up the gun.

He had to move past me to get to it and I instinctively kicked out with my left foot. He tripped over and fell against the table. But he recovered quickly and snapped his head towards me.

'Bitch,' he screamed.

There was no way I could avoid his fist, though I did manage to turn away so that it struck my left ear instead of hitting me full in the face. The pain was no less intense, however. It was like a nail bomb going off inside my head.

My vision blurred and my mouth flew open in a silent scream of agony.

Through the tears I saw Bishop lining up another slap or punch and I tried to brace myself.

But instead of lashing out he went for my throat and drove his thumbs into my windpipe.

The bastard was going to throttle me and I couldn't fight back. I could feel him choking off the air supply and a burning sensation rose up through my chest.

Then his hands suddenly fell away and the breath spluttered out of me.

It was a couple of seconds before I realised that I had Danny to thank for saving my life. He had managed to get up and grab hold of the gun.

And I watched as he used it like a hammer to batter Bishop's head into a bloody mess.

Danny finally stopped smashing Bishop's face and head with the grip of the gun. He must have struck him five times before dropping the weapon on the floor.

By then Bishop was sprawled out on his back, his face almost unrecognisable. Even my untrained eye could see the man was never going to get up again.

Danny stood above him, his chest rising and falling dramatically with every breath. His lips quivered and his face was clown-pale.

For several seconds the silence was deafening and the only sound was the rapid beating of my own heart. My gut swirled with nausea and my throat throbbed from where Bishop had squeezed it.

Danny eventually turned to me and put a hand on my shoulder.

'I had to do it,' he said. 'He would have killed you. I've seen him like that before. Like he's fucking possessed.'

Danny then knelt beside Bishop and checked for a pulse.

'He's dead,' he said.

I nodded. 'I'd say that was bleeding obvious.'

'I'll get something to cut those ties.'

He found a pair of strong scissors in one of the drawers and used it to sever the zip-ties around my hands and ankle. Then he took my arm and led me out of the kitchen and into the living room, where the furniture was draped in white sheets.

The shock of what I'd witnessed hit me then with a vengeance. I dropped onto the sofa and let my head fall into my hands. There were more tears, and I started gagging. But I brought up only bile.

Danny went and got me a glass of water and insisted I drink it. He patted my back. Told me I was going to be okay.

I started taking slow breaths, trying to get a handle on my emotions. Everything seemed to be moving in slow motion, and the room felt hot and airless.

Danny left me to it for a few minutes and went into the kitchen. I heard his voice and assumed he was speaking to someone on the phone.

When he reappeared he was holding his mobile in one hand

and the gun in the other. I noticed it had been wiped clean of blood.

'Who were you talking to?' I asked him.

'Some people who will come here in the morning to clean up the mess and dispose of the body.'

He stood looking down at me, waiting for a reaction, for me to tell him that I couldn't let that happen, that we had to call the police. But my brain was numb and clouded and I spluttered out some words that made no sense even to me.

'We can't let the police get involved, Beth,' he said. 'There'll be too much explaining and everyone will suffer, including your ex-husband who helped me find you. This way we get to carry on with our lives and the world will be a better place without that nutcase anyway.'

He held out his phone to me. 'Just be grateful that you're alive and call your mum. She must be worried sick.'

I reached out, took the phone, flinched at the sight of Bishop's blood on his sleeve.

'We can't just act like it didn't happen,' I said.

Danny shrugged. 'Why not? Nobody needs to know. Frankie had no family and he wasn't married. He was a loner. So no one is going to miss him. And, trust me, the filth will be glad he's gone.'

I didn't know what to think so I decided not to. Instead, I tapped our home number into the phone and called Mum. She gasped when she heard my voice and broke down after I told her I was all right.

'How's Rosie?' I said.

'She's fast asleep. I didn't bother putting her to bed because she was too upset.'

'Have you spoken to anyone?'

'Only Ethan. He called me. He knew what had happened, Beth.'

'I know. He helped me, Mum. It was thanks to him that Danny found me.'

'Danny?'

'It's a long story,' I said. 'I'll tell you all about it when I get home. Don't talk to anyone in the meantime.'

I hung up and handed the phone back to Danny.

'So can I depend on you, Beth?' he said. 'Will you keep what's happened and what you've heard to yourself?'

I stared up at him, my sight still blurry with tears. Some of the colour had returned to his cheeks and he'd wiped the sweat from his face. He was back to being handsome again and more like the man who used to prance around London with a soap star on his arm.

It was hard to believe that he was a notorious criminal and harder still to think that we shared the same father.

'I need to know, Beth,' he said. 'Because if you insist on going to the police then I'm done for.'

I took a deep breath and nodded. 'I won't tell them. It's the least I can do since you came after me and saved my life.'

The most horrendous day of my life was over. The day during which I discovered that my real father was a gangster. The day someone tried to strangle me. The day I witnessed a man being beaten to death.

But the nightmare continued into the early hours of the following morning. Midnight had come and gone and now I had to face up to the prospect of living with what I had seen and agreed to. There was no going back once we left the house and the firm's 'clean-up' crew moved in to destroy all evidence of what had happened here. Despite my reservations and the guilt that sat inside me I knew I wouldn't tell the police.

Danny Shapiro had in no way redeemed himself in my eyes. He remained an unscrupulous villain with Peter Kline's blood on his hands. Yet if it hadn't been for him I'd be dead and Rosie would be without a mother.

'It's time to go,' he said.

I'd been sitting as if in a trancelike state in the living room while he got things sorted. He destroyed Bishop's two pay-as-you-go phones and wiped our prints from everything we had both touched. He said he would dump Bishop's gun on the way back to London. When we went outside he picked up the revolver that Bishop had made him drop on the driveway.

I sat next to him in the front of his BMW and that in itself was a surreal experience. Danny Shapiro and me in the same car! Who would have thought it would ever be possible?

Neither of us spoke as we left Bishop's house and drove out of the city. He kept within the speed limit so as not to draw attention to us.

My mind was sludgy and my eyes burned. I could still feel Bishop's fingers on my throat and hear the crack of his skull as Danny laid into him. But at least my heart had slowed down and the tears had dried up.

When we hit the motorway and headed north we started speaking to each other. Danny asked what Bishop had said to me.

'He told me you got him to kill Peter Kline and that you made Ethan go with him,' I said.

He didn't respond, just kept his eyes on the road ahead.

'I take some responsibility for what happened to Mr Kline,' I said. 'If I hadn't found out that Tamara had spent Friday night at his place then he wouldn't have become a target. And he'd still be alive.'

'It wasn't your fault, Beth,' he said. 'You were doing your job. Nothing more.'

'You didn't have to kill him. He was an innocent bystander.'

'I panicked. I knew the coppers would think I killed Megan and they'd pin it on me. I'm not proud of what I did, but then there's not much I do that I'm ever proud of. It's what I am, though. What I've become. We may well have the same father but from an early age our lives went in entirely different directions.'

'Did you have any idea that you had a half-sister?' I asked.

He shook his head. 'There were rumours years ago that he'd fathered a child by someone else. But he told me and my mum that they weren't true and we believed him.'

'What was your mother like?'

'She was terrific. Far too good for Callum. She did everything she could to try to stop me following in his footsteps, but he insisted on moulding me in his image. And he desperately wanted me to take over the business. So that's what I did when he went down. I didn't feel I had a choice. It was the main reason my marriage to Megan broke up.'

We drove in silence for a while. Then he pulled over onto the hard shoulder and dumped Bishop's gun under a pile of earth on the wooded embankment.

When we were on the move again I asked him how long Ethan Cain had been taking bribes from the firm.

'About four years,' he said. 'How do you feel about that?'

'Numb,' I said.

'Still, it was thanks in part to him that you're alive. He was really worried and he came through with the location of Bishop's house. In fact I ought to call him and tell him you're okay.'

'There's something else you need to tell him,' I said. 'Bishop told me he'd sent a flash drive to the police with evidence on it that will incriminate Ethan.'

He shook his head. 'The git.'

'Do you know what he was talking about?'

Danny nodded. 'It's something we put together. Photos, video and audio of Ethan in compromising positions. We do it with all the coppers on our books. It helps to keep them in check.'

'So what will happen to Ethan when the police see what's on it?'

Danny cleared his throat. 'They'll throw the book at him and I expect he'll go to prison for a long time.'

I didn't want to talk after that. I was hit by another wave of anger and revulsion. It wasn't that I felt sorry for Ethan. It seemed to me that he deserved what was going to happen to him, but I saw it as another example of the dirty, squalid, vicious world of Danny Shapiro.

A world I had only seen from the outside. A world I'd written about and talked about. But until this moment I had never fully appreciated just how ugly it really was.

58

Beth Chambers

Danny took me all the way home to Peckham and we arrived at the house at half four in the morning.

'You should come in,' I said. 'I think it's only right that you should meet my mother.'

'I'm not sure that's a good idea,' he said.

'But aren't you curious? She's the woman your father had a six-year affair with.'

'All the more reason to keep a wide berth I think.'

'Nonsense. After tonight you and me may never see each other again. So I'd like her to meet the man who saved my life.'

I got quickly out of the car before he could respond and he followed me. My mother opened the front door as we approached it. She seemed not to notice Danny at first as she flung her arms around me and cried tears of relief into my shoulder.

'Oh my God, Beth. I thought we'd lost you.'

I squeezed her back. 'I'm here because this man saved me, Mum.'

She stood back and looked at Danny and I feared she was going to say something nasty to him. But instead she smiled and said a little stiffly, 'Thank you, Mr Shapiro. I'm very grateful.'

We followed my mother into the house. Rosie was asleep on the sofa under her comfort blanket but I couldn't resist taking her in my arms even though I knew she'd wake up. She was relieved and delighted to see me and I had to reassure her that the bad man was gone.

'Who's that?' she said, pointing at Danny.

'He's a friend, sweetheart,' I said. 'He's the person who brought me back.'

Danny stared at her like he had never seen a child before and it occurred to me that he was probably a pretty lonely guy. Apart from his father, Rosie and I were the nearest he had to a family.

Mum made us tea and the next hour was pretty weird. After I put Rosie to bed I told Mum what had happened and it made her shiver.

'So we can never talk about it,' I said. 'We'll all be in trouble if it gets out.'

'I understand,' she said. Then to Danny, she added, 'You look just like your father did when I knew him.'

Danny cleared his throat. 'He told me he loved you, Miss Chambers.'

My mother nodded solemnly. 'But he loved your mum more. I can't complain, though. He gave me Beth.'

An awkward pause. Then Danny said, 'He wasn't responsible for what happened to Tony. He really wants you to know that.'

She thought about it and shrugged. 'That won't be easy. I've believed it for a long time.'

'Well, maybe you should go and see him. He might convince you that he's been telling the truth all along.'

My mother shifted her gaze away from him and sipped at her tea. I could tell she didn't know what to say.

Danny's phone rang then and he checked it before he answered it.

'It's Ethan,' he said. 'I'd better take it.'

He stayed in the room with us and we heard him tell Cain what had happened. He also broke the news about the flash drive that Bishop had supposedly sent to the police.

'He might have been lying, mate,' Danny said. 'I don't know.'

I thought that would bring the conversation to an end, but Cain was saying something that had Danny listening intently.

After a minute Danny handed the phone to me. 'He's got something to tell you.'

Ethan began by telling me that he was glad I was safe and that he was sorry for all the lies he'd told me.

'I know what you think of me, Beth,' he said. 'And I deserve what's coming my way. But before the shit hits the fan I want you to know that there's been a development in the Megan Fuller murder case and I'm telling you before anyone else finds out. It'll be another exclusive.'

'What is it?' I said.

'We're about to interview the man who killed Megan,' he said. 'And you'll never believe who it is.'

59

Ethan Cain

Cain told Beth what he could in the short time he had. Then DCI Redwood summoned him to the interview room.

He had to force himself not to think about the flash drive. If that bastard Bishop had been telling the truth to Beth he was fucked.

But there was no time to dwell on it now. The suspect they had brought in last night was ready to be questioned. He'd been given time to talk to his lawyer and his house had been searched.

The evidence against him was coming together nicely. They had CCTV footage of his car near Megan's house on Friday evening and they'd found traces of blood on a pair of his shoes. Now they were going to throw everything at him in the hope of extracting a confession.

Nigel Fuller was already waiting for them in the interview room. He was sitting beside a thin guy in a light grey suit, who introduced himself as Paul Barton.

'I'm Mr Fuller's legal representative,' he said. 'And I'd like to make clear at the outset that I'm not happy with the way my client has been treated. He's been here for a number of hours now and he still hasn't been told what it's about.'

'I beg to differ, Mr Barton,' Redwood said. 'It's been made clear to him that we need to ask him some questions in connection with the murder of his daughter, Megan.'

'But he's already told you everything he knows,' Barton said.

'That was before he became a suspect. Now we've got a different set of questions for him.'

Sweat beaded on Fuller's upper lip and a muscle twitched under his left eye.

'This is ridiculous,' he said. 'How can I be a suspect? I was the one who found her. I was nowhere near Balham on Friday night.'

Redwood looked at Cain and raised his brow, the cue for Cain to take over.

'So remind us where you were on Friday night when Megan was killed,' Cain said.

'I told you. I was at home in bed with Amy. She told you that as well.'

'So how come you left your house in Lewisham just after nine and drove to Balham?'

'I didn't.'

'In that case who else has access to your car?'

'What do you mean?'

'Well, we have CCTV footage which shows your Vauxhall Astra travelling between Lewisham and Balham on Friday evening.'

'That's not possible. It must be a mistake.'

'It's not a mistake,' Cain said. 'And it's not the only evidence we have that convinces us you stabbed your daughter to death.'

A frown tightened Fuller's forehead, and he swallowed a lump the size of a plum.

377

'You played the grieving father really well, Mr Fuller,' Cain said. 'You had everyone convinced, including me.'

'You're wrong. I swear I had nothing to do with it. I loved Megan. She was—'

His voice broke then and he started to cry.

'We found a shoe at your house with blood on it,' Cain said. 'A black slip-on that you must have worn when you went to Megan's house on Friday.'

Barton chipped in, saying, 'If it is indeed the victim's blood then that can easily be explained. My client's shoes were contaminated when he found his daughter's body on the Saturday morning.'

Cain shook his head. 'The shoes he was wearing on Saturday were taken away by the scene-of-crime officers.'

Cain turned back to Fuller. 'So how come your other shoes have blood on them?'

Fuller couldn't explain it so he didn't try. He wiped his eyes and said, 'I can't believe you're accusing me of killing my own daughter. Why would I? It makes no sense.'

Cain curled his lips contemptuously. 'It does if she was black-mailing you. And we believe she was. In the same way she was blackmailing Danny Shapiro.'

'You can't be serious.'

'Oh, but I am. I believe your daughter told you that she was writing her autobiography and that she was going to reveal the truth about you unless you paid her money. You decided that you had too much to lose, including marriage to the new woman in your life.'

'You're making this up,' Fuller said. 'What possible reason would Megan have to blackmail me?'

Cain's mouth tightened a little. 'What about the fact that you

378

repeatedly abused her as a child? You raped her from the age of five until she was ten. And you threatened to hurt her if she told her mother. She believed you because there were times when you were violent towards her. Isn't that right, Mr Fuller?'

Fuller stared at the detective, mesmerised, in shock.

'Megan told her psychiatrist everything,' Cain said. 'It all came out after she started seeing him about her depression. She told him what you did to her as a child and about your violent rages. It blighted her life. At the last session with him she indicated that she'd finally come up with a way to get her own back, but she didn't tell him what it was. Now we know, don't we?'

Cain fully expected Fuller to deny it, to say that what Megan had told the shrink wasn't true. But he didn't because at that point he must have realised the game was up.

He stopped crying and closed his eyes. Then he inhaled slowly, deeply, and said, 'I warned her not to push it. I told her I wouldn't let her destroy my life. But she wouldn't listen. She was determined to dig up the past and I couldn't let her do it. I knew that if I paid her what she asked for then that wouldn't be the end of it. She'd only come back for more.'

It took another hour for the full story to come out. He said it began when Megan called him a month ago, having not been in touch for years. She told him she was going to reveal the secrets of her childhood in her book unless he paid her £30,000. She phoned him on the Friday to tell him the price had gone up to £40,000. She knew he had the money in the bank from the sale of his house before he moved in with Amy.

'We went to bed as usual on Friday night at about eight,' he said. 'And as usual Amy had a mug of drinking chocolate beforehand with a couple of sleeping pills. Once she drops off it's impossible to wake her. But I couldn't sleep. I was so angry. So I decided to go and have it out with Megan and at the back of my mind I knew that I was going to hurt her.'

He said he drove to Balham and parked some distance from Ramsden Road. He walked to Megan's house, via a route not covered by CCTV cameras.

'When I was approaching the house I saw Danny Shapiro coming out,' he said. 'He looked angry and I wondered if he'd gone there for the same reason I had. I didn't let him see me, though. As soon as he disappeared I rang Megan's bell and she let me in. I tried reasoning with her, but she refused to back down over the book and the money. It made me snap and I grabbed the knife from the worktop and stabbed her. It wasn't my fault. It was hers.'

After killing Megan he used her phone to send a text to himself asking him to come over in the morning because she needed to talk to him.

'It was a way of making sure I wasn't a suspect,' he said. 'And it meant there was a legitimate reason for my prints and DNA to be in the kitchen. I didn't notice the blood on my shoes.'

He quickly searched the house for Megan's manuscript and notes relating to her book, but didn't find anything. Then he saw an opportunity to put the blame on Danny Shapiro and lied about Megan claiming that he'd threatened her. He went on to act as the distraught father.

Fuller finally finished his confession at 7 a.m. He then crossed his arms, locked his lips together and stared at the ceiling, his face stark and emotionless.

At 7.15 a.m. he was charged with murdering his daughter.

There was a lot of back-slapping in the incident room after Fuller was charged. Cain was given most of the credit for solving the case. But he didn't feel like celebrating. He knew that he wasn't going to be the blue-eyed boy for very long.

He made two quick calls to Beth and to Danny and filled them in. Then he was called into Redwood's office.

'You did well, Ethan,' the DCI said. 'You should go home and get some sleep. It was a long night. I'll take care of all the paperwork.'

Cain didn't argue. He felt knackered. But once outside the station he decided not to go straight home. He needed time to think through his options.

Trouble was they were few and far between. Despite the successful resolution to the case he was still wading up to his neck in shit. And he was still filled with self-loathing.

Try as he might he couldn't will away the image of Peter Kline being garrotted by Frankie Bishop. The guilt had settled in his chest like a sack of bricks.

As he walked he was oblivious to those around him and his limbs felt as heavy as lead. He heard an ominous crack of thunder overhead but ignored it. Even when it started to rain he carried on walking until it became a belting downpour.

He was walking past Wandsworth Road station so he ducked inside. A voice in his head told him to get on a train and ride around for a bit. Perhaps he could get some perspective on things in the company of commuters who would all be reflecting on their own trials and tribulations.

He bought a Travelcard and as he walked onto the platform he thought about what a disappointment he was to himself as well as to everyone else. What he had done to Beth and Rosie was unforgivable. And once he was arrested and charged with corruption they would be right in the thick of the scandal. It wasn't fair and it wasn't right.

He loved Rosie too much to put her through that. His feelings for Beth were still strong too. They both deserved better.

He felt the emotion well up in his throat. He couldn't believe he'd fucked up his life – and their lives – in such a spectacular way. What happened? he asked himself. Why did he allow that idealistic young police officer that he once was to be sucked into a downward spiral of betrayal and debauchery?

Why couldn't he have been satisfied with what he had? Why couldn't he have embraced the luck and good fortune that came his way?

Why had it never been enough?

He heard the announcer informing those who were waiting that the train now approaching would not be stopping and to stand back from the platform edge.

Cain looked up and suddenly realised what he had to do. For Beth's sake and for Rosie's.

He saw the train coming towards him. Waited until it had almost reached him.

And then he jumped.

60

Beth Chambers

I had just stepped out of the shower when Ethan rang to tell me that they'd charged Nigel Fuller with his daughter's murder.

I got straight onto *The Post*'s newsroom. Grant Scott took the call and began to ask me if I was feeling better, but I talked over him.

'I've got an update on the Megan Fuller murder,' I said. 'And it's an exclusive.'

Grant was as shocked as I'd been to learn that Megan had been killed by her father.

'I'll put a story together from here,' I said.

'That's great, Beth. Give us the headlines for the website and then a longer piece for the front page.'

I filed it all before getting dressed and it wasn't until afterwards that I thought about how we had all been taken in by Nigel Fuller. He'd convinced me and everyone else that he'd been a loving father when in fact he'd subjected his daughter to years of vile sexual abuse.

After Cain told me on the phone that Fuller was their man I'd been forced to apologise to Danny for having convinced myself that he'd done it.

'Don't worry about it,' Danny had said. 'It was the obvious conclusion to draw after you found out about the alibi.'

It occurred to me then that Peter Kline had died for nothing – the victim of a callous cover-up that would not have been necessary if the police had got at the truth sooner.

Before Danny left our house I'd told him I would never forgive myself for not telling the police I knew that Peter Kline was dead. It was unfair on his family, who would always live in hope. I also said that I would never be able to forgive him and Cain for the parts they had played in Kline's death.

'I wouldn't expect you to,' he'd said.

That was how it was left when he went home. But I did thank him again for saving my life. And I did let him hug me even though I didn't want him to.

Two Weeks Later

There was a good turnout for Ethan's funeral. That was because the Met decided to cover up the truth about what kind of police officer he was.

I was told off the record that the flash drive that Frankie Bishop had put in the post had ended up on the commissioner's desk and he saw no point in making it public. So it was buried along with the secrets it contained.

I was glad and, as I stood in the crematorium with Ethan's fellow officers, I tried to focus on the good years before it all went belly-up.

Ethan may have turned into a filthy, lying scumbag, but he had given me the one thing I treasured above all else and that was Rosie.

The shock of his suicide had worn off and my mother had summed it up perfectly when she'd said it was probably the best thing for all concerned that he had chosen the easy way out.

I couldn't disagree with her, but it didn't bring about any kind of closure. My life had been turned inside out and the future seemed more uncertain than ever.

After the funeral I did what I had told myself I wouldn't do – which was to meet up with Danny. We hadn't seen each other since we returned from Southampton, but he'd called me twice asking if we could get together because there were things he wanted to say. Curiosity had finally got the better of me and in any case there was something I needed to say to him. So I'd agreed.

The venue was his luxury mews house in the heart of London's West End. He said I was the first person to visit there, and it made me realise again that despite his wealth and power he was a pretty sad and lonely man.

He explained why he lived there and that it was a safe haven. And then he passed on a message from Callum.

'He wants to know if you'll go and see him again and if you can maybe persuade your mother to go as well.'

'You can tell him that my mother is thinking about it,' I said. 'I'm sure she won't be able to resist talking to him one last time, if only to give him a piece of her mind.'

'So what about you, Beth? Will you visit him?'

I'd given a great deal of thought to what I should do now I knew that Callum Shapiro was my father. In fact it was pretty much all I'd been thinking about for the past couple of weeks.

'No, I won't,' I said after a beat. 'I don't want any further contact with the man. And the same goes for you, Danny.'

'I was hoping that we might stay in touch. Build up a relationship.'

I shook my head. 'That's not going to happen. I don't want you as a brother, Danny, and the thought of you being an uncle to my daughter appals me.'

He didn't look shocked, just disappointed. 'Do you really mean that?' he said.

'Of course I do. You're a bad man, Danny. You're a gangster and a killer. You've done terrible things and you'll no doubt carry on doing them. It's who you are and I wouldn't be able to live with that.'

'Won't you at least think about it?'

'There's no point. I've made up my mind and I'm not going to change it. But I promise I'll never tell anyone about what happened to Peter Kline and Frankie Bishop. And I want you to promise me that you won't tell anyone I'm your half-sister.'

He nodded slowly. 'If that's what you want.'

'It is.'

Danny pursed his lips. 'And there was me thinking that I'd suddenly been blessed with a ready-made family.'

I wasn't sure how to respond to that so I didn't try. Instead, I picked up my bag from the floor and slipped on my sunglasses.

'I have to go,' I said. 'But before I do I want you to know that I'll never forget that you saved my life. I'll be forever grateful and so will my mother.'

'It was my pleasure,' he said. 'And I want *you* to know that if you ever have second thoughts about staying in touch then just give me a call. Things change and so do people, Beth. It'd be great to hear from you.'

I held his gaze for a few moments and realised that a part of me felt sorry for the man. But it was only a small part.

Then I turned and walked out of the room and along the hallway to the front door. As I let myself out I glanced back over my shoulder and saw him standing in the doorway, staring at me, his head tilted slightly to one side.

In that moment I knew I had made the right decision. Danny

Shapiro was never going to change. He would continue to be a cold, heartless villain just like his father was.

In fairness to Danny he really had no choice – not if he was determined to remain the most powerful figure in the London underworld.

Your next bestseller awaits . . .

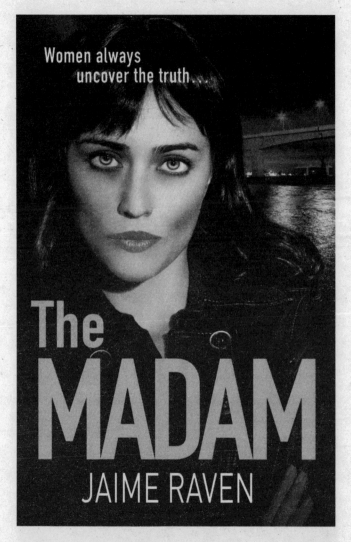

Women always
uncover the truth...

The MADAM

JAIME RAVEN

Murder, loyalty, and vengeance collide in this gritty read. Perfect
for fans of Martina Cole and Kimberley Chambers.

Bad things are going down in Soho. Someone's going to
have to pay the price . . .

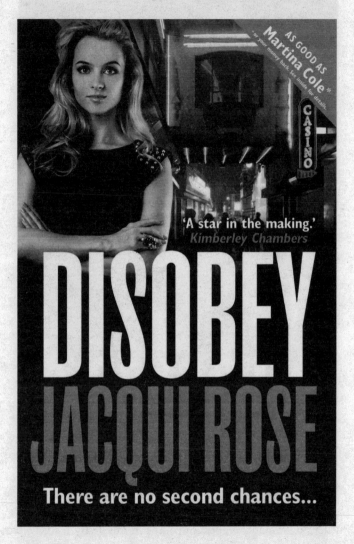

AS GOOD AS
Martina Cole *
or your money back. See inside for details.

CASINO

'A star in the making.'
Kimberley Chambers

DISOBEY

JACQUI ROSE

There are no second chances...

A hard-hitting thriller that you won't forget in a hurry.

You make a deal with the devil; you pay your dues . . .

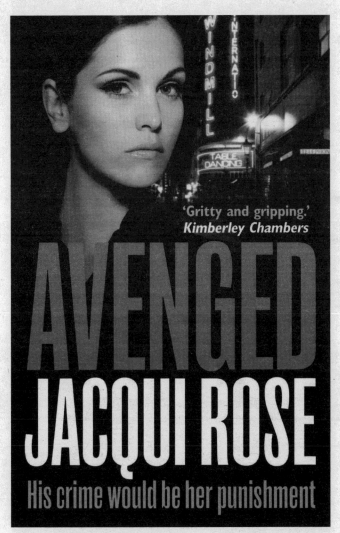

'Gritty and gripping.'
Kimberley Chambers

AVENGED

JACQUI ROSE

His crime would be her punishment

Thrilling, dangerous and compulsive: if you loved
The Alibi, you'll love this!